ORSON SCOTT CARD'S
InterGalactic
Medicine Show

By Orson Scott Card From Tom Doherty Associates

Empire
The Folk of the Fringe
Future on Fire (editor)
Future on Ice (editor)
Invasive Procedures (with Aaron Johnston)
Keeper of Dreams
Lovelock (with Kathryn Kidd)
Maps in a Mirror: The Short Fiction of
    Orson Scott Card
Orson Scott Card's InterGalactic
    Medicine Show
Pastwatch: The Redemption of
    Christopher Columbus
Saints
Songmaster
Treason
A War of Gifts
The Worthing Saga
Wyrms

THE TALES OF ALVIN MAKER

Seventh Son
Red Prophet
Prentice Alvin
Alvin Journeyman
Heartfire
The Crystal City

ENDER

Ender's Game
Ender's Shadow
Shadow of the Hegemon
Shadow Puppets
Shadow of the Giant
Speaker for the Dead
Xenocide
Children of the Mind
First Meetings

HOMECOMING

The Memory of Earth
The Call of Earth
The Ships of Earth
Earthfall
Earthborn

WOMEN OF GENESIS

Sarah
Rebekah
Rachel & Leah

From Other Publishers

Enchantment
Homebody
Lost Boys
Magic Street
Stone Tables

Treasure Box
How to Write Science Fiction and
    Fantasy
Characters and Viewpoint

ORSON SCOTT CARD'S
InterGalactic
Medicine Show

EDMUND R. SCHUBERT
AND
ORSON SCOTT CARD

A TOM DOHERTY ASSOCIATES BOOK
NEW YORK

This is a work of fiction. All of the characters, organizations, and events portrayed in the stories in this collection are either products of the authors' imaginations or are used fictitiously.

ORSON SCOTT CARD'S INTERGALACTIC MEDICINE SHOW

A Tor Book
Published by Tom Doherty Associates, LLC
175 Fifth Avenue
New York, NY 10010

www.tor-forge.com

Tor® is a registered trademark of Tom Doherty Associates, LLC.

ISBN-13: 978-0-7653-2000-1
ISBN-10: 0-7653-2000-2

First Edition: August 2008

Printed in the United States of America

0 9 8 7 6 5 4 3 2 1

Contents

Foreword

BY ORSON SCOTT CARD

The medicine wagon rolls into town. With brightly painted signs, it advertises cures for every ailment, from cancer to impotence to senility to drought. The man on the wagon can do miracles.

Of course, they're all fake. You'll get a bottle of *something,* but it's a sure thing it won't cure any of the things he's said it will cure.

He'll keep only one of his promises, and that one is the unstated one: He'll put on a great show.

He stops the wagon; he stands on top of it, or at the top step at its back, and he makes his pitch.

And here's where his talents have to shine. He has to have a voice that can be heard all through a town square, in order to draw a crowd. He has to have a face that knows how to zero in on an audience, member by member, so that they take his words seriously, so that their eyes are drawn to him and can't escape.

Even if they know he's lying, even if they're determined not to believe, they can't bear to miss the *show.*

We fiction writers are all medicine men. All we have to sell are lies. Everyone knows they're lies. We *admit* they're lies. If somebody sues us for libel, we *insist* they're lies. We made it up. None of it ever happened anywhere, to anybody.

So why do people buy these tales of ours?

One reason is the voice. We fiction writers speak with confidence. We declare that we *know* the answers to the great mysteries, and we can tell you with certainty:

Why people do the strange, hurtful, terrible, wonderful, cruel, kind things they do.

That's the miracle of our made-up stories. When we tell you *why* a person does something, nobody can argue with us. Nobody can say, "No, the *real* reason he did it is something else entirely."

Because the person doesn't exist. It's a character, existing only in the storyteller's mind. There is no authority but the author.

And yet . . . when the author gets it right, the characters he made up resonate with us. They feel true and right: Yes, this is why people do what they do. Now I understand. Things make sense. And in the midst of fiction, awash with lies, we tie ourselves to the mast of a kind of truth we cannot ever find in the real world.

So we authors speak with a voice of command. And as we weave our tales out of thin air, if you believe in them, you allow us to spin threads in your own mind and begin to weave a fabric in your memory. It is composed of pieces of your own experience that we cannot see, but when we say certain things, your own memories are awakened and fibers of this and that from your real life get twisted into the threads and woven into the textiles that our text creates.

It's magic. When we're done, you have memories implanted

in your minds—vivid ones, powerful ones, treasured ones, if we've done our job aright—and these memories we've given you are clearer than anything in real life.

That's the medicine in our bottles. That's the show we put on.

Short stories are the treasurehouse of fiction. Few writers are ready to tackle a novel as their first venture into fiction. It is in the short stories that they can try out their voice, make their first tentative explorations into new worlds, and test new ideas to see if there's any truth in them.

In recent years, the market for short fiction has shrunk to a shocking degree. Yet the need for it has not. I believe that the reason is not that the audience does not want short stories, but rather that the marketplace offers no easy way to reach an audience.

Printing magazines is expensive—even on the cheap pulp paper that has typified the magazines in the speculative fiction genre. Publishing online carries far less risk, and a far higher percentage of earnings can go to the writers.

That's why I launched *Orson Scott Card's InterGalactic Medicine Show* a few years ago, at http://www.oscIGMS.com.

From the start, I determined that even though it's expensive, our stories would all be illustrated. For me, that's one of the hallmarks of magazine publication. The story begins with a splash of evocative art to set the tone.

At first I edited the magazine myself, but quickly discovered that editing a magazine takes more time than I could devote to the task—not if I wanted to do it well. I was doing a bad job of keeping up with submissions and getting issues out on time. So I fired me.

That's when I invited Ed Schubert to take the helm. He is

doing a superb job, except, of course, for the problem of working with me. I have promised an *Ender's Game* story in every issue, in the hopes that we can draw some of the readers of that series of books to this magazine. Sometimes Ed has to wring my ear a little to squeeze the story out anywhere near the due date. But that's why he gets the big bucks.

Oh, wait. He doesn't get big bucks. He gets paid with bags of dirt. But it's *good* dirt. Magical dirt. Dirt just right for growing magic beans. If you know where to get magic beans.

Even with the low overhead of an online magazine, there are few ways to get the word out that the website even exists. That's why I proposed to my publisher, Tom Doherty of Tor, that we bring out an anthology of stories that will show the variety and quality of what our magazine offers.

So please, don't just sample our wares here in this book. Come to our website and see the latest issues and read the latest stories. We think you'll find that *our* kind of patent medicine really does deliver.

Introduction
The Story Behind the Stories
by Edmund R. Schubert

Everyone loves the line from the end of *The Wizard of Oz* when the wizard booms out in his most ominous voice, *"Pay no attention to that man behind the curtain!"*

But if you think for a moment, you'll recall that the wizard's booming quickly turned to blustering and ultimately did nothing to stop Dorothy and her friends from pulling back the curtain to see what secrets it hid.

That's because there's something basic to human nature that wants—almost needs—to know what's going on behind the veil. Even when the wizard turns out to be a charlatan, there's something about a charlatan behind the veil that is far more interesting than a wizard in front of it.

That's why when it comes to short story collections and anthologies, my favorites have always been those filled with stories written by the late, great Dr. Isaac Asimov. I know that sounds terribly disjointed, but stay with me for a moment. Did I seek out the good doctor's collections because he wrote such wonderful stories? (He did, there's no question about that.)

No, the reason those collections enthralled me so was because Asimov always took the time to write anywhere from a few lines to a few paragraphs about each story. The story *behind* his stories.

To get a glimpse into Asimov's mind, to find out what he was trying to accomplish, or why he wrote a particular story, or the trials and tribulations the story endured on its way to publication—that fascinated me. I couldn't get enough. And given how much I have always loved stories—long, short, printed, on the big screen, it doesn't matter; I just love stories—the opportunity to be a fly on Isaac Asimov's wall was a beautiful gift.

Why, maybe it was that secret part of my soul that, even at the age of fourteen, longed to be a writer, a storyteller. Or maybe it was nothing more than the fundamental aspect of human nature that simply relishes feeling like we're "in" on someone else's secrets. Or maybe it was: C) all of the above. Did it matter? Not really. Not to me. I freely admit I was addicted.

To me the best stories have a life of their own. They breathe, they think, they move, and in so doing they move *me*. You should also have no trouble, then, understanding why it was absolutely necessary, once I had found these living, breathing stories, to find out how they came to be born and what kinds of lives they've led before arriving on my doorstep.

The problem, I must confess, is that I enjoy these moments of insight so much that sometimes, going back to Asimov's collections, for instance, I'd go through his books and read all the essays before I read any of the stories.

If you are also the kind of person who does that sort of thing, let me take this opportunity to warn you against doing so in this anthology. With this assemblage of stories, all of the authors have written their "stories behind the stories." The catch is that some of these essays contain spoilers—tidbits of information you don't want to know until after you've read the stories. That's why the essays are published as afterwords, not introductions. Trust me when I say there are a few stories herein where you *really* don't want to spoil the surprise. Just a couple, but if I tell you which ones, we both know you'll go look. So no peeking, now. I mean it.

The afterwords will make re-reading these stories even richer—and there are stories here that you will definitely want to read more than once—but let them stand on their own the first time around.

Yes, *even though* they're standing behind a curtain and the wizard just told you to pay them no attention . . .

ORSON SCOTT CARD'S
InterGalactic
Medicine Show

In the Eyes of the Empress's Cat
by Bradley P. Beaulieu

Al-Ashmar sat cross-legged in the tent of Gadn ak Hulavar
and placed his patient, a spotted cat, onto a velvet pillow. Gadn
lounged on the far side of the spacious tent, puffing on his
hookah and waiting for the diagnosis of his grossly thin cat.

Al-Ashmar held his fingers near the cat's nose. She sniffed
his hand and raked her whiskers over his knuckles. When the
cat raised her head and stared into his eyes, Al-Ashmar found a
brown, triangle-shaped splotch in the right eye, along the left
side of the green-and-gold iris. The location of the mark indicated the cat's liver, but in this case it was the strong color that
was most disturbing.

"What have you been feeding her?" Al-Ashmar asked as he
stroked the cat, noting its muscle tone.

Gadn shrugged his massive shoulders. "Nothing. Cats find
food."

Al-Ashmar smiled, if only to hide his annoyance. The wealthy always wanted cats of status, but when it came time to care for them, they hadn't an idea worth its weight in sand.

"Not this one," Al-Ashmar said as he picked up the cat and stood, absently continuing to stroke its ears. "Please, go to the bazaar; buy a large cage and some swallows. Once a day, put her in the cage with one bird. The activity should interest her enough to induce appetite. Do this for a week and her normal eating pattern should return. If it doesn't, send me word."

A bald servant boy rushed into the room and bowed deeply. "Master, if you please, there is a messenger."

"We are done?" Gadn asked Al-Ashmar.

"Yes."

"Then bring the messenger here, Mousaf." Gadn handed Al-Ashmar three coins and then embraced him, kissing one cheek, then the other.

But the servant boy remained. "Begging your mercy, master, but they are asking for Al-Ashmar ak Kulhadn."

Al-Ashmar frowned. "*Who* is, boy?"

"A man, from the palace."

Gadn shoved the boy aside and rushed from the tent. "Why didn't you say so?"

Al-Ashmar was right behind him. Moments later, they reached the edge of the caravan grounds, near the pens holding dozens of Gadn's camels and donkeys and goats. A balding man with a reed-thin beard—the current rage in the Empress's courts—and wearing blue silk finery stood just outside the caravan grounds, on the sandy road leading back toward the city proper. Behind him stood four palace guards.

The first thought through Al-Ashmar's mind was the sort

of beating Gadn's servant would get for referring to Djazir ak
Benkada as a "messenger."

The second was what sort of emergency would require the
Empress's own spiritual guide and physician to personally come
asking for *him,* a simple physic. At the least it would be to at-
tend to a courtier's cat—after all, he'd been to the palace a
handful of times for just such a purpose—but since Djazir had
come personally, he could only assume it was for Bela, the Empress's cat.

Gadn ak Hulavar, as the caravan's master, stepped forward
to meet Djazir. "Please, Eminence, would you care to join us?
A smoke, perhaps?"

But Gadn stopped when Djazir held up an open palm and
stared at Al-Ashmar.

"You will accompany me," Djazir said.

"Of course, Eminence," Al-Ashmar replied.

He left the confused and slightly hurt Gadn and followed
the royal guards and physician toward the palace. The climb
through the city streets was not long, but neither was it easy.
Al-Ashmar didn't consider himself old, but he didn't have sharp
climbs like this in him anymore—not without becoming
winded, in any case. Djazir, on the other hand, a good fifteen
years older than Al-Ashmar, seemed hardly winded at all.

They walked through the Grand Hallway with its long
pool of water and lily pads, up four sets of stairs to reach the
Empress's personal wing, through a small garden of palm trees
and beds of sand sculptures, and finally reached the waiting
chamber of the Empress herself.

Even though it had been nearly ten years since he'd had the
honor of visiting the Empress's wing, Al-Ashmar was surprised
to find so many memories in conflict with reality. The room

was as opulent as he remembered, but almost completely stripped of furniture—the only furnishings were the throne itself and a marble table crouched next to it, the only entertainment the three books stacked on top of the table.

Djazir turned to Al-Ashmar and spoke softly. "Understand, ak Kulhadn, you are here to examine the Empress's cat, that is all. You will do your business and you will leave. Is that understood?"

Al-Ashmar tipped his head low. "Of course, Eminence."

"If the Empress decides to speak to you, it will be through her handmaid. But it is taxing on her, and you will formulate brief answers, answers that will not invite further comment."

"Of course."

Djazir studied Al-Ashmar's eyes and finally, apparently satisfied, turned to the guard nearest the rear door of the room and nodded. The guard rang a small brass cymbal. Minutes passed, and Al-Ashmar began to wonder if the cymbal had been heard, but then the door opened, and two huge eunuchs walked in carrying a palanquin between them. The Empress sat inside the covered palanquin, but her form was obscured by the green veils hanging down from the palanquin's roof. The only thing Al-Ashmar could discern was the golden headdress resting over her brown hair.

They set the palanquin down near the padded throne and, after pulling the fabric away on the far side, cradled the Empress from inside and set her gently on the throne. The pair of eunuchs—for only eunuch guards were allowed this close to the Empress—then moved to stand behind her, one on each side.

The Empress's eyes drooped, the left lower than the right;

she sat tilted to one side, her head arching back the other way; her thin arms rested ineffectually in her lap. She had a face Al-Ashmar barely recognized—another memory that appeared to have faded to the point of uselessness. Then again, the last time he'd seen her had been years before the malady that had left her in such a state.

Al-Ashmar suddenly realized that someone else had entered the room. A woman—young, but no child, she. She moved with a subtle grace, hips swaying as she did so, but she stared at no one until she reached the Empress's side. Thus positioned, she turned and regarded Al-Ashmar with impassive, kohl-rimmed eyes. How stunning those green eyes were. How beautiful.

Much of Al-Ashmar's mind wanted to compare her to another beauty in his life—dear Nara, his wife who'd passed years ago—but those memories were still tender, and so he left the comparisons where they lay. Buried.

With no one performing introductions, Al-Ashmar took one knee to the Empress and woman both. "I am Al-Ashmar ak Kulhadn, humble physic."

"The Empress knows who you are," the woman said.

Movement pulled Al-Ashmar's attention away from the Empress. From inside the safety of the palanquin leapt a cat, Bela, the bright one, ninth and final companion to the Empress Waharra before she alights for the heavens. Like the cat Al-Ashmar had just treated, Bela was long and lean, but she had the muscle tone of a cat treated well. Her smooth coat was ivory with onyx spots coating her sides and back. Stripes slid down her face, giving her an innocent but regal look. She roamed the room and croaked out a meow as if she had just woken from a long nap. She seemed wary of Al-Ashmar and

Djazir, but then she slunk to the foot of the throne, curled up in a ball, and began licking one outstretched leg.

Djazir moved to the palanquin and retrieved a crimson pillow dusted with short white hair. He set the pillow down several paces away from the throne and then set Bela upon it.

"Please," Djazir said to Al-Ashmar, motioning to Bela, "tell us what you can."

Al-Ashmar hesitated—how rude not to introduce him to the woman!—but there was nothing for it. He couldn't afford to insult Djazir.

As Al-Ashmar stepped forward and knelt before the cat, he felt the Empress's eyes watching his every move. Her body might have failed her, but her mind, he was sure, was as sharp as ever. Al-Ashmar stroked Bela's side and stomach. Bela stretched and purred.

"Her symptoms?" he asked.

He expected Djazir to answer, but it was the woman who spoke. "Her feces are loose and runny. She eats less, though she still eats. She's listless much of the day."

Bela's purr intensified, a rasping sound everyone in the room could hear.

"Anything else? Anything you noticed days ago, even weeks?"

"Her eyes started watering and crusting eight or nine days ago. But that stopped a few days back."

"Has her diet changed?"

"She began eating less, but Djazir administered cream from the Empress's reserve herd, laced with fennel."

"She's kept her appetite since?"

"Somewhat, but she still seems to eat too little."

Al-Ashmar scratched Bela under the chin. Bela stretched

her neck and squinted, but when she opened her eyes wide
again, Al-Ashmar started. He leaned closer while continuing to
scratch, tilting Bela's head from side to side while doing so. Bela
seemed amused, but on the inside of her iris was a raised, curl-
ing mark. It retained the golden color of the iris, but something
was obviously there, just beneath the surface.

Al-Ashmar sat upright, confused.

But the woman . . . She held an expression that said she'd
rather this sullied business be over and done with.

"Do you have a name," Al-Ashmar asked, "or shall I continue to treat you like a talking palm?"

Was there a hint of a smile from the Empress?

"You may call me Rabiah," the woman said crisply.

The height of rudeness! What civilized person withholds
her mother's name?

"Where has this cat been, *Rabiah*?" Al-Ashmar asked.

Her eyes narrowed. "What do you mean?"

"I asked where the Empress's cat has been, in the last
month."

"In the palace only. She has never left."

"Never?"

"Of course not."

"Enough, ak Kulhadn," Djazir said. "What is it you see?"

"Forgive me. I ask these questions because Bela—long may
the sun shine on her life—has snakeworm."

"What?" Djazir asked. He kneeled beside Al-Ashmar and
stared into Bela's eyes.

"Look for the raised area. There."

While Djazir inspected her eyes, Al-Ashmar couldn't help
but wonder how this could have happened. Snakeworm was
common in his homeland, but that was far to the south, and the

worm came from *goats*. There were caravans, of course, like Gadn's, that brought livestock northward. It was conceivable that a cat could get it from a transplanted goat, but the worm seemed to have trouble thriving in the north. In nearly twenty years in the capital, he'd seen only three cases, and all of them had been near the caravan landings or the bazaar. How could Bela, a cat that would never be allowed away from the palace grounds, have contracted the worm?

Al-Ashmar stood. "I can make a tonic and return tomorrow."

"No," Djazir said, standing as well. "You will tell me how to make it."

Al-Ashmar dipped his head until he could no longer make eye contact with Djazir. "With due respect, it cannot be taught in so short a time. The balance is tricky, and I wouldn't wish to jeopardize Bela's life over a formula crudely made."

Djazir bristled. "Then you will do it immediately and return here when it's done."

"Of course, but it will take nearly a day. The ingredients are rare, and it will take me time to find those of proper quality. And then I must boil—"

Al-Ashmar stopped at a disturbing noise coming from the Empress. The sounds from her throat could hardly be construed as words, and yet Rabiah leaned over and listened attentively as if she *were* speaking.

Rabiah stood. "Her Highness, Waharra sut Shahmat, wishes for Al-Ashmar to make the tonic. Alone. He will return tomorrow when it is ready, and every day after until Bela's recovery is judged complete."

Djazir bowed to the Empress, as did Al-Ashmar. Again, he saw a quirky smile from her lips and wondered if it could be such a thing. She had enough control still to speak to Rabiah. Could she not show amusement if she so chose?

He supposed she could. But the real question was: Why? Why him? And why amusement?

Al-Ashmar rose to his feet and turned to Djazir. "Anyone in close contact with Bela may have contracted the worm, so it would be wise to examine everyone, even wiser for everyone to take the same tonic as Bela will receive."

After Djazir nodded his assent, Al-Ashmar inspected the hulking guards, then Djazir. As he held Rabiah's head and gazed into her irises, more than anything else he sensed the scent of jasmine and the warmth of her face through his fingertips. He had to force himself to examine her complex green eyes closely to make sure there were no signs of infection.

Al-Ashmar knelt before the Empress next. It took him a moment, for the two guards were watching him as the cobra spies the mongoose. The Empress's eyes were free of the worm, but she kept glancing toward the stack of books on the nearby marble table.

When Al-Ashmar stepped away, he noticed the binding of the top book; it was inlaid with a cursive pattern—a pattern often used in the south, Al-Ashmar's home. In the center of the leather cover rested a tiger-eye stone with a silver, diamond-shaped setting.

Bela, sitting beneath the table, watched him closely. It was strange how utterly human Bela looked for that brief instant.

Al-Ashmar nodded to the Empress. "Our Exalted has fine taste in books."

She spoke to Rabiah. Rabiah said not a word, but it was a long time before she moved to the stack of books and retrieved the top one. She held it out to Al-Ashmar.

"My lady?" Al-Ashmar said.

"The Blessed One wishes to gift you."

Al-Ashmar nearly raised his hands to refuse, but how grave an insult to reject such an offer. "The Empress is too kind," he said at last.

Rabiah shoved it into his chest, forcing him to take it.

And now there could be no doubt.

The Empress *was* smiling.

Late that night, within his workroom, Al-Ashmar poured three heaping spoonfuls of ground black walnut husk into the boiling pot before him. The sounds of the evening meal being cleared by the children came from behind. Mia, his second youngest, sat on a stool, watching, as she so often did. She picked up the glass phial of clove juice and removed the stopper, but immediately after recoiled from the sharp smell and wrinkled her nose.

Al-Ashmar laughed. "Then stop smelling it."

"It smells so *weird*."

"Well, weird or not, it's the Empress's, so leave it alone." Al-Ashmar added the minced wormwood root and mixed it thoroughly with the ground husks. That done, he flipped his hourglass over, and the sand began spilling into the empty chamber.

Mia leaned over the table and retrieved a thin piece of coal and the papyrus scrap she'd been writing on. "How long after the bark?"

"Four hours, covered. It will boil down, nearly to a paste."

She wrote chicken prints on the scroll. Al-Ashmar tried to hide his smile, for if she caught him, she always got upset. She didn't know how to write more than a few letters, but still she created her own recipes as Al-Ashmar made things she hadn't learned about yet.

"Then what?"

"I told you, the clove juice, then the elixir, then they steep."

"Oh," she said while writing more, "I forgot." She sat up then and fixed him with a child's most-serious expression. "Doesn't she have people to heal cats in the palace?"

Al-Ashmar found himself hiding another smile. He often told his seven children about his day over their evening meal, but Mia was the one who listened most often. "She does, Mia, but they rarely see such things."

"Snakeworm?"

"Yes."

"From where you and Memma came from."

"Yes."

"Then how did it get here?"

Al-Ashmar shrugged. He still hadn't been able to piece together a plausible story. "I don't know."

"Tell me about the woman again. She sounded pretty."

"I told you, pet, she wasn't pretty. She was mean."

Mia shrugged and tugged the Empress's book closer. "She sounded pretty to *me*." She flipped through the pages, pretending to read each one. "What's this?"

"A gift, from the Empress," Al-Ashmar said.

"What does it teach?"

Al-Ashmar smiled. It was a retelling of several fables from his homeland—four of them, all simple tales of the spirits of the southern lands and how they helped or harmed wayward travelers.

"Nothing," he finally said. "Now off to bed."

Mia ignored him, as she often did on his first warning. "What's this?"

Al-Ashmar snatched the book away and stared at the scribbles Mia had been looking at. He hadn't noticed it earlier. He'd had too much to do, and since it had seemed so innocuous, he'd left it until he had more time to sift through its pages. On the last page were the words *save her* written in an appalling, jittery hand. The letters were oversized as well, as if writing any smaller either was impossible or would have rendered the final text unreadable.

The Empress, surely. But why? Save who?

And from what?

Mia dropped from her stool and fought next to him for a view. "Enough, Mia. To bed."

After tucking the children in for the night, Al-Ashmar stayed up, nursing the tonic and thinking. *Save her.* Save Bela? But that made no sense. He had already been summoned, had already been directed to heal the Empress's cat. Why write a note for that?

Then again, there was no logical reason that the cat would have the worm. Coincidence was too unlikely. So it had to have been intentional. But who would dare infect the Empress's cat? Did the Empress fear that the next attempt would be bolder? Was something afoot even now?

Bela, after all, was the Empress's ninth cat—her last—and when she died, so would the Empress, and her closest servants with her. That might explain Djazir's tense mood, might even explain Rabiah's sullenness. But it wouldn't explain the smile on the Empress's lips. For whatever reason, it seemed most logical that the Empress had arranged this.

Al-Ashmar paged through the tale in which the jagged words had been written. It was a tale of a child that had wandered too far and was destined to die alone in the mountains. But then a legendary shepherd found her and brought her to live with him—him and his eighty-nine children, others who'd been found wandering in the same manner.

Hours later, Al-Ashmar added the clove juice and a honey-ginger elixir to the tonic and left it to steep. After his mind struggled through a thousand dead-end possibilities, Father Sleep finally found him.

The Following day, Al-Ashmar was led to the Empress's garden. Strands of wispy clouds marked the blue sky as a pleasant breeze rattled the palm leaves. Bela sat at the foot of the Empress's throne, which had been moved from inside the cold and empty room. The cat lapped at the cream laced with the tonic.

Odd, Al-Ashmar thought. Cats usually detested the remedy no matter how carefully it was hidden. Al-Ashmar's other patients, however, were not so pliant. Nearby, Rabiah took a deep breath and downed the last of her phial. The eunuchs, thank goodness, had swallowed theirs at a word from Rabiah.

"Bela will need two more doses today," Al-Ashmar said, "and three more tomorrow."

Djazir stared at his half-empty phial, a look of complete disgust on his face.

"Please," Al-Ashmar said to Djazir, "I know it is distasteful, but you need to drink the entire phial."

"I will drink it, physic, but we will not subject the Empress to such a thing."

Al-Ashmar hid his eyes from Djazir. "Of course you know best, but if the Empress has the worm, the effects will only worsen."

The Empress spoke to Rabiah. Al-Ashmar, listening more closely than the day before, could still understand not a single word.

"Of course, Exalted," Rabiah said, and she retrieved the phial meant for the Empress.

Djazir gritted his jaw as Rabiah tilted the phial into the Empress's mouth. The Empress's eyes watered, and she coughed, causing some of it to spill onto Rabiah's hands.

"Be careful of her eyes," Al-Ashmar said, stepping forward. "The tonic will sting horribly for quite some time—"

But Rabiah waved him away. At least she took more care how she supported the Empress's head as she dispensed the liquid. The Empress's coughing slowed the process to a crawl, but eventually the ordeal was over.

Djazir took Al-Ashmar by the elbow, ready to lead him from the garden and out of the palace.

"I wonder if we might speak," Al-Ashmar said. "Alone, so as not to disturb the Empress."

Djazir seemed doubtful, but he released Al-Ashmar's elbow. "What about?"

"A few questions only, in order to narrow down the source of the worms. If we cannot find it, the infection may simply recur."

Djazir brought him up a set of stairs to a railed patio on the roof of the palace. Around them the entire city sprawled over the land for miles. The river glistened as it crawled like the snakeworm through the flesh of the city until reaching the glittering sea several miles away.

Al-Ashmar spoke, asking questions about Bela's activities, the Empress's, even Rabiah's, but this was all a ruse. He'd wanted to get Djazir to agree to questioning simply so he could ask the same of Rabiah. He had to get her alone, for only in her did he have a chance of unwrapping this riddle.

Djazir agreed to send Rabiah up to speak to him as well, and several minutes later, she came and stood a safe distance away from him, staring out over the city. It took him a moment,

but Al-Ashmar realized that Rabiah was staring at the fourteen
spires standing at attention along the shore. Thirteen Empresses
lay buried beneath thirteen obelisks, and the fourteenth stood
empty, waiting. Al-Ashmar thought at first she was simply ignoring him, but there was so much anxiety on her face as she
stared at the obelisk.

"She won't die from the worm, my lady. We've caught it in
time."

Rabiah turned to him and nodded, her face blank now. "I
know, physic."

Then realization struck. Rabiah wasn't afraid because of
the worm, never had been. She was afraid for something else,
something much more serious. Like riddles within riddles, the
answer to this one simple curiosity led to a host of answers he'd
struggled with late into the night.

He hesitated to voice his thoughts—they were thoughts
that could get one killed—but he had no true choice. He could
no more bury this question than he could have denied any of
his children a home when they'd needed it.

"How much longer?"

A muscle twitched along Rabiah's neck. She turned away
from him and stared out over the sharp, rolling landscape. For a
long, long time the only sound he heard was the call of a lone
gull and the pounding of stone hammers in the distance.

"Months, perhaps," she said, "but I fear it will be less."

"You know what she's asking of me, don't you?"

"Yes, physic, but you will do nothing of the sort. I will die
with her. I will help her on the other shore as I have helped her
here."

This was ludicrous, Al-Ashmar thought. He jeopardized
his entire family with this one conversation. He should leave.

He should instruct Djazir in the creation of the tonic, heal Bela, and be done with this foul mess.

But as he stared at Rabiah, he realized how lost she was. She would die the day after the Empress did, would be buried in the Empress's tomb, which waited beneath the newest obelisk along the shores of the Dengkut.

The ways of the Empresses had always seemed strange when he'd been growing up in the southlands, and little had changed since coming to the capital to find his fortune. In fact, the opposite had happened. Each year found him more and more confused.

But that was him. His opinion mattered little. What mattered was why the *Empress* would go against tradition and ask him to save Rabiah from her fate.

The answer, Al-Ashmar realized, could be found by looking no further than his adopted children. Rabiah had cared for the Empress, most likely day and night, ever since her attacks had left her stricken. Rabiah would have become part daughter, part mother. And when the Empress died, Rabiah's bright young life would be forfeit. How could the Empress not try to protect her?

Al-Ashmar regarded Rabiah with new eyes. She had cared for the Empress in life, and she was willing to do so in death, no matter what it might mean for her personally.

"You are noble," Al-Ashmar said.

Rabiah turned to him, a confused look on her beautiful face. "You don't believe that."

Al-Ashmar smiled. "I may not understand much, Rabiah of No Mother, but I know devotion when I see it."

Rabiah stared, saying nothing, but her eyes softened ever so slowly.

"I will need to come for a week, to ensure Bela's restoration is complete. Perhaps we can come here and talk. Perhaps play a hand of river."

"I don't play games, physic."

"Then perhaps just the talk."

Rabiah held his gaze, and then nodded.

The next week passed by quickly. Al-Ashmar's oldest son, Fakhir, was forced to take the summonses Al-Ashmar would have normally taken himself; Tayyeb, his oldest girl, did what she could for those who brought their cats to his home; and though they hated it, it was up to Hilal and Yusuf to watch over the young ones, Shafiq and Badra and Mia.

The family conversed each night over dinner. Al-Ashmar helped them learn from things they did wrong, but in truth his pride swelled over their performances in tasks he had thought them incapable of only days ago.

Most of his time, however, was spent creating the tonic for Bela and the Empress, administering it, and teaching the technique to Djazir. Bela continued her uncanny acceptance of the tonic, as Djazir continued his complaints, but the cure progressed smoothly.

Rabiah held true to her word. She accompanied him to the roof, sometimes for nearly an hour, and spoke to him. She was reserved at first, unwilling to speak, and so it was often Al-Ashmar who told stories of the south, of his travels, of his early days in the capital. It was uncomfortable to speak of Nara, but to speak of his children, he had no choice but to speak of his wife.

"You loved her?" Rabiah asked one day.

"My wife? Of course."

"You couldn't have children of your own?"

Al-Ashmar smiled and jutted his chin toward the city. "She knew what it was like, out there. Why have our own when there are so many in need?"

Rabiah regarded him for a long time then, and finally said, "You wanted one of your own, didn't you?"

Al-Ashmar paused, embarrassed. "Am I so shallow?"

"No, but such a thing is hard to hide when you speak of subjects so close to the heart."

He shrugged, though the gesture felt like a clear betrayal of Nara. "I did want my own, once, but I regret nothing. How would I have found my Mia if I hadn't? My Fakhir and Tayyeb?"

The silence grew uncomfortable, and Al-Ashmar was sure he'd made a mistake by discussing his children. But how could he not? They were his loves. His life.

"*You* are the noble one," Rabiah said, and left him standing near the railing.

Al-Ashmar, hugging Mia against his hip, stood before the palace, unsure of himself with the palace so near.

The eighth day had come—the last day Al-Ashmar would be allowed into the palace. Djazir had mastered the tonic well enough, and he'd grown increasingly insistent that no one, least of all the Empress, needed to take such a distasteful brew any longer.

Al-Ashmar could hardly argue. The snake-like trails in Bela's eyes were gone, and her feces had returned to a proper level of density.

"Let's *go*," Mia said.

"All right, pet, we'll go."

They entered the palace. The guards were a bit disturbed by

the unexpected addition of Mia, but Al-Ashmar explained to
them calmly that Rabiah had permitted it. He made it to the Empress's garden, where he relieved his aching arms of Mia's weight.

Djazir marched forward. "What is this?"

"Eminence, my sincere apologies. With my absence, my
business is in a shambles. My other children are old enough to
run my errands, but I had no one to watch Mia. She will sit
quietly, here, and bother no one."

"She had best not, physic." Djazir frowned and stared at
Mia. "Don't touch a thing, child. Do you hear me?"

Mia hugged Al-Ashmar's waist and nodded.

Al-Ashmar calmed Mia down enough that he could leave
her on a bench near the rear of the garden, mostly out of sight of
the Empress's three peaked doorways. He made his way inside
the room, where the Empress sat waiting on her throne. The
four guards stood at the corners of the room, two more behind
the throne, but Rabiah was not to be found. Where was she?

The Empress stared out through the gauzy curtains hanging over the doorways. She studied the garden, perhaps watching Mia play. Then her eyes took in Al-Ashmar.

And a hint of a smile came to her lips.

Al-Ashmar couldn't help but return the smile, but he hid it
as quickly as it had come.

Bela strutted around from the back of the throne and moved
to the bowl of cream placed there by Djazir.

"Come, physic."

Al-Ashmar nodded. From inside his vest he retrieved one
of the eight phials he'd brought for their final day, but Djazir
held up his hand to forestall him.

"I've administered my own tonic," Djazir said. "All that's
left is for you to examine Bela."

Al-Ashmar began to worry. He needed to speak to Rabiah this one last time for he would never have the chance again, but with the tonic already administered there was only so far he could extend the examination before Djazir caught on. He did what he could: He kneeled and studied Bela's golden eyes closely even though they were obviously clear of the worm; he checked her muscle tone and reflexes; he examined her teeth.

"Enough," Djazir said, stepping to Al-Ashmar's side. "We both know Bela is fine. The Empress thanks you for your time."

Just then the Empress began to cough, a wracking, hoarse affair, and it nearly shook her from the throne. The guards moved to hold her, but Djazir waved them away as he rushed to her side. Al-Ashmar waited, hoping that Rabiah would step from the rear of the room.

"That will be all, ak Kulhadn."

Al-Ashmar bowed and retreated to the sounds of the Empress's horrible coughing. How painful it sounded. Painful, but also a touch forced to Al-Ashmar's ear.

He reached the garden, but could not find Mia.

"Mia," he called softly, hoping Djazir wouldn't hear.

She wasn't in the garden, so he moved up the stairs leading to the rooftop patio. He allowed himself to smile. Rabiah was crouched next to Mia, and her gaze followed Mia's outstretched finger through the balustrades of the marble railing to the city beyond.

"Is that so?" Rabiah asked.

Mia nodded. "And then Peppa brought it to our house. It was big as me—at least, big as I was then, which is still pretty big."

Mia noticed Al-Ashmar approach. "I *told* you she was pretty," Mia said.

Al-Ashmar smiled as his face flushed. He wished he could say the same thing to her, but Nara's memory stayed his tongue.

"You could help others," Al-Ashmar said as he tussled Mia's dark hair, "and the Empress will be waiting for you on the other side."

"She'll need me."

"She'll have your predecessor, Rabiah. She'll have the others." He motioned down toward the Empress's coughing, which was starting to subside. "She'll be whole once she reaches the far shore."

Her eyes were pleading, as if she *wanted* a reason to come with him. "This is blasphemy."

"Not where we're from," Mia said, as if she, too, were from the south.

Rabiah looked down at Mia, and a sad smile came to her lips. "That's just it, child. It *is,* even where your peppa's from." When she again met Al-Ashmar's eyes, her expression was resolute. "Please, go."

Al-Ashmar hesitated. Words always seemed to flee in the important moments of his life, and this time he knew the reason why. No matter how foolish he considered Rabiah's choice to be, he would never force his beliefs on another. She would have to embrace the Empress's wish before she could be saved.

"You would be loved," he said to Rabiah, and then he picked up Mia and left the palace.

When they were back in the streets, Mia said, "Is she coming to live with us?"

"No, pet, she's not."

Al-Ashmar woke upon hearing the great bell on top of the Hall of Ancients ring. A gentle rain pattered against the roof.

The bell rang again and again. Al-Ashmar knew, well before it had reached the fourteenth peal, that the Empress had died.

When it was over, he sat there in the silence, feeling as if one of his own family had been lost. No, not one. Two. The Empress, even in her state, had smiled upon him in more ways than one—how could he not consider her family? And Rabiah. She'd been so close to walking away from her pointless fate.

A soft knock came at the door.

He opened it in a rush and found Rabiah standing outside, drenched.

"I don't want to die," she said.

Al-Ashmar stepped aside and ushered her into his house. He motioned her to his workroom, where the hearth still had enough embers to stoke some warmth from them. He got a blanket for Rabiah and wrapped it around her shoulders.

Fakhir walked into the room, hair disheveled with a blanket around his shoulders. "Everything all right, Peppa?"

"Fine, Fakhir. Go to bed."

Fakhir retired, leaving Al-Ashmar alone with this beauty and the sounds of the pattering rain. He prepared some lime tea for her, but by the time he handed it to her, she looked confused, as if coming to him might have been a terrible mistake.

"There is no shame in living a longer life, Rabiah. There's so much good you can do. For these children." He paused. "For me."

She looked at him then. Her eyes, no longer rimmed with kohl, looked just as beautiful in the ruddy light of the hearth. "For you?"

A harsh knock came at the front door.

Al-Ashmar's heart beat faster in his chest. "Were you followed?"

Rabiah glanced around, as if specters would take form from the shadows around them. "I—I took precautions."

Djazir's voice bellowed from the other side of the door. "Open, ak Kulhadn, or we'll break the door in."

Al-Ashmar scrambled for a proper hiding place, but there would be none. He couldn't even spirit her out the rear door. There was no telling what Djazir would do if they were caught running.

"It will be all right," Al-Ashmar said as he stood and moved to the door. "Stay by my side."

Four of his children stood in the doorway of their bed-room. "Fakhir, get them to bed, now. Close your door."

Before he could reach the front door, it crashed open. Al-Ashmar shivered. Three guards stormed into the room. Two more stood outside with Djazir. After the guards had po-sitioned themselves about the room, Djazir strode in as if it were his own home. He looked Al-Ashmar up and down, then Rabiah, who stood nearby.

"Rabiah, come."

She stayed planted, gaze darting between Al-Ashmar and Djazir.

"Djazir, please. We can discuss this."

Djazir motioned to the nearest guard. Al-Ashmar barely registered the fist from the corner of his eye, and then every-thing was pain and disorientation. He fell, his shoulder and neck striking the low eating table in the center of the room. A piercing ache stormed up his neck to the base of his skull.

Before he could make sense of what had happened, the guard closest to Rabiah grabbed the back of her neck and man-handled her toward the exit.

"Stop!"

"Dear physic, you have made this *more* than necessary." He knelt next to Al-Ashmar, daring him to rise. "Now, I will assume, for the sake of your children, that Rabiah has come to you for a bit of advice, that she has come to spill her fears of the time to come. It is natural, after all; you of all people should know this. I'll also assume that you kindly told her that everything will be fine, that her sacred voyage will be painless, and that she should return to the palace, as any good citizen would."

Al-Ashmar opened his mouth to speak, but Djazir talked over him.

"But if I find differently, or if I see you again before I guide the Empress to the opposite shore, I'll have your head." Djazir stood. "Do we understand one another?"

The door to the children's room was cracked open. Mia's whimpering filtered into the room. He had no choice. He had to protect them, and though it burned his gut to do so, he nodded to Djazir.

Djazir smiled, though his eyes still pierced. "I see we have an understanding. It would be a pity for seven orphans to become orphaned all over again."

And with that he left. The door stood open, and Al-Ashmar could only watch as Rabiah was forced to accompany them up the street, toward the palace.

The sun had not yet risen. It was hours since Rabiah had been taken away, but still Al-Ashmar could think of nothing to do. He was powerless to stop Djazir.

"Peppa?" It was Mia, standing in the doorway to his workroom.

"Go to bed," Al-Ashmar said.

"Nobody can sleep, and it's almost morning."

Several of the other children were preparing breakfast in the main room behind Mia.

"Then eat."

Mia sat on the stool nearby and picked up the Empress's book. "Is she coming back?"

Al-Ashmar wanted to cry. "No, Mia. She's not."

Just then a cat entered through the rear door of the workroom and rubbed against Mia's leg. "Bela!" Mia said.

Indeed, the cat looked just like the Empress's. Al-Ashmar picked the animal up and examined her eyes, removing any doubt. This was certainly Bela, but how was it possible? The cat should have died with the Empress.

Bela bit the meat of Al-Ashmar's thumb, and he dropped her in surprise. Bela walked from the room as if she'd never intended to be here in the first place.

Al-Ashmar followed her out the rear door. Bela had already slunk beneath the gate of their small yard and out to the alley behind. Al-Ashmar followed and called back to Mia, who was trying to trail him. "Go back, Mia. I'll return when I can."

Al-Ashmar trailed Bela through the pale light of pre-dawn. She wound her way through the streets, and it gradually became clear she was leading him toward the palace. But she avoided the main western road. She traveled instead to the rear of the tall hill that housed it. She climbed the rocks, often leaving her human companion behind, but she would stop when Al-Ashmar fell too far back and then continue before he could catch up to her.

The eastern face of the hill held a shallow ravine with plants dotting a trail—most likely from the waste it carried from the palace to the river. Bela found a crook in the hillside, whereupon she stopped. When Al-Ashmar finally caught up, she circled his legs and meowed.

Al-Ashmar parted the wall of vines clinging to the nearby boulder. A low, dark tunnel entrance stood there. Al-Ashmar rushed through, realizing that Bela—or more likely the soul of the Empress—was leading him up to the palace. In utter darkness, he climbed the spiral stairs as quickly as his burning lungs would allow. Occasionally the stairwell would end, forcing him to take a short passage to find another that led him upward once more, but by and large it was strictly a grueling uphill climb.

His legs threatened to give out, forcing him to stop, but dawn would arrive soon, and Al-Ashmar feared that would be when the Empress's retinue would be killed.

Finally, dim light came from above, and the peal of a bell filtered down to him. Dawn had arrived. Bela meowed somewhere ahead. He felt sure he'd climbed treble the height of the palace, but still he pushed harder. The light intensified, and he came to a wall with a grate embedded into it. Though the brightness hurt his eyes, he surveyed what he realized was the Empress's garden.

Visible through the three peaked doorways, Djazir paced along the Empress's throne room. Six of the Empress's personal guard stood nearby, each wearing ornate leather armor with a sword and dagger hanging from a silver belt. Djazir wore a white silk robe embroidered with crimson thread, and a ceremonial dagger hung from a golden belt at his waist. The Empress was wrapped in folds of white cloth, her face still exposed. Five bolts of white cloth waited on the marble floor to her left.

To her right, on another bolt of cloth, was Rabiah, unconscious or dead.

Please, Rabiah, be alive.

Djazir continued to pace and wring his hands. A young

man, wearing clothes similar to but not so grand as Djazir's, entered the garden and reported to Djazir.

As the two of them conversed, too low to be heard, Bela strolled out from the grate. Al-Ashmar tried to prevent it, but Bela sped up just before his fingers could reach her. She walked up to Djazir as if she were asking for a bit of cream.

"By the spirits, thank you," Djazir said loudly as he picked Bela up. "Now please," he said. "Prepare yourselves." Then he turned to the young man. "Prepare the procession immediately. You will find everything ready by the time you return."

The young man bowed and walked back through the garden. Al-Ashmar heard a heavy wooden door close. Moments later, the palace's bell pealed once more.

Al-Ashmar, heart quickening, searched the landscape of the grate, looking for any sign of a catch. He found something hard and irregular about halfway down on the left side, but had no idea how to release it.

As the Empress's guards positioned themselves on their white cloths, Djazir ladled a thick white liquid from a ceramic bowl using an ornate spoon. He held the spoon to Bela's lips and waited as she lapped at it. Then he set Bela down on a silk pillow on the Empress's throne and petted her until her movements slowed.

Bela rested her head on her crossed paws and stared directly at Al-Ashmar. Her eyes blinked, twice, before slowly closing for the last time. Her lungs ceased to draw breath mere moments later.

The bell pealed again, long and slow.

Djazir moved to each of the guards in turn and administered a spoonful of the liquid. Their bodies were already lying down, but each fell slack less than three breaths after imbibing the poison.

Al-Ashmar worked frantically at the catch. Open, damn it! Open!

Djazir moved next to Rabiah's motionless form.

"Stop it, Djazir!"

Djazir turned. He moved toward the grate, squinting.

The catch released.

Al-Ashmar stepped out into the light, ready to charge for Djazir should he make a move toward Rabiah. Instead Djazir dropped the spoon and pulled his dagger free of its sheath.

"I was willing to let your children live, Al-Ashmar, but an affront such as this demands their deaths."

Al-Ashmar, heart beating wildly, patted his vest for anything he might use as a weapon and found only the leftover phials of Bela's tonic. He swallowed hard and pulled one of them from his vest pocket.

Djazir chuckled. "Are you going to heal me, physic?"

Al-Ashmar unstoppered the phial and waited for Djazir to come close, but Djazir lunged much faster than Al-Ashmar had anticipated. Al-Ashmar dodged, but still the steel bit deep into his shoulder. He flung the phial's contents at Djazir's face, aiming for the eyes. Enough of the acerbic liquid struck home, and Djazir screamed and fell backward.

Al-Ashmar fell on top of Djazir, driving his good shoulder into Djazir's gut. A long, deep, noisy exhalation was forced from Djazir's lungs, giving Al-Ashmar time to scramble on top of him. Holding the knife to one side, Al-Ashmar seized Djazir's neck and applied all the leverage he could as the older man writhed beneath him, sputtering and choking, eyes pinched tight. Finally, as the palace bell pealed over the city, Djazir's body lost all tension.

Al-Ashmar breathed heavily, wincing from the pain in his screaming shoulder. He cleaned Djazir as best he could and tugged him into position on the remaining bolt of white cloth. Then he rushed to Rabiah's side and tried to wake her. He thought surely she was dead, thought surely this had all been for naught, but no, she still had a faint heartbeat. She still drew breath, however slowly. He slapped her, but she would not wake.

The bell pealed. They would return soon.

Al-Ashmar took a bit of the tonic still left in the phial and spread it under and inside Rabiah's nostrils. She jerked and her eyes opened. She was slow in focusing, but eventually she seemed to recognize Al-Ashmar.

"Where am I?" she asked, rubbing the tonic from her nose.

"Not now. I will explain all later."

Al-Ashmar helped Rabiah through the grate, but before he could take the first of the steps down, she turned him around and wrapped her arms around him.

"Thank you for my life," she said.

He freed himself from her embrace and pulled her toward the stairs. "Thank me when you have your new one."

Al-Ashmar knew they would have to leave for foreign lands, but it couldn't be helped. He hadn't expected this change in fortune, but neither had he expected his wife to die or to raise seven children on his own. He would take what fate gave him and deal with it as best he could.

With Rabiah.

Yes, with Rabiah it would all be just a little bit easier.

Afterword by Bradley P. Beaulieu

I heard an analogy years ago: that you draw yourself toward a goal similar to the way a rubber band pulls a weight across a table. If the pull is too slack, you end up moving toward your goal too slowly (or not at all); too fast and the rubber band breaks. It's at those in-between times where the pull is not too strong and not too slack that you work at peak efficiency. I believe this is what happened to me with this story.

"In the Eyes of the Empress's Cat" was written during Uncle Orson's Literary Bootcamp in the summer of 2005. In Bootcamp, the campers are asked to write one story—in twenty-four hours. Well, that's not exactly true. You take one day to brainstorm and develop the story idea; the story idea is critiqued by the group the following day; and *then* you're expected to write the story in twenty-four hours.

The guidelines we were given were interesting and may give some insight into how easy it can be to generate story ideas. First, we were told to interview random people. We were allowed to say *why* we were interviewing them, but beyond that it was simply a conversation with a person I didn't know that would eventually (inevitably) reveal something insightful or enigmatic or thought-provoking—in other words: something I could use in my story. The thing to note here is that this was not only true of the person I ended up interviewing, but of *anyone* I might have interviewed.

The young woman I met was a college student, still trying to find her way in life but interested in medicine. She spoke of a family friend who had had a stroke. During her recovery this woman would *try* to say one word, but a completely different yet perfectly intelligible word would come out of her mouth, as if the wires to the one word had been rerouted to the other. Out of this conversation, as you may have guessed, came the Empress.

Another brainstorming technique was to visit a library or bookstore and simply browse. Just like a conversation with a stranger, this will eventually produce something that can complicate or enhance a story. I found a book on iridology, the discipline of assessing one's health through examination of the iris and white of the eye. I'll leave you to determine how this affected the story.

I'm embarrassed to admit that I didn't complete the story in the allotted time frame. I took an extra day, but I'm still very proud of the result. That's not to say that I did this alone. I have all my fellow '05 Bootcampers to thank and, of course, Card himself. As I recall, Card was critical of my initial story idea, and rightly so. It was with his insights and all the excellent advice I received during Bootcamp that "Cat" was conceived, created, and refined. My heartfelt thanks to all those involved.

Mazer in Prison
BY ORSON SCOTT CARD

Being the last best hope of humanity was a lousy job.

Sure, the pay was great, but it had to pile up in a bank back on Earth, because there was no place out here to shop.

There was no place to *walk*. When your official exercise program consisted of having your muscles electrically stimulated while you slept, then getting spun around in a centrifuge so your bones wouldn't dissolve, there wasn't much to look forward to in an average day.

To Mazer Rackham, it felt as though he was being punished for having won the last war.

After the defeat of the invading Formics—or "Buggers," as they were commonly called—the International Fleet learned everything they could from the alien technology. Then, as fast as they could build the newly designed starships, the IF launched them toward the Formic home world, and the other planets that had been identified as Formic colonies.

But they hadn't sent Mazer out with any of *those* ships. If they had, then he wouldn't be completely alone. There'd be other people to talk to—fighter pilots, crew. Primates with faces and hands and voices and *smells,* was that asking so much?

No, he had a much more important mission. He was supposed to command *all* the fleets in their attacks on all the Formic worlds. That meant he would need to be back in the solar system, communicating with all the fleets by ansible.

Great. A cushy desk job. He was old enough to relish that.

Except for one hitch.

Since space travel could only approach but never quite reach three hundred million meters per second, it would take many years for the fleets to reach their target worlds. During those years of waiting back at International Fleet headquarters—IF-COM—Mazer would grow old and frail, physically *and* mentally.

So to keep him young enough to be useful, they shut him up in a near-lightspeed courier ship and launched him on a completely meaningless outbound journey. At some arbitrary point in space, they decreed, he would decelerate, turn around, and then return to Earth at the same speed, arriving home only a few years before the fleets arrived and all hell broke loose. He would have aged no more than five years during the voyage, even though decades would have passed on Earth.

A lot of good he'd do them as a commander, if he lost his mind during the voyage.

Sure, he had plenty of books in the onboard database. Millions of them. And announcements of new books were sent to him by ansible; any he wanted, he could ask for and have them in moments.

What he couldn't have was a conversation.

He had tried. After all, how different was the ansible from regular email over the nets? The problem was the time differential. To him, it seemed he sent out a message and it was answered immediately. But to the person on the other end, Mazer's message was spread out over days, coming in a bit at a time. Once his whole message had been received and assembled, the person could write an answer immediately. But to be received by the ansible on Mazer's little boat, the answer would be spaced out a bit at a time, as well.

The result was that for the person Mazer was conversing with, many days intervened between the parts of the conversation. It had to be like talking with somebody with such an incredible stammer that you could walk away, live your life for a week, and then come back before he had finally spit out whatever it was he had to say.

A few people had tried, but by now, with Mazer nearing the point where he would decelerate to turn the ship around, his communications with IF-COM on the asteroid Eros were mostly limited to book and holo and movie requests, plus his daily blip—the message he sent just to assure the IF that he wasn't dead.

He could even have automated the daily blip—it's not as if Mazer didn't know how to get around their firewalls and reprogram the shipboard computer. But he dutifully composed a new and unique message every day that he knew would barely be glanced at back at IF-COM. As far as anyone there cared, he might as well be dead; they would all have retired or even died before he got back.

The problem of loneliness wasn't a surprise, of course. They had even suggested sending someone with him. Mazer himself had vetoed the idea, because it seemed to him to be stupid and cruel to tell a person that he was so completely useless to the fleet, to the whole war effort, that he could be sent out on Mazer's aimless voyage just to hold his hand. "What will your recruiting poster be next year?" Mazer had asked. "'Join the International Fleet and spend a couple of years as a paid companion to an aging space captain!'?"

To Mazer it was only going to *be* a few years. He was a private person who didn't mind being alone. He was sure he could handle it.

What he hadn't taken into account was how long two years of solitary confinement would *be*. They do this, he realized, to prisoners who've misbehaved, as the worst punishment they could give. Think of that—to be completely alone for long periods of time is *worse* than having to keep company with the vilest, stupidest felons known to man.

We evolved to be social creatures; the Formics, by their hivemind nature, are never alone. They can travel this way with impunity. To a lone human, it's torture.

And of course there was the tiny matter of leaving his family behind. But he wouldn't think about that. He was making no greater sacrifice than any of the other warriors who took off in the fleets sent to destroy the enemy. Win or lose, none of *them* would see their families again. In this, at least, he was one with the men he would be commanding.

The real problem was one that only he recognized: He didn't have a clue how to save the human race, once he got back.

That was the part that nobody seemed to understand. He

explained it to them, that he was not a particularly good commander, that he had won that crucial battle on a fluke, that there was no reason to think he could do such a thing again. His superior officers agreed that he might be right. They promised to recruit and train new officers while Mazer was gone, trying to find a better commander. But in case they didn't find one, Mazer *was* the guy who fired the single missile that ended the previous war. People believed in him. Even if he didn't believe in himself.

Of course, knowing the military mind, Mazer knew that they would completely screw up the search for a new commander. The only way they would take the search seriously was if they did *not* believe they had Mazer Rackham as their ace in the hole.

Mazer sat in the confined space behind the pilot seat and extended his left leg, stretching it up, then bringing it behind his head. Not every man his age could do this. Definitely not every *Maori,* not those with the traditional bulk of the fully adult male. Of course, he was only half Maori, but it wasn't as if people of European blood were known for their extraordinary physical flexibility.

The console speaker said, "Incoming message."

"I'm listening," said Mazer. "Make it voice and read it now."

"Male or female?" asked the computer.

"Who cares?" said Mazer.

"Male or female?" the computer repeated.

"Random," said Mazer.

So the message was read out to him in a female voice.

"Admiral Rackham, my name is Hyrum Graff. I've been assigned to head recruitment for Battle School, the first step in our training program for gifted young officers. My job is to scour the Earth looking for someone to head our forces during the coming conflict—instead of you. I was told by everyone who bothered to answer me at all that the criterion was simple: Find someone just like Mazer Rackham."

Mazer found himself interested in what this guy was saying. They were actually looking for his replacement. This man was in charge of the search. To listen to him in a voice of a different gender seemed mocking and disrespectful.

"Male voice," said Mazer.

Immediately the voice changed to a robust baritone. "The trouble I'm having, Admiral, is that when I ask them specifically what *traits* of yours I should try to identify for my recruits, everything becomes quite vague. The only conclusion I can reach is this: The attribute of yours that they want the new commander to have is 'victorious.' In vain do I point out that I need better guidelines than that.

"So I have turned to you for help. You know as well as I do that there was a certain component of luck involved in your victory. At the same time, you saw what no one else could see, and you acted—against orders—at exactly the right moment for your thrust to be unnoticed by the Hive Queen. Boldness, courage, iconoclasm—maybe we can identify those traits. But how do we test for vision?

"There's a social component, too. The men in your crew trusted you enough to obey your disobedient orders and put their careers, if not their lives, in your hands.

"Your record of reprimands for insubordination suggests, also, that you are an experienced critic of incompetent commanders. So you must also have very clear ideas of what your future replacement should *not* be.

"Therefore I have obtained permission to use the ansible to query you about the attributes we need to look for—or avoid—in the recruits we find. In the hope that you will find this project more interesting than whatever it is you're doing out there in space, I eagerly await your reply."

Mazer sighed. This Graff sounded like exactly the kind of officer who should be put in charge of finding Mazer's replacement. But Mazer also knew enough about military bureaucracy to know that Graff would be chewed up and spit out the first time he actually tried to accomplish something. Getting permission to communicate by ansible with an old geezer who was effectively dead was easy enough.

"What was the sender's rank?" Mazer asked the console.

"Lieutenant."

Poor Lieutenant Graff had obviously underestimated the terror that incompetent officers feel in the presence of young, intelligent, energetic *replacements*.

At least it would be a conversation.

"Take down this answer, please," said Mazer. "Dear Lieutenant Graff, I'm sorry for the time you have to waste waiting for this message . . . no, scratch that, why *increase* the wasted time by sending a message stuffed with useless chat?" Then again, doing a whole bunch of editing would delay the message just as long.

Mazer sighed, unwound himself from his stretch, and went to the console. "I'll type it in myself," said Mazer. "It'll go faster that way."

He found the words he had just dictated waiting for him on the screen of his message console, with the edge of Graff's message just behind it. He flipped that message to the front, read it again, and then picked up his own message where he had left off.

"I am not an expert in identifying the traits of leadership. Your message reveals that you have already thought more about it than I have. Much as I might hope your endeavor is successful, since it would relieve me of the burden of command upon my return, I cannot help you."

He toyed with adding "God could not help you," but decided to let the boy find out how the world worked without dire and useless warnings from Mazer.

Instead he said "Send" and the console replied, "Message sent by ansible."

And that, thought Mazer, is the end of that.

The answer did not come for more than three hours. What was that, a month back on Earth?

"Who is it from?" asked Mazer, knowing perfectly well who it would turn out to be. So the boy had taken his time before pushing the matter. Time enough to learn how impossible his task was? Probably not.

Mazer was sitting on the toilet—which, thanks to the Formics' gravitic technology, was a standard gravity-dependent chemical model. Mazer was one of the few still in the service who remembered the days of air-suction toilets in weightless spaceships, which worked about half the time. That was the era when ship captains would sometimes be cashiered for wasting fuel by accelerating their ships just so they could take a dump that would actually get pulled away from their backside by something like gravity.

"Lieutenant Hyrum Graff."

And now he had the pestiferous Hyrum Graff, who would probably be even more annoying than null-g toilets.

"Erase it."

"I am not allowed to erase ansible communications," said

the female voice blandly. It was always bland, of course, but it *felt* particularly bland when saying irritating things.

I could make you erase it, if I wanted to go to the trouble of reprogramming you. But Mazer didn't say it, in case it might alert the program safeguards in some way. "Read it."

"Male voice?"

"Female," snapped Mazer.

"Admiral Rackham, I'm not sure you understood the gravity of our situation. We have two possibilities: Either we will identify the best possible commanders for our war against the Formics, or we will have you as our commander. So either you will help us identify the traits that are most likely to be present in the ideal commander, or you will *be* the commander on whom all the responsibility rests."

"I understand that, you little twit," said Mazer. "I understood it before you were born."

"Would you like me to take down your remarks as a reply?" asked the computer.

"Just read it and ignore my carping."

The computer returned to the message from Lieutenant Graff. "I have located your wife and children. They are all in good health, and it may be that some or all of them might be glad of an opportunity to converse with you by ansible, if you so desire. I offer this, not as a bribe for your cooperation, but as a reminder, perhaps, that more is at stake here than the importunities of an upstart lieutenant pestering an admiral and a war hero on a voyage into the future."

Mazer roared out his answer. "As if I had need of reminders from *you*!"

"Would you like me to take down your remarks as—"

"I'd like you to shut yourself down and leave me in—"

"A reply?" finished the computer, ignoring his carping.

"Peace!" Mazer sighed. "Take down *this* answer: I'm divorced, and my ex-wife and children have made their lives without me. To them I'm dead. It's despicable for you to attempt to raise me from the grave to burden their lives. When I tell you that I have nothing to tell you about command it's because I truly do not know any answers that you could possibly implement.

"I'm desperate for you to find a replacement for me, but in all my experience in the military, I saw no example of the kind of commander that we need. So figure it out for yourself—I haven't any idea."

For a moment he allowed his anger to flare. "And leave my family out of it, you contemptible . . ."

Then he decided not to flame the poor git. "Delete everything after 'leave my family out of it.'"

"Do you wish me to read it back to you?"

"I'm on the toilet!"

Since his answer was nonresponsive, the computer repeated the question verbatim.

"No. Just send it. I don't want to have the zealous Lieutenant Graff wait an extra hour or day just so I can turn my letter into a prizewinning school essay."

But Graff's question nagged at him. What *should* they look for in a commander?

What did it matter? As soon as they developed a list of desirable traits, all the bureaucratic buttsniffs would immediately figure out how to fake having them, and they'd be right back where they started, with the best bureaucrats at the top of every military hierarchy, and all the genuinely brilliant leaders either discharged or demoralized.

The way I was demoralized, piloting a barely-armed supply ship in the rear echelons of our formation.

Which was in itself a mark of the stupidity of our commanders—the fact that they thought there could *be* such a thing as a "rear echelon" during a war in three-dimensional space.

There might have been dozens of men who could have seen what I saw—the point of vulnerability in the Formics' formation—but they had long since left the service. The only reason *I* was there was because I couldn't afford to quit before vesting in my pension. So I put up with spiteful commanders who would punish me for being a better officer than they would ever be. I took the abuse, the contempt, and so there I was piloting a ship with only two weapons—slow missiles at that.

Turned out I only needed one.

But who could have predicted that I'd be there, that I'd see what I saw, and that I'd commit career suicide by firing my missiles against orders—and then I'd turn out to be right? What process can test for *that*? Might as well resort to prayer—either God is looking out for the human race or he doesn't care. If he cares, then we'll go on surviving despite our stupidity. If he doesn't, then we won't.

In a universe that works like *that,* any attempt to identify in advance the traits of great commanders is utterly wasted.

"Incoming visuals," said the computer.

Mazer looked down at his desk screen, where he had jotted

Desperation
Intuition (test for *that,* sucker!)
Tolerance for the orders of fools
~~Borderline~~-insane sense of personal mission

Yeah, *that's* the list Graff's hoping I'll send him.

And now the boy was sending him visuals. Who approved *that*?

But the head that flickered in the holospace above his desk wasn't an eagerbeaver young lieutenant. It was a young woman with light-colored hair like her mother's and only a few traces of her father's part-Maori appearance. Still, the traces *were* there, and she was beautiful.

"Stop," said Mazer.

"I am required to show you—"

"This is personal. This is an *intrusion*."

"—all ansible communications."

"Later."

"This is a visual and therefore has high priority. Sufficient ansible bandwidth for full-motion visuals will only be used for communications of the—"

Mazer gave up. "Just play it."

"Father," said the young woman in the holospace.

Mazer looked away from her, reflexively hiding his face, though of course she couldn't see him anyway. His daughter, Pai Mahutanga. When he last saw her, she was a tree-climbing five-year-old. She used to have nightmares, but with her father always on duty with the fleet, there was no one to drive away the bad dreams.

"I brought your grandchildren with me," she was saying. "Pahu Rangi hasn't found a woman yet who will let him reproduce." She grinned wickedly at someone out of frame. Her brother. Mazer's son. Just a baby, conceived on his last leave before the final battle.

"We've told the children all about you. I know you can't see them all at once, but if they each come into frame with me for just a few moments—it's so generous of them to let me—

"But he said that you might not be happy to see me. Even if that's true, Father, I know you'll want to see your grandchildren. They'll still be alive when you return. *I* might even be. Please don't hide from us. We know that when you divorced Mother it was for her sake, and ours. We know that you never stopped loving us. See? Here's Kahui Kura. And Pao Pao Te Rangi. They also have English names, Mirth and Glad, but they're proud to be children of the Maori. Through you. But your grandson Mazer Taka Aho Howarth insists on using the name you went . . . *go* by. And as for baby Struan Maeroero, he'll make the choice when he gets older." She sighed. "I suppose he's our last child, if the New Zealand courts uphold the Hegemony's new population rules."

As each of the children stepped into frame, shyly or boldly, depending on their personality, Mazer tried to feel something toward them. Two daughters first, shy, lovely. The little boy named for him. Finally the baby that someone held into the frame.

They were strangers, and before he ever met them they would be parents themselves. Perhaps grandparents. What was the *point*? I told your mother that we had to be dead to each other. She had to think of me as a casualty of war, even if the paperwork said DIVORCE DECREE instead of KILLED IN ACTION.

She was so angry she told me that she would rather I had died. She was going to tell our children that I was dead. Or that I just left them, without giving them any reason, so they'd hate me.

Now it turns out she turned my departure into a sentimental

memory of sacrifice for God and country. Or at least for planet and species.

Mazer forced himself not to wonder if this meant that she had forgiven him. She was the one with children to raise—what she decided to tell them was none of his business. Whatever helped her raise the children without a father.

He didn't marry and have children until he was already middle-aged; he'd been afraid to start a family when he knew he'd be gone on voyages lasting years at a time. Then he met Kim, and all that rational process went out the window. He wanted—his DNA wanted—their children to exist, even if he couldn't be there to raise them. Pai Mahutanga and Pahu Rangi—he wanted the children's lives to be stable and good, rich with opportunity, so he stayed in the service in order to earn the separation bonuses that would pay to put them through college.

Then he fought in the war to keep them safe. But he was going to retire when the war ended and go home to them at last, while they were still young enough to welcome a father. Then he got *this* assignment.

Why couldn't you just *decide,* you bastards? Decide you were going to replace me, and then let me go home and have my hero's welcome and then retire to Christchurch and listen to the ringing of the bells to tell me God's in his heaven and all's right with the world. You could have left me home with my family, to raise my children, to be there so I could talk Pai out of naming her firstborn son after me.

I could have given all the advice and training you wanted—more than you'd ever use, that's for sure—and then *left* the fleet and had some kind of life. But no, I had to leave everything and come out here in this miserable box while you dither.

Mazer noticed that Pai's face was frozen and she was making no sound. "You stopped the playback," said Mazer.

"You weren't paying attention," said the computer. "This is a *visual* ansible transmission, and you are required to—"

"I'm watching *now*," said Mazer.

Pai's voice came again, and the visual moved again. "They're going to slow this down to transmit it to you. But you know all about time dilation. The bandwidth is expensive, too, so I guess I'm done with the visual part of this. I've written you a letter, and so have the kids. And Pahu swears that someday he'll learn to read and write." She laughed again, looking at someone out of frame. It had to be his son, the baby he had never seen. Tantalizingly close, but not coming into frame. Someone was controlling that. Someone decided not to let him see his son. Graff? How closely was he manipulating this? Or was it Kim who decided? Or Pahu himself?

"Mother has written to you, too. Actually, quite a few letters. She wouldn't come, though. She doesn't want you to see her looking so old. But she's still beautiful, Father. More beautiful than ever, with white hair and—she still loves you. She wants you to remember her younger. She told me once, 'I was never *beautiful,* and when I met a man who thought I was, I married him over his most heartfelt objections.'"

Her imitation of her mother was so accurate that it stopped Mazer's breath for a moment. Could it truly be that Kim had refused to come because of some foolish vanity about how she looked? As if he would care!

But he *would* care. Because she would be old, and that would prove that it was true, that she would surely be dead before he made it back to Earth. And because of that, it would not be *home* he came back to. There was no such place.

"I love you, Father," Pai was saying. "Not just because you saved the world. We honor you for that, of course. But we love you because you made Mother so happy. She would tell us stories about you. It's as if we knew you. And your old mates would visit sometimes, and then we knew that Mother wasn't exaggerating about you. Either that or they *all* were." She laughed. "You *have* been part of our lives. We may be strangers to you, but you're not a stranger to us."

The image flickered, and when it came back, she was not in quite the same position. There had been an edit. Perhaps because she didn't want him to see her cry. He knew she had been about to, because her face still worked before weeping the same way as when she was little. It had not been so very long, for him, since she was small. He remembered very well.

"You don't have to answer this," she said. "Lieutenant Graff told us that you might not welcome this transmission. Might even refuse to watch it. We don't want to make your voyage harder. But Father, when you come home—when you come back to us—you *have* a home. In our hearts. Even if I'm gone, even if only *our* children are here to meet you, our arms are open. Not to greet the conquering hero. But to welcome home our papa and grandpa, however old we are. I love you. We *all* do. *All.*"

And then, almost as an afterthought: "Please read our letters."

"I have letters for you," said the computer, as the holospace went empty.

"Save them," said Mazer. "I'll get to them."

"You are authorized to send a visual reply," said the computer.

"That will not happen," said Mazer. But even as he said it, he was wondering what he could possibly say, if he changed his mind and did send them his image. Some heroic speech about the nobility of sacrifice? Or an apology for accepting the assignment?

He would never show his face to them. Would never let Kim see that he was *not* changed.

He would read the letters. He would answer them. There were duties you owed to family, even if the reason they got involved was because of some meddling jerk of a lieutenant.

"My first letter," said Mazer, "will be to that git, Graff. It's very brief. 'Bugger off, gitling.' Sign it 'respectfully yours.'"

"'Bugger' is a noun. 'Git' is a substandard verb, and 'gitling' is not in any of my wordbases. I cannot spell or parse the message properly without explanation . . . Do you mean 'Leave this place, alien enemy'?"

"I made 'gitling' up, but it's an excellent word, so use it. And I can't believe they programmed you without 'bugger off' in the wordbase."

"I detect stress," said the computer. "Will you accept mild sedation?"

"The stress is being caused by your forcing me to view a message I did not want to see. *You* are causing my stress. So give me some time to myself to calm down."

"Incoming message."

Mazer felt his stress levels rising even higher. So he sighed and sat back and said, "Read it. It's from Graff, right? Always use a male voice for the gitling."

"Admiral Rackham, I apologize for the intrusion," the computer baritoned. "Once I broached the possibility of letting your family contact you, my superiors would not give up on the idea, even though I warned them it would be more likely to be counterproductive if you hadn't agreed in advance. Still, it was my idea and I take full responsibility for that, but it was also clumsily handled without waiting for your permission, and that was not my responsibility. Though it *was* completely predictable, because this is the military. There is no idea so stupid that it won't be seized upon and made the basis of policy, and no idea so wise that it won't be perceived as threatening by some paper pusher, who'll kill it if he can, or claim complete credit for it if it works. Am I describing the military you know?"

Clever boy, thought Mazer. Deflect my anger to the IF. Make me *his* friend.

"However, the decision was made to send you only those letters that you would find encouraging. You're being 'handled,' Admiral Rackham. But if you want *all* the letters, I'll make sure you get the whole picture. It won't make you happier, but at least you'll know I'm not trying to manipulate you."

"Oh, right," said Mazer.

"Or at least I'm not trying to trick you," said the computer. "I'm trying to persuade you by winning your trust, if I can, and then your cooperation. I will not lie to you or leave out information in order to deceive you. Tell me if you want all the letters or are content with the comfortable version of your family's life."

Mazer knew then that Graff had won—Mazer would have no choice but to answer, and no choice but to request the omitted letters. Then he would be beholden to the gitling. Angry, but in debt.

The real question was this: Was Graff staging the whole thing? Was *he* the one who withheld the *un*comfortable letters, only so he could gain points with Mazer for then releasing them?

Or was Graff taking some kind of risk, scamming the system in order to send him the full set of letters?

Or did Graff, a mere lieutenant, have a degree of power that allowed him to flout the orders of his superiors with impunity?

"Don't send the bugger-off letter," said Mazer.

"I already sent it and receipt has been confirmed."

"I'm actually quite happy that you did that," said Mazer. "So here's my next message: Send the letters, gitling."

Within a few minutes, the reply came, and this time the number of letters was much higher.

And with nothing else to do, Mazer opened them and began to read them silently, in the order they were sent. Which meant that the first hundred were all from Kim.

The progression of the early letters was predictable, but no less painful to read. She was hurt, angry, grief-stricken, resentful, filled with longing. She tried to hurt him with invective, or with guilt, or by tormenting him with sexually charged memories. Maybe she was tormenting herself.

Her letters, even the angry ones, were reminders of what he had lost, of the life he once had. It's not as if she invented her temper for this occasion. She had it all along, and he had been lashed by it before, and bore a few old scars. But now it all combined to make him miss her.

Her words hurt him, tantalized him, made him grieve, and often he had to stop reading and listen to something—music, poetry, or the drones and clicks of subtle machinery in the seemingly motionless craft that was hurtling through space in, the physicists assured him, a wavelike way, though he could not detect any lack of solidity in any of the objects inside the ship. Except, of course, himself. He could dissolve at a word, if it was from her, and then be remade by another.

I was right to marry her, he thought again and again as he read. And wrong to leave her. I cheated her and myself and my children, and for what? So I could be trapped here in space while she grows old and dies, and then come back and watch some clever young lad take his rightful place as commander of all the fleets, while I hover behind him, a relic of an old war, who lived out the wrong cliché. Instead of him coming home in a bag for his family to bury, it was his family who grew old and died while he came back still . . . still young. Young and utterly alone, purposeless except for the little matter of saving the human race, which wouldn't even be in his hands.

Her letters calmed down after a while. They became monthly reports on the family. As if he had become a sort of diary for her. A place where she could wonder if she was doing the right thing in her raising of the children—too stern, too strict, too indulgent. If her decisions could have a wrong outcome or a wrong motive, then she wondered constantly if she should have done it differently. That, too, was the woman he had known and loved and reassured endlessly.

How did she hold together without him? Apparently she remembered the conversations they used to have, or imagined new ones. She inserted his side of the conversation into the letters. "I know you'd tell me that I did the right thing . . . that I had no choice . . . of course you'd say . . . you always told me . . . I'm still doing the same old . . ."

The things that a widow would tell herself about her dead husband.

But widows could still love their husbands. She *has* forgiven me.

And finally, in a letter written not so long ago—last week; half a year ago—she said it outright. "I hope you have forgiven me for being so angry with you when you divorced me. I know you had no choice but to go, and you were trying to be kind by cutting all ties so I could go on with life. And I *have* gone on, exactly as you said I should. Let us please forgive one another."

The words hit him like three-g acceleration. He gasped and wept, and the computer became concerned. "What's wrong?" the computer asked. "Sedation seems necessary."

"I'm reading a letter from my wife," he said. "I'm fine. No sedation."

But he wasn't fine. Because he knew what Graff and the IF could not have known when they let this message go through. Graff *had* lied to him. He *had* withheld information.

For what Mazer had told his wife was that she should go on with life *and marry again.*

That's what she was telling him. Somebody had forbidden them to say or write anything that would tell him that Kim had married another man and probably had more children—but he knew, because that's the only thing she could mean when she said, "I *have* gone on, exactly as you said I should." That had been the crux of the argument. Her insisting that divorce only made sense if she intended to remarry, him saying that of course she didn't think of remarrying *now,* but later, when she finally realized that he would never come back as long as she lived, she wouldn't have to write and ask him for a divorce, it would already be done and she could go ahead, knowing that she had his blessing—and she had slapped him and burst into tears because he thought so little of her and her love for him that he thought she could *forget* and marry someone else . . .

But she had, and it was breaking his heart, because even though he had been noble about insisting on the divorce, he had believed her when she said she could never love any other man.

She did love another man. He was gone only a year, and she . . .

No, he had been gone three decades now. Maybe it took her ten years before she found another man. Maybe . . .

"I will have to report this physical response," said the computer.

"You do whatever you have to," said Mazer. "What are they going to do, send me to the hospital? Or—I know—they could cancel the mission!"

He calmed down, though—barking at the computer made him feel marginally better. Even though his thoughts raced far beyond the words he was reading, he did read all the other letters, and now he could see hints and overtones. A lot of unexplained references to "we" and "us" in the letters. She wanted him to know.

"Send this to Graff. Tell him I know he broke his word almost as soon as he gave it."

The answer came back in a moment. "Do you think I don't know exactly what I sent?"

Did he know? Or had he only just now realized that Kim had slipped a message through, and now Graff was pretending that he knew it all along . . .

Another message from Graff: "Just heard from your computer that you have had a strong emotional response to the letters. I'm deeply sorry for that. It must be a challenge, to live in the presence of a computer that reports everything you do to us, and then a team of shrinks tries to figure out how to respond in order to get the desired result. My own feeling is that if we intend to trust the future of the human race to this man, maybe we ought to tell him everything we know and converse with him like an adult. But my own letters have to be passed through the same panel of shrinks. For instance, they're letting me tell you about them because they hope that you will come to trust me more by knowing that I don't like what they do. They're even letting me tell you *this* as a further attempt to allow the building of trust through recursive confession of trickery and deception. I bet it's working, too. You can't possibly read any secret meanings into *this* letter."

What game is he playing? Which parts of his letters are true? The panel of shrinks made sense. The military mind: Find a way to negate your own assets so they fail even before you begin to use them. But if Graff really did let Kim's admission that she had remarried sneak through, knowing that the shrinks would miss it, then did that mean he was on Mazer's side? Or that he was merely *better* than the shrinks at figuring out how to manipulate him?

"You can't possibly read any secret meanings into *this* letter," Graff had said. Did that mean that there *was* a secret meaning? Mazer read it over again, and now what he said in the third sentence took on another possible meaning. "To live in the presence of a computer that reports everything you do to us." At first he had read it as if it meant "reports *to us* everything you do." But what if he literally meant that the computer would report everything Mazer *did to them.*

That would mean they had detected his undetectable reprogramming of the computer.

Which would explain the panel of shrinks and the sudden new urgency about finding a replacement for Mazer as commander.

So the cat was out of the bag. But they weren't going to tell him they *knew* what he had done, because he was the volatile one who had done something insane, and so they couldn't believe he had a rational purpose and speak to him openly.

He had to let them see him and realize that he was not insane. He had to get control of this situation. And in order to accomplish that, he had to trust Graff to be what he so obviously wanted Mazer to think he was: an ally in the effort to find the best possible commander for the IF when the final campaign finally began.

Mazer looked in the mirror and debated whether to clean up his appearance. There were plenty of insane people who tried, pathetically, to look saner by dressing like regular people. Then again, he *had* let himself get awfully tangle-haired, and he *was* naked all the time. At least he could wash and dress and try to look like the kind of person that military people could regard with respect.

When he was ready, he rotated into position and told the computer to begin recording his visual for later transmission. He suspected, though, that there would be no point in editing it—the raw recording was what the computer would transmit, since it had obviously reported his earlier reprogramming.

"I have reason to believe that you already know of the change I made in the onboard computer's programming. Apparently I could take the computer's navigational system out of your control, but couldn't keep it from reporting the fact to you. Which suggests that you *meant* this box to be a prison, but you weren't very good at it.

"So I will now tell you exactly what you need to know. You—or, by now, your predecessors—refused to believe me when I told them that I was not the right man to command the International Fleet during the final campaign. I was told that there would be a search for an adequate replacement, but I knew better.

"I knew that any 'search' would be perfunctory or illusory. You were betting everything on me. However, I also know how the military works. Those who made the decision to rely on me would be long since retired before I came back. And the closer we got to the time of my return, the more the new bureaucracy would dread my arrival. When I got there, I would find myself at the head of a completely unfit military organization whose primary purpose was to prevent me from doing anything that might cost somebody his job. Thus I would be powerless, even if I was retained as a figurehead. And all the pilots who gave up everything they knew and loved on Earth in order to go out and confront the Formics in their own space would be under the actual command of the usual gang of bureaucratic climbers.

"It always takes six months of war and a few dreadful defeats to clear out the deadwood. But we don't have time for that in this war, any more than we did in the last one. My insubordination fortunately ended things abruptly. This time, though, if we lose *any* battle then we have lost the war. We will have no second chance. We have no margin of error. We can't afford to waste time getting rid of you—you, the idiots who are watching me right now, the idiots who are going to let the human race be destroyed in order to preserve your pathetic bureaucratic jobs.

"So I reprogrammed my ship's navigational program so that I have complete control over it. You can't override my decision. And my decision is this: I am not coming back. I will not decelerate and turn around. I will keep going on and on.

"My plan was simple. Without me to count on as your future commander, you would have no choice but to search for a new one. Not go through the motions, but really search.

"And I think you must have guessed that this was my plan,

because you started letting me get messages from Lieutenant Graff.

"So now I have the problem of trying to make sense of what you're doing. My guess is that Graff is trained as a shrink. Perhaps he works as an intelligence analyst. My guess is that he is actually very bright and innovative and has got spectacular results at . . . at something. So you decided to see if he could get me back on track. Only he is exactly the kind of wild man that terrifies you. He's smarter than you, and so you have to make sure you keep him from getting the power to do anything that looks to you like it might be dangerous. And since everything remotely effective will frighten you, his main project has been figuring out how to get around you in order to establish honest communication between him and me.

"So here we are, at something of an impasse. And all the power is in your hands at this moment. So let me tell you your choices. There are only two of them.

"The first choice is the hard one. It will make your skin crawl. Some of you will go home and sleep for three days in fetal position with your thumbs in your mouths. But there's no negotiation. This is what you'll do:

"You'll give Lieutenant Graff real power. Don't give him a high rank and a desk and a bureaucracy. Give him genuine authority. Everything he wants, he gets. Because the whole reason he is alive will be this: to find the best possible commander for the fleets that will decide the future of the human race.

"To do this he first has to find out how to identify those with the best potential. You'll give him all the help he asks for. All the *people* he asks for, regardless of their rank, training, or how much some idiot admiral hates or loves them.

"Then Graff will figure out how to *train* the candidates he identifies. Again, you'll do whatever he wants. Nothing is too expensive. Nothing is too difficult. Nothing requires a single committee meeting to agree. Everybody in the IF and everybody in the government is Graff's servant, and all they should ever ask him is to clarify his instructions.

"What I require of Graff is that he work on nothing but the identification and training of my replacement as battle commander of the International Fleet. If he starts bureaucratic kingdom building—in other words, if he turns out to be just another idiot—I'll know it, and I'll stop talking to him.

"My quid pro for your giving Graff this authority is that once I'm satisfied he *has* it and is using it correctly, then I'll turn this ship around immediately. I'll get home a few years earlier than the original plan. I'll be part of training whatever commander you have. I'll evaluate Graff's work. I'll help choose among the candidates for the job, if you have more than one that might potentially do the job.

"And all along the way, Graff will communicate with me constantly by ansible, so that everything he does will be done with my counsel and approval. Thus, through Graff, I am taking command of the search for our war leader *now*.

"But if you act like the idiots who led the fleet during the war *I* won, and try to obfuscate and prevaricate and procrastinate and misdirect and manipulate and lie your way out of letting Graff and me control the choice and training of the battle commander, then I won't turn this ship around, ever.

"I'll just sail on out into oblivion. Our campaign will fail. The Buggers will come back to Earth and they'll finish the job this time. And I, in this ship, will be the last living human being.

But it won't be my fault. It will be yours, because you did not have the decency and intelligence to step aside and let the people who know how to do the job of saving the human race *do* it.

"Think about it as long as you want. I've got all the time in the world. But keep this in mind: Whoever tries to take control of this situation and set up committees to study your response to this vid—*those* are the people you need to assign to remote desk jobs and get them out of the IF right now. They are the allies of the Buggers—they're the ones who will end up getting us all killed. I have already designated the only possible leader for this program: Lieutenant Graff. There's no compromise. No maneuvering. Make him a captain, give him more actual authority than any other living human, stand ready to do whatever he tells you to do, and let him and me get to work.

"Do I believe you'll actually do this? No. That's why I reprogrammed my ship. Just remember that I *am* the guy who saved the human race, and I did it because I was able to see exactly how the Buggers' military system worked and find its weak spot. I have also seen how the human military system works, and I know the weak spot, and I know how to fix it. I've just told you how. Either you'll do it or you won't. Now make your decisions and don't bother me again unless you've made the right one."

Mazer turned back to the desk and selected SAVE and SEND.

When he was sure the message was sent, he returned to his sleeping space and let himself think again about Kim and Pai and Pahu, about his grandchildren, about his wife's new husband and what children they might have. What he did not let himself think about was the possibility of returning to Earth to meet these babies as adults and try to find a place among them as if he were still alive, as if there were anyone left on Earth for him to know and love.

The answer did not come for a full twelve hours. Mazer imagined with amusement the struggles that must be going on. People fighting for their jobs. Filing reports proving that Mazer was insane and therefore should not be listened to. Struggling to neutralize Graff—or suck up to him, or get themselves assigned as his immediate supervisor. Trying to figure out a way to fool Mazer into thinking they had complied without actually having to do it.

The answer, when it came, was from Graff. It was a visual. Mazer was pleased to see that while Graff was, in fact, young, he wore the uniform in a slovenly way that suggested that looking like an officer wasn't a particularly high priority for him.

He wore a captain's insignia and a serious expression that was only a split second away from a smile.

"Once again, Admiral Rackham, with only one weapon in your arsenal, you knew right where to aim it."

"I had two missiles the first time," said Mazer.

"Do you wish me to record—" began the computer.

"Shut up and continue the message," growled Mazer.

"You should know that your former wife, Kim Arnsbrach Rackham Summers—and yes, she does keep your name as part of her legal name—was instrumental in making this happen. Because whenever somebody came up with a plan for how to fool you and me into thinking they were in compliance with your orders, I would bring her to the meeting. Whenever they said, 'We'll get Admiral Rackham to believe' some lie or other, she would laugh. And the discussion would pretty much end there.

"I can't tell you how long it will last, but at this point, the

IF seems to be ready to comply fully. You should know that has involved about two hundred early retirements and nearly a thousand reassignments, including forty officers of flag rank. You still know how to blow things up.

"There are things I already know about selection and training, and over the next few years we'll talk constantly. But I can't wait to take actions until you and I have conferred on everything, simply because there's no time to waste and time dilation adds weeks to all our conversations.

"However, if I do something wrong, tell me and I'll change it. I'll never tell you that we've already done this or that as if that were a reason *not* to do it the right way after all. I will show you that you have not made a mistake in trusting this to me.

"The thing that puzzles me, though, is how you decided to trust me. My communications to you were full of lies or I couldn't have written to you at all. I didn't know you and had no clue how to tell you the truth in a way that would get past the committees that had to approve everything. The worst thing is that in fact I'm very good at the bureaucratic game or I couldn't have got to the position to communicate directly with you in the first place.

"So let me tell you—now that no one will be censoring my messages—that yes, I think the highest priority is finding the right replacement for you as battle commander of the International Fleet. But once we've done that—and I know that's a big if—I have plans of my own.

"Because winning this particular war against this particular enemy is important, of course. But I want to win all future wars the only way we can—by getting the human race off this one planet and out of this one star system. The Formics already figured it out—you have to disperse. You have to spread out until you're unkillable.

"I hope they turn out to have failed. I hope we can destroy them so thoroughly they can't challenge us for a thousand years.

"But by the end of that thousand years, when another Bugger fleet comes back for vengeance, I want them to discover that humans have spread to a thousand worlds and there is no hope of finding us all.

"I guess I'm just a big-picture guy, Admiral Rackham. But whatever my long-range goals are, this much is certain: If we don't have the right commander and win this war, it won't matter what other plans anybody has.

"And *you* are that commander, sir. Not the battle commander, but the commander who found a way to get the military to reshape itself in order to find the right battle commander without wasting the lives of countless soldiers in meaningless defeats in order to find him.

"Sir, I will not address this topic again. But I have come to know your family in the past few weeks. I know now something of what you gave up in order to be in the position you're in now. And I promise you, sir, that I will do everything in my power to make your sacrifices and theirs worth the cost."

Graff saluted, and then disappeared from the holospace.

And even though he could not be seen by anybody, Mazer Rackham saluted him back.

Afterword by Orson Scott Card

I've always been fascinated by the issues involved in relativistic space travel. To me it seemed that any kind of voyage that was long enough for relativistic effects to kick in would be a kind of death. Your body would still be alive, but you would be cut off from the community around you for long enough that by the time you returned—if you returned—all the people you knew would either be dead, or would have lived so many years without you that you would not know them.

This is particularly poignant when it comes to parents and children, or siblings. I remember how powerfully William Sleator's brilliant novel *Singularity* dealt with that issue, when he had one of a pair of twins use a backyard singularity to age himself, deliberately, a full year in a single night. Because he did it at the onset of puberty, he emerged markedly larger and older than his brother. But he had also tricked himself, because it was a year spent in utter solitude, except for the books he was reading. He had not had a year of growth through interaction with other people. Fortunately, though, he had used the time to understand himself a little better and gain some perspective.

When I gave myself the assignment of writing one *Ender's Game* story per issue of the *InterGalactic Medicine Show,* I was quickly drawn to Mazer's dilemma. Because he was regarded as essential to the survival of the human race in the next war with the Formics, he was sent out at (near) lightspeed on an empty voyage; he would then bring himself back, again at lightspeed, so that when the war came, he would hardly have aged.

In one sense, this is no more than we ask of any soldiers in combat—they go away from their homes, knowing that a certain percentage of them will not come back.

But when you send a fleet of soldiers on a relativistic journey, *none* of them will return to the world, and the people, that they knew. Even though their bodies remain alive, it's a suicide mission.

So in a way it's merciful that the fleets were ordered to stay and colonize the planets they conquered; there was no point in bringing them home. Only Mazer had to face the bittersweet dilemma of meeting his family again.

The challenge, then, was to determine how Mazer would feel about all this and then what he would do. Because one thing was certain: Mazer was smart enough to know that he was *not* the right man to command the human fleet. So if he did come back, he would face a burden that he knew he could not handle. What does a good soldier do then?

Tabloid Reporter to the Stars

BY ERIC JAMES STONE

When I was fired after ten years as a science reporter for the *New York Times,* the editor told me I'd never get a job with a decent paper again. He was right, at first: No one wanted to hire a reporter who had taken bribes to write a series of articles about a nonexistent technology in order to inflate the value of a company being used in a stock swindle—even if I had managed to get off without serving time.

And that's the only reason I took the job with the *Midnight Observer* tabloid. They didn't care that I'd made up a news story—they were impressed that I'd managed to write something that had fooled experts for over a year. So began my new career under the pseudonym of Dr. Lance Jorgensen. The doctorate was phony, of course, and I never did decide what it was in. I worked that gig for three years before I caught the break that let me get back into real journalism.

When the United Nations Space Agency decided to hold a lottery to choose a reporter to travel on board the first interstellar ship, they set strict qualifications: a college degree in journalism, at least five years of experience as a science reporter, and current employment with a periodical or news show with circulation or viewership of at least one million.

Technically, I qualified. So I entered. And a random number generator on an UNSA computer picked my number.

Less than five minutes after UNSA announced the crew of the *Starfarer I,* including yours truly as the only journalist, the calls began. The first was from my old editor at the *Times.* He wanted me back on an exclusive basis—I could name my own price. I'll admit I was bitter: I told him that my price was full ownership of the paper and that I'd fire him as soon as I had it. He sputtered; I hung up.

By the end of that week, I had a TV deal with CNN and a print/Web deal with the *Washington Post.* And so, without a gram of regret, Dr. Lance Jorgensen gave the *Midnight Observer* his two weeks' notice. I was once again Lawrence Jensen, science reporter.

A lot of journalists squawked that I didn't deserve to be on the mission because of my scrape with the law, even if I had managed to avoid a conviction by turning state's evidence. But the rules were on my side for a change: My degree from the Columbia School of Journalism, my experience at the *Times,* and the *Midnight Observer*'s seven-million-plus circulation fit the letter, if not the spirit, of the rules. Despite their fervent wishes, I made it through spaceflight training without a hitch, and proudly boarded the *Starfarer* as the world looked on.

This mission was my chance for redemption. I'd made one big mistake, and I planned to make up for it with accurate, well-written science reporting that made the wonders of space travel understandable to everyone. I had loved science since I was a kid; if I'd had the brains to do the math, I might have chosen a career as a scientist instead of a reporter. Reporting this mission was my dream job, and I was determined not to mess things up.

The day we launched, the *Midnight Observer* ran a cover story claiming that I had been selected for this mission because while working undercover for them I had already met the aliens the *Starfarer* would encounter, and they had requested that I serve as Earth's ambassador. They had even 'shopped a picture of me shaking hands with a stereotypical short, gray, bald, bulge-headed alien.

During all two hundred and twenty-three days of hyperspace travel, my crewmates refused to let me live that down.

Fortunately, when we found the aliens, they didn't look anything like that picture.

The theory behind hyperspace travel involves several dimensions beyond the usual four we humans can perceive. The mathematical formulas involved in actually making a hyperspace drive work surpass the understanding of the unenhanced human brain. But what the formulas and the theory don't mention is that traveling by hyperspace is beautiful. The harsh radiation that fills the hyperspacial void becomes a kaleidoscope of infinite variety as it washes upon our magnetic shields.

Observations from Hubble III had indicated the possibility of a planet with an oxygen-nitrogen atmosphere in this system, and now that we had arrived, our onboard telescopes had confirmed that the fourth planet had such an atmosphere. I had just finished my third column for this week's homelink, explaining about nonequilibrium gases and why this meant there was life of some sort on the planet, when Singh began pounding on my cabin door.

"Hey, Ambassador, you in there?"

I didn't dignify that by responding.

"Come on, Jensen, open up. I've got a scoop for you."

Narinder Singh was one of *Starfarer's* xenobiologists, and until we actually got down on the ground, he didn't have much to do except make guesses based on the limited data our telescopes could gather. So it was unlikely that he had anything important. Besides, since I was the only reporter on board, there wasn't anyone who could scoop me. But I said, "Come in," anyway.

He opened the hatch and came in. "Look at these." He shoved a handful of eight-by-ten photos in front of my face.

I took the photos and began leafing through them. They showed a thin sunlit crescent of planet, which I assumed to be Aurora, the planet with the good atmosphere. "So, it's nighttime on half the planet. Excuse me while I call my editor and tell him to stop the presses."

"No, look closer at the nighttime side. Over here." He pointed to a region along the equator near the edge of the darkness.

Peering at the photo, I noticed that there were a dozen or so little clumps of bright spots. "You think these are the lights of cities?"

"Yes. There's a civilization on that planet. And I want you to remember I came to you with this discovery first."

I looked over at the column I had just finished. I could rewrite a bit to mention Singh's speculations, with plenty of caveats. But it still seemed a little too flimsy—and the whole situation with the *Midnight Observer* story made me leery of anything involving aliens. "Yeah, I'll remember, if it turns out to be anything. It's probably volcanoes or forest fires or something. Did you run this by Khadil?" Iqrit Khadil was our geologist. "I mean, if it's really a civilization down there, how come there's no radio traffic?"

"Maybe they haven't developed radio yet. Or maybe they've moved beyond it. But I'm telling you, this is it: a sentient species with at least rudimentary civilization."

"Look, if you can get Khadil to agree that those are not volcanoes or any other geological phenomenon within the next half hour, I'll put your speculations in today's column. Otherwise, you'll have to wait till next week, which might be better anyway, since by then there might be more evidence one way or the other."

He grabbed the photos back. "I know what I know. I'll talk to Khadil."

Now that the Starfarer *is out of hyperspace, normal radio transmissions would take over one hundred and thirty years to travel to Earth, making direct two-way communication impossible. So the* Starfarer's *designers came up with a solution. When we arrived in this solar system, our ship split into two modules. The Hyperspace Module (HM) and two members of the crew remain in the outer system, where they can make the jump to hyperspace, while the Orbital Module (OM) heads in toward the planets with the rest of the crew. We send all our data—including this column—to the HM.*

It takes six days for the nuclear reactor on the HM to store enough power in the capacitors for the jump to hyperspace. So

once a week, they make the jump and send a radio signal to a
ship in hyperspace near Earth. Instead of one hundred and
thirty years, the signal only takes eighteen hours to travel to
Earth. The receiving ship then returns to normal space and
transmits the data to UNSA headquarters on Earth, which
sends my columns to the Washington Post, *who delivers*
them to your doorstep.

By the time the OM reached planetary orbit five days later,
all the evidence pointed to a developing civilization on Aurora, so I decided it was a good thing I'd included Singh's
speculations in my column. We didn't know what the reaction
from Earth was yet—the HM was still charging its capacitors
for its weekly jump into hyperspace to transmit our reports
and download communications from home. But first contact
with an alien species, which had always been considered only a
slight possibility, transformed our mission from one of simple
exploration into something far greater. I'd already written and
rewritten and discarded several columns about the meaning of
all this. It was probably the biggest news story ever; I was writing history, and I wanted to get the words right.

I wasn't the only one. Commander Inez Gutierrez de la
Peña, who was in overall command of our mission, commed me
in my quarters in the middle of the night. The next morning
most of the crew would be taking the Landing Module down to
an isolated island in the middle of Aurora's larger ocean, and she
would take the first human step on a planet outside our solar
system. She wanted my opinion on what she would say upon
taking that step.

I was flattered, but feigned irritation out of habit. "It's two
in the morning. How'd you know I wasn't sleeping?"

"I checked the power consumption in your quarters and could tell the lights and your computer were on." UNSA hadn't picked Gutierrez by lottery; she knew this ship six ways from zero.

"Okay. Tell me what you've got so far."

She hesitated a moment. "It's no 'One small step,' but . . . 'Humanity has always been a race of explorers. Though in the past we have not always lived up to our aspirations, letting fear and exploitation rule our encounters with the unknown, today on this new world we have a chance—"

"Blah blah blah. Are you looking to write a pamphlet on social responsibility, or do you want to say something that will still be quoted a thousand years from now?"

"I was thinking that putting the event in its historical context—"

"Leave that to the historians and people like me. What you need is a sound bite. Short. To the point, yet something that recalls the dreams of our first ancestors, who looked up at the stars and wondered what lay beyond them."

On my com screen, her face nodded. "I see what you mean. You going to be up a while longer?"

"Yeah. Call me when you come up with something."

I may not have sounded very respectful, but Commander Gutierrez had my respect. Not only was she almost irritatingly competent at her job, but out of the thirty-seven other members of the crew, she was the only one who had never called me "Ambassador."

It took her six more tries over the next three hours before I thought she had it about right.

The next morning, precisely on schedule, she climbed down the ladder outside the LM's airlock. We could hear her steady breathing over her spacesuit's com system. When she reached the bottom and took that first step onto Aurora's soil, her voice came in loud and clear.

"Today humanity walks among the stars. Where will we walk tomorrow?"

As those of us on board the LM clapped and cheered, I felt twin twinges of pride and jealousy. Every word I had ever written would be long forgotten, and still those words would be remembered. They were not mine, but at least I had helped shape them.

I took my little shares of immortality wherever I could.

Like the generation who as children saw the Wright Brothers fly and as adults saw man walk on the moon, or those who watched the latter as children and lived to see the first colony on Mars, we are witnesses to the dawn of a new age of humanity. Who knows how far we will go, following the footsteps of Commander Gutierrez?

Our landing spot's isolation allowed the biologists to analyze the native life with the least risk of contaminating the planetary biosphere. Seven days after landing, I got a chance to take a five-minute walk around the island. Aurora's light gravity—78 percent of Earth's—gave a spring to my step despite the weight of the spacesuit.

I daydreamed of spotting something significant during my walk, a scientific discovery of my own that I could reveal to a waiting world, but in the end all that I had discovered for myself was the sensation of walking beneath an aquamarine sky and looking up at a sun that seemed too blue and too small.

As far as important discoveries went, I had to settle for the daily breakthroughs of the biologists. The biggest one was the fact that life on Aurora was not based on DNA, but rather on a previously unknown nucleic acid molecule with a hexagonal cross-section. A few days later came the finding that the protein building blocks of Auroran life consisted of twenty-two amino acids instead of just twenty.

Exciting and heady information though these details might be for the fraction of Earth's population who were molecular biologists, I needed a subject that would grab the average reader's attention. That meant either danger or sex or both—suitably phrased for the *Washington Post,* of course. I abandoned my half-written amino acid column and went down to the biolab to wheedle something worth writing about out of the biologists.

Singh was in the middle of something delicate and didn't have time to talk, but Rachel Zalcberg said she could spare a few minutes while she waited for some test results.

About three months into the hyperspace flight, I'd made a pass at Rachel. She'd shot me down in no uncertain terms. Asking her about alien sex was definitely not the right place to start, so I focused on danger. "Since life here on Aurora is so different, how likely is it that there's some sort of disease organism that our immune system can't handle?"

She waved a hand dismissively. "Most disease organisms have trouble crossing the species barrier. Genetically, you're closer to an elm tree than to anything here, and you don't have to worry about Dutch elm disease. Our biochemistry is so different, the Auroran equivalents of bacteria and viruses wouldn't be able to reproduce inside us, assuming they even managed to survive at all."

That ruled out the danger angle, but since she'd brought up

the subject of reproduction . . . "How do the animals here reproduce?"

She surprised me by grinning. "You will not believe how different it is. It's very exciting. I haven't had a chance to write this up yet, but I will before the next homelink. Just be sure to credit me with the discovery when you talk about it in your column."

"Of course." I leaned forward.

"Our initial examination showed that all the life here is asexual: There are no divisions between male and female."

"I know what asexual means." It meant *biologist* exciting, not *reader* exciting.

"We are isolated here, so it may not hold true for the whole planet, but for now it's all we have. Some of the life here reproduces by budding, essentially splitting off a little clone of itself. However, that doesn't account for the genetic diversity we've seen within species. And then we caught some of our lab specimens being naughty."

"Naughty? I thought they didn't have sex."

"Not exactly. One of our furry slugs—we haven't come up with a scientific name for it yet—ate another one. Swallowed it whole."

"Cannibalism?" Maybe there was something here after all.

"Reproduction. After a few hours, that slug's skin hardened into a sort of cocoon. Two days later the cocoon cracked, and out came four smaller furry slugs. And each of the four is genetically different, with two-thirds of the genetic material from one slug, one-third from the other. Two slugs died and four were born."

It was good enough for one of those more-things-in-heaven-and-earth-than-are-dreamt-of-in-your-philosophy columns. I even got some footage of the new furry slugs for my CNN commentary.

I had the biologists to thank for the other highlight of that week. Coupled with the chemists' analysis of the atmosphere, which showed there were no threatening toxins, the biologists' report that there was no significant disease threat meant we were authorized to go outside without spacesuits, and breathe fresh air for the first time since we'd left Earth almost nine months before.

I jumped at the chance to be one of the first group to breathe the unfiltered air of another planet. The airlock door hissed open. I took a deep breath—and gagged on an aroma reminiscent of wet dirty socks.

That footage did not make it into my CNN commentary.

Opponents of contact with the Auroran civilization point to the tragic experiences of indigenous societies on Earth after contact with more technologically advanced societies. Indeed, the histories of Native American tribes, Australian aborigines, Native Siberians, and many others prove that such contact can be disastrous. But isn't the whole point of learning from history the idea that we can do better? If humanity could not progress, if we were forever destined to remain the same barbaric species that came out of the caves, then we would not even be debating this issue: We would be out conquering the Aurorans to use them as slave labor. Yes, our past demands that we proceed with caution, but our future demands that we proceed.

Perhaps the approval from UNSA would have come anyway, although I like to think my columns in favor of contact with the Aurorans had some effect. Our supplies limited us to only six months on the planet before we would have to begin the return journey to Earth, but we would be able to spend the last two of those months near an Auroran city.

We had refilled our fuel tanks by using electricity from our nuclear power plant to derive hydrogen and oxygen from seawater, and we would need to do so again before leaving, so we selected a coastal city as our destination and began our suborbital flight toward first contact.

"How you think they look?" asked Gianni Cacciatore, our climatologist, a few minutes after we launched. "If they are gray humanoids with bulging heads, they greet you as an old friend, *ehi, paesano?*"

There was Italian ancestry on my mother's side, so he'd taken to calling me *paesano,* countryman. At least it was better than Ambassador. I couldn't avoid talking to him, since we were strapped into seats next to each other for the duration of the flight. "Look, that ambassador thing is getting about as old as someone asking you to go do something about the weather instead of just talking about it."

He thought a moment, then laughed. "*Buffo.* But what you think? I want to say, you are the only that knows something of the research of everyone. You have the grand picture."

It was a good question, actually. Our only pictures of the Auroran cities came from the Orbital Module, and its orbit was too high up to show individual Aurorans as anything more than a few pixels. In order to avoid any possible contamination, our initial landing site had intentionally been far from any sign of Auroran civilization. So none of us knew what an actual Auroran looked like. I'd discussed the issue with the biologists but hadn't written it up because it was pure speculation.

"Well, based on the animals we've discovered so far, the

Aurorans are probably bilaterally symmetrical, although it could be quadrilateral. Since they have a civilization, they must be tool users, which means they must have something like our arms and hands, though it could be tentacles with claws for all we really know. They must have a way of getting around, so legs are probable, but we can't really know how many. Or maybe they move like snakes or snails." I sighed. "What I'm basically trying to say is that there are so many possibilities that we haven't got a really good idea of what they will look like, but they probably will not look as much like us as the stupid fake alien in that photo does."

He nodded. *"Interessante."*

I shifted the conversation to some of the unusual things he had discovered about Aurora's climate and thus kept myself occupied until our pilot, Zhao Xia, announced that we should prepare for a jolt when she activated the engines to slow us for landing.

The LM's cabin was mostly silent as we watched the ground grow ever closer on our screens. When we touched down, there was some clapping and cheering, though not as much as there had been the first time we landed.

Commander Gutierrez's firm voice came over the intercom. "I'm sure the Aurorans nearby must have seen us coming, and some of them will probably arrive soon. Those who were chosen for the first contact party, please prepare to exit the ship."

I had demanded to be included in the party, and Gutierrez had refused. Although it seemed unlikely, there was no way to be sure the Aurorans would not react with xenophobic violence, so she had decided to send only two people: Singh, because of his xenobiological expertise, and Tinochika Murerwa, because prior to becoming an astrophysicist he had seen combat while serving in the UN Special Forces.

My arguments in favor of freedom of the press did not persuade her, but I made enough of a fuss that her superiors on Earth had ordered her to include me. I don't know why they overrode her; I suspect the real reason had nothing to do with freedom of the press and everything to do with the fact that the United States shouldered 40 percent of the cost of this mission, and U.S. politicians wanted an American involved in the biggest news to come out of it. It didn't matter why—I was in.

Singh, Murerwa, and I gathered our equipment and entered the airlock. As the pressure equalized, I said, "Good luck, Singh," because he was the one in command of our little party.

"Thanks."

We climbed down the ladder and started preparing for our hosts to arrive and greet their unexpected visitors.

Murerwa looked over his shoulder at the videocam I was setting up on a tripod. He let out a deep bass laugh. "Planning to get a picture of yourself shaking hands with a real alien?"

"Yes." Somehow I felt that getting a real picture would be my compensation for all the grief I'd taken over the fake one.

After a very long five minutes, something came over a small ridge east of us. As it got closer, I began to make out details of its physiology. It looked like a scaly brown headless camel with four tentacles instead of a neck. As it got closer, I could see a wide opening between the top and bottom pairs of tentacles that I presumed to be its mouth.

It stopped about ten meters away from us. It wasn't very large; although it certainly weighed more than me, the hump on its back only came up to about the middle of my chest. As if responding to that thought, the hump rose a few inches on a thick stalk, and the creature seemed to stare at us out of two glossy blue-black openings on the front of the hump.

Singh said something in Hindi that I didn't understand.

"Is it one of the Aurorans or just an animal?" I asked.

"I think it's sentient. It's wearing something like a tool belt around one of its forelegs."

Now that he pointed it out, I saw the belt, which appeared to be made of a thick woven fabric. And one of the tools was undoubtedly a hammer, even if I wasn't sure what the rest were.

We stared at him while he stared at us. Now we knew what an Auroran looked like.

Or rather, we thought we did until more creatures began coming over the hill. Some came on four legs, some on two. I was fairly sure I saw one with eight. Some had tentacles; others had jointed arms with hand-like appendages. All had scaly skins, but some had patches of fur that appeared to be part of their bodies, not clothing, and all had heads similar to the hump on the first one, though it didn't seem to be in the same place on the different anatomies. Some were bilaterally symmetrical, but some were not—I spotted one that had anemone-like tendrils on one side and a crab-like pincer on the other. And of the fifty or more arrivals, there didn't appear to be more than a handful that looked like they belonged to the same species.

As the crowd grew, they began singing to each other. At least that's what it sounded like to me—wordless tunes that harmonized rather than creating a cacophony.

Then one of them said some words, and the others silenced almost immediately.

"Did you catch what he said?" asked Singh.

"Sounded like 'Alla Beeth' to me," I answered.

A voice in the crowd repeated it, and suddenly all of them were chanting, "Alla Beeth."

They didn't stop chanting until the soldiers showed up. Their civilization might be very different from ours, but a sword still looks like a sword, even if it is strapped to the waist of a tentacled reptilian centaur.

The soldiers sang to the crowd, and the crowd quieted down, parting in the middle to allow the half-dozen soldiers through.

Their leader trotted forward through the buffer zone the crowd had left around us and stopped about two meters away. His wide, expressionless eyes looked at each of the three of us in turn. Then he edged sideways until he was standing in front of me. Slowly he drew his sword.

I bravely stood my ground to show the aliens that humans were not intimidated. Or else I was frightened into immobility. Either way, the result was the same.

The leader bent one of his forelegs and sort of knelt on one knee. He placed his sword on the ground, looked at me, and said, "Alla Beeth."

The crowd took up the chant once more.

Murerwa laughed again. "Looks like you've been chosen as the first ambassador to Aurora."

The failure to include a linguistics expert on this mission is not as unreasonable as critics of UNSA are claiming. The evidence showed a high likelihood of a planet with an oxygen-nitrogen atmosphere, but before the Starfarer *arrived there was not a scintilla of evidence for a sentient, civilized life-form in this system. Earth has had an oxygen-nitrogen atmosphere for perhaps 1.5 billion years. The chances that an alien ship visiting Earth during that time would have found humans are only a third of 1 percent. The chances it would find us civilized are less than half a thousandth of a percent.*

Iqrit Khadil was the first to bring up religion. During a lull in mess-hall conversation as the crew ate dinner the night of first contact, he said, "I do not think it can be merely coincidence that one of the two words we have heard these aliens speak is 'Allah.'"

"You can't be serious!" Rachel said.

"Why not? These primitives obviously seemed to think Jensen was a god, or a messenger sent by a god. And though they seem to communicate among themselves by singing, they knew to speak words to us. And one of those words was 'Allah.'"

Rachel's knuckles tightened around her fork. "All right, O wise one, then what does 'Beeth' mean?"

Khadil shrugged. "Maybe it means messenger. 'Allah Beeth,' messenger of Allah."

I almost said that if I was anyone's messenger, I was the *Washington Post*'s, but several people began talking at once.

Rachel pounded the table with her fist until everyone turned to look at her. "First of all, we don't know how the words are divided, or even that it's more than one word, or even that it's a word at all. Maybe the first word is 'Al', but they're really just mispronouncing 'El', and so they're actually referring to the God of the Jews, not the God of Islam." She raised her voice over the beginnings of objections. "But coincidence is the most likely explanation. If we are going to speculate based on the idea that they spoke to us because they have seen humans before—which I find hard to believe—then there are other reasonable explanations. For example, they were trying to say the first two letters of the alphabet. Everyone here is familiar with the first two letters of the Greek alphabet: *alpha, beta*. In Hebrew, they are *aleph, bet*." She turned to Khadil. "What are they in Arabic?"

"*Alif, ba.*" He nodded. "I spoke too soon. I was just excited to hear what sounded like 'Allah.' But it is most likely a coincidence."

During the rest of dinner I thought about what Khadil and Rachel had said. Coincidence. The possible meaning of the words didn't really matter to me. But if the Aurorans communicated through song, why did they have words to use with us? And why only two words?

I tried to avoid wondering why their leader had chosen me to bow to, but I wasn't very successful.

Imagine if eating an octopus in a certain way would allow you to grow tentacles on your body. Or if by eating a horse, you could replace your two human legs with four horse legs. According to Singh and Zalcberg's observations of our newfound friends, that is essentially what the Aurorans can do: manipulate their own bodies by absorbing an animal and using its genetic code to recreate some aspect of that animal's body. The wide variety of body shapes and parts among the Aurorans comes from deliberate change, not from their inherited genes.

Within a few days, the Aurorans remedied our failure to bring a linguistics expert by providing one of their own. His name was a short trill that most of us could not reproduce, so someone called him Mozart. I pointed out that, given "Beeth" was one of the two words he knew, Beethoven might have been more appropriate, but by then the name had already stuck.

Biologically speaking, Mozart was neither a he nor a she, but none of us really felt comfortable calling it "it." Since the real Mozart had been a he, we defaulted to that usage for the most part.

Through trial and error, we determined that the Auroran vocal apparatus simply was incapable of making most of the sounds of human languages. Fortunately, Mozart had brought rough sheets of a paper-like substance, inks of various colors, and a collection of clay stamps that could be used to imprint various symbols on the paper. While a few of the simpler symbols bore a resemblance to letters in various Earth alphabets—X, O, I, T, Δ, Λ, Γ—there did not appear to be any connection between them and their Earthly sounds, so Rachel's *aleph-bet* explanation for "Alla Beeth" was a dead end.

Since Mozart understood the concept of written symbols representing ideas, once he got over his astonishment at the interaction between a computer keyboard and monitor, we were able to teach him to use his tentacles to type. We would communicate back by typing and saying words at the same time, so he could learn to associate the text of a word with its sound.

Whoever had decided to send Mozart to communicate with us had made a good choice. After only four days, he had learned enough English to carry on simple conversations, so during my shift for teaching him, I asked him the question that had been bothering me. "Why did your leader bow to me?"

<What is my leader?>

"One of your people with swords. The most important one."

<Commander Gutierrez is your leader?>

"Yes."

<What is bow?>

I demonstrated a bow.

<Not my leader. Leader close people. I is far.>

The nearest town, which someone had imaginatively dubbed Neartown, was not the place Mozart was from. That was new information, and I felt a little pleased with myself for discovering it. Still, I pressed on to find out more about what was bothering me. "Why did the leader of the close people bow to me?"

<He think you is How do you spell?> He stopped typing and said, "Alla Beeth."

I typed it out for him.

<He think you is Alla Beeth.>

"You do not think I am Alla Beeth?"

<No. You look like but not same.>

"Who is Alla Beeth?"

Mozart whistled a staccato tune. <You not know Alla Beeth?>

I thought fast. If Alla Beeth was some sort of deity and I denied knowledge of it, I wasn't sure what sort of complications that would cause. "Our language is so different from yours that our name for Alla Beeth may be different, too." I hoped that wasn't some sort of heresy.

<Alla Beeth is first of your people to visit our people.>

I felt the tremble in my stomach that I get when I realize I'm on the verge of a major story. "When did Alla Beeth visit your people?"

<Is fifty years more.>

Fifty years. Their planet's year was more than two Earth years long, so he was claiming a human had visited Aurora over a hundred years ago, back before we'd even walked on Mars.

"Wait a minute." Even though this was being recorded, I wanted someone else with me before I proceeded any further. I commed Commander Gutierrez and asked her to come join us.

After reading the transcript of our conversation to that point, she asked, "Is this a joke?"

"If it is, someone's setting me up. I swear I had no idea he was going to say this."

She nodded, then turned to Mozart. "Did someone tell you to say that Alla Beeth was human?"

<I not know Alla Beeth is human before I see humans. Then I know. No one tell me.>

Gutierrez typed and spoke slowly. "Mozart, we are the first humans to visit your people."

Mozart let out a long, descending note, and began typing furiously. <No. Alla Beeth is first. Is long time. Six my mergings but I remember. He come sky. He clothes all white. He like bright. He talk our language but we slow understand. He here small time. He go sky. Fifty years more you come.>

Gutierrez and I looked at each other.

<You not believe Alla Beeth? How not believe Alla Beeth?>

I looked into Mozart's shiny black eyes. "I believe you, Mozart." He believed that this Alla Beeth had visited his world, and even if I couldn't believe it was a human, I was sure that something must have visited the Aurorans.

Merging requires much more commitment than human mating, because neither of the Aurorans involved will survive. The larger of the two Aurorans swallows the other whole to begin the reproductive process, then hardens its skin into a thick shell. After about eighty days of cocoon-like existence, four small Aurorans break out of the shell to begin their lives. But their minds are not blank slates. In addition to a genetic heritage from both adults, each new Auroran carries a portion of the memories from the brains of its parents. Some Aurorans can remember events from over a thousand years ago.

This time it was Cacciatore who brought up religion, breaking the stunned silence after Commander Gutierrez and I had shown the rest of the crew the recordings of our conversation with Mozart. "If nobody else say it, I will. Technology could not have brought a human here before us. Only the power of God."

The racial and religious proportionality requirements during the crew selection process had been intended to represent all of Earth in our tiny ship. Not surprisingly, the scientific community had undergone a small religious revival when those requirements were announced. So, no matter how recently converted, we had a good cross-section of religious belief on board.

Some of the Christians in the crew backed Cacciatore's theory that the visitor had been an angel; others thought it had been Jesus himself. A few of the Muslims could accept the idea of an angel but insisted that Allah must have sent the angel. The rest of the Muslims supported Khadil, who insisted that the visitor must have been Mohammed. The Hindus spoke of the possibility that it had been one of the avatars of Vishnu. Rachel, as the only Jew on board, was arguing against all sides at once, while admitting the barest possibility that the visitor was an angel.

Commander Gutierrez mostly succeeded in remaining

above the fray. The atheists and agnostics stayed out of it, as did the Buddhists.

As for me? From when I was four years old until I was eighteen, I alternated weekends between my mom and my dad. Sundays with my mom meant going to church; Sundays with my dad meant watching TV on the couch or playing catch in the yard while listening to his old-time music collection. By the time I was fourteen, I pretty much felt that I took after my dad more than my mom, at least as far as preferred Sunday activities went, and my mom eventually quit asking me to go with her.

So I stuck with the atheists and agnostics in trying to ignore the potential religious aspect of Alla Beeth.

Nothing was settled that night, of course. But the hard feelings engendered by the argument disrupted the work the various scientific teams had been doing. Over the next few days, as I tried interviewing different scientists about their work, I could see that the crew had fractured: Whenever possible, they avoided their colleagues who were on the "wrong" side.

Mozart didn't help in resolving the dispute. In fact, when he revealed that he could not show us a picture of Alla Beeth because the Creator had commanded against making images of living things, the arguments erupted with new fervor.

There are several possible rational scientific explanations for the Aurorans' visitor, none of which involve the intervention of any god or other supernatural entity. Since the Aurorans have no pictures of the visitor and are relying on memories passed through several generations of mergings, it is possible that some significant details have become distorted, and a natural event has been imbued with mystical significance. Our descent from the sky was then connected to memories of that event. Another possibility is that the visitor was from another alien race, one that is humanoid in appearance. Under the theory of convergent evolution, it is quite possible that an intelligent, tool-using species could look superficially like us—even some of the Aurorans walk on two legs, have two arms, and have a head with two forward-facing eyes. Perhaps we will encounter such a race in a few years and be able to resolve this mystery. Until we have actual evidence, though, nothing about "Alla Beeth" can be said with any certainty.

"He trusts you more than any of the rest of us." Commander Gutierrez sat on my bed, facing me in my chair. Her voice was tired.

"Maybe so, but he believes Alla Beeth was a human, and I don't think I can change his mind."

"There has got to be more evidence than these memories and traditions. Some artifact left behind. Something. The crew is splitting apart: I spend all day ordering people to share their data with each other. Some of them have actually gotten physical. I'm sure part of it is just the stress of the mission, but this mystery has pushed us to the breaking point. We need proof that this is something explainable by the laws of science, like you said in your column. Then, I think, people will calm down."

I shrugged. "What can I do? I'm just a science reporter, not a scientist."

"Mozart and his people see you as our ambassador." She gave a half laugh, half sigh. "I've been careful never to call you that, you know. But I didn't try to put a stop to it, either. Interpersonal dynamics: People need a scapegoat, and I felt you could take the jokes. But now, I need you to be the ambassador. Ambassador Lawrence Jensen, descending from the sky with the full unity of Earth behind you. Push Mozart, push his people, until they show you everything they know, everything they have. Find the truth."

Find the truth. Scientist or reporter, it distills to that: Find the truth.

The nearest large city, which we call Metropolis, has a massive building near its center that rivals the old cathedrals of Europe in its intricate craftsmanship. Since only members of a certain priest class are allowed to enter, most Aurorans have never seen what it looks like from the inside. Mozart is a member of that class, and he explains that it is a place of scholarship. It was from that building that he was sent to find out if "Alla Beeth" had truly returned. Though we proved to be a disappointment to that hope, he stayed on to learn from us, as we learn from him. Despite the vast evolutionary and cultural gulf between our people and his, he has become our friend and has come to trust us. I leave it to you, the reader, to draw your own conclusion from that.

<Ambassador means you are the representative of all humans?>

"Yes," I lied.

<Then you are the most important one, not Commander Gutierrez?>

"She is in charge of the ship that brought me here, but I am the ambassador."

He bobbed his head affirmatively, a gesture he had learned from us.

"One of my functions is to find the truth, and report that truth to my people."

Mozart piped surprise. <You are a Seeker of Truth?>

After six weeks, his English was good enough that I knew the capitalization was not accidental. "Yes, I am a Seeker of Truth." And I'm willing to lie in order to get it.

<The Seekers of Truth is the name of my order.>

"What you have told us about Alla Beeth is causing arguments among my people. I must find a way to resolve those arguments. I must find the truth. Is there anything more you can tell me or show me about Alla Beeth?"

He tapped the tips of his tentacles against his forelegs for a few moments. <You must come with me to the place of my order. Since you are a Seeker of Truth, you should be allowed to hear the message of Alla Beeth directly.>

I suppressed a grin and replied gravely, "I would be most honored."

Commander Gutierrez had one of the pilots take us in the blimp, so we arrived in Metropolis before sundown.

It took him nearly half an hour of consultation with members of his order before he came over to me and began typing on the portable computer we'd brought with us.

<They have agreed that since you are a Seeker of Truth from your world, it is permitted for you to enter our church.>

"I thank them."

<Though they are in our language, the messages of Alla Beeth are difficult for us to understand, even after years of study. That is why only members of my order are allowed to hear them directly, and we then pass on what we learn to the rest of the people. Since you do not understand our language, I

do not know that you will find any truth in them. Yet Alla Beeth was human, so perhaps you will. And there is something more, something that I cannot tell you, only show.>

He led the way, and I followed him into the cathedral.

I probably hadn't been in a church more than a dozen times since I stopped going with my mom, mostly as a tourist. I could tell that the Aurorans had spent years of painstaking effort in creating this building, carving delicate patterns into solid stone. We passed through various archways and doors, and I started to hear Auroran voices harmonizing. Finally we entered a round room; about twenty Aurorans stood in the middle, singing.

I felt a chill on the back of my neck, like I used to get sometimes listening to the choir at my mom's church. But there was something more; there was something about this tune that made me nostalgic, homesick even. It felt like a memory that I couldn't quite pull from the depths of my mind.

Then Mozart walked to a curtain that hung on one of the walls and pulled it back.

There, in violation of one of their commandments, was a painting of a man—definitely human—dressed all in white.

My childhood Sunday memories came flooding back, and between the music and the picture there was no doubt in my mind as to who had been the first ambassador from Earth.

"Alla Beeth" was the Aurorans' way of saying "Elvis."

Anyone else on this expedition would have to be taken seriously. But not me. I'm a proven liar. Even worse—I'm a tabloid reporter. I would be accused of fabrication, of planting the evidence, of corrupting Auroran culture as part of some tabloid hoax.

The biggest story of my career had fallen in my lap, and I couldn't tell anyone without ruining whatever credibility I had managed to regain. Whatever powers that be must not want the publicity.

Of course, my mom would say this was punishment for having lied.

Thank you for sharing the secrets of Alla Beeth with me," I told Mozart as we left the cathedral.

<Did you find what you need to stop the arguments among your people?>

"You were right: Alla Beeth is human."

Mozart trilled joyfully.

"But his message is intended for your people, not mine." I sighed. "You were right to keep the image hidden. You must keep it hidden, because my people would not understand. They would reject your belief in him."

After a pause, Mozart asked, <Then what will you tell your people?>

"The truth," I said. "I will tell them the truth."

I refused Commander Gutierrez's request for a private briefing on what I'd found, insisting instead on speaking to the assembled scientists. After everyone gathered outside the LM, I sat on the rim of the airlock and recounted exactly what happened up until the moment Mozart pulled back the curtain and revealed the picture of Alla Beeth. Then I stopped.

After a long pause, Khadil said, "Did you recognize the person?"

"He was a human," I said. "Unmistakably. We are not the

first to travel the stars. But as for who it was . . . You really want to know the truth?"

"Yes," said Cacciatore.

"Do you?" I looked at him. "If I say it was Mohammed, will you become a Muslim?" I turned to Khadil. "If I say it was Moses or Elijah, will you become a Jew?" I shook my head. "You want me to give you scientific proof of your religious beliefs? Well, I'm not going to; it's called 'faith' for a reason. Here's the real truth: You've all been acting like a bunch of ig- norant yahoos, not the cream of Earth's scientists. So quit bick- ering and get back to work."

I rose, turned my back on them, and stalked through the airlock into the LM.

Commander Gutierrez caught up with me just outside my quarters. "That's it? That's all you're going to say?"

I stopped. "Yes."

She looked at me appraisingly. "You know they'll all hate you for that little show-and-not-tell."

I shrugged. "As long as they're united again . . . That's what you wanted, right?"

Gutierrez nodded. "Just between you and me, though, who was it in the picture?"

Cocking an eyebrow, I said, "Assuming it was one of the great religious leaders of the past, how on Earth—or Aurora—would I know him from Adam?" I hit the button to open the hatch to my quarters. "Now, if you'll excuse me, Commander, I have a column to file."

The mystery of just who Alla Beeth was and how he got to Aurora may never be fully explained. But as Earth's first

ambassador to Aurora, he prepared the way for peaceful rela-
tions between our two worlds. And for that, we can only say,
"Thank you, thank you very much."

Afterword by Eric James Stone

In early 2004 I sold a story called "The Man Who Moved the
Moon." It was a combination of some fairly hard science fiction
and a fairly ridiculous premise, and to this day it remains one of
my favorites. Having succeeded with that rather strange combination, I decided to try it again in time for the next Writers of
the Future contest deadline.

So I wrote a first-contact story, using some speculative ex-
obiology for the hard-science parts. For the ridiculous premise,
I dredged up an idle thought I'd had years before about Elvis
appearing to aliens.

But what made the story work for me was the narrator.
Less than a year before I wrote the story, reporter Jayson Blair
was fired by the *New York Times* for having fabricated stories,
and that's what gave me the idea of a disgraced reporter looking
to redeem himself. The narrative voice allowed me to inject
self-deprecating humor into the story.

Having finished the story, I titled it "The First Ambassador" and sent it off to Writers of the Future.

I was extremely happy when it was rejected seven days
later. Why? The reason they rejected it was that I had become
ineligible for the contest—my previous submission had just
won second place in its quarter.

Without the pressure of the contest deadline, I submitted
the story to some of my usual critiquers. The feedback I got was
generally positive, but many people had a real problem with the

ending. As originally written, the revelation of Alla Beeth's identity came in the last line of the story, which made it feel like a punch line.

In order to set up the punch line a little more, I changed the title to "Tabloid Reporter to the Stars," but that wasn't enough to fix the problem. The story got rejected in several markets because they felt the ending was unsatisfactory.

When Orson Scott Card asked me if I had anything I could submit for the new online magazine he was starting (and let me tell you, being asked was one of the biggest compliments of my writing career), this story was one I sent for his consideration.

After Ed Schubert took over as *IGMS* editor, he read the story and asked if I would rewrite the ending to make it less like a punch line. We had a good discussion about the story when we met at Dragon*Con, and over the next few weeks I wrote a new ending that kept the Elvis element but added a resolution to the conflict between the scientists.

Audience

by Ty Franck

Linus watched his personal assistant bustle through the door
of his immense bedroom at exactly the right time. He had been
awake long enough that he was no longer bleary-headed, but
not long enough to start thinking about doing things for himself. This was the perfect time for someone to come talk to him
about the day's plans, and this particular assistant had arrived at
exactly that moment every day for the last six years.

Of course, Linus thought, his very perfection is why he is
my personal assistant.

"Slept well, I hope? Good, let's talk about the day's appointments," said Michael as he walked across the room and drew
back the curtains. Every morning it was the same. A quick, im-
personal greeting and on to business. Linus sighed and decided
not to make too much fuss today.

"Yes, Michael, I slept very well. The bed was very

comfortable, and the comforter is wonderful. Please send my compliments to everyone."

"Excellent," said Michael, making a few quick notes on his pad. "You have a very full schedule today; shall we go over it?"

"Will there be much traveling today, Michael? I'm not feeling up to traveling. I think I might be getting a headache."

Michael merely gave him the blank stare he used when he thought Linus was being petulant. When just enough time had passed that Linus began to feel silly, but before he felt the need to become truly obstinate, Michael said, "All of your appointments today are here in New York. We will be traveling by car from here to the museum for an art exhibit, paintings, I believe. We will then travel by car to your luncheon. A new restaurant called the Orange Garden. There are three chefs there, and all are in contention for top rankings this year. It is your most important stop of the day. After, we will travel by car to the opera. The composer is Lisa Takei. She is a relatively new talent to the rankings, but some are saying the finest since Whitworth last year. It has a highly ranked cast."

Michael was giving him the other look now, the one that asked whether he was going to behave or not. "I do try to appreciate Japanese opera, Michael, you know I do. I'll be very attentive, I promise," said Linus.

"After the opera is a dinner party in your honor. You have not been to New York in some time, and the mayor felt it necessary for the city to show its appreciation. All of the top-ranked talent will be there. Naturally, there will be some trying for unscheduled showings, but I needn't remind you that appreciating any of their works without an appointment is a bad idea. It is getting hard enough to move you from place to place without crowds of unranked talent disrupting things."

Linus knew how bad it could get. Michael had been his assistant for six years now, but he was actually a replacement. Linus's first assistant had nearly been killed when an unranked stone carver threw one of his works off an overpass onto their moving car. Of course, security was much better now, but there were still those so desperate for appreciation that they would throw themselves in front of his car just to get him to view their work.

"Yes, Michael, I'll be a pillar of inobservation for the entire evening."

"Inobservation is not a word, Linus. You might want to refrain from using it in public," said Michael as he moved toward the door. "Your tailor will be here shortly. Breakfast is in one hour. Please call if you need anything." With that he bustled efficiently away.

Before Linus had time to decide whether he should get up or not, a large mound of moving fabrics shuffled into the room. It took him a few seconds to realize there were legs at the bottom of the pile, and then the clothes were quickly being hung up all over the room on nearly anything with an edge on it.

A tall, gangly man slowly appeared as the clothes were distributed. When his face was visible, he started to talk. "I hope you like a more formal look. I know that everyone has been putting you in lighter colors this year, but I've always thought that you had the right kind of dignity for a darker, more classic look. And pleats, your figure is very good for pleats. Something in a dark maroon color, maybe?"

"Ummm, could you wait a second? I just woke up, and I need to use the restroom. I think I'd like a shower, too. I promise I'll be right out, okay?"

The gangly man deflated. "I am so sorry. I just didn't think. What's wrong with me? Please, take as much time as you need." He moved closer with a terrible look of desperation on his face. For a second, Linus felt an irrational fear that the man might hurt him. "Please, don't let my unforgivable rudeness keep you from appreciating these clothes. I have worked very hard on them. This is the greatest moment of my life. Please don't let my excitement and lack of social grace destroy everything I've worked for . . . please."

Linus breathed a sigh of relief and felt a little shiver go down his back as sadness, and a little pity, replaced the fear. "Of course not. The clothes look wonderful. I can't wait to try them on. Just let me shower really quick, and I'll be right back. Okay?"

The clothier smiled and nodded, but still looked defeated. Linus went into the bathroom and locked the door behind him. While he was showering, he thought about how desperate some were to be appreciated. They work so hard to get here, and the playing field is far from level. Every single person on Earth is doing whatever they are best at. They read it right off our genes before we are even born.

The left-brain talents weren't so bad. They accounted or assisted or researched, and they were happy. The right-brain talents were the problem. They needed to be noticed, they needed to be compared, they needed to be appreciated. No wonder this poor tailor is scared. He thinks he has blown his one shot at immortality. Well, I can fix that; I can make him happy again.

The tailor was still waiting and looking flat when Linus came out of the bathroom in his robe. He always wore his own robe, and it was the only thing he took with him from place to place. Linus liked to wear something familiar and comforting each day, before putting on a suit of clothes he would wear once and never see again.

Well, time to put on my game face.

"Hey, that maroon suit is really nice. I saw it when you first came in, but it's really grabbing me now. Can I try that one on first?"

When the tailor realized that he might still get a chance at appreciation, he seemed to regain some of his former energy. "Absolutely, sir. An excellent choice, and the one I myself thought would be most flattering on you. You have a very good eye for fashion, sir." Which technically was not true.

If I had a good eye for fashion, thought Linus, I would be a fashion designer like you.

Linus tried the suit, declared it to be one of the finest he had ever worn, both for look and comfort, and sent the tailor away beaming. The tailor took none of the other clothes away with him. Why take them? Each item had been painstakingly designed with Linus himself in mind. If he wasn't going to wear them, no one would. It always seems such a waste, he thought. But no one ever goes without anything they need anymore, so maybe the world can afford to be a little wasteful in the interests of art.

As soon as he was dressed and the tailor had left, Michael came back. "All ready for breakfast? Very good. Come this way, please."

Michael led him out of the room and down to an elaborate dining area. Michael always led him everywhere. Since Linus slept in a different place nearly every night, he could not be expected to keep track of where things were. It was Michael's job to know how to get around. Every now and then, Linus would try to wander off, but he almost always got immediately lost. When Michael found him, he would never scold, of course, but he would give that look. Linus wondered if the ability to reprove without speaking was one of those genetic markers they looked for when deciding who was best suited to be a personal assistant.

Once in the dining area, Linus sat on a very comfortable chair and ate an elaborate, yet surprisingly nonfilling, breakfast. Afterward, he was offered a tray covered in sugary pastries. Linus was widely rumored to love sugary pastries. In truth, he was indifferent to them, but took one anyway. The baker who had made it was watching from the doorway and gave a loud whoop when Linus took it. Michael looked exasperated because such displays during appreciation were considered the height of vulgarity. Linus, however, secretly loved to break someone's composure like that. Good for you, Mr. Baker; live it up, man.

Just to rub it in, instead of taking one bite and putting the pastry down, he ate the whole thing while looking right at Michael.

"All finished? Very good, let's move on. The car is waiting," Michael said without a hint of impatience.

"Yeah, ready to go," Linus replied around a mouthful of pastry. On the way out, he winked at the baker.

The ride to the museum was very comfortable. Of course it was. Linus tried to think of how many people had worked on this car so he could ride in it this one day. Someone to design the outside and make it visually pleasing, yet functional. Maybe some other person designed the inside, made it roomy and comfortable, without being cavernous. Some engineering genius to design the engine and other mechanical parts; an electronics wizard to design the sound system and video monitors. Maybe even someone to design the seats.

And those are just the designers, Linus thought. Then there are people who machine and build and stitch. It was all hand-built, of course. Linus had never ridden in a mass-produced car.

All those people, picked at birth to be designers and mechanical engineers and leather workers and mechanics. They work their whole lives to be the best in their field, and everyone they are competing with was also picked at birth, given the same education, raised practically from the first moment of consciousness to be that thing. No wonder they are all starving for attention. So focused on what they do, they never see what anyone else is doing. But they all need someone to see them.

The thought put him in a melancholy mood.

"Michael."

"Yes, Linus?" Michael seemed far away, reading something on his pad. Probably tomorrow's schedule, or the weather in Amsterdam, or even the lunch menu. Always working, but the most famous personal assistant in the world because he works for me.

"How many paintings will I see today?"

"Several dozen, I would think. We have you scheduled for three hours. Why?" And now Michael was giving him the questioning look. He is wondering what I am getting at, what I plan to do. I still scare him a little.

"A few dozen paintings . . . I see so little of what they do, Michael. How many paintings were created today, I wonder? How many last year? How many of them do I ever see?"

"You only see the best of them, Linus."

"But who decides that? The other painters? Blinded by envy, always competing, how can they judge the others' work?"

"And yet some are deemed worthy of your attention, so the system must work."

"But what about all those others, the thousands of other painters who never make it high enough in the rankings to show me their work? Who appreciates it?"

"Their work is shown at the regional levels. Others of their talent see it. The better pieces are purchased and put in homes or other buildings."

"Purchased. By who? Doctors, physicists, personal assistants? How many paintings do you own, Michael?"

Michael put down his pad. He sat back in his seat and relaxed. This conversation was going in a familiar direction now. He knew what to say. He was no longer worried. "You know perfectly well that I do not own any paintings. I do not have a dwelling of my own. My life is working with you, assisting you in your work. If I ever settle down and own a home, perhaps I will purchase paintings."

"Is that enough, Michael? Following me around? Making sure I get to my appointments on time? Do you ever look at the paintings we go to see?"

Michael looked out the window at the rain and wet streets going by. The conversation was still going where he expected, but it required a gentle touch, and a bit of truth. "It is enough, Linus. I have always known that this is what I would do. I was raised from birth to be a perfect companion, confidant, secretary, protector. The better I was at my job, the more important the person I assisted would be. And I assist the most important person in the world, so I must have become very good at my job. Mock me if you like, but that is a satisfaction I cannot explain to you."

Linus sat quietly. He knew that Michael was speaking the

plain truth to him now, and he treasured such openness because it happened so rarely. He honored it with his silence. After a while, Michael spoke again.

"The world revolves around you, Linus. You only see the top, the tip of the iceberg, but you are the reason for so many things. These paintings we are going to see? They may only be twenty or thirty out of all that were painted. But when you look at them, you justify the painting of them all. Every one of those artists knew that maybe, just maybe, theirs would be the painting that made it all the way here. And for perhaps the first time, their work would be looked at by someone who does not judge, only appreciates."

"How could I judge? Half the time I don't even understand," Linus replied.

"That is your gift. You are the world's most unique genetic combination. A man with virtually no talents. Median-level intelligence, average physical skills, and no genetic predisposition for anything."

"The luckiest man in the world, because I'm nothing."

"The luckiest man in the world, because you can *see* everything. You still have a sense of wonder. You will never look at the work of another human and say, 'My own work is better.' And so you are the only person people want to show their work to. You can appreciate, and that is the only talent left that is in short supply."

"I promise to try very hard to appreciate the Japanese opera. I really will," Linus said quietly. "I'm sure they must work very hard on those complex arrangements."

Michael smiled at him for a moment, then picked up his pad and returned to work.

Linus sat back in the seat. He felt his clothes on him, and

they were comfortable and flattering. And he felt the seat, all the soft leather. The precise hum of the engine, the smooth glide of the car, the breakfast sitting lightly in his stomach, all easy to appreciate. He would try hard to look like he enjoyed the opera, so they felt appreciated as well.

He remembered a play he saw once, written by someone who died long before they had talents and rankings. There was a character, who later died stupidly if Linus remembered correctly, who was strutting around onstage ranting about how all the world is a stage, and we are merely players on it. And sitting all alone in the darkened theater, Linus had thought, *All except me: I am the audience of one.*

Afterword by Ty Franck

The seed of this story was planted when I read an article in a science magazine (I've forgotten which one) that described the increasing specialization in science, and the loss of the Thomas Edison–type generalist. This is not surprising, given the increasingly competitive nature of scientific investigation where multiple labs race for the same end result, and often millions or billions of dollars hang in the balance.

But we also see the always intimidating and sometimes outright predatory nature of the peer review process. You'd better know what you're talking about when you publish your findings, or legions of competitors will rush to be the first to poke holes in your theory. Extreme specialization is the natural outcome of this environment, and the truth is that science has grown so vast and complicated that to achieve expertise in even a tiny portion of it is a lifetime's work. And often, scientists in one narrow field of endeavor will be totally ignorant of the advances taking place in closely related fields.

I got another idea, the one that made me write the story, watching the early reality TV shows. We humans are so hungry for attention that we will suffer starvation on a desert island, eat live bugs, and sell ourselves into a marriage decided by a contest. As someone who writes and associates a great deal with writers, I know how desperate for recognition and validation the artistic personality can be.

These two ideas became "Audience." What if everyone in the world is at the absolute top of their game? What if they are raised right from birth to be the very best at whatever it is that they have the greatest genetic predisposition toward? Who decides what the very best is?

We hear a lot about the mythical "everyman." Joe Sixpack, who doesn't do anything but buy the products or services that smarter or more talented people want to sell. While I dislike the cliché a great deal (I have yet to meet Joe), I decided to do what speculative fiction always does: take the extreme of an idea and make it real. Linus is Joe Everyman. Utterly lacking in talent himself, the one service he can provide to an ultra-competitive world is impartial observation and professional consumerism.

In a funny twist, it is that very desire to be appreciated that led to the sale of this story. Through a bulletin board we both frequented, I had developed an online friendship with a writer named Kathryn Kidd. After finishing the first draft of "Audience," I sent it to her for feedback. Apparently, Card stays at her and her husband's house when he's in that part of the country, and he happened to be there not long after she received the story. Without asking me, she gave him the story. This led to him inviting me to participate in his Uncle Orson's Literary Bootcamp. When he started his magazine a couple of years later, he asked me for a story, and I sent in a later draft of "Audience," which he bought.

Thanks for liking the story, Kathy.

The Mooncalfe

BY DAVID FARLAND

It was late evening on a sultry summer's day when three riders appeared at the edge of the woods on the road southwest of
Tintagel castle. The sentries did not see them riding up the
muddy track that led from Beronsglade. The knights merely
appeared, just as the sun dipped below the sea, as if they'd coalesced from mist near a line of beech trees.

The manner of their appearance did not seem odd, on that
day of oddities. The tide was very low, and the whole ocean lay
as placid as a mountain pool. To the castle's residents, who were
used to the constant pounding of the surf upon the craggy
rocks outside the castle walls, the silence seemed thunderous.
Even the gulls had given up their incessant screeching and now
huddled low on the rocks, making an easy dinner of cockles
and green kelp crabs.

All around the castle, the air was somber. Smoke from

cooking fires and from the candles hung in a blue haze all about Tintagel's four towers. The air seemed leaden.

So it was that the sentries, when they spotted the three knights, frowned and studied the men's unfamiliar garb. The leader of the trio wore a fantastical helm shaped like a dragon's head, and his enameled mail glimmered red like a dragon's scales. He rode a huge black destrier, and as for the device on his shield, he carried only blank iron strapped to a pack on a palfrey.

Beside him rode a big fellow in oiled ringmail, while the third knight wore nothing but a cuirass of boiled leather, yet carried himself with a calmness and certainty that made him more frightening than if he rode at the head of a Saxon horde.

"'Tis Uther Pendragon!" one of the boys at the castle walls cried at first. The lad hefted his halberd as if he would take a swing, but stepped back in fright.

Pendragon was, of course, the guards' worst nightmare. At the Easter feast, King Uther Pendragon had made advances on the Duke Gorlois's wife, the Lady Igraine. He had courted her in her husband's company with all the grace and courtesy of a bull trying to mount a heifer. At last the duke felt constrained to flee the king's presence. The king demanded that Gorlois return with his wife, but Gorlois knew that if he ever set foot in the king's palace again, he'd lose his head. So he locked his wife safely in Tintagel, began fortifying his castles, and prayed that he could hire enough Irish mercenaries to back him before the king could bring him down.

Last anyone had heard, Duke Gorlois was holed up like a badger at his fortress in Dimilioc, where Uther Pendragon had laid siege. It was said that Pendragon had employed Welsh miners as sappers, vowing to dig down the castle walls and skin Gorlois for his pelt within forty days.

So when the lad atop the castle wall thought he saw Pendragon, immediately someone raised a horn and began to blow
wildly, calling for reinforcements, though none would likely be
needed. Tintagel was a small keep, situated by the sea on a pile
of rocks that could only be reached over a narrow causeway. It
was said that three men could hold it from an army of any size,
and no fewer than two dozen guards now manned the wall.

The captain of the guard, a stout old knight named Sir Ventias who could no longer ride due to a game leg, squinted through
the smoke that clung around the castle. Something seemed afoul.
He knew fat King Pendragon's features well, and as he peered
through the gloom and the smoke that burned his eyes, he saw
immediately that it was not Pendragon on the mount. It was a
young man with a flaxen beard and a hatchet face.

Ventias squinted, trying to pierce the haze until he felt
sure: It was Duke Gorlois. He rode in company with his true
friend Sir Jordans and the stout knight Sir Brastias.

Ventias smiled. "Tell the duchess that her husband is home."

The celebration that night was remarkable. The duke's pen-
nant was hoisted on the wall, and everywhere the people made
merry. Sir Brastias himself told the miraculous tale of their
escape—how they had spied Pendragon leave the siege and the
duke had issued out from the castle with his knights. After a
brief battle, Gorlois had broken Pendragon's lines and had hurried toward Tintagel, only to discover Pendragon himself a few
miles up the road, frolicking with some maiden in a pool. Since
King Pendragon was naked and unarmed, it became an easy
matter to capture the lecher, both arms and armor, and force his
surrender.

Thus Gorlois rode home in Pendragon's suit of mail.

So it was that the celebration began at Tintagel. Suckling

pigs were spitted and cooked over a bonfire in the lower bailey, while every lad who had a hand with the pipe or the tambor made music as best he could. New ale flowed into mugs like golden honey. Young squires fought mock combats to impress their lord and entertain the audience. And everywhere the people began to dance.

But Duke Gorlois could not relish it. Instead, he went to his great hall before the festivities began and gazed upon his glorious young bride with a sultry stare. He never even took his seat at the head of the table. Instead, he studied her for less than a minute before he grabbed one of her breasts as if it were a third hand and began to lead her to the bedchamber.

This he did in front of some eighty people. When the priest quietly complained about this impropriety to the duke, Gorlois, who was normally a very reserved fellow, merely said, "Let the people frolic as they see fit, and I will frolic as I see fit."

Though everyone was astonished at this crude display, no one other than the priest dared speak against it. Even Sir Jordans, a man who could normally be counted on to pass judgment fairly on any matter, merely sat in the great hall and did not eat. Instead, he played with his heavy serpent-handled dagger, stabbing it over and over again into the wooden table beside his trencher.

Then Duke Gorlois dragged his wife up the stairs against her will, stripping off his armor as he went.

Or at least that is the way that my mother tells the tale, and she should know, for she was a young woman who served tables there at Tintagel.

It seems surprising that no one found it odd.

The evening star that night shone as red as a bloodstone,

and all the dogs somehow quietly slipped from the castle gates.

There was a new horned moon, and though the people danced, they did not do so long. Somehow their feet seemed heavy, and the celebration seemed more trouble than it was worth, and so the crowds began to break off early.

Some went home, while most seemed more eager to drink themselves into a stupor. Yet no one at the time remarked about the queer mood at Castle Tintagel.

Late that night, my mother found Sir Jordans still on his bench, where he'd sat quietly for hours. He was letting the flame of a candle lick his left forefinger in a display that left my mother horrified and set her heart to hammering.

Dozens of knights lay drunk and snoring on the floor around him, while a pair of cats on the table gnawed the bones of a roast swan.

My mother wondered if Sir Jordans performed this remarkable feat for her benefit, as young men often will when trying to impress a young woman.

If so, he'd gone too far. She feared for Sir Jordan's health, so she quietly scurried to the long oaken table. She could not smell burning flesh above the scents of ale and grease and fresh loaves, though Sir Jordans had been holding his finger under the flame for a long minute.

"What are you doing?" my mother asked in astonishment. "If it's cooking yourself that you're after, there's a bonfire still burning out in the bailey!"

Sir Jordans merely sat at the table, a hooded traveling robe pulled low over his head, and held his finger beneath the flickering flame. Candlelight glimmered in his eyes. My mother thought the silence odd, for in the past Sir Jordans had always been such a garrulous fellow, a man whose laugh sounded like the winter's surf booming on the escarpment at the base of the castle walls.

"Do you hear me? You'll lose the finger," my mother warned. "Are you drunk, or fey?" she asked, and she thought of rousing some besotted knight from the floor to help her subdue the man.

Sir Jordans looked up at her with a dreamy smile. "I'll not lose my finger, nor burn it," he said. "I could hold it thus all night. It is a simple trick, really. I could teach you—if you like?"

Something about his manner unnerved my mother. She was beautiful then. Though she was but a scullery maid, at the age of fourteen she was lovely—with long raven hair, eyes of smoke, and a full figure that drew appreciative gazes from men. Sir Jordans studied her now with open admiration, and she grew frightened.

She crossed herself. "This is no trick, this is sorcery!" my mother accused. "It's evil! If the father found out, he'd make you do penance."

But Sir Jordans merely smiled as if she were a child. He had a broad, pleasant face that could give no insult. "It's not evil," he affirmed reasonably. "Did not god save the three righteous Israelites when the infidels threw them into the fire?"

My mother wondered then. He was right, of course. Sir Jordans was a virtuous man, she knew, and if god could save men who were thrown whole into a fire, then surely Sir Jordans was upright enough so that god could spare his finger.

"Let me teach you," Sir Jordans whispered.

My mother nodded, still frightened, but enticed by his gentle manner.

"The trick," Sir Jordans said, withdrawing his finger from the candle flame, "is to learn to take the fire into yourself without getting burned."

He held up his finger for her inspection, and my mother drew close, trying to see it in the dim light, to make sure that it was not oozing or blistered.

"Once you learn how to hold the fire within," Sir Jordans whispered, "you must then learn to release the flames when— and how—you will. Like this . . ."

He reached out his finger then and touched between my mother's ample breasts. His finger itself was cold to the touch, so cold that it startled her. Yet after he drew it away, she felt as if flames began to build inside her, pulsing through her breasts in waves, sending cinders of pleasure to burn hot in the back of her brain. Unimaginable embers, as hot as coals from a blacksmith's forge, flared to life in her groin.

As the flames took her, she gasped in astonishment, so thoroughly inflamed by lust that she dropped to her knees in agony, barely able to suppress her screams.

Sir Jordans smiled at her and asked playfully, "You're a virgin, aren't you?"

Numb with pain, my mother nodded, and knelt before him, sweating and panting from desire. This is hell, she thought. This is how it will be, me burning with desires so staggering that they can never be sated. This is my destiny now and hereafter.

"I could teach you more," Sir Jordans whispered, leaning close. "I could teach you how to make love, how to satisfy every sensual desire. There are arts to be learned—pleasurable beyond your keenest imagining. Only when I teach you can the flames inside you be quenched."

My mother merely nodded, struck dumb with grief and

lust. She would have given anything for one moment of release, for any degree of satisfaction. Sir Jordans smiled and leaned forward, until his lips met hers.

At dawn, my mother woke outside the castle. She found herself sprawled dazed and naked like some human sacrifice upon a black rock on the ocean's shore.

The whole world was silent, with a silence so profound that it seemed to weigh like an ingot of lead on her chest. The only noise came from the cries of gulls that winged about the castle towers, as if afraid to land.

She searched for a long while until she found her clothes, then made her way back to the castle.

Two hours later, riders came charging hard from Dimilioc. They bore the ill tidings that Duke Gorlois had been slain in battle the day before. Among the dead were found Sir Brastias and Sir Jordans.

Everyone at Tintagel took the news in awe, speaking well only because they feared to speak ill.

" 'Twas a shade," they said. "Duke Gorlois so loved his wife that he came at sunset to see her one last time."

Even the Lady Igraine repeated this tale of shades as if it were true, for her husband had slipped from her bed before dawn, as if he were indeed a shade, as had the other dead men who walked in his retinue.

But my mother did not believe the tale. The man she'd slept with the night before had been clothed in flesh, and she felt his living seed burn her womb. She knew that she had been seduced by sorcery, under the horned moon.

Two children were conceived on that fell night. I was one of them, the girl.

You have surely heard of the boy.

King Uther Pendragon soon forced the widowed Igraine to be his wife and removed her to Canterbury. When the boy was born, Pendragon ripped the newborn son from its mother's breast and gave it to a pale-eyed Welsh sorcerer who slung it over his back and carried it like a bundle of firewood into the forest.

I have heard it said that Igraine feared that the sorcerer would bury the infant alive, so she prayed ceaselessly that god would soften the sorcerer's heart, so that he would abandon it rather than do it harm.

Some say that in time Igraine became deluded into believing that her son was being raised by peasants or wolves. She was often seen wandering the fairs, looking deep into the eyes of boy children, as if trying to find something of herself or Duke Gorlois there.

As for my mother, she fled Tintagel well before her stomach began to bulge. She loved a stableboy in Tintagel, and had even promised herself to him in marriage, so it was a hard thing for her to leave, and she slunk away one night without saying any good-byes.

For she constantly feared that the false Sir Jordans would return. It is well known, after all, that devils cannot leave their own offspring alone.

My mother went into labor three hundred and thirty-three days later, after a term so long that she knew there would be something wrong with me.

My mother took no midwife, for she rightly feared what I would look like. I would have a tail, she thought, and a goat's pelt, and cloven hooves for feet. She feared that I might even be born with horns that would rip her as I came through the birth canal.

No priest would have baptized a bastard and a monstrosity, she knew, and she hoped that I would be born dead, or would die soon, so that she could rid herself of the evidence of her sin.

So she went into the forest while the labor pains wracked her, and she gouged a little hole to bury me in, and she laid a huge rock beside it to crush me with, if it came to that.

Then she squatted in the ferns beneath an oak. Thus I dropped into the world, and the only cries to ring from the woods that day came from my mother.

For when I touched the soil, I merely lay quietly gazing about. My mother looked down between her legs in trepidation and saw at once that I was no common girl. I was not as homely as her sin. I was not born with a pelt or a twisted visage.

Instead, she said, I was radiant, with skin that smelled of honeysuckle and eyes as pale as ice. I did not have the cheesy covering of a newborn, and my mother's blood did not cling to me.

I looked out at her, as if I were very old and wise and knowing, and I did not cry. I reached out and grasped her bloody heel, as if to comfort her, and I smiled.

When my mother was a little girl herself, she told me, she had often tried to visualize angels who were so pure and good, so wise and beautiful, so innocent and powerful that the mind revolted from trying to imagine them. Now a newborn angel grasped her heel, and it broke my mother's heart.

No human child had ever had a skin so pale, or hair that so nearly matched the blush of a rose.

Thus my mother knew that I was a fairy child as well as a bastard born under the horned moon, and though she loved me, she dared not name me. Instead, though I bore no lump like a hunchback nor any disfigurement of any kind that made me seem monstrous or ill-favored, she merely called me "Moon-calfe."

IF beauty and wisdom can be said to be curses, no one was more accursed than I.

My mother feared for me. She feared what lusty men might do to me if ever I were found.

So she fled from villages and castles into an abandoned cottage deep in the wooded hills, and perhaps that was for the best. The Saxons were moving north, and on her rare trips to the nearest village, she came back distressed by the news.

At nights I could hear her lying awake, the beads of her rosary clacking as she muttered prayers to her vengeful god, hoping that he would heal me. I knew even then that she prayed in vain, that her god had nothing to do with me.

Mother raised me alone. Time and again she would plead, "Don't wander from the cottage. Never let your face be seen, and never let any man touch you!"

She loved me fiercely, and well. She taught me games and fed me as best she could. She punished me when I did wrong, and she slept with me wrapped in her arms at night.

But if she let me outside to play at all, she did so only briefly, and even then I was forced to cover myself with a robe and a shawl, so that I might hide my face.

Sometimes, at night, she would kneel beneath a cross she had planted in front of the cottage and raise her voice, pleading with her god and his mother. She begged forgiveness, and asked him that I might be healed and made like any other child. She would sometimes cut herself or pull out her own hair, or beat herself mercilessly, hoping that her god would show pity on her for such self-abuse.

I admit that at times, I too prayed to the Blessed Virgin, but never for myself—only for my mother's comfort.

She sought to cure me of my affliction. She rubbed me with healing leaves, like evening star and wizard's violet.

When I was three, my mother took a long journey of several days, the first and only one she ever took with me. She had learned in the village that a holy man had died, a bishop who was everywhere named a man of good report, and she badly wanted his bones to burn for me.

So she bundled me up and carried me through the endless woods. Her prayers poured out from her as copiously as did her sweat.

We skirted villages and towns for nearly a week, traveling mostly at night by the light of the stars and a waxing moon, until at last we reached an abbey. My mother found his tomb, and had work prying the stone from his grave. If the bishop was truly a good man, I do not know. His spirit had already fled the place.

But we found his rotting corpse, and my mother severed his hand, and then we scurried away into the night. The abbot must have set his hounds on us, for I remember my mother splashing through the creek, me clinging to her back, while the hounds bayed.

Two nights later, when the moon had waxed full, we found a hilltop far from any habitation, and she set the bone fire.

We piled up tree limbs and wadded grass into a great circle, and all the time that we did so, mother prayed to her god in my behalf.

"god can heal you, Mooncalfe," she would mutter. "god loves you and can heal you. He can make you look like a common child, I am sure. But in order to gain his greatest blessings, you must say your prayers and walk through the fire of bones.

Only then, as the smoke ascends into heaven, will the Father and his handmaid Mary hear your most heartfelt prayer."

It seemed a lot of trouble to me. I was happy and carefree as a child. My greatest concern was for my mother. Having seen all the work she had done, I consented at last.

When the fire burned its brightest, and columns of smoke lit the sky, my mother threw the bishop's severed hand atop the mix, and we waited until we could smell his charred flesh.

Then my mother and I said our prayers, and my mother bid me to leap through the fire.

I did so, begging the blessing of the Virgin and leaping through the flames seven times.

Even as a child, I never burned. Until that time, I had thought myself fortunate.

But though the fire was so hot that my mother dared not approach it, I leapt through unharmed, untouched by the heat.

On my last attempt, when I saw that the bone fire had still not made me look human, I merely leapt into the conflagration and stood.

I hoped that the flames would blister me and scar me, so that I might look more like a mortal.

My mother screamed in terror and kept trying to draw near, to pull me from the fire, but it burned her badly.

I cried aloud to the Virgin, begging her blessing, but though the flames licked the clothing from my flesh, so that my skirts and cloak all turned to stringy ashes, I took no hurt.

I waited for nearly an hour for the flames to die low before I wearied of the game. Then I helped my mother down to the stream, to bathe her own fire-blistered flesh and ease her torment.

She wept and prayed bitterly, and by dawn she was not fit for travel. She had great black welts on her face, and bubbles beneath the skin, and her skin had gone all red—all because she sought to save me from the flames. But as for me, my skin was unblemished. If anything, it looked more translucent. My mother sobbed and confirmed my fears. "You look more pure than before."

So it was that I foraged for us both, and after several days we began to amble home in defeat.

After that, Mother seemed to lose all hope of ever healing me. She confided a few days later, "I will raise you until you are thirteen, but I can do no more after that."

She wanted a life for herself.

She took to making trips to the village more, and I knew that she fell in love, for often when she returned, she would mention a young miller who lived there, a man named Andelin, and she would sometimes fall silent and stare off into the distance and smile.

I am sure that she never mentioned her accursed daughter to him, and I suppose that he could not have helped but love my mother in kind.

One night, late in the summer, my mother returned from the village crying. I asked her why she wept, and she said that Andelin had begged for her hand in marriage, but she had spurned him.

She did not say why. She thought I was still too young to understand how I stood in the way of her love.

Later that night, Andelin himself rode into the woods and called for my mother, seeking our cottage. But it was far from the lonely track that ran through the wood, and my mother was careful not to leave a trail, and so he never found us.

Though I felt sorry for my mother, I was glad when Andelin gave up looking for us.

The thought terrified me that my mother might leave someday. She was my truest companion, my best friend.

But if I was raised alone as a child, the truth is that I seldom felt lonely. In a dark glen not a quarter mile from my home was a barren place where a woodsman's cottage had once stood. A young boy, Daffyth, had died in the cottage, and his shade still hovered near the spot, for he longed for his mother who would never return.

I could speak with him on all but the sunniest of days, and he taught me many games and rhymes that he'd learned at his mother's knee. He was a desolate boy, lost and frightened. He needed my comfort more than I ever needed his.

For in addition to conversing with him and my mother, I could also speak to animals. I listened to the hungry confabulations of trout in the stream, or the useless prattle of squirrels, or the fearful musings of mice. The rooks that lived against the chimney of our cottage often berated me, accusing me of pilfering their food, but then they would chortle even louder when they managed to snatch a bright piece of blue string from my frock to add to their nests.

But it was not the small animals that gave me the most pleasure. As a child of four, I learned to love a shaggy old wolf bitch who was kind and companionable, and who would warn me when hunters or outlaws roamed the forest.

When, as a small girl, I told my mother what the birds or foxes were saying, she refused to believe me. I was lonely, she thought, and therefore given to vain imaginings. Like any other child, I tended to chatter incessantly, and it was only natural that I would take what company I could find.

Or maybe she feared to admit even to herself that she knew what I could do.

Certainly, she had to have had an intimation.

I know that she believed me when I turned five, for that

was the year that I met the white hart. He was old and venerable and wiser than even the wolf or owls. He was the one who first taught me to walk invisibly, and showed me the luminous pathways in the air that led toward the Bright Lady.

"You are one of them," he said. "In time, you must go to her." But I did not feel the goddess's call at that early age.

It was that very year that my mother became ill one drear midwinter's day—deathly ill, though I did not understand death. Flecks of blood sprayed from her mouth when she coughed, and while her flesh burned with inner fire, she shivered violently, even though I piled all of our coats and blankets on her and left her beside the roaring fire.

"Listen to me," my mother cried one night after a bout of coughing had left her blankets all red around her throat. "I am going to die," she said. "I'm going to die, my sweet Mooncalfe, and I'm afraid you'll die because of it."

I had seen death, of course. I'd seen the cold bodies of squirrels, but I'd also seen their shades hopping about merrily in the trees afterward, completely unconcerned. I did not share my mother's fear.

"All right," I said, accepting death.

"No!" my mother shouted, fighting for breath. Tears coursed from her eyes. "It's not all right." Her voice sounded marvelously hoarse and full of pain. "You must promise me to stay alive. Food. We have plenty of food. But you must keep the fire lit, stay warm. In the spring, you must go north to the nunnery at the edge of the wood."

"All right," I answered with equanimity, prepared to live or die as she willed.

She grew weak quickly.

In those days, I knew little of herb lore or magic. If I'd

known then what I do now, perhaps I would have walked the path to the Endless Summer and gathered lungwort and elderflower to combat her cough, and willow and catmint to help ease her pain and gently sweat out the fever.

But as a child I only prayed with her. She prayed to live; I prayed for a quick cessation of her agony.

Her god granted my prayer—the only one that he ever granted me—and she died within hours.

But death did not end my mother's torment. Her shade was restless and longed to watch over me. She thought me abused because of her sin.

So she remained with me in that house, wailing her grief. Each night was a new beginning to her, for like most shades, she would forget all that had happened the night before. I took her to see Daffyth on some occasions, hoping that they might comfort one another, but she gained nothing from it.

She cursed herself for her weakness in allowing herself to be seduced by Sir Jordans, and she often breathed out threats of vengeance.

She loved me and wept over me, and I could not comfort her. Nor did I ever seek out the nunnery, for my mother seemed as alive to me as ever.

I lived and grew. The she-wolf brought me hares and piglets and young deer to eat, until she herself grew old and died. I gathered mushrooms from the forest floor, and the white hart showed me where an old orchard still stood, so that I filled up stores of plums and apples to help me last through each winter.

I foraged and fed myself. As I did, I began to roam the woods and explore. I would leave the old cottage for days at a time, letting my mother stay alone in her torment. On such occasions, she wandered, too, searching for her little lost girl.

I found her once, there at the edge of the village, staring at Andelin's house. The miller had grown older and had married some girl who was not my mother's equal. Their child cried within, and my mother dared not disturb them.

Yet, like me, she stood there at the edge of the forest, craving another person's touch.

I often kept myself invisible on my journeys, and at times, I confess, I enjoyed sneaking up on the poachers and outlaws that hid in the wood, merely to watch them, to see what common people looked like, how they acted when they thought themselves alone.

But in my fourteenth summer, I once made the mistake of stepping on a twig as I watched a handsome young man stalking the white hart through tall ferns. The boy spun and released his bow so fast that I did not have time to dodge his shot.

The cold iron tip of his arrow only nicked my arm. Though the wound was slight, still the iron dispelled my charms, and I suddenly found myself standing before him naked (for I had no need of clothes). My heart pounded in terror and desire.

I suddenly imagined what the boy would do, having seen me. I imagined his lips against mine, and his hands pressing firmly into my buttocks, and that he would ravish me. After all, night after night my mother had warned me what men would do if they saw me.

So I anticipated his advances. In fact, in that moment I imagined that I might actually be in love, and so determined that I would endure his passion if not enjoy it.

But to my dismay, when he saw me suddenly standing there naked, he merely fainted. Though I tried to revive him for nearly an hour, each time I did so, he gazed at me in awe and then passed out again.

When night came, I wrapped myself in a cloak of invisibility and let him regain his wits. Then I followed him to his home at the edge of a village. He kept listening for me, and he begged me not to follow, thinking me a succubus or some other demon.

He made the sign of the cross against me, and I begged him to tarry. But he shot arrows at me and seemed so frightened that I dared not follow him farther, for his sake as well as mine.

Soon thereafter I met Wiglan, the wise woman of the barrow. She was a lumpy old thing, almost like a tree trunk with arms. She had been dead for four hundred years, and still her spirit had not flickered out and faded, as so many do, but instead had ripened into something warped and strange and eerie. Moreover, she did not grow forgetful during the days as my mother's shade did, and so she offered me a more even level of companionship.

One night under the bright eternal stars, I told Wiglan of my problem, of how my mother longed for me to look mortal, and how I now longed for it, too. I could no longer take comfort in the company of cold shades or in conversations with animals. I craved the touch of real flesh against mine, the kiss of warm lips, the touch of hands, and the thrust of hips.

"Perhaps," Wiglan said, "you should seek out the healing pools up north. If the goddess can heal you at all, there is where you will find her blessing."

"What pools?" I asked, heart pounding with a hope that I had never felt so keenly before.

"There are ancient pools in Wales," she said, "called the Maiden's Fount. While I yet lived, the Romans built a city there, called Caerleon. I heard that they enclosed the fount and built a temple to their goddess Minerva. The fount has great powers, and the Romans honored the goddess in their way, but even then it was a sin, for in honoring the goddess, they sought to hedge her in."

"That was hundreds of years ago," I said. "Are you sure that the fount still springs forth?"

"It is a sacred place to the Lady and all of her kin," Wiglan said. "It will still be there. Go by the light of a horned moon and ask of her what you will. Make an offering of water lilies and lavender. Perhaps your petition will be granted."

Bursting with hope, I set off at once. I set my course by the River or Stars, and journeyed for many days over fields and hills, through dank forest and over the fetid bogs. At night I would sometimes seek directions from the dead, who were plentiful in those days of unrest, until at last after many weeks I reached the derelict temple.

The Saxons had been to Caerleon and burned the city a few years before. A castle stood not far from the ancient temple, but the villages around Caerleon had been burned and looted, their citizens murdered. Little remained of it, and for the moment the castle was staffed by a handful of soldiers who huddled on its walls in fear.

The temple on the hills above the fortress was in worse condition than was the castle. Some of the temple's pillars had been knocked down, and moon disks above its facade lay broken and in ruins. Perhaps the Saxons had sensed the Lady's power here and sought to put an end to it, or at least sully it.

The pools were overgrown and reedy, while owls hooted and flew on silent wings among the few standing pillars.

There I took my offerings and went to bathe under the crescent moon.

I knelt in the damp mud above the warm pool, cast out a

handful of lavender into the brackish water, and stood with a
white water lily cupped in my left palm. I whispered my prayers
to the goddess, thanking her for the gifts that the Earth gave
me, for her breasts that were hills, for the fruit of the fields and
of the forest. I pleaded with her and named my desire before
making my final offering of lily.

As I prayed, a man's voice spoke up behind me. "She's not
that strong anymore. The new god is gaining power over this
land, and the Great Mother hides. You seek a powerful magic,
one that will change the very essence of what you are—and
that is beyond her power. Perhaps you should seek a smaller
blessing, ask her to do something easy, like change the future?
Still, pray to her as you will. It hurts nothing, and I'm glad that
some still talk to her."

I turned and looked into the ice-pale eyes of a Welshman—and
recognized at once my features in his face. He was my father. I
did not feel surprised to meet him here. After all, my mother
had taught me well that demons always seek out and torment
their own children.

He stared right at me, his eyes caressing my naked flesh,
even though I had been walking invisible.

"Sir Jordans?" I asked. "Or do you have a truer name?"

The fellow smiled wistfully and drew back his hood so that
I could see his silvered hair in the moonlight. "I called myself
that—but only once. How is your mother? Well, I hope."

"Dead," I answered, then waited in the cold silence for him
to show some reaction.

When he saw that he must speak, he finally said, "Well,
that happens."

I demanded, "By the Bright Lady, what is your name?" I
do not know if the goddess forced him to reveal it because we

were at the pool, or if he would have told me anyway, but he answered.

"Merlin. Some call me Merlin the Prophet, or Merlin the Seer. Others name me a Magician."

"Not Merlin the Procurer? Not Merlin the Seducer? Not Merlin the Merciless?"

"What I did, I did only once," Merlin said, as if that should buy a measure of forgiveness. "The omens were good that night, for one who wished to produce offspring strong in the old powers. It was the first horned moon of the new summer, after all."

"Is that the only reason you took my mother, because the moon was right?"

"I was not at Tintagel on my own errand," Merlin defended himself. "Uther Pendragon wanted to bed the Duchess Igraine, and he would have killed her husband for the chance. Call me a procurer if you will, but I tried only to save the duke's life—and I foresaw in the process that Pendragon's loins would produce a son who could be a truer and greater king than Uther could ever be."

"Igraine's son? You did not kill the boy?"

"No, Arthur lives with me now, and follows me in my travels. In a year or two, he will learn his destiny," Merlin said. "He will unite all of England and drive back the Saxons, and he will rule this stubborn realm with a gentle hand . . ." He hunched in the tall grass beside the pool, staring thoughtfully into water that reflected moon and stars.

"So you helped seduce the Lady Igraine for a noble cause. But why did you bed my mother?"

"For you!" Merlin said in surprise, as if it were obvious. "I saw that night that your mother had fey blood, and all of the omens were right. I saw that you would be wise and beautiful, and the thought came to me that Arthur would need a fair maiden by his side. The old blood is strong in you, both from me and your mother. If you marry Arthur Pendragon, perhaps together we can build a realm where the old gods are worshipped beside the new."

"Didn't you think before you mounted her?" I asked. "Didn't you think about how it would destroy her?"

Merlin said, "I looked down the path of her future. She would have married a stableboy and borne him five fine sons and a brace of daughters. She would have been happier, perhaps—but she would not have had you!"

"My mother died in torment because of you!" I shouted. "She died alone in the woods, because she feared letting anyone see me alive. She died friendless, because I was too young and silly to know how to save her. Her spirit is in torment still!"

"Yes, yes," Merlin cajoled as if I did not quite see some greater point, "I'm sure it all seems a tragedy. But you are here, are you not? You—"

I saw then that he would not listen, that my mother's suffering, her loneliness and shame, all meant nothing to him. She was but a pawn in his hand, a piece to be sacrificed for the sake of some greater game.

I knew then that I hated him, and that I could never allow Merlin to use his powers against a woman this way again. And suddenly I glanced up at a shooting star, and I knew that I had the power, that the old blood was strong enough in me, that I could stop him.

"Father," I interrupted him, holding the lily high in my left hand. Merlin shut his mouth. "In the name of the Bright Lady I curse you: Though you shall love a woman fiercely, the greater your desire for her grows, the more lame shall be your groin. Never shall you sire a child again. Never shall you use a woman as your pawn, or your seed as a tool."

I stepped through the rushes to the side of the warm pool at Minerva's failing temple, felt the living power of the goddess there as my toe touched the water.

"No!" Merlin shouted and raised his hand with little finger and thumb splayed in a horn as he tried to ward off my spell.

But either he was too late or the spell was too strong for him. In any case, I tossed the white lily into the still waters.

As the wavelets rolled away from the lily, bouncing against the edges of the pool, Merlin screamed in agony and put his hands over his face.

I believe that he was peering into his own bleak future as he cried in horror, "No! No! No!"

I knelt and dipped my hand in the pool seven times, cupping the water and letting it run down my breasts and between my legs.

Then I stood and merely walked away.

Sometimes near dawn, I waken and think that I can still hear Merlin's cries ringing in my ears. I listen then, and smile a fey smile.

In time I made it back to my cottage in the woods, and I told the shade of my mother about all that had transpired. She seemed more at peace that night than ever before, and so before daybreak, I introduced her to the child Daffyth once again.

I told Daffyth that she was his mother, and convinced my mother's shade that Daffyth was a forgotten son, born from her love for a man named Andelin.

In the still night I coaxed them to the edge of the woods, and let them go.

When last I saw them, they were walking hand in hand on the road to Tintagel.

As for me, I learned in time to praise the goddess for her goodness and for what I am and always hope to be—a mooncalfe, and no sorcerer's pawn.

Afterword by David Farland

One day I happened to pick up a book on "extinct" English words, in which a linguist discussed words that had fallen out of use in our language. One of those words was "mooncalfe," and the other was "bone fire," and as I was reading, a brief image flashed through my mind of a young woman sending her prayers to heaven upon the smoke that rose from burning bones. I knew that she was a mooncalfe, and that she was twisted—but twisted in a way that left her with the unearthly beauty of a Faery on the outside and an unquenchable rage on the inside.

At the time, I was thinking about some of the moral ambiguity in Arthurian legend. Arthur's tale is, without a doubt, a classic "fairy tale," in the sense that it was a cautionary tale devised to show good Christians the folly of becoming involved with fairies or taking their gifts.

As we look at it today, we imagine that when Arthur pulls Excalibur from the stone, it is a great accomplishment. But a thousand years ago, our ancestors would have known that no good could come from such an unnatural thing. You can't go about consorting with wizards and fairies and hope to come to a happy end. You can't go about hoping to be more than what you are.

So when Arthur pulls the sword from the stone, it is the beginning of his downfall, and we are left to watch him through the rest of his tale—a young Christian with a heart of gold—doggedly treading the road to ruin.

Of course, over time, I'm sure, as Celtic beliefs were forgotten, the story changed. Arthur became a beloved hero, and Merlin was said to be a "prophet" and was twisted in such a way that Disney was able to show him as a harmless old tutor who only happened to have vast magical powers.

But I've always been bothered by that disturbing genesis of Arthur's story—where Merlin uses his shape-changing abilities to help an evil king rape a good man's wife.

And as the tale progresses, we see that no good can come from Merlin's actions.

I've often thought that it would be fun to rewrite the Arthur story in such a way that the modern audience would experience the sense of horror that it was meant to evoke. "The Mooncalfe," I suppose, would be the first chapter of that story.

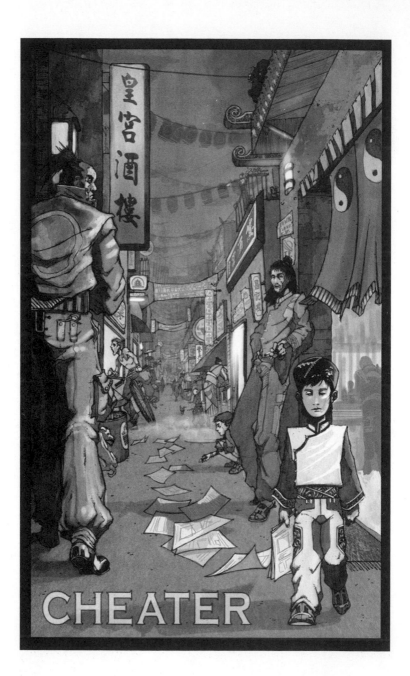

CHEATER

Cheater

BY ORSON SCOTT CARD

Han Tzu was the bright and shining hope of his family. He wore a monitor embedded in the back of his skull, near the top of his spine. Once, when he was very little, his father held him between mirrors in the bathroom. He saw that a little red light glowed there. He asked his father why he had a light on him when he had never seen another child with a light.

"Because you're important," said Father. "You will bring our family back to the position that was taken from us many years ago by the Communists."

Tzu was not sure how a little red light on his neck would raise his family up. Nor did he know what a Communist was. But he remembered the words, and when he learned to read, he tried to find stories about Communists or about the family Han or about children with little red lights. There were none to be found.

His father played with him several times a day. He grew up with his father's loving hands caressing him, cuffing him playfully; he grew up with his father's smile. His father praised him whenever he learned something; it became Tzu's endeavor every day to learn something so he could tell Father.

"You spell my name Tzu," said Tzu, "even though it's pronounced just like the word 'zi.' T-Z-U is the old way of spelling, called . . . 'Wade-Giles.' The new way is 'pinyin.'"

"Very good, my Tzu, my Little Master," said Father.

"There's another way of writing even older than *that,* where each word has its own letter. It was very hard to learn and even harder to put on computer so the government changed all the books to pinyin."

"You are a brilliant little boy," said Father.

"So now people give their children names spelled the old Wade-Giles way because they don't want to let go of the lost glories of ancient China."

Father stopped smiling. "Who told you that?"

"It was in the book," said Tzu. He was worried that somehow he had disappointed Father.

"Well, it's true. China has lost its glory. But someday it will have that glory back and all the world will see that we are still the Middle Kingdom. And do you know who will bring that glory back to China?"

"Who, Father?"

"My son, my Little Master, Han Tzu."

"Where did China's glory go, so I can bring it back?"

"China was the center of the world," said Father. "We invented everything. All the barbarian kingdoms around China stole our ideas and turned them into terrible weapons. We left them in peace, but they would not leave *us* in peace, so they came and broke the power of the emperors. But still the Chinese resisted. Our glorious ancestor, Yuan Shikai, was the greatest general in the last age of the emperors.

"The emperors were weak, and the revolutionaries were strong. Yuan Shikai could see that weak emperors could not protect China. So he took control of the government. He pretended to agree with the revolutionaries of Sun Yat-sen, but then destroyed them and seized the imperial throne. He started a new dynasty, but then he was poisoned by traitors and died, just as the Japanese invaded.

"The Chinese people were punished for the death of Yuan Shikai. First the Japanese invaded China and many died. Then the Communists took over the government and ruled as evil emperors for a hundred years, growing rich from the slavery of the Chinese people. Oh how they yearned for the day of Yuan Shikai! Oh how they wished he had not been slain before he could unite China against the barbarians and the oppressors!"

There was a light in Father's eyes that made Tzu a little afraid and yet also very excited. "Why would they poison him if our glorious ancestor was so good for China?" he asked.

"Because they wanted China to fail," said Father. "They wanted China to be weak among the nations. They wanted China to be ruled by America and Russia, by India and Japan. But China always swallows up the barbarians and rises again, triumphant over all. Don't you forget that." Father tapped Tzu's temples. "The hope of China is in *there.*"

"In my head?"

"To do what Yuan Shikai did, you must first become a great general. *That's* why you have that monitor on the back of your neck."

Tzu touched the little black box. "Do great generals all have these?"

"You are being watched. This monitor will protect you and keep you safe. I made sure you had the perfect mama to make you very, very smart. Someday they'll give you tests. They'll see that the blood of Yuan Shikai runs true in your veins."

"Where's Mama?" asked Tzu, who at that age had no idea of what "tests" were or why someone else's blood would be in his veins.

"She's at the university, of course, doing all the smart things she does. Your mother is one of the reasons that our city of Nanyang and our province of Henan are now leaders in Chinese manufacturing."

Tzu had heard of manufacturing. "Does she make cars?"

"Your mother invented the process that allows almost half of the light of the sun to be converted directly to electricity. That's why the air in Nanyang is always clean and our cars sell better than any others in the world."

"Then Mama should be emperor!" said Tzu.

"But your father is very important, too," said Father. "Because I worked hard when I was young, and I made a lot of money, and I used that money to pay for her research when nobody else thought it would lead to anything."

"Then *you* be emperor," said Tzu.

"I am one of the richest men in China," said Father, "certainly the richest in Henan province. But being rich is not enough to be emperor. Neither is being smart. Though from your mother and me, you will grow up to be both."

"What does it take to be emperor?"

"You must crush all your enemies and win the love and obedience of the people."

Tzu made a fist with his hand, as tight and strong a fist as he could. "I can crush bugs," he said. "I crushed a beetle once."

"You're very strong," said Father. "I'm proud of you all the time."

Tzu got to his feet and went around the garden looking for things to crush. He tried a stone, but it wasn't crushable. He broke a twig, but when he tried to crush the pieces, it hurt his hand. He crushed a worm and it made his hands smeary with ichor. The worm was dead. What good was a crushed worm? What was an enemy? Would it look like this when he crushed one?

He hoped his enemies were softer than stone. He couldn't crush stones at all. But it was messy and unpleasant to crush worms, too. It was much more fun to let them crawl across his hand.

Tutors began to come to the house. None of them played with him for very long at a time, and each one had his own kind of games. Some of them were fun, and Tzu was very good at many of them. Children were also brought to him, boys who liked to wrestle and race, girls who wanted to play with dolls and dress up in adult clothing. "I don't like to play with girls so much," said Tzu to his father, but Father only answered, "You must know all kinds of people when you rule over them someday. Girls will show you what to care about. Boys will show you how to win."

So Tzu learned he should care about tending babies and bringing home things for the pretend mama to cook, though his own mama never cooked. He also learned to run as fast as he could and to wrestle hard and cleverly and never give up.

When he was five years old, he read and did his numbers far better than the average for his age, and his tutors were well-satisfied with his progress. Each of them told him so.

Then one day he had a new tutor. This tutor seemed to be more important than all the others. Tzu played with him five or six times a day, fifteen minutes at a time. And the games were new ones. There would be shapes. He would be given a red one that was eight small blocks stuck together, and then from a group of pictures of blocks he had to choose which one was the same shape. "Not the same color—it can be a different color. The same shape," said the tutor. Soon Tzu was very good at finding that shape no matter how the picture was turned around and twisted, and no matter what color it was. Then the tutor would bring out a new shape, and they'd start over.

He was also given logic questions that made him think for a long time, but soon he learned to find the classifications that were being used. All dogs have four legs. This animal has four legs. Is it a dog? Maybe. Only mammals have fur. This animal has fur. Is it a mammal? Yes. All dogs have four legs. This animal has three legs. Is it a dog? It might be an injured dog—some injured dogs have only three legs. But I said all dogs have four legs. And I said some dogs have only three legs because they're *broken* but they're still dogs! And the tutor smiled and agreed with him.

Then there were the memorization tests. He learned to memorize longer and longer lists of things by putting them inside a toy cupboard the tutor told him to create in his mind, or by mentally stacking them on top of each other, or putting them inside each other. This was fun for a while, though pretty soon he got sick of having all kinds of meaningless lists perfectly memorized. It wasn't funny after a while to have the ball come out of the fish which came out of the tree which came out of the car which came out of the briefcase, but he couldn't get it out of his memory.

Once he had played them often enough, Tzu became bored with all the games. That was when he realized that they were

not games at all. "But you must go on," the tutor would say.
"Your father wants you to."

"He didn't say so."

"He told *me*. That's why he brought me here. So you would
become very good at these games."

"I *am* very good at them."

"But we want you to be the *best*."

"Who is better? You?"

"I'm an adult."

"How can I be best if nobody is worst?"

"We want you to be one of the best of all the five-year-old
children in the world."

"Why?"

The tutor paused, considering. Tzu knew that this meant
he would probably tell a lie. "There are people who go around
playing these games with children, and they give a prize to the
best ones."

"What's the prize?" asked Tzu suspiciously.

"What do you want it to be?" asked the tutor playfully. Tzu
hated it when he acted playful.

"Mama to be home more. She never plays with me."

"Your mama is very busy. And that can't be the prize because the people who give the prize aren't your mama."

"That's what I want."

"What if the prize was a ride in a spaceship?" said the tutor.

"I don't care about a ride in a spaceship," said Tzu. "I saw
the pictures. It's just more stars out there, the same as you see
from here in Nanyang. Only Earth is little and far away. I don't
want to be far away."

"Don't worry," said the tutor. "The prize will make you
very happy and it will make your father very proud."

"If I win," said Tzu. He thought of the times that other children beat him in races and wrestling. He usually won but not always. He tried to think how they would turn these games into a contest. Would he have to make shapes for the other child to guess, and the child would make shapes for him? He tried to think up logic questions and lists to memorize. Lists that you *couldn't* put inside each other or stack up. Except that he could always imagine something going inside something else. He could imagine *anything*. He just ended up with more stupid lists he couldn't forget.

Life was getting dull. He wanted to go outside of the garden walls and walk around the noisy streets. He could hear cars and people and bicycles on the other side of the gate, and when he stuck his eye right up against the crack in the gate he could see them whiz by on the street. Most of the pedestrians were talking Chinese, like the servants, instead of Common, like Father and the tutors, but he understood both languages very well, and Father was proud of that, too. "Chinese is the language of emperors," said Father, "but Common is the language that the rest of the world understands. You will be fluent in both."

But even though Tzu knew Chinese, he could hardly understand what was said by the passersby. They spoke so quickly and their voices rose and fell in pitch, so it was hard to hear, and they were talking about things he didn't understand. There was a whole world he knew nothing about, and he never got to see it because he was always inside the garden playing with tutors.

"Let's go outside the walls today," he said to his Common tutor.

"But I'm here for us to read together," she said.

"Let's go outside the walls and read today," said Tzu.

"I can't," she said. "I don't have the key."

"Mu-ren has a key," said Tzu. He had seen the cook go out of the gate to shop for food in the market and come back with a cart. "Pei-tian has a key, too." That was Father's driver, who brought the car in and out through the gate.

"But *I* don't have a key."

Was she really this stupid? Tzu ran to Mu-ren and said, "Wei Dun-nuan needs a key to the gate."

"She does?" said Mu-ren. "Whatever for."

"So we can go outside and read."

By then Mu-ren had caught up with him. She shook her head at Mu-ren. Mu-ren squatted in front of Tzu. "Little Master," she said, "you don't need to go outside. Your papa doesn't want you out on the street."

That was when Tzu realized he was a prisoner.

They come here and teach me what Father wants me to learn. I'm supposed to become the best child. Even the children that come here are the ones they pick for me. How do I know if I'm the best, when I never get to find children on my own? And what does it matter if I'm best at boring games? Why can't I ever leave this house and garden?

"To keep you safe," Father explained that evening. Mu-ren or the tutor must have told him about the key. "You're a very important little boy. I don't want you to be hurt."

"I won't be hurt."

"That's because you won't go out there until you're ready," said Father. "Right now you have more important things to do. Our garden is very large. You can explore anywhere you want."

"I've looked at all of it."

"Look again," said Father. "There's always more to find."

"I don't want to be the best child," said Tzu. "I want to see what's outside the gate."

"After you take the tests," said Father, laughing. "Plenty of time. You're still very, very young. Your life isn't over yet."

The tests. He had to take the tests first. He had to be best child before he could go out of the garden.

So he worked hard at his games with the tutors, trying to get better and better so he could win the tests and go outside. Meanwhile, he also studied all the walls of the garden to see if there was a way to get through or under or over them without waiting.

Once he thought he found a place where he could squeeze under a fence, but he no sooner had his arm through than one of the tutors found him and dragged him back in. The next time, that place had tight metal mesh between the bottom of the fence and the ground.

Another time he tried to climb a box set on top of a bin, and when he got to the top he could see the street, and it was glorious, hundreds of people moving in all directions but almost never bumping into each other, the bicycles zipping along and not falling over, and the silent cars crawling through as people moved out of the way for them. Everyone wore bright colors and looked happy or at least interested. Every single person had more freedom than Tzu did. What kind of emperor will I be if I let people keep me inside a cage like a pet bird?

So he tried to swing his leg up onto the top of the wall, but once again, before he could even get his body weight onto the top, along came a tutor, all in a dither, to drag him down and scold him. And when he came back to the place, the bin was no longer near the wall. Nothing was ever near the garden walls again.

Hurry up with the tests, then, thought Tzu. I want to be out there with all the people. There were children out there, some of them holding on to their mothers' hands, but some of them not holding on to anybody. Just . . . loose. I want to be loose.

Then one day the newest tutor, Shen Guo-rong, the one with the logic games and lists, stood outside Tzu's room and talked with his father in a low voice for a long time. He came in with a paper, which he looked at long and hard.

"What's on that paper?"

"A note from your father."

"Can I read it?" asked Tzu.

"It's not a note to you, it's a note to me," said Guo-rong.

But when he set it down, it wasn't a note at all. It was covered with diagrams and words. And that day, all their games were chosen by Guo-rong after consulting with the paper.

It went like that for days. Always the same answers, until Tzu knew them all in order and could start reciting them before the questions were asked.

"No," said Guo-rong. "You must always wait for the question to be completely finished before you answer."

"Why?"

"That's the rule of the game," he said. "If you answer any question too fast, then the whole game is over and you lose."

That was a stupid rule, but Tzu obeyed it. "This is boring," he said. "The test will be soon," said Guo-rong. "And you'll be completely ready for it. But don't tell the testers about any of your practice with me."

"Why not?"

"It will look better for you if they don't know about me, that's all."

That was the first time that Tzu realized that there might be something wrong with the way he was being prepared for the tests. But he had little time to think about it, because the very next day, a strange woman and a strange man came to the house. They had no folds over their eyes and had strange ruddy skin, and they wore uniforms he recognized from the vids. They were with the IF, the International Fleet.

"He's fluent in Common?" the man said.

"Yes," said Father—Father was home! Tzu ran into the room and hugged his father. "This is a special day," Father told him as he hugged him back. "These people are going to play some games with you. A kind of test."

Tzu turned and looked at them. He didn't know the test was from soldiers. But now it became clear to him. Father wanted him to become a great general like Yuan Shikai. The beginning of that would be to enter the military. Not the Chinese army, but the fleet of the whole world.

But he didn't want to go into space. He just wanted to go out on the street.

He knew Father would not want him to ask about this, however. So he smiled at the man and the woman and bowed to each in turn. They bowed back, smiling also.

Soon Tzu was alone in his playroom with the two of them. No tutors, no servants, no Father.

The woman spread out some papers and brought out shapes, just like the ones he had practiced with.

"Have you seen these before?" she asked.

He nodded.

"Where?"

Then he remembered he wasn't supposed to talk about Guo-rong, so he just shrugged.

"You don't remember?"

He shrugged again.

She explained the game to him—it was just like the one

Guo-rong had played. And when she held up a shape, it was the very one they had practiced with, and he instantly recognized it from the choices on the paper. He pointed.

"Good," she said.

And so it went with the next two shapes. They were exactly the ones Guo-rong had shown him, and the answer was exactly the one that had been on the note from Father.

Suddenly Tzu understood it all. Father had cheated. Father had found out the answers to the test and had given them to Guo-rong so that Tzu would know all the answers to all the questions.

It took only a moment to make the next leap. In a way, it was a logic problem. The best child is the one who scores the best on this test. He wants me to be best child. So I must score the best on this test.

But if I score the best because I was given the answers in advance and trained to memorize them, then this test won't prove I'm the best child, it will only prove that I can memorize answers.

If Father believed I was the best child, then he would not need to get these answers in advance. But he did get the answers. Therefore he must believe that I would not have won the test without having special help. Therefore Father does not believe I am best child, he just wants to fool other people into believing that I am.

It was all he could do to keep from crying. But even though his eyes burned and he felt a sob gathering behind his nose and in his throat, he kept his face calm. He would not let the people know that his father had given him the answers. But he would also not pretend to be best child when he really wasn't.

So the next question he got wrong.

And the next.

And all the others.

Even though he knew the answer to every single one, before they even finished the question, he got every one of them wrong.

The woman and man from the International Fleet showed no sign of whether they liked his answers or not. They smiled cheerfully all the time, and when they were done, they thanked him and left.

Afterward, Father and Guo-rong came into the room where Tzu waited for them. "How did it go?" asked Father.

"Did you know the answers?" asked Guo-rong.

"Yes," said Tzu.

"All of them?" asked Father.

"Yes," said Tzu.

"Did you answer all the questions?" asked Guo-rong.

"Yes," said Tzu.

"Then you did very well," said Father. "I'm proud of you."

You're not proud of me, thought Tzu as his father hugged him. You didn't believe I'd pass the test on my own. You didn't think I was best child. Even now, you're not proud of *me,* you're proud of yourself for getting all the answers.

There was a special dinner that night. All the tutors ate with Father and Tzu at the main table. Father was laughing and happy. Tzu could not help but smile at all the smiling people. But he knew that he had answered all but the first three questions wrong, and Father would not be happy when he found that out.

When dinner was over, Tzu asked, "Can I go outside the gate now?"

"Tomorrow," said Father. "In daylight."

"The sun is still up," said Tzu. "Take me now, Father."

"Why not?" said Father. He rose to his feet and took Tzu by the hand and they walked, not to the gate where the car came in and out, but to the front door of the house. It let out onto another garden, and for a moment Tzu thought his father was going to try to fool him into thinking this was the outside when it was really more garden. But soon the path led to a metal gate which opened at Father's touch, and beyond the gate was a wide road with many cars on it—more cars than people. It was a different world from what Tzu had seen over the back fence. It was so quiet. The cars glided silently by, their tires hissing on the pavement, though there were some that had no tires and merely hovered over the concrete of the road.

"Where are all the people and bicycles?" asked Tzu.

"Behind the house is a back road," said Father. "Where poor people go about their business. This is the main road. It connects to the highway. These cars could be going anywhere. Xiangfan. Zhengzhou. Kaifeng. Even Wuhan or Beijing or Shanghai. Great cities, where powerful people live. Millions of them. In the richest and greatest of all nations." Then Father picked Tzu up and held him on his hip so their faces were close. "But you are the best child in all those cities."

"No I'm not," said Tzu.

"Of course you are," said Father.

"You know that I'm not," said Tzu.

"What makes you say that?"

"If you thought I was best child, you wouldn't have given Guo-rong all the answers."

Father just looked at him for a moment. "I was just making sure. You didn't need them."

"Then why did you have him teach them to me?" said Tzu.

"To be sure."

"So you weren't sure."

"Of course I was," said Father.

But Tzu had been studying logic. "If you were sure I would know the answers on my own, then you wouldn't have to *make* it sure by getting the answers. But you got the answers. So you weren't sure."

Father looked a little bit upset.

"I'm sorry, Father, but it's how we play the logic game. Maybe you need to play it more."

"I *am* sure that you're the best child," said Father. "Don't you ever doubt it." He set Tzu down and took his hand again. They went through the gate and walked up the street.

Tzu wasn't interested in this road. There were no people here, except in cars, and they went by too fast for Tzu to hear them. There were no children. So when they came to a side street, Tzu began to pull his father that direction. "This way," he said. "Here's all the people!"

"That's why it isn't safe," said Father. But then he laughed and let Tzu lead him on into the crowds. After a while it was so jammed with people and bicycles that Father picked him up. That was much better. Tzu could see the people's faces. He could hear their conversations. Some of them looked at Tzu, being held up by his father, and smiled at them both. Tzu smiled and waved back.

Father walked slowly alongside a high fence, which Tzu realized was the back fence around their garden. Eventually they came to a gate, which Tzu knew was the gate to their garden. "Don't go in yet," said Tzu.

"What?"

"This is our gate, but don't go in."

"How did you know it was our gate? You've never been on this side of it before."

"Father," said Tzu impatiently, "I'm very smart. I know this is our gate. What else could it be? We've just made a circle. Let me see more before we go in."

So they walked past the gate, and on into one of the streets that seemed to go on forever, more and more people, flowing into and out of the buildings. Starting and stopping, buying and selling, calling out and keeping still, laughing and serious-faced, talking on phones and gesturing, or listening to music and dancing as they walked.

"Is this China, Father?" asked Tzu.

"A very small part of it. There are hundreds of cities, and lots of open country, too. Farmland and mountains, forest and beaches. Seaports and manufacturing centers and highways and deserts and rice paddies and wheatfields and millions and millions and millions of people."

"Thank you," said Tzu.

"For what?"

"For letting me see China before I go off into space."

"What are you talking about?"

"The man and woman with the test, they were from the International Fleet."

"Who told you that?"

"They wore the uniforms," said Tzu impatiently. But then he realized: He *hadn't* passed the test. He answered the questions wrong. He wouldn't be going to space after all. "Never mind," he said. "I'm staying."

Father laughed and held him close. "Sometimes I have no idea what you're talking about, Little Master."

Tzu wondered if he should tell him that he answered the

questions wrong, but he decided against it. Father was so happy. Tzu didn't want to make him angry tonight.

The next morning, Tzu was eating breakfast in the kitchen with Mu-ren when someone came to the door. The visitor did not wait for old Iron-head, as Mu-ren and Tzu secretly called the houseman, to fetch Father. Instead, many feet began walking briskly through the house.

The kitchen door was flung open. A soldier with a weapon in his hand stepped in and looked around. "Is Han Pei-mu here?" he asked sternly. Mu-ren shook her head.

"What about Shen Guo-rong?"

Again, the head shake.

"Guo-rong doesn't come till later," said Tzu.

"You two stay right here in the kitchen, please," said the soldier. He continued to stand in the doorway. "Keep eating, please."

Tzu continued eating, trying to think what the soldiers were there for. Mu-ren's hands were shaking. "Are you cold?" asked Tzu. "Or are you scared?"

Mu-ren only shook her head and kept eating.

After a while he could hear his father shouting. "Let me at least explain to the boy!" he was saying. "Let me see my son!"

Tzu got up from his mat on the floor and jogged toward the kitchen door. The soldier put his hand on his shoulder to stop him.

Tzu slapped his hand and said to him fiercely, "Don't touch me!" Then he jogged on down the hallway to Father's room, the soldier right behind him.

The door opened just before Tzu got to it, and there was the man from the test yesterday. "Apparently someone already decided," said the man. He ushered Tzu into the room.

Father's hands were bound together behind his back, but now one of the soldiers loosed them and he reached out to Tzu. Tzu ran to him and hugged him. "Are you under arrest?" asked Tzu. He had seen arrests on the vids.

"Yes," said Father.

"Is it because of the answers?" asked Tzu. It was the only thing he could think of that his father had ever done wrong.

"Yes," said Father.

Tzu pulled away from him and faced the man from the tests. "But it was all right," said Tzu. "I didn't use those answers."

"I know you didn't," said the man.

"What?" said Father.

Tzu turned around to face him. "I didn't like it that you were only going to pretend I was best child. So I didn't use any of the answers. I didn't want to be called best child if I wasn't really." He turned back to the man from the fleet. "Why are you arresting him when I didn't use the answers?"

The man smiled confidently. "It doesn't matter whether you used them or not. What matters is that he obtained them."

"I'm sorry," said Father. "But if my son did not answer the questions correctly, how can you prove that any cheating took place?"

"For one thing, we've been recording this entire interview," said the man from the fleet. "The fact that he knew he had been given the right answers and chose to answer incorrectly does not change the fact that you trained him to take the test."

"Maybe what you need is a little better security with the answers," said Father angrily.

"Sir," said the man from the fleet, "we always allow people

to buy the test if they try to get it. Then we watch and see what they do with it. A child as bright as this one could not possibly have answered every question wrong unless he absolutely had the entire test down cold."

"I got the first three right," said Tzu.

"Yes, all but three were wrong," said the man from the fleet. "Even children of very limited intellect get some of them right by random chance."

Father's demeanor changed again. "The blame is entirely mine," he said. "The boy's mother had no idea I was doing this."

"We're quite aware of that. She will not be bothered, except of course to inform her. The penalty is not severe, sir, but you will certainly be convicted and serve the days in prison. The fleet makes no exceptions for anyone. We need to make a public example of those who try to cheat."

"Why, if you let them cheat whenever they want?" said Father bitterly.

"If we didn't let people buy the answers, they might figure out much cleverer ways to cheat the test. Ways we wouldn't necessarily catch."

"Aren't you smart."

Father was being sarcastic, but Tzu thought they *were* smart. He wished he had thought of that.

"Father," said Tzu. "I'm sorry about Yuan Shikai."

Father glanced furtively toward the soldiers. "Don't worry about that," he said.

"But I was thinking. It's been so many hundred years since Yuan Shikai lived that he must have *hundreds* of descendants now. Maybe thousands. It doesn't have to be me, does it? It could be one of *them*."

"Only you," said Father softly. He kissed him good-bye.

They bound his wrists behind his back and led him out of the house.

The woman from the test stayed with Tzu and kept him from following to watch them take Father away. "Where will they take him?" asked Tzu.

"Not far," said the woman. "He won't be imprisoned for very long, and he'll be quite comfortable there."

"But he'll be ashamed," said Tzu.

"For a man with so much pride in his family," said the woman, "that is the harshest penalty."

"I should have answered most of the questions right," said Tzu. "It's my fault."

"It's not your fault," said the woman. "You're only a child."

"I'm almost six," said Tzu.

"Besides," said the woman, "we watched Guo-rong coaching you. Teaching you the test."

"How?" asked Tzu.

She tapped the little monitor on the back of his neck.

"Father said that was just to keep me safe. To make sure my heart was beating and I didn't get lost."

"Everything your eyes see," said the woman, "we see. Everything you hear, we hear."

"You lied, then," said Tzu. "You cheated, too."

"Yes," said the woman. "But we're fighting a war. We're allowed to."

"It must have been boring, watching everything I see. I never get to see *anything*."

"Until last night," she said.

He nodded.

"So many people on the streets," she said. "More than you can count."

"I didn't try to count them," said Tzu. "They were going all different directions and in and out of buildings and up and down the side streets. I stopped after three thousand."

"You counted three thousand?"

"I'm always counting," said Tzu. "I mean my counter is."

"Your counter?"

"In my head. It counts everything and tells me the number when I need it."

"Ah," she said. She took his hand. "Let's go back to your room and take another test."

"Why?"

"*This* test you don't know the answers to."

"I bet I do," said Tzu. "I bet I figure them out."

"Ah," said the woman. "A different kind of pride."

Tzu sat down and waited for her to set up the test.

Afterword by Orson Scott Card

Smart kids fascinate me, because even when they function at genius levels, there are still things they don't know. Intelligence is about capacity; sophistication is about experience and knowledge and understanding of context.

Knowing that having a child chosen for Battle School would be a matter of very high prestige, I realized that it is inevitable that someone would cheat. How would Battle School deal with this? Was it possible for anyone to beat the system? I decided not—especially when they had the option of installing monitors to watch the genius children all the time.

Or perhaps the monitors were installed *because* of cheaters, to make sure that the children who did well were the real thing.

Anyway, once I realized that the testers from Battle School

would have a system in place to trap cheaters and deal with them, I then tried to imagine how a genius child might react to his parents' assumption that he would need to cheat in order to get into Battle School.

That's when I decided that Han Tzu—Hot Soup—was going to be the kid who had to deal with his father's lack of confidence in him.

Then the problem became one of deciding what life would be like in China more than a century in the future. Of course, predicting the future is not what sci-fi writers are good at. Heinlein outlived large swaths of his "future history," and even though there's zero chance I'll outlive mine, it's still annoying when things happen that make little details in a story wrong.

Still, there are continuities in Chinese culture that transcend the politics of history. I hope I gave Han Tzu a world that rings true, now and in years to come.

Dream Engine

BY TIM PRATT

The Stolen State, The Magpie City, The Nex, The Ax—this is the place where I live, and hover, and chafe in my service; the place where I take my small bodiless pleasures where I may. Nexington-on-Axis is the proper name, the one the Regent uses in his infrequent public addresses, but most of the residents call it other things, and my—prisoner? partner? charge? trust?—my associate, Howlaa Moor, calls it The Cage, at least when zie is feeling sorry for zimself.

The day the fat man began his killing spree, I woke early, while Howlaa slept on, in a human form that snored. I looked down on the streets of our neighborhood, home to low-level government servants and the wretchedly poor. The sky was bleak, and rain filled the potholes. The royal orphans had snatched a storm from somewhere, which was good, as the district's roof gardens needed rain.

I saw a messenger approach through the cratered street. I didn't recognize his species—he was bipedal, with a tail, and his skin glistened like a salamander's, though his gait was bird-like—but I recognized the red plume jutting from his headband, which allowed him to go unmolested through this rough quarter.

"Howlaa," I said. "Wake. A messenger approaches."

Howlaa stirred on the heaped bedding, furs and silks piled indiscriminately with burlap and canvas and even coarser fabrics, because Howlaa's kind enjoy having as much tactile variety as possible. And, I suspect, because Howlaa likes to taunt me with reminders of the physical sensations I cannot experience.

"Shushit, Wisp," Howlaa said. My name is not Wisp, but that is what zie calls me, and I have long since given up on changing the habit. "The messenger could be coming for anyone. There are four score civil servants on this block alone. Let me sleep." Howlaa picked up a piece of half-eaten globe-fruit and hurled it at me. It passed through me without effect, of course, but it annoyed me, which was Howlaa's intent.

"The messenger has a red plume, skinshifter," I said, making my voice resonate, making it creep and rattle in tissues and bones, so sleep or shutting-me-out would be impossible.

"Ah. Blood business, then." Howlaa threw off furs, rose, and stretched, arms growing more joints and bends as zie moved, unfolding like origami in flesh. I could not help a little subvocal gasp of wonder as zir skin rippled and shifted and settled into Howlaa's chosen morning shape. I have no body, and am filled with wonder at Howlaa's mastery of physical form.

Howlaa settled into the form of a male Nagalinda, a biped with long limbs, a broad face with opalescent eyes, and a lip-

less mouth full of triangular teeth. Nagalinda are fearsome
creatures with a reputation for viciousness, though I have
found them no more uniformly monstrous than any other
species; their cultural penchant for devouring their enemies
has earned them a certain amount of notoriety even in the
Ax, though. Howlaa liked to take on such forms to terrify
government messengers if zie could. Such behavior was in-
subordinate, but it was such a small rebellion that the Regent
didn't even bother to reprimand Howlaa for it—and having
such willfully rude behavior so completely disregarded only
served to annoy Howlaa further.

The Regent knew how to control us, which levers to tug
and which leads to jerk, which is why he was the Regent, and
we were in his employ. I often think the Regent controls the
city as skillfully as Howlaa controls zir own form, and it is a
pretty analogy, for the Ax is almost as mutable as Howlaa's
body.

The buzzer buzzed. "Why don't you get that?" Howlaa
said, grinning. "Oh, yes, right, no hands, makes opening the
door tricky. I'll get it, then."

Howlaa opened the door to the messenger, who didn't find
the Nagalinda form especially terrifying. The messenger was
too frightened of the fat man and the Regent to spare any fear
for Howlaa.

I Floated. Howlaa ambled. The messenger hurried ahead,
hurried back, hurried ahead again, like an anxious pet. Howlaa
could not be rushed, and I went at the pace Howlaa chose, of
necessity, but I sympathized with the messenger's discomfort.
Being bound so closely to the Regent's will made even tardi-
ness cause for bone-deep anxiety.

"He's a fat human, with no shirt on, carrying a giant battle-ax, and he chopped up a brace of Beetleboys armed with dung-muskets?" Howlaa's voice was blandly curious, but I knew zie was incredulous, just as I was.

"So the messenger reports," I said.

"And then he disappeared, in full view of everyone in Moth Moon Market?"

"Why do you repeat things?" I asked.

"I just wondered if it would sound more plausible coming from my own mouth. But even my vast reserves of personal conviction fail to lend the story weight. Perhaps the Regent made it all up, and plans to execute me when I arrive." Howlaa sounded almost hopeful. "Would you tell me, little Wisp, if that were his plan?"

Howlaa imagines I have a closer relationship with the Regent than I do, and has always believed I willingly became a civil servant. Howlaa does not know I am bound to community service for my past crimes, just as Howlaa is, and I allow this misconception because it allows me to act superior and, on occasion, even condescend, which is one of the small pleasures available to us bodiless ones. "I think you are still too valuable and tractable for the Regent to kill," I said.

"Perhaps. But I find the whole tale rather unlikely."

Howlaa walked along with zir mouth open, letting the rain fall into zir mouth, tasting the weather of other worlds, looking at the clouds.

I looked everywhere at once, because it is my duty and burden to look, and record, and, when called upon, to bear witness. I never sleep, but every day I go into a small dark closet and look at the darkness for hours, to escape my own senses. So I saw everything in the streets we passed, for the thousandth time, and though details were changed, the essential nature of the neighborhood was the same. The buildings were mostly brute and functional, structures stolen from dockyards, ghettos, and public housing projects, taken from the worst parts of the thousand thousand worlds that grind around and above Nexington-on-Axis in the complicated gearwork that supports the structure of all the universes. We live in the pivot, and all times and places turn past us eventually, and we residents of the Ax grab what we can from those worlds in the moment of their passing—and so our city grows, and our traders trade, and our government prospers. It is kleptocracy on a grand scale.

But sometimes we grasp too hastily, and the great snatch-engines tended by the Regent's brood of royal orphans become overzealous in their cross-dimensional thieving, and we take things we didn't want after all, things the other worlds must be glad to have lost. Unfortunate imports of that sort can be a problem, because they sometimes disrupt the profitable chaos of the city, which the Regent cannot allow. Solving such problems is Howlaa's job.

We passed out of our neighborhood into a more flamboyant one, filled with emptied crypts, tombs, and other oddments of necropoli, from chipped marble angels to fragments of ornamental wrought iron. To counteract this funereal air, the residents had decorated their few square blocks as brightly and ostentatiously as possible, so that great papier-mâché birds clung to railings, and tombs were painted yellow and red and blue. In the central plaza, where the pavement was made of ancient headstones laid flat, a midday market was well under way. The pale vendors sold the usual trinkets, obtained with privately owned low-yield snatch-engines, along with the district's sole specialty, the exotic mushrooms grown in cadaver-earth deep in the underground catacombs. Citizens shied away from the red-plumed messenger, bearer of bloody news, and shied farther away at the sight of Howlaa, because Nagalinda seldom strayed from their own part of the city, except on errands of menace.

As we neared the edge of the plaza there was a great crack and whoosh, and a wind whipped through the square, eddying the weakly linked charged particles that made up my barely physical form.

A naked man appeared in the center of the square. He did not rise from a hidden trapdoor, did not drop from a passing airship, did not slip in from an adjoining alley. Anyone else might have thought he'd arrived by such an avenue, but I see in all directions, to the limits of vision, and the man was simply there.

Such magics were not unheard of, but they were never associated with someone like this. He appeared human, about six feet tall, bare-chested and obese, pale skin smeared with blood. He was bald, and his features were brutish, almost like a child's clay figure of a man.

He held an absurd sword in his right hand, the blade as long as he was tall, but curved like a scimitar in a theatrical production about air-pirates, and it appeared to be made of gold, an impractical metal for weaponry. When he smiled, his lips peeled back to show an amazing array of yellow stump-teeth. He reared back his right arm and swung the sword, striking a merrow-woman swaddled all over in wet towels, nearly severing her arm. The square plunged into chaos, with vendors, customers, and passersby screaming and fleeing in all directions, while the fat man kept swinging his sword, moving no more than a step or two in any direction, chopping people down as they ran.

"The reports were accurate after all," Howlaa said. "I'll go sort this." The messenger stood behind us, whimpering, tugging at Howlaa's arm, trying to get zim to leave.

"No," I said. "We were ordered to report to the Regent, and that's what we'll do."

Howlaa spoke with exaggerated patience. "The Regent will only tell me to find and kill this man. Why not spare myself the walk, and kill him now? Or do you think the Regent would prefer that I let him kill more of the city's residents?"

We both knew the Regent was uninterested in the well-being of individual citizens—more residents were just a snatch-and-grab away, after all—but I could tell Howlaa would not be swayed. I considered invoking my sole real power over Howlaa, but I was under orders to take that extreme step only in the event that Howlaa tried to escape the Ax or harm one of the royal orphans. "I do not condone this," I said.

"I don't care." Howlaa strode into the still-flurrying mass of people. In a few moments zie was within range of the fat man's swinging sword. Howlaa ducked under the man's wild swings and reached up with a long arm to grab his wrist. By now most of the people able to escape the square had done so, and I had a clear view of the action.

The fat man looked down at Howlaa as if zie were a minor annoyance, then shook his arm as if to displace a biting fly.

Howlaa flew through the air and struck a red-and-white-striped crypt headfirst, landing in a heap.

The fat man caught sight of the messenger—who was now rather pointlessly trying to cower behind me—and sauntered over. The fat man was extraordinarily bowlegged, his chest hair was gray, and his genitals were entirely hidden under the generous flop of his belly-rolls.

As always in these situations, I wondered what it would be like to fear for my physical existence, and regretted that I would never know.

Behind the fat man, Howlaa rose, rippled, and transformed, taking on zir most fearsome shape, a creature I had never otherwise encountered, that Howlaa called a Rendigo. It was reptilian, armored in sharpened bony plates, with a long snout reminiscent of the were-crocodiles that lived in the sewer labyrinths below the Regent's palace. The Rendigo's four arms were useless for anything but killing, paws gauntleted in razor scales, with claws that dripped blinding toxins, and its four legs were capable of great speed and leaps. Howlaa seldom resorted to this form, because it came with a heavy freight of biochemical killing rage that could be hard to shake off afterward. Howlaa leapt at the fat man, landing on his back with unimaginable force, poison-wet claws flashing.

The fat man swiveled at the waist and flung Howlaa off his back, not even breaking stride, raising his sword over the messenger. The fat man was uninjured; all the blood and nastiness that streaked his body came from his victims. His sword passed through me and cleaved the messenger nearly in two.

The fat man smiled, looking at his work, then frowned, and blinked. His body flickered, becoming transparent in places, and he moaned before disappearing.

Howlaa, back in Nagalinda form, crouched and vomited out a sizzling stream of Rendigo venom and biochemical rage-agents.

Howlaa wiped zir mouth, then stood up, glancing at the dead messenger. "Let's try it your way, Wisp. On to the Regent's palace. Perhaps he has an idea for . . . another approach to the problem."

I thought about saying "I told you so." I couldn't think of any reason to refrain. "I told you so," I said.

"Shushit," Howlaa said, preoccupied, thinking, doing what zie did best, assessing complex problems and trying to figure out the easiest way to kill the source of those problems, so I let zim be, and didn't taunt further.

Before we entered the palace, Howlaa took on one of zir common working shapes, that of a human woman with a trim assassin-athlete's body, short dark hair, and deceptively innocent-looking brown eyes. The Regent—who had begun his life as human, though long contact with the royal orphans had wrought certain changes in him physiologically and otherwise—found this form attractive, as I had often sensed from fluctuations in his body heat. I'd made the mistake of sharing that information with Howlaa once, and now Howlaa wore this shape every time we met with the Regent, in hopes of discomforting him. I thought it was a wasted effort, as the Regent simply looked, and enjoyed, and was untroubled by Howlaa's unavailability.

We went up the cloudy white stone steps of the palace, which had been a great king's residence in some world far away, and was unlike any other architecture in Nexington-on-Axis. Some said the palace was alive, a growing thing, which seemed borne out by the ever-shifting arrangement of minarets and spires, the way the hallways meandered organically, and walls that appeared and disappeared. Others said it was not alive but simply magical. I had been reliably informed that the palace, unable to grow out because of the press of other government

buildings on all sides, was growing down, adding a new
sub-basement every five years or so. No one knew where the
excavated dirt went, or where the building materials came
from—no one, that is, except possibly the royal orphans, who
were not likely to share the knowledge with anyone.

Two armored Nagalinda guards escorted us into the palace.
That was a better reason for Howlaa to change shape—Nagalinda
didn't like seeing skinshifters wearing their forms, because it
meant that at some point the skinshifter had ingested some portion of a Nagalinda's body, and while their species enjoyed eating their enemies, they didn't tolerate being eaten by others.

We were escorted, not to the audience room, but into one
of the sub-basements. We were working members of the government and received no pomp or ceremony. As we walked,
the Nagalinda guards muttered to one another, complaining of
bad dreams that had kept them up all night. I hadn't even realized that Nagalinda could dream.

We reached the underground heart of the palace, where the
Regent stood at a railing looking down into the great pit that
held the royal snatch-engines. He was tall, dressed in simple
linen, white-haired, old but not elderly. We joined him, waiting to be spoken to, and as always I was staggered at the scale of
the machinery that brought new buildings and land and large
flora and fauna to the Ax.

The snatch-engines were towering coils of copper and silver and gleaming adamant, baroque machines that wheezed
and rumbled and squealed, with huge gears turning, stacks
venting steam, and catwalks crisscrossing down to the unseen
bottom of the engine-shaft. The royal orphans scuttled along
the catwalks and on the machinery itself, their bodies feathered
and insect-like, scaled and horned, multi-legged, some winged,

all of them chittering and squeaking to one another, making subtle and gross refinements to the engines their long-dead parents, the Queen and Kings of Nexington-on-Axis, had built so many centuries ago. The orphans all had the inherent ability to steal things from passing worlds, but the engines augmented their powers by many orders of magnitude. The Queen and Kings had been able to communicate with other species, it was said, though they'd seldom bothered to do so; their orphans, each unlike its siblings except for the bizarre chimera-like makeup of their bodies, communicated with no one except the Regent.

"I understand you attempted to stop the killer on your way here," the Regent said, turning to face us. While his eyes were alert, his bearing was less upright than usual. He looked tired. "That was profoundly stupid."

"I've never encountered anything my Rendigo form couldn't kill," Howlaa said.

"I don't think that's a true statement anymore. You should have come to me first. I have something that might help you." The Regent stifled a yawn, then snapped his fingers. One of the royal orphans—a trundling thing with translucent skin through which deep blue organs could be seen—scrambled up to the railing, carrying a smoked-glass vial in one tiny hand. The Regent bowed formally, took the vial, and shooed the orphan away. "This is the blood of a questing beast. You may drink it."

"A questing beast!" I said. "How did you ever capture one?"

"We have our secrets," the Regent said.

Howlaa snorted. "Even questing beasts die sometime, Wisp. The snatch-engines probably grabbed the corpse of one."

Howlaa was pretending to be unimpressed, but I saw zir hands shake as they took the vial.

Questing beasts were near-legendary apex predators, the only creatures able to hunt extra-dimensional creatures. They could pursue prey across dimensions, grasping their victims with tendrils of math and magic, and chasing them forever, even across branching worlds.

"Wherever the killer disappears to, you'll be able to follow him, once you shift into the skin of a questing beast," the Regent said.

"Yes, I've grasped the implications," Howlaa said.

"Then you've also grasped the possible avenues of escape this skin will provide you," the Regent said. "But if you think of leaving this world for frivolous reasons, or of not returning when your mission is complete, there will be . . . consequences."

"I know," Howlaa said, squeezing the vial. "That's what my little Wisp is for."

"I will be vigilant, Regent," I said.

"Oh, indeed, I'm sure," the Regent said. "Away, then. Go into the city. The killer seems to favor marketplaces and restaurants, places with a high concentration of victims—he has appeared in five such locations since yesterday. Take this." He passed Howlaa a misshapen sapphire, cloudy and cracked, dangling on a thin metal chain. "If any civil servants see the killer, they will notify you through this, and, once you drink the blood of the questing beast, you will be able to 'port yourself to the location instantly."

Howlaa nodded. I would go wherever Howlaa did, for my particulate substance was inextricably entangled with zir gross anatomy. Howlaa uncapped the vial and drank the blood. Zir body, through the arcane processes of the skinshifter race, sequenced the genetic information of the questing beast, the macro-in-the-micro implicit in the blood, and incorporated the properties of the beast. Howlaa shivered, closed zir eyes, swallowed, and whined deep in zir throat. Then, with a little sigh of pleasure, Howlaa opened zir eyes and said, voice only slightly trembling, "Let's go, Wisp. On with the hunt."

The killer did not reappear that day. Howlaa and I went to the Western Outskirts, one of the few safe open spaces in the Ax, so zie could practice being the questing beast. It's dangerous to loiter in empty lots in the city proper, because the royal snatch-engines are configured to look for buildings that can fill available gaps. Thus, a space that is at one moment a weed-filled lot can in another instant be occupied by an apartment building full of bewildered humans, or a plaster-hive of angrily jostled buzz-men, or stranger things—and anyone who happened to be standing in the empty lot when the building appeared would be flattened. But the Western Outskirts are set aside for outdoor recreations, acre upon acre of playing fields, ramshackle wooden skydiving platforms, lakes of various liquids for swimming or bathing or dueling, obstacle courses, consensual-cannibalism hunting grounds, and similar public spaces. Howlaa chose an empty field marked off with white lines for some unknown game, and transformed into the questing beast.

As one of the bodiless, dedicated to observation, it shames me to admit I could make little sense of Howlaa's new form; too much of zir body occupied nonvisible dimensions. I saw limbs, golden fur, the impression of claws, something flickering that might have been a tail pendulum-swinging in and out of phase, but nothing my vision could settle on or hold. Looking at Howlaa in this form agitated me. If I had a stomach, I might have found it nauseating.

Howlaa flickered back to female human form and spent some minutes curled on the ground, moaning. "Coming back to this body is a bit of a shock," zie said after a while. "But I think I get the general idea. I can go anywhere just by finding the right trail of scent."

"But you won't go anywhere. You won't try to escape."

Howlaa threw a clod of dirt at me. "Correct, Wisp, I won't. But not because you'd try to stop me—"

"I would stop you."

"—only because I don't like being tossed aside in a fight. I'm going to follow this fat bastard, and I'm going to chew on him. You can't lose a questing beast once it gets its claws in you."

"So . . . now we wait."

"Now you wait. I'm going to drink. One of the advantages of wearing a human skin is that something as cheap and plentiful as alcohol provides such a fine buzz."

"Is this the best time to become intoxicated?" We bodiless have a reputation for being prudish and judgmental, which is not unwarranted. I can never get drunk, can never pleasantly impair my own faculties, and I am resentful of (and confused by) those bodied creatures that can.

"Which time? This time, when I might be killed by a fat man with a golden sword tomorrow? Yes, I'd say that's the best time for intoxication."

The next morning, we went to a den of vile iniquity near the palace. While Howlaa drank, I observed, and listened. I learned that a plague of nightmares was troubling the city center, and many of the bar's patrons had gone to stay with relatives in more far-flung districts in order to get some sleep. At least Howlaa and I wouldn't be called upon to deal with that crisis—bad dreams were rather too metaphysical a problem for Howlaa's methods to solve.

After a morning of Howlaa's hard drinking, the sing-charm the Regent had given us began to sound. Howlaa was underneath a table, talking to zimself, and seemed oblivious to the gem's keening, though everyone else in the bar heard, and went silent.

"Howlaa," I said, rumbling my voice in zir bones. Howlaa scowled, then skinshifted into a Nagalinda form, becoming instantly sober. Nagalinda process alcohol as easily as humans process water.

"Off we go," Howlaa said, and rushed into the street, transforming into the questing beast once zie was far enough away to avoid inadvertently snagging any of the bar patrons with extra-dimensional tendrils.

We traveled, the city folding and flickering around us, buildings bleeding light, darkness pressing in from odd angles until I was hopelessly disoriented. Seconds later we were in the middle of the Landlock Sea, on a floating wooden platform so large it barely seemed to move. The sea-market nearby was in chaos, fishermen and hunters of various species—Manipogos, Hydrans, Mhorags, others—running wildly for boats and bridges or diving into the water to get away from the fat man, who was now armed with a golden trident. He speared people, laughing, and Howlaa went for him and grappled, flashing tendrils wrapping around the fat man's bulk, barely seen limbs knocking aside his weapon. The fat man stumbled, staggered, and fell to his knees. Howlaa's ferocious lashings didn't penetrate the man's impossibly durable flesh, but at least he'd been prevented from further acts of murder.

Then the man vanished, and Howlaa with him, and I was pulled along in their wake, on my way to wherever the fat man went when he wasn't killing residents of the Ax for sport.

For a moment, I looked down on the Ax, which spun as sedately as a gear in a great machine, and other universes flashed past, their edges blue- and red-shifting as they went by at tremendous speeds, briefly touching the Ax, sparks flying at the contact, the royal snatch-engines making their cross-dimensional depredations. Then we plummeted into an oncoming blur of blue-green-white, and after a period of blackness, I found myself in another world.

"Wisp," Howlaa hissed as I came back into focus. I had never been unconscious before—even my "sleep" is just a blessed respite from sensory input, not a loss of consciousness—and I did not like the sensation. Our passage from the Ax to this other plane had agitated my particles so severely that I'd lost cohesion and, thus, awareness.

Now that my faculties were in control of me again, I saw a star-flecked night sky above, and Howlaa in human-female form, crouching by bushes beside a brick wall. I did not see the fat man anywhere.

"What—" I began.

"Quiet," Howlaa whispered, looking around nervously. I looked, but saw nothing to worry about. Grass, flowerbeds, and beside us a single-story brick house of a sort sometimes seen in the blander sections of the Middling Residential District. "The fat man got away," Howlaa said. "Only he actually melted away, or misted away, or . . . My tentacles didn't slip. He didn't slip through them. He just disappeared. Nothing can escape a questing beast."

"Perhaps the legends exaggerate the beast's powers," I said.

"Perhaps you'd best shushit and listen, Wisp. There's an open window just over there, and I can almost hear . . ."

I did not have to settle for almost. I floated above the bushes a few feet to the window, which opened onto a bedroom occupied by two humans, neither of them the fat man. The man and woman were both in bed, illuminated by a single bedside lamp. The man, who was pigeon-chested and had thinning hair, gestured excitedly, and the woman, an exhausted-looking blonde, lay propped on one elbow, looking at him through half-closed eyelids.

I listened, and because Howlaa is (I grudgingly admit) better at data analysis than I am, I let zir listen, too, by extending a portion of my attenuated substance down toward zim, a probing presence that Howlaa sensed and accepted. My vision blurred, and sounds took on strange echoes, but then I found my focus and stopped picking up residuals of Howlaa's sensory input—still, zie would see and hear everything as clearly as I did.

"It's amazing," the man was saying. "They get more real all the time. I know you think it's stupid, but lucid dreaming is amazing. I'm so glad I took that seminar. It's like living a whole other life while I'm asleep!"

"What did you do this time?" She leaned back and closed her eyes.

The man hesitated. "I was in a sort of fish-market. There were fish-people, mermaids, selkies, things like that, and ordinary people, too, all buying and selling things. There was a lake, or an inland sea, and we were all on a wooden platform floating on the water . . ."

"You get seasick just stepping over a puddle," she said.

He looked at her, mouth a tense line, eyes narrowed, and I think if she had seen his expression she would have leapt from the bed in fear for her life. Unless long association with this man had dulled her awareness to the dark currents in him I saw so clearly.

"My dream body doesn't get sick," he said. "It's part of my positive visualization technique. My dream body is impervious to harm."

"And I bet you look like a movie star, too."

Another hesitation, this one accompanied by a troubled frown. "Something like that."

I wondered what his dream self really looked like—his father? An old enemy? A figure from a childhood nightmare that he could not escape, but was eventually able to embody?

He continued. "The only problem is, I can't seem to control where I go. The teacher at the seminar said that was the best part, being able to go to the mountains or the beach or outer space as easily as thinking it. But I just find myself in this city full of strange people and creatures, and . . ."

"Do you sleep with any of those strange people?" she asked.

"No. It's not like that."

"What good's having control of your dreams if you can't wish yourself into an erotic dream? Seems like that would be the best part."

"I want to go back to sleep," he said. "I want to try again."

"You don't have to ask my permission. I was sleeping fine until you sat up and started yelling. Doesn't sound like lucid dreaming is doing you much good—you're still having night-mares."

"The nightmares are different now," he said. "I'm in control."

She just turned over and pulled the sheet up to her neck.

"He's the fat man," Howlaa said, speaking silently into me, able to share thoughts as easily as we shared senses. "He goes to the Ax in his dreams, and he kills us for pleasure. That's why the questing beast couldn't hold the killer, why he melted away, because he has no substance beyond the borders of the Ax."

"Madness," I said, though Howlaa's intuitive leaps had proven right more often than my skepticism.

"No, I think I've figured it. The Regent has consulted with many oneiromancers, lucid dreamers, and archetype-hunters over the years—I know, because I was sent to kidnap and press-gang many of them into civil service. I never knew why he wanted them before. I think that, with the Regent's help, the royal orphans have constructed a machine to steal dreams. A dream engine, that grabs mental figments and makes them real. But they locked on to this madman's dream, and now his dream-self will keep coming, and killing, until this world spirals too far from the Ax for the engine to reach, which could take years."

"A dream engine," I repeated. "The activity of such a machine might explain the plague of nightmares in the city center."

"I doubt the Regent would worry overmuch about properly shielding any strange radiations," Howlaa said. "This is a new low for him. It's not enough that he grows rich through the orphans' thefts—now he wants to pillage our dreams, too."

The man lay on his back, staring at the ceiling. Despite his words, he did not seem eager to sleep again. If Howlaa was right, the man had just been chased out of his fantasy of infinite strength by the monstrous questing beast, which would be enough to give any dreamer pause.

"If you're right, we have to kill him," I said.

"Or not," Howlaa said.

Howlaa severed our connection, swirling my motes, and so it took me a moment to realize zie was transforming into the questing beast again—and I knew why. To jump away from this world, to another plane, adjacent to this one but not necessarily adjacent to the Ax. A few dimensional leaps, a little time, and Howlaa would be far beyond the Ax's influence, beyond the grasp of even the greatest snatch-engines.

But I still had a chance, this brief moment between transformations, to strike, and I did. I performed the one act that Howlaa could not resist, the power I was given permission to use only in circumstances as extreme as these.

I took possession of Howlaa's body.

Howlaa Fought, and I batted zir efforts aside, then simply reveled in having a body, especially a body as sensitive as the questing beast's, seeing into higher dimensions, seeing colors that only exist between worlds. I wanted to fly through suns, roll across jagged stones, immerse myself in lava, feel feel feel this forever.

Howlaa was laughing at me, a tinny internal sound. "Shushit," I said, not speaking aloud. I didn't even know if this body had vocal cords. "You didn't escape. You failed. We're going to kill this man, and then return to the Ax."

"Go on, then," Howlaa said. "Best of luck."

I attempted to take a step forward, and everything blurred. My head rang with odd chimes, and bizarre scents assailed me. I had never been in a body so sensitive to smell—each scent was like a line attached to me, tugging me in one direction or another. I paused, and the chaos of sensory input lessened. I took another step toward the dream-killer's window, and this time a whole new set of sensations struck me, making me fall to the ground.

"This form will not do," I said.

"Why not? Because you have no finesse, Wisp? Because you can control gross motor functions, but the intricacies are lost to you? In the questing beast's form, even the most trivial movement is intricate. Then why not take another form, a simpler one?"

I felt rage—glandular rage, pumping up from somewhere in this body, a biological response to a mental state. I never get used to that, the feedback loop of mind and body that the corporeal undergo constantly, and I tried to dismiss its effects. I couldn't shift into another form. That was far too intricate a task for my understanding of how to control a body. If Howlaa had been in a human form, I could have broken into the man's house, stabbed him with a knife, and walked out again—such simple physical manipulation was within my powers. But as the questing beast . . .

"We have reached an impasse," I said.

"And what do you propose?"

"Kill this man," I said, "and I will not report your attempt to escape."

Howlaa laughed. "Oh, please, don't report me. What will they do? Sentence me to another lifetime of servitude?"

"Just kill him! That's why we came."

"I came to kill an invulnerable fat man with the golden weapons, Wisp, not a mentally disturbed human in his bed."

ORSON SCOTT CARD'S INTERGALACTIC MEDICINE SHOW

"They are the same!"

"They are not the same. This man is mad, but he is not the killer—he simply dreams of killing."

"But . . . his dreams are evil . . ."

"You would hold us responsible for our dreams now? If so, I am a regicide a thousand times over, for in my dreams, I rip the Regent and his orphans to wet bits every night. The Regent is the guilty party in this—he has made a machine that steals dreams, and he brought the killer to our city."

"What do you recommend?"

"Fixing this problem at the source. Which is what I was trying to do when you so rudely possessed me."

"You were trying to escape," I said.

"No, Wisp, I was trying to return to Nexington-on-Axis. Sorry I didn't consult you—my understanding was that you're an observer, here to lend me support."

"I am here to make sure you do your duty," I replied, wondering if zie was telling the truth.

"I will. But my duty is not to the Regent. I serve the welfare of Nexington-on-Axis. Come, Wisp, and I'll show you I do have a sense of responsibility. Such a strong one, in fact, that I won't kill an innocent madman for the Regent's crimes."

I gave up control of Howlaa's body, and with more shifting, we returned to the Ax.

We appeared in the Regent's private chambers, which should have been impossible, as there were safeguards against teleportation there. The Regent sat in a wingback chair, holding a ledger in his lap, and he raised his eyebrows when we appeared.

Howlaa shifted to female-human form, only swaying a bit on zir feet in the aftermath of being the beast. "Huh," zie said.

"I wondered if that would work. It's said nothing can stop a questing beast from coming and going as it pleases."

"Mmm," the Regent said. "I trust you solved our problem, and disposed of the fat man? I'll see you get something extra in your next pay allotment. Now, go away. I'm busy." He looked back down at his ledger.

Howlaa cleared zir throat. "Regent. I require your assistance in the fulfillment of my duties."

The Regent looked up. "You didn't kill the fat man?"

"My investigation is ongoing. I need to see the new snatch-engine, the one that steals dreams, and I may have some questions regarding its operation."

The Regent set his ledger aside and stared at Howlaa for a long moment. "Well," he said. "You are not famed for your powers of deduction, Howlaa Moor, but for your powers of destruction. I had not expected you to make inquiries, and I did not ask you to. You are dismissed from this case. I will assign someone else to deal with the fat man."

"Respectfully, sir, you may not interfere with any legitimate inquiries I care to make in an ongoing investigation. My contract prohibits such interference. Again, please have me escorted to the new snatch-engine, and provide someone knowledgeable to answer any questions I might have. Or do you believe this line of inquiry is without cause? If so, I would be happy to bring my evidence before the magisters." Howlaa smiled.

I was in awe at zir audacity. To confront the Regent this way! And zie had no evidence, just intuition and inference. If the Regent called the bluff . . . But no. He didn't want any evidence Howlaa might possess brought before the magisters and, indirectly, the citizens of the Ax.

"I am the Regent, Moor. You take orders from me."

"Indeed. But my contract states that I serve the city, and not the ruler. You may not lawfully inhibit me. Break my contract, if you like, and I'll not trouble you again. Otherwise, you are obliged to cooperate."

"I could have you executed for treason."

Howlaa bowed. "You are welcome to try, sir." Skinshifters could be executed, but it was difficult, since a long-lived member of the species would have forms resistant to most obvious methods of execution. "But if you choose not to execute me or break my contract, then I must ask, for the third time, that you take me to the dream engine and provide—"

"Yes," the Regent snapped. "Fine."

I was astonished. Howlaa's bluff had succeeded. Zie was too valuable for the Regent to dismiss from duty or to kill, and his own laws prevented any other action.

The Regent couldn't simply disregard these laws, for they were the source of his power. Without his laws, there would be no city of Nexington-on-Axis, just a giant junkheap full of things snatched at random by the orphans, indiscriminate slaves to their magpie impulses. "But I am about to show you a state secret."

"That's fine," Howlaa said. "My contract gives me any necessary clearances to fulfill my duties—"

"I know what your contract says, Moor. I wrote it myself, so you would be forced to serve the city in perpetuity, even in the event of my death. Now shut up about it. I'm taking you where you want to go. If you speak a word about this device to anyone, you will be executed for treason. We have methods designed for your kind. There's a special chamber in one of the basements for disposing of skinshifters."

"I serve the state," Howlaa said. "I will not betray it."

I wondered what kind of execution chamber the Regent had that could hold a questing beast, since the safeguards on his private chambers had been insufficient to keep the beast out. I didn't think the Regent realized what kind of power he was giving Howlaa by letting zim drink the questing beast's blood.

We set off down the shifting opalescent corridors of the palace, and the walls groaned around us as they moved.

"You think the killer is a dream-being, snatched here by the experimental engine," the Regent said as we walked.

"I'll submit my report when my investigation is complete," Howlaa said. "Along with my recommendations for how to rectify the problem."

The Regent scowled, but kept walking. Finally we reached a door of black iron. The stone around it was discolored and cracked—the substance of the palace apparently had an allergy to iron, but the heavy metal had certain shielding properties that made its use necessary on occasion. The Regent knocked, a complex rhythm, his unbreakable adamant signet ring clanging against the metal with each rap.

The door swung open silently, and the Regent ushered us into the dimly lit place beyond.

"This is the dream engine," the Regent said. "Not what you expected, I wager."

"No," Howlaa murmured. "It's not."

Unlike the snatch-engines, there were no gears here, no oiled pistons, no sparking ladders of electricity, no bell-shaped domes of glass, no miles of copper pipes for coolant. There was only a throbbing organic mass in a web of wires, a red-and-green slick thing with no visible eyes or limbs, though it did have vestigial wings, prismatic like a dragonfly's, which drooped to the floor. A royal orphan, pinned in a web of wires.

Howlaa crossed zir arms. "So it's psychic, then."

The Regent smiled. "In a way. It sees dreams. More importantly, it covets dreams. And what the royal orphans covet, they get. Much of the process of governing Nexington-on-Axis is making sure the orphans want things the city needs. They don't care what happens to the things they snatch. They simply live for the process of snatching. This one is no different, except for the sorts of thing it snatches."

"You haven't been successful making this one want things the city needs, since it pulled a madman's murderous dream to this world."

"You're certain of that?" the Regent said.

Howlaa just nodded, and the Regent sighed. "I'll have to spend some time tuning the process. It's still experimental. I trust you found and killed the dreamer, to prevent another incident?"

"I did not," Howlaa said. "If I had known for certain about the existence of this dream engine, I would have tried, but I only had suspicions. When I grabbed the fat man, I was carried to another world, surrounded by houses filled with sleeping humans, with no sign of the fat man anywhere. That's when I began to suspect that I'd grabbed a dream-figment—I remembered your studies with various experts on dreaming, Platonic ideals, the collective unconscious, things of that nature."

"You have quite a memory," the Regent said.

"I drank the blood of an elephant once," Howlaa said, and I almost laughed. "Since I wasn't sure the killer was a dream-thing, I came back here to inquire further."

"We should talk in the hall," the Regent said abruptly. "Vibrations disturb the engine." Indeed, the vestigial wings were flickering, weakly, and we left the room. Once in the hall, the Regent said, "How do you intend to proceed?"

"When the killer appears again, I'll grab him, and when he sweeps me back to the human world with him again . . . well, I think it's safe to assume that the dangerous dreamer will be somewhere in the general vicinity of the place where I land. I'll simply kill everyone within a mile or so. It will take time, but I have some forms that are suited to the task."

I was stunned. I knew Howlaa was lying. We knew very well who the dreamer was, and Howlaa had shown no inclination to kill him. So what was zie planning?

"Very good," the Regent said. "But if you mention a word about the contents of that room, I'll have you flayed into your component atoms. Understood?"

"The authorities appreciate your cooperation," Howlaa said. The Regent sniffed and walked away.

"Come, Wisp. Back to our eternal vigilance."

"Back to the bar, you mean."

"Just so." Howlaa grimaced, touching zir stomach. "Shit. I've got a pain in my gut."

"Are you all right?"

"Probably something I ate in another form that doesn't agree with this one. I'll be all right." Howlaa shivered, stretched, and became the questing beast. We traveled.

I tried to get some sense out of Howlaa at the bar, before zie drank too many red bulldozers, primal screams, and gravity wells to maintain a coherent conversation. I slipped a tendril into zir mind and said, "What is your plan?"

"Assume what I told the Regent is true," Howlaa said,

smiling at the human bartender, who looked appreciatively at Howlaa's human breasts as she mixed drinks. "If things work out, it won't matter, but if things go badly, you'll need all the plausible deniability you can get. No reason for you to go down with me if I fail. This way you can honestly claim ignorance of my plans."

"You want to protect me from getting in trouble with the Regent?" I said, almost touched.

Zie laughed aloud and gulped a fizzing reddish concoction. "No, Wisp. But on the off chance that they imprison me instead of putting me to death, I don't want to be stuck in a cell with you forever."

After that, zie wouldn't talk to me at all, but had fun as only Howlaa on the eve of potential death can.

Zie vomited more often than usual, though.

A day passed, and Howlaa was sober and bored at home, playing five-deck solitaire while I made desultory suggestions, before the fat man reappeared. The singing gem keened at midday. Howlaa cocked zir head, taking information from the gem.

Zie became the questing beast, and we were away.

This time we landed in the city center. The fat man sat on the obsidian steps of the Courthouse of Lesser Infractions, face turned up to the sun, smiling up at the light. He held a golden scythe across his knees, and blood and bodies lay strewn all over the steps around him, many wearing the star-patterned robes of magisters.

Howlaa did not hesitate, but traveled again, this time appearing directly in front of the fat man and lashing out with barely visible hooked appendages to grasp the killer. Then Howlaa traveled again. We reappeared in the racing precinct, startling the spectators and scattering the thoroughbred chimeras. The fat man struggled in the hoof-churned mud, his weapon gone.

I had barely overcome my disorientation before Howlaa traveled again. I knew it was Howlaa controlling the movement, for the sensation was quite different from the swirling transcendence that came when the fat man dragged us to that other world. This time we appeared in another populated area, the vaulted gray halls of the Chapel of Blessed Increase in the monastic quarter. We flickered again, Howlaa and the fat man still locked in struggle, and flashed briefly through another dozen places around the city, all filled with startled citizens—in the adder's pit, the ladder to the stars, the moss forest, the monster farm, the glass park, the burning island. We even passed through the Regent's inner chamber, briefly, though he was not there, and through other rooms in the palace, courtrooms, dungeons, and chambers of government. There was a fair amount of incidental damage in many of these instances, as the fat man rolled around, kicked, and thrashed.

Then we appeared in the dream engine's chamber, and everything in my full-circle visual field wobbled and ran, either as an aftereffect of all that spatial violation, or because bringing a dream into such proximity with the dream engine set up unstable resonances.

Howlaa and the fat man thrashed right into the pulsing royal orphan in its tangle of wires. The orphan's wings fluttered as it broke free from the mountings, and the ovoid body fell to the floor with a sick, liquid sound, like a piece of rotten fruit dropping onto pavement. The fat man broke free of Howlaa—though that wasn't possible, so Howlaa must have let him go. He attacked Howlaa, who flickered and reappeared on the far side of the weakly pulsing royal orphan. The fat man roared and strode forward, a new weapon suddenly in his hand, a six-foot polearm covered in barbs and hooks. He tread on the royal orphan, which popped and deflated, a wet, ripe odor filling the room. The fat man swung at the unmoving Howlaa, but the weapon disappeared in mid-arc. The fat man stumbled, falling to one knee, then moaned and came apart. It was like seeing a shadow-sculpture dissolve at the wave of an artist's hand, his substance darkening, becoming transparent, and finally melting away.

Howlaa became human, fell to zir knees, and shivered. "Feel sick," zie said, grimacing.

I was terrified. The Regent might kill us for this. We'd stopped the fat man, yes, but at the cost of a royal orphan's life. "We have to go, Howlaa," I said. "Become the questing beast. I won't try to stop you—let's flee across the worlds. We have to get away."

But Howlaa did not hear, for zie was vomiting now, violently, zir whole body heaving, red and milky white and translucent syrupy stuff coming from zir mouth, mingling with the ichor from the dead orphan on the floor.

The door opened. The Regent and two Nagalinda guards entered. "No!" the Regent cried. "No, no, no!" The guards seized Howlaa, who was still vomiting, and dragged zim away. I floated along inexorably behind. The Regent stayed, kneeling by the dead orphan, gently touching its unmoving rainbow wings.

"Feeling better, traitor?" the Regent said. Howlaa sat, pale and still unwell, on a hard wooden bench before the Regent's desk.

"A bit," Howlaa said.

The Regent smiled. "You didn't think I'd let you be the questing beast forever, did you? I couldn't risk your escape.

Wisp is one line of defense against that, but I felt another was needed, so I laced the blood with poison and bound their substances together. When the poison activated, your body expelled it, along with all the questing beast's genetic material. You've lost the power to take that form."

"I've never vomited up an entire shape before," Howlaa said. "It was an unpleasant experience."

"The first of many, for a traitor like you."

"Regent," I said, "as Howlaa's witness, I must inform you that you are incorrect. Howlaa did not mean to harm the orphan. The fat man appeared and disappeared, and Howlaa and I were simply carried along with him. Surely there are others who can attest to that, testify that we appeared all over the city, fighting? Howlaa held on, hoping the fat man would fade and we would be taken to the world of the dreamer, but before that could happen . . . well. The dream engine was damaged."

"The orphan was killed," the Regent said. "You expect me to believe that, by coincidence, the last place Howlaa and the killer appeared was in that room?"

"We could hardly appear anywhere after that, Regent, since the dream engine was destroyed, dissolving the fat man in the process." I spoke respectfully. "Had that not happened, I cannot tell you where the fat man might have traveled next."

"He was a lucid dreamer," Howlaa said. "He'd learned to move around at will. He was trying to shake me off, bouncing all over the city."

The Regent stared at Howlaa. "That orphan was the result of decades of research, cloning, cross-breeding—the pinnacle of the bloodline. With a bit of practice, it would have been the most powerful of the orphans, and this city would have flourished as never before. We would have entered an age of dreams."

"It is a great loss, Regent," Howlaa said. "And we certainly deserve no honor or glory for our work—I failed to kill the dreamer. He killed himself. But I did not kill the orphan, either. The fat man trod upon it."

"Wisp," the Regent said. "You affirm, on your honor as a witness, that this is true?"

My honor as a witness. My honor demanded that I respect Howlaa's elegant solution, which had saved the city further murder and also destroyed the Regent's wicked dream engine. I think the Regent misunderstood the oath he requested. "Yes," I said.

"Get out of here, both of you," he said. "There will be no bonus pay for this farce. No pay at all, in fact, until I decide to reinstate you to active duty."

"As you say, Regent," Howlaa and I said together, and took our leave.

"**You lied** for me, Wisp," Howlaa said that night, reclining on a heap of soft furs and coarse fabrics.

"I provided an interpretation that fit the objectively available facts," I said.

"You knew I was the one dragging the killer around the city, not vice versa."

"So it seemed to me subjectively," I said. "But if the Regent chose to access my memory and see things as I had seen them, there would be no such subjectivity, so it hardly seemed relevant to the discussion."

"I owe you one, Wisp," Howlaa said.

"I did what I thought best. We are partners."

"No, you misunderstand. I owe you one, and I want you to take it, right now." Howlaa held out zir hand.

After a moment, I understood. I drifted down to Howlaa's

body, and into it, taking over zir body. Howlaa did not resist, and the sensation was utterly different from the other times I had taken possession, when most of my attention went to fighting for control. I sank back in the furs and fabrics, shivering in ecstasy at the sensations on zir—on my—skin.

"The body is yours for the night," Howlaa said in my—our—mind. "Do with it what you will."

"Thank you."

"You had the right of it," Howlaa said. "We are partners. Finally, and for the first time, partners."

I buried myself in furs, and reveled in the tactile experience until the exquisite, never-before-experienced sensation of drowsiness overtook me. I fell asleep in that body, and in sleep I dreamed my own dreams, the first dreams of my life. They were beautiful, and lush, and could not be stolen.

Afterword by Tim Pratt

"Dream Engine" is a hodgepodge story, combining various free-floating ideas I've had for years.

I've always liked weird cities—from Edward Bryant's Cinnabar to M. John Harrison's Viriconium to China Miéville's New Crobuzon, and I've long wanted to create my own bizarre urban setting. I came up with the idea of a city at the center of a multiverse, a big messy organic sprawl built on the spinning axis of the great wheel of the multiverse, with whole discrete universes whirling around it on all sides. Conceiving of such a place raised obvious questions. How would this linchpin city be populated? How would the citizens feed and shelter themselves, how would they trade, etc.? At some point, reading about the collapse of the former Soviet Union, I came across the word "kleptocracy," to describe a state ruled by thieves. That seemed perfect. The denizens of my city, Nexington-on-Axis, are magpies of the multiverse, snatching buildings, people, animals, and even hunks of land from passing planets, planes, and dimensions. I knew I'd hit upon a great setting, one where I could do almost anything. I wanted the city to have weirdly alien rulers and a Regent with a hidden agenda, and so I created them.

But a setting isn't a story.

The notion of a man who kills people in his dreams—and the question of whether he would bear a moral responsibility for those murders—has fascinated me since high school, and I made a few failed attempts at writing that story over the years. I realized how I could apply that idea to my new setting, so I decided to give it a try. At that point, I had a setting, and something that could become a plot. All I needed was a protagonist.

I like detectives, from literary ones like C. Auguste Dupin, Sherlock Holmes, and Sam Spade to newer media detectives like Veronica Mars. (I'm also fond of bounty hunters, assassins, and secret agents.) A weird city like Nexington-on-Axis would need some kind of detective/enforcer, and who better than Howlaa Moor, a shapeshifting rogue of no fixed gender, who serves the state because the only alternative is death or imprisonment? (The no-fixed-gender thing did provide a challenge when it came to pronouns, so I chose to use one of the several invented gender-neutral sets of terms: "zim" instead of "him" or "her"; "zir" instead of "his" or "hers," etc.)

I'm a big fan of sidekicks, so it seemed natural to give Howlaa zir own Dr. Watson, in this case, the bodiless tattletale know-it-all Wisp. They seemed like perfect foils—Howlaa can

transform into virtually any living shape, while Wisp has no
physical body at all, just a charged field of floating motes.

Once I had setting, plot, and characters in mind, the story
was remarkably easy to write, and it's a world I expect to explore further. Howlaa and Wisp have a lot more adventures in
them, I think.

Hats Off

BY DAVID LUBAR

Freddy and I were busting our butts cleaning out his parents' toolshed. Freddy's father had offered us each a couple of bucks to do the work, which was fine with me. Of course, it turned out to be a lot more work than either of us counted on.

"Man, it's amazing how much junk you can put in one of these sheds," I said as I collapsed on the ground next to a huge stack of tools and boxes.

"Tell me about it," Freddy said. He opened a small box. I remembered it since it had weighed about eight million pounds and I'd nearly busted my gut carrying it out of the shed.

"What's in it?" I asked.

"Fishing magazines," Freddy said. "Dad hasn't fished in years. Guess it goes in the recycling pile."

I helped him drag it over. We'd decided to sort every-thing into three piles: recycle, keep, and throw out. Toward the end of the cleanup, I opened a box that was filled with hats.

"Hey, Dad!" Freddy yelled toward the house. "You want any hats?"

"No," his father called back through the open window. "Toss 'em."

"We should keep these," I said, lifting one of the hats from the box. It looked like a baseball cap, but it didn't have a team name. All it said over the brim was ENERGY. I put it on.

And I felt great.

"Hey, let's load those recyclables into your dad's van," I said.

"Hold on," Freddy said. "I'm beat."

"Not me," I said, lifting the box of magazines. "I've got tons of—"

"Tons of what?" Freddy asked.

"Weird," I muttered. I'd been about to say "energy."

"What?" Freddy asked again.

I reached into the hat box and grabbed another hat. This one promised HAPPINESS. Before Freddy could say anything, I plunked the hat on his head.

"All right!" Freddy shouted, grinning at me. "Come on. Let's get moving. Man, I'm glad we're doing this." He laughed and grabbed a box.

That was fine with me. We loaded the van. I'd just put in the last box when I heard Freddy say, "Hey, what a great surprise. There's Millard Thwaxton. Hey, Millard, how ya doing?"

"Hold it," I said, grabbing Freddy by the arm. But it was too late. Millard was the meanest kid in town—and Freddy just got his attention.

I snatched at Freddy's hat, figuring he was too happy for our own good. It was stuck. I reached up and tried to get mine off. It was stuck, too, like a jar lid that's threaded on the wrong way. I thought it might come off if I worked on it, but I didn't have the time right now. Millard was rumbling our way.

"Keep talking," I said, running toward the backyard. I tore through the box of hats and searched for one that might save us. I passed on ANGER and CURIOSITY. The first would get us killed and the second didn't seem too promising, especially if it made Millard curious about the best way to cause us pain. I grabbed KINDNESS. That would do the trick, and make the world a better place.

I got to the front yard just in time. Millard had reached Freddy and was playing that bully game where the other player always loses.

"What did you say to me?" he asked.

"I said hi," Freddy told him. "And I meant it. I'm awful happy to see you."

"That some kind of a joke?" Millard asked.

"Hey, have a hat," I said, tossing the cap to Millard.

He grabbed it and stared at me. I was afraid he'd just throw the hat away. Or throw me away. But he put it on.

He shoved it on his head. Backwards. With the brim facing away. I wondered what that would do to the kindness.

I found out right away.

"I'm gonna smash both of you," Millard said.

Freddy and I took off. At least I had lots of energy for running. And Freddy seemed pretty happy. For the moment. But when meanness caught up with him, it wouldn't be pretty.

Afterword by David Lubar

My first writing task each morning is to add something to my "what if" file. (OK—that's a lie. My first writing task is to make coffee.) I have about fifty-five pages' worth of ideas there. When I need inspiration, I'll scroll through the entries and look for something that grabs me. "Hats Off" sprang from this entry: "What if kids get some hats that give them magical powers, but they wear the hats backwards and get the opposite effect?"

The next step of the process reminds me of playing chess. (One of the many things I do just well enough to know how bad I really am at it.) A beginner has to think through each possible move. An experienced player processes a lot of factors automatically. When I'm thinking about a story idea, the same thing happens. My mind shuffles through settings, plots, and characters, discarding weak moves and dead-end paths. I liked the idea of the kids finding the hats while cleaning a shed, but I wasn't thrilled with the simple twist of having one of them put the hat on backwards.

I realized it would be fun for them to try to use the hat against an enemy and have the plan backfire. On a different day, with stronger coffee, the enemy could have been an ax murderer or a vampire. That day, it was a bully. You might have noticed I made another slight change to the idea. While the hats are magical, the powers they grant are mundane. I felt there was no need to double up on the magic.

So I had everything I needed. I could have built a bigger world around the idea. The characters are admittedly slight. The reader has no reason to care what happens to them. But I strongly believe two things about stories. First, they should have plots. This isn't a problem in the genre world, but it infects the literary world to such a degree that much of what gets printed isn't worth reading. (See davidlubar.com/litfic.html for a parody of this.) Second, any story that relies entirely on a simple twist should be extremely short. O. Henry knew this. So did Saki. It's fine to encounter a twist after several pages. It's annoying to meet one after reading for an hour. Or a week.

There you have it—an explanation nearly as long as the story itself. And no twist at all. As for the original venue of this piece, I'm thrilled that He Who Is Often Mentioned invited me to contribute two stories to each issue of his *InterGalactic Medicine Show*. What a joy. I've tried hard to give the readers a variety of stories, from light and goofy to truly twisted. For a much darker sample of my work, try "Running Out of Air" in the October 2006 issue of *IGMS*. I really hope it will take your breath away.

Eviction Notice

BY SCOTT M. ROBERTS

Another eviction notice. Not really a notice, though—a note. Just a couple of lines scrawled out in Ernesto's handwriting, amounting to little more than "Hey, Mr. Rick Manchester, you're a filthy, lazy, S.O.B., get out in four days." That's all it was. A note and a signature, Ernesto Ruiz Montalvo. The fourth this month, counting down the days. And then, he'd have to abandon Tommy. He'd have to leave his little son here alone.

Rick's fingers shook as he closed the front door. He needed a drink, but last night's bottle was half gone. If he drank it now, he'd have nothing left after he visited Tommy. Rick brushed his hands over his beard and stood and trembled at the weight of the eviction note in his hand until he let it fall to the floor. Upstairs, that's where he had to go now. Tommy would have to see him now, wouldn't he? Because it was all about to end. Everything was about to be torn to pieces by Ernesto Ruiz Montalvo and his damn eviction notes.

He touched the wall reverently as he made his way up the stairs. Even though he'd put plaster over every spot, he knew right where to lay the tips of his fingers. This was where Tommy's head hit the wall. This was where his *Dukes of Hazzard* watch tore into the wallpaper. This was where Rick picked his little son up by the neck and threw him down the stairs. The top step. It squeaked today just as loudly as it had fifteen years ago. In four days, he'd never be allowed to touch these walls again. Never hear the squeak of the step that warned him too late to save Tommy.

The bedroom. He'd had his last dream here. The very last one. Sergeant Davies screaming in the rain while men were flashed into gore by Vietnamese bullets, and poor, scrawny Private Rick Manchester curled up under a bush, too scared to scream or run, and he knew it was a dream because Sergeant Davies had been killed by a grenade outside Dong Hoi, but here he was impaled on a stake, and Timmons and Rosas were trying to put their guts back in their stomachs, but in that other Vietnam, that *real* Vietnam, they had been crushed underneath a jeep that flipped, and all their blood was running down toward him in the rain, and it was pooling at his feet, and it hissed and something dark and cold as iron rose up from out of it, but that never happened in the *real* Vietnam, and this thing coming out of their blood and pain, it was worse than war and Hell, and if it touched him, Rick knew he'd spend all his soul's days devoted to it, and then a hand on his neck, a little hand like Charlie's hands were, and now he screamed at last, and leaped on his attacker, strangling him like he was about to be strangled, only he realized too late the hand was soft and the fingers weren't just little, they were tiny, and the step squeaked, and Marie screamed and Sergeant Davies screamed and little Tommy opened his mouth but didn't make a sound just like Private Rick Manchester. But the thing in the pool of blood laughed.

No more dreams. Not even on the lonely, angry nights in the mental hospital. Not even when they put him on suicide watch and doped him up so much he couldn't do anything else but sleep.

Rick crossed the room to the dumbwaiter. It had been here when he and Marie had first rented the place. When Tommy had been a baby, they'd put him on the little sliding tray, and haul him up and down, up and down . . . it was the only way, sometimes, to get him to sleep. It became their favorite indoor game. Five years, he'd hauled Tommy up and down. Five years, Tommy's laughter echoed up the chute while Rick's laughter chased him down. Then the welding accident, the morphine, the flashbacks . . . In one year, it was all gone. Tommy, Marie, life—gone like an echo with no one to hear it.

The door to the dumbwaiter was about at waist level. Rick slid it open. It was barely big enough for him to fit his shoulders through. That was fine—Rick had learned he didn't have to even put his shoulders through, just his face. Close eyes, insert head, and hold breath: a little safety drill. He waited a moment, and then opened his eyes.

All the world spun and swirled like a million dark butterflies blown by a breeze into Rick's face.

He was somewhere else. It was nighttime, and the moon was big and silver in the sky, brighter than it ever was in any sky Rick had seen. He was in a wheat field, and a breeze made the stalks dance softly. There was no eviction notice here, no Ernesto Ruiz Montalvo. Just the moon, the wheat, the breeze.

And Tommy.

He was sitting up on a little rise. Rick could see his red overalls. He pushed away the desire to run to his son—just moved forward easy through the wheat, his back straight. Slow and calm and maybe this time Tommy would stay. Maybe he'd let Rick hold him again. Maybe they could sit down together on that little rise, and Rick could smell him, and wrap his arms around him and hug him, and feel the smoothness of that little six-year-old face against his grizzled cheek.

He was walking too quickly. Tommy saw him coming and jumped up. His eyes were wide and dark, as black as the starless sky. He turned and ran. Rick could see his head just over the bobbing wheat, a loose tangle of brown curls.

"Tommy! Tommy, please stop! Stop!"

He had to catch him this time. He had to make Tommy understand that this was the end. So Rick ran, too, following Tommy under the bright moon, through the whispering, rushing wheat and the warm breeze. He tried to make it a game—Tommy wasn't really terrified of him. This was play. A daddy and his boy playing tag. But the breeze carried Tommy's sobbing back to his ears.

"Go away!" Tommy screamed when Rick was close enough to put his hand out, just an inch from Tommy's bright red overalls. "Go away!"

And then Rick tripped over nothing he could see. He fell, and fell, and fell, until he was back in the bedroom, looking down the dark chute.

Rick stood there numbly, willing the wheat field back. It wouldn't come. It never did. Tommy had told him to go away, and so he did, and he couldn't come back until tomorrow. Tomorrow . . . maybe tomorrow Tommy would listen to him.

But he wouldn't. Rick knew it. Tommy hadn't listened the first day Rick had put his head into the chute, looking to see why the tray had stuck. He had gone back every day since then, even when he was bone tired from medication and liquor and work, even when he knew all he could do was watch his son run off into the wheat field.

Tommy never listened.

Ernesto was at the front door. Rick could hear him pounding and shouting his name. Little rat's key didn't work, now, did it? Must have something to do with the new lock Rick had installed after getting the last eviction note. Rick lay on the nappy old couch in the living room, and smiled, listening to Ernesto. Let him try the back door, too. Let him go on back there and see how Rick had fixed it, too. Let him bang away, and scream and shout.

Rick got up to get a drink of water—and the front door swung inward, without even making a squeak. Ernesto looked in at Rick, surprised.

"Hi, Ernesto," Rick managed slowly. How had the door been opened? There was someone else standing behind the Mexican, someone tall and broad shouldered, with graying hair. The stranger had a face like a retired army general. Apple pie and industry and discipline all rolled into one.

Ernesto came in. "Took you long enough to open the door."

Rick shrugged. "I was asleep."

"You was drunk. It's eleven o'clock, man. Why ain't you working?"

"I don't see the point, Ernesto. You're evicting me, remember? I've got nothing to work for now, since I don't have to pay rent." Mr. Army General was still standing outside. "Come in if you're coming in, mister. Don't just stand there with the door open—you'll let the flies in."

"You invite him in, but not me, Rick? After all I've done for you?"

Ernesto was in his face now. Rick backed off a bit. "He's not evicting me."

Mr. Army General came in and closed the door softly. When he moved up, Ernesto moved aside. Like he was obeying an unspoken order. Mr. Army General stuck out a hand. "Quincy Umble, Mr. Manchester."

Rick took his hand slowly. Quincy Umble had hands as cool as iron. "Rick. Just Rick."

"Rick." Quincy Umble nodded. "I am going to be purchasing this home from Mr. Montalvo."

Ernesto guffawed. "See? He is evicting you. In a way."

Rick sagged away. "Oh."

Quincy Umble did not look at Ernesto. "I'd like to take a look around your home, Rick. Ernesto, I don't think you need to stay—why don't you go get the car started up? I won't be long."

And just like that, not a word spoken back, Ernesto left them alone. Rick watched him go. He turned to look at Quincy Umble, and his breath caught in his throat. Quincy Umble's eyes were as large as moons, as dark as a starless night sky. And they were hungry.

"So," Quincy Umble said. "Rick. Show me around."

He shouldn't do it. He didn't want to do it. Men with hunger like that in their eyes—Rick knew that look. Like some of the soldiers he'd known, looking at the pretty young Vietnamese girls and licking their lips. Like the child molesters he'd seen in the hospital. Like the kids he'd seen in some alleyways, hunkered over needles and syringes. Hunger that doesn't ever, ever die, and here it was right in his own home, asking him to show it around. It had no place here.

"I don't want to," Rick said. His voice got swallowed up in those black eyes.

Quincy Umble smiled, showing his white, even teeth. He clapped Rick on the shoulder. "I understand perfectly. But you should. Be a good host. Show me around."

Quincy Umble's hand was on his shoulder still. Rick felt his head getting light. "This is the kitchen," he said, pointing. "And, uh, this is the living room. I had to sell my TV. You know, to, uh, buy food."

"I see. I like the pyramid of liquor bottles that has taken its place."

"Uh, yeah. See, I know I have a problem. I do. I've been to AA, you know."

"I can imagine. Won't you show me upstairs?"

Rick led him upstairs. Quincy Umble's arm never left his shoulder. Rick felt his arms twitching, wanting to touch the sacred places he'd covered with plaster. But he couldn't. Not with Quincy Umble watching. Not with Quincy Umble's arm on his shoulder.

They came to the bedroom. "Exquisite," Quincy Umble said, and his black eyes were on the dumbwaiter. "Beautiful." He swallowed, and Rick watched his Adam's apple bob up, down, up. He whispered, "Sweet."

Quincy Umble let him go, and Rick felt all strength ebb right out of his body. Quincy Umble crossed over to the dumb-waiter, laid his hands on the door, and opened it slowly. Tenderly. But Rick knew his eyes were hungry, and they were peering down the chute.

"Beautiful boy," Quincy Umble muttered. "So tragic. So sad."

"Get away from him!" Rick hauled himself to his feet, lurching against the wall until he stood at the dumbwaiter. "Get away!"

He struck at Quincy Umble, knocking him away from the dumbwaiter. Was Tommy all right? What had Quincy Umble done? How had he known about the dumbwaiter?

Quincy Umble straightened himself, and those terrible black eyes fixed themselves on Rick. He didn't say a word. But suddenly, his hand was around Rick's throat, squeezing, until it felt like his eyes were going to burst out of their sockets. No matter how hard he flailed and beat at Quincy Umble, he couldn't breathe, he couldn't get free.

The top stair was squeaking.

"Irony," Quincy Umble said. Then he heaved Rick through the air.

Rick's head cracked against the wall as he fell. He crumbled into a heap at the bottom of the stairs. Everything was a madness of rushing blood and spinning lights. He tried to see the steps—they were right in front of him, they had to be. He had to get up there, and get that *thing* away from the dumbwaiter, away from Tommy. Rick's fingers scrabbled at the edge of the step, but he was too weak to push himself up.

The sound of footsteps coming down. Quincy Umble wasn't going after Tommy right now—Rick felt big hands close around his arms and drag him into the living room. Then, a breath on his eyes, as damp as November rain, and frigid. Rick felt something snap together in his skull, and the pounding blood stopped, and the lights stopped spinning. Quincy Umble let him fall to the floor, then sat heavily on his chest, straddling him so his knees held Rick's arms pinned to the floor.

"Get off of me," Rick grunted.

Quincy Umble pulled something out of his jacket. It looked at first like an ugly stone knife, its edges caked with blood; but as Quincy Umble turned it, Rick saw that it was a long, thick spike, its head worn from being hammered; but at last he saw, *really* saw, what it was: a combat knife. One edge keen and honed, the other serrated. Quincy Umble lowered the knife to Rick's temple and made a quick little *snick!* Rick felt tufts of his beard fall away onto his ear.

"What do you want?" Rick demanded. "Why are you doing this to me?"

Quincy Umble did not look at him. *Snick, snick!* More of his beard fell away. "I know you, Richard Manchester. I've known you since . . . Vietnam. Yes. You got away from me for a bit when you married Marie, but I found you again. When you burned your hands, I found you." His voice was low, teasing. Soft. The knife scraped against Rick's face. "When you became addicted to morphine, how delicious, I knew how things would end. I was with you when you had your last dream, when you lifted poor little Tommy and threw his body down the stairs. I was with you through your divorce, through your trial, when despite your best efforts, they found you *not guilty.* I stayed close to you every night in the asylum. I was with you when you visited Tommy's grave, and Marie and her new husband found you and she slapped you, and he kicked you in the crotch. I knew you'd come back to this house. I knew you'd find a way to pull Tommy back to you. I knew your misery would bring you to him, and him to you. It's all about misery, Rick. You understand *that,* don't you? Misery can do terrible, terrible things. People forget what misery can do. I do not. I know all the wounds, all the depth, all the ache of your misery. It is . . . sweet to me, Rick.

"But now, old man, you're tapped out." Quincy Umble had finished shaving off Rick's beard. "Your misery has just about reached its peak. I don't want you now. Tommy—well, Tommy, trapped up in that dumbwaiter, no way to get free. Capture a ghost, and its capacity for misery is endless, because it cannot die. Absolutely. So I'm going to take your boy with me. I'm going to pull him right out of that chute, and place him in my strongest butterfly-box so he will never get away."

Rick wailed and struggled, but Quincy Umble just chuckled. He wiped his cold hands on Rick's smooth, bare face. "Your beard will never grow back now, Rick. Never. Go on. Take a look at yourself."

Quincy Umble pulled him up to the window so he could see his reflection. There was no strength in Rick to move against him. The face in the window was old, tired. But it was Tommy. Tommy, as if he had aged, and been through years of pain and trial. His eyes were full of failure and alcoholism. His reflection was Tommy, in misery. Rick choked back a scream, and Quincy Umble pushed him away.

"It'd be a shame if you killed yourself just to get away from living a failed life, Rick," said Quincy Umble. "So don't. I'm serious. Really. I'm going to leave now, but I'll be back. In two days. I have to get an early start, you know, so please have your things moved out before nine A.M. The demolition equipment will probably be here tomorrow evening—I don't think I mentioned I was destroying this house, did I? Anyway, just please be out by nine A.M. on Friday.

"And say hello to that sweet little boy of yours for me Rick, if you go visit him. I'll be seeing him soon."

The door to the dumbwaiter was still open. Rick sat opposite to it, on the far side of the room. The moon had risen once, and set once, and now it was getting dark again. Rick's head was buzzing for liquor. But he didn't leave. What if Quincy Umble came back, with his black eyes and iron hands? What if he looked in the chute?

The motors of big machines pulling into his driveway interrupted his thoughts, made his heart jump. But he didn't get up. Not even to see Tommy.

What was the point? He was a fool to think Tommy would ever love him. Love the man who had choked him, thrown him, killed him? Good daddies don't choke their little boys. Good daddies don't have dreams about men being impaled on sticks, and dark things rising from their misery. Good daddies don't get addicted to morphine, even if their hands are raw flesh and burn every second of every day so they can't sleep, can't think, can't do anything but be in agony.

The machines outside were as silent as the moonless sky now. Rick didn't move from his spot on the floor, just sat and stared at the open door of the dumbwaiter. Before the welding accident, there had been good times with Marie and Tommy. The trip to Kansas to see buffalo and antelope. The daily games of catch and tag. If he had known . . .

Misery. That's what Quincy Umble had said this was all about. His misery had drawn Tommy to him. Like drawing the tray up the dumbwaiter. Only now, the dumbwaiter was stuck in the middle of the chute, so Tommy couldn't ever come all the way out . . . Or maybe, Rick's misery had drawn him here, and Tommy was too scared to come all the way through. And that's why the dumbwaiter stuck. And why Quincy Umble could strip him out, maybe, because he was caught in the dumbwaiter and couldn't get up to Rick, or down to escape.

If Tommy was stuck . . . why couldn't Rick pull him out?

Rick crossed the room and gave the draw rope attached to the dumbwaiter a tug. The dumbwaiter wouldn't budge. He did it again, hard this time—and the dumbwaiter slid up in the chute a little. Rick cried out, but the rope snapped taut suddenly, then dragged downward a couple of inches. No matter how hard he struggled with the rope now, the dumbwaiter wouldn't budge.

Could he push it down? Maybe with a stick or a long pole . . . but Rick didn't have either. He'd have to climb into the chute if he wanted to push it down.

Impossible. He couldn't fit through the opening. Only to his shoulders. The chute looked wide enough, but the door . . . If he lifted his arms above his head and edged in, he could do it. Rick ran his hand around the opening. He could get out the same way.

Rick felt his heart thumping hard. What time was it? Rick raced downstairs to the clock on the oven—4:30. Four and a half hours. He could manage that. On the way back up the steps, he took them two at a time.

He forgot to touch the sacred wall places.

Rick took off all his clothes but his shoes and skivvies, and tucked his shoelaces securely back into the shoes. If there were any sharp edges in the chute, he didn't want clothes snagging on them and slowing him down. Better to scrape himself bloody than to be slow. Almost as an afterthought, he tied a knot in the end of the draw rope to keep it from slipping through the pul-

ley. And that way, he could use the rope to pull himself back up
the chute.

"Close eyes. Deep breath. In we go," he muttered.

He scraped his shoulders and ribs on the opening, but was
able to brace his arms against either wall of the chute and pull
his waist and legs in. It was a tight fit. Eyes still closed, he
pulled on the draw rope until the knot caught on the pulley
and it was secure. Then he began to descend.

The chute was close and hot. Rick was soon bathed in
sweat, and his bare skin kept slipping and chafing on the walls.
But he kept his eyes closed as he worked his way down. This
would be his farewell to Tommy. He'd set him free. This was
Tommy's eviction day. No—this was Tommy's day of *emancipation*. He would be free of Rick, free of Quincy Umble, free of
the misery that they had both imposed and wanted to impose
on him.

His feet touched something solid. The dumbwaiter. Rick
resisted the urge to open his eyes, resisted the trigger that
would take him to his son and the wheat field. Instead, he took
a breath of the hot, stuffy air, and pushed with all his might
down, down, down for Tommy—

"Rick. What the hell are you doing?"

Quincy Umble's voice caught Rick by surprise. He felt his
eyelids trembling, felt them opening, and saw him grinning
down.

The world broke apart into thousands of dark butterflies.
The sound of their wings swallowed Rick's cry of dismay.

He was in the wheat field. The moon was as bright as ever, the
wheat just as gold—but the wind was as cold as rain. Tommy
lay shivering at his feet.

"I'm waiting for Daddy," Tommy said. His lips were blue. "Leave me alone. Go away. I'm waiting for my daddy."

But this time, Rick found he did not go away.

"Tommy, is there someone else here?" Rick asked. "Is Quincy Umble here?"

"He left. You leave, too. I'm waiting for my daddy."

The wind stopped. Out at the edge of the wheat, Rick saw something moving—not through the wheat, but on top of it. Where its feet touched, the wheat froze in place, seeping blood from the roots. The creature had no features, no fingers or toes, but was all jagged blackness. Arms and legs and a torso of dark shards, and its head was a massive, gaping blackness that devoured the moonlight around it.

Tommy whimpered as it got close. Rick put himself between his son and the creature.

"Little man," the thing said in Quincy Umble's voice, "get out of my way."

It never moved, but suddenly Rick's hands and arms were covered in a wash of molten metal. Rick screamed and thrust his hands into the ground, but it had already become hard from the creature's presence. His flesh dropped away from his hands, leaving gobs on the ground as he tried to find something to wipe off the metal.

"I will allow you to wipe your hands on Tommy," said the creature. "You may be free of the pain that way, and no other."

Tommy wasn't moving. His lips gave a sudden twitch—a whisper. Rick knew what he was saying. I'm waiting for my daddy.

Pain—that's all this was. Just pain. Not misery. And he could live with pain. Rick knelt to the ground and let the metal eat right through to his bone. He cried. He wailed and whimpered and screamed. But he did not move an inch closer to Tommy.

Something formed at the end of the creature's arm—a stone dagger, a spike, a knife, a black box with a butterfly pattern on it. And last of all, a squat spider coiling and uncoiling its legs. The creature whispered, "Tommy, come to me now."

Tommy's lips moved. I'm waiting for my daddy.

"I said, come."

Tommy screamed. Something black and crawling was eating away at his feet, creeping up to his thighs, a slick darkness that devoured him. Just a moment, then it was gone, leaving the boy whole but whimpering.

"Come to me, Tommy." The creature gestured, and the black spider on its hand quivered.

I am waiting for my daddy.

The black goop appeared again, moving slower now, creeping up Tommy's feet, hissing up his ankles. Tommy gurgled and screamed and cried, and writhed on the hard, cold ground.

Rick struggled to speak. "It's just pain, Tommy." The metal on his arms flashed hotter suddenly, splashing onto his chest. "Like shots! Remember how your butt hurt after the shots for kindergarten? It's just pain, Tommy, and pain goes away. It isn't like losing Grandma, right? It won't hurt forever, it isn't misery! Dammit, Quincy Umble, leave him alone, he's a child!"

The metal on Rick's arms surged upward, searing through his eyes, filling his nasal cavity, burning through his eardrums. Rick tried to scream, would have screamed, but he choked on hot metal as it poured over his tongue and down his throat, into his lungs.

"Touch your son, Rick Manchester. Touch him, just lay

one little finger on his leg, and I will release you. No more pain. No more misery. One touch, Rick."

He burned and burned and burned, but Rick didn't move. He endured. And deep in his chest, something burst. Everything that had gone before was nothing, was just a little burn, compared to this. This was Sergeant Davies suffering on the end of a punji stick, Rosas and Timmons eviscerated by shrapnel, and they all looked at him, Private Rick Manchester cowering in the bushes, and he didn't move to help them. This was Marie screaming for thirty minutes until the ambulance came to take Tommy's body away while Rick stood at the top of the stairs and looked down at her anguish and Tommy's broken neck, afraid to move a muscle. This was living every day of eternity with Tommy's ghost, never able to touch him. This was the failure and shame of his whole life, and it *seared* him more deeply and more horribly than molten metal.

"Touch your boy, Rick."

Jagged words, softly spoken.

"He is right there, your sweet boy. You can hold him close now, Rick. Let him share your misery."

But Rick lay still beneath his shame and agony. His misery would never be Tommy's.

The wheat field shook with a warm wind. Everything spun.

Rick was in the chute. His chest burned madly within him, his heart seizing. The left side of his body was completely numb.

Emancipation.

He lifted one foot and then let it fall hard on the top of the dumbwaiter. Fall, he prayed above the pain in his chest and the misery in his mind. Fall and free my boy.

It fell.

Rick gulped his last breath and closed his eyes.

And opened them.

The world exploded into butterflies. They came from all directions at once as the chute dissolved. On his arms, on his hands, between his legs, under his feet, a wash of every color, every size—they swarmed and floated all over him.

Far away, something dark and jagged squealed and was broken on their wings.

"Daddy. You came."

A small hand on his neck. A warm little hand, as tender and welcome as sunlight.

Rick took a breath, and the air was full of Tommy-scent. That unique, peculiar boy-smell, like grass and good earth, and sweat. And he felt Tommy's face on his face, smooth and warm. Eyes brown as honey looked into his eyes, and Rick lifted his hands to stroke Tommy's hair and touch his cheek.

They settled down in that field of rushing, hushing wheat. The moon set; the wind grew warmer. And they talked. They talked about Rick's war, and they talked about how Tommy had died. They talked about pain, and misery. They wept together, as fathers and sons should do, and do not often enough. And when the moon rose again, they settled against one another, Tommy's head on Rick's chest, Rick's arm snug around his son's waist.

And they slept.

And they both dreamed good dreams.

Afterword by Scott M. Roberts

The old man wore a maroon cap with a battleship's name on it, and a denim jacket in the dead heat of summer. The jacket was pocked with pins proclaiming the validity of this conspiracy or that political stance—often at odds with each other. He was short and scrawny, and the skin on his face was peculiarly loose. He seemed an odd duck to be sitting in a trendy coffee shop just outside the campus of a small southern college—but then, I'm not a big patron of coffee shops, or small colleges, so what do I know?

We struck up a conversation. We talked about the Korean War (he was a veteran; I'd seen a couple of episodes of *M*A*S*H*), bees (I'm an amateur beekeeper; he thought insects would eventually unite to destroy humanity), and science fiction (he, a fan of the genre; me, an aspiring writer). He offered me advice on what to write about; I offered to pay for his coffee.

He mentioned that he was about to be evicted from the apartment he rented from his son. "I'm drunk all the time" was his approximate explanation.

That old man was the seed for "Eviction Notice."

Stories come from strange places. "Eviction Notice" was germinated in a trendy coffee shop, by talking with an old man. It also came from my understanding of fathers and sons (having been both) and of misery (having once been a teenager). Stephen Vincent Benét's butterflies from *The Devil and Daniel Webster* make an appearance here, and so do a few late-night memories of the television series *China Beach* (as viewed through a crack in my bedroom door, when my parents were sure I was asleep). Not that I plotted these things into the story—and not that anyone else would ever recognize them on paper.

A day after I met that old man, I was typing out "Eviction Notice" on a borrowed laptop in a dorm room at the University of North Carolina at Greensboro. I finished in about eight hours of typing. To date, that's the fastest I've ever completed a story. It is also, to date, the most traumatic writing experience I've ever had. My oldest son was two at the time "Eviction

Notice" was written, and . . . well, it was difficult for me to keep a professional, clinical distance. I think that the only reason I was able to get through it at all was because, writing it, I knew how it was going to end.

I can't guess how *you* made it through . . .

To Know All Things That Are in the Earth

BY JAMES MAXEY

Allen Frost assumed the first cherub he spotted was part of the restaurant's Valentine's decorations. He and Mary sat on the enclosed patio at Zorba's. He'd taken a pause to sip his wine when he first saw the cherub behind the string of red foil hearts that hung in the window. The cherub was outside, looking like a baby doll with pasted-on wings.

A second cherub fluttered down, wings flapping. A third descended to join them, then a fourth. Allen thought it was a little late in the evening to still be putting up decorations, but he appreciated the work someone had put into the dolls. Their wings moved in a way that struck him as quite realistic, if "realistic" was a word that could be used to describe a flying baby.

Then the first cherub punched the window and the glass shattered. Everyone in the room started screaming. The cherubs darted into the restaurant, followed by a half dozen more swooping from the sky. Mary jumped up, her chair falling. Before it clattered against the tile floor, a cherub had grabbed her arm. She shrieked, hitting it with her free hand, trying to knock it loose, until another cherub grabbed her by the wrist.

Allen lunged forward, grabbing one of the cherubs by the leg, trying to pull it free. He felt insane—the higher parts of his brain protested that this couldn't be happening. Nonetheless, his sensory, animal self knew what was real. His fingers were wrapped around the warm, soft skin of a baby's leg. White swan wings held the infant aloft. A ring of golden light the size of a coffee-cup rim hovered above the angel's wispy locks. The whole room smelled of ozone and honeysuckle. The cherub's fat baby belly jiggled as Allen punched it.

The angel cast a disapproving gaze at Allen, its dark blue eyes looking right down to Allen's soul. Allen suddenly stopped struggling. He felt inexplicably naked and ashamed in the face of this creature. He averted his eyes, only to find himself staring at the angel's penis, the tiny organ simultaneously mundane and divine and rude. He still had a death grip on the cherub's leg. Gently, the cherub's stubby hands wrapped around Allen's middle and ring fingers. The cherub jerked Allen's fingers back with a *snap,* leaving his fingernails flat against the back of his wrist.

Allen fell to his knees in pain. Mary disappeared behind a rush of angels, a flurry of wings white as the cotton in a bottle of aspirin. Her screams vanished beneath the flapping cacophony. Somewhere far in the distance, a trumpet sounded.

The Rapture was badly timed for Allen Frost. He taught biology at the local community college while working on his doctorate. This semester, he had a girl in his class, Rachael Young, who wouldn't shut up about intelligent design. She monopolized his classroom time. Her leading questions were thinly disguised arguments trying to prove Darwin was crap. He'd been blowing off steam about Rachael when he'd said something really stupid, in retrospect.

"People who believe in intelligent design are mush-brained idiots," he said. "The idea that some God—"

"I believe in God," Mary said.

"But, you know, not in *God* God," Allen explained. "You're open-minded. You're spiritual, but not religious."

Mary's eyes narrowed into little slits. "I have very strong beliefs. You just never take the time to listen to them."

Allen sighed. "Don't be like this," he said. "I'm only saying you're not a fundamentalist."

Mary still looked wounded.

Allen felt trapped. Most of the time, he and Mary enjoyed a good relationship. They agreed on so much. But when talk turned to religion, he felt, deep in his heart, they were doomed. Their most sincere beliefs could never be reconciled.

Allen lifted his wineglass to his lips and took a long sip, not so much to taste the wine as to shut up before he dug his hole any deeper. He turned his attention to the cherubs outside the window. Then his brains turned to mush.

Because, when you're wrestling an angel—its powerful wings beating the air, its dark, all-knowing eyes looking right through you—you can't help but notice evolution really doesn't explain such a creature. The most die-hard atheist must swallow his pride and admit the obvious. An angel is the product of intelligent design.

A year after the Rapture, Allen tossed his grandmother's living room furniture onto the lawn, then whitewashed the floor.

When he was done, Allen went out to the porch to read while the floor dried. It had been four hours, eleven minutes since he'd put his current book down. He'd grown addicted to reading, feeling as uncomfortable without a book in hand as a smoker without a cigarette. He purchased his reading material, and the occasional groceries, with income he made reading tarot cards; he was well known to his neighbors as a magician. He always informed his hopeful visitors he didn't know any real magic. They came anyway. The arcane symbols painted all over the house gave people certain ideas about him.

The books that lined the shelves of his library only added to his reputation for mysticism. He was forever studying some new system of magic—from voodoo to alchemy to cabala. Much of the global economy had collapsed after the Rapture, but supernatural literature experienced a boom.

He did most of his trading over the Internet. The world, for the most part, was intact. It wasn't as if the angels came down and ripped out power lines or burned cities. They had simply dragged off God's chosen. No one was even certain how many people were gone—some said a billion, but the official UN estimate was a comically understated one hundred thousand. The real hit to the economy came in the aftermath of the Rapture; a lot of people didn't show up for work the next day. Allen suspected he could have found a reason to do his job if he'd been a fireman or a cop or a doctor. But a biology teacher? There was no reason for him to get out of bed. He'd spent the day hugging Mary's pillow, wondering how he'd been so wrong. He spent the day after that reading her Bible.

He hadn't understood it. Even in the aftermath of the Rapture, it didn't make sense to him. So he'd begun reading books written to explain the symbolic language of the Bible, which

led him to study cabala, which set him on his quest to understand the world he lived in by understanding its underlying
magical foundations.

Jobless, unable to pay his rent, he'd moved into his grandmother's abandoned house, where he'd studied every book he
could buy, trade, or borrow to learn magic. So far, every book
was crap. Alchemy, astrology, chaos magic, witchcraft—bullshit
of the highest order. Yet he kept reading. He tested the various
theories, chanting spells, mixing potions, and divining tea
leaves. He was hungry for answers. How did the world really
work? Pre-Rapture, science answered that question.

But science, quite bluntly, had been falsified. The army of
angels had carried away his understanding of the world.

Allen now lived in a universe unbounded by natural laws.
He lived in a reality where everything was possible. Books
were his only maps into this terra incognita.

The whitewash dried, leaving a blank sheet twenty feet across.
It was pristine as angel wings. Allen crept carefully across it,
having bathed his feet in rainwater. He wore pale, threadbare
cotton. He'd shaved his head, even his eyebrows. The only
dark things in the room were his eyes and the shaft of charcoal
he carried. He crouched, recited the prayer he'd studied, then
used his left hand to trace the outer arc of the summoning circle. The last rays of daylight faded from the window. His goal
was to speak with an angel before dawn.

With the circle complete, he started scribing arcane glyphs
around its edges. This part was nerve-wracking; a single mis-
placed stroke could ruin the spell. When the glyphs were done,
Allen filled the ring with questions. Where was Mary? Would
he see her again? Was there hope of reunion? These and a dozen

other queries were marked in shaky, scrawled letters. His hand ached. His legs cramped from crouching. He pushed through the pain to craft graceful angelic script.

It was past midnight when he finished. He placed seven cones of incense along the edge of the circle and lit them. The air smelled like cheap aftershave.

He retrieved the polished sword from his bedroom and carried it into the circle, along with Solomon's Manual. He opened to the bookmarked incantation. Almost immediately, a bright light approached the house. Shadows danced on the wall. A low bass rumble rattled the windows.

A large truck with no muffler was clawing its way up the gravel driveway.

Disgusted by the interruption, Allen stepped outside the circle and went to the front porch, book and sword still in hand. The air was bracing—the kind of chill February night where every last bit of moisture has frozen out of the sky, leaving the stars crisp. The bright moon cast stark shadows over the couch, end tables, and lamps cluttering the lawn.

Allen lived in the mountains of southern Virginia, miles from the nearest town. His remote location let him know all his neighbors—and the vehicle in his driveway didn't belong to any of them. It was a flatbed truck. Like many vehicles these days, it was heavily armed. A gunner sat on the back, manning a giant machine gun bolted to the truck bed. The fact that the gunner sat in a rocking chair took an edge from the menace a gun this large should have projected. Gear and luggage were stacked on the truck bed precariously. A giant, wolfish dog stood next to the gunner, its eyes golden in the moonlight.

The truck shuddered to a halt, the motor sputtering into silence. Loud bluegrass music seeped through the cab windows.

It clicked off and the passenger door opened. A woman got out, dressed in camouflage fatigues. She looked toward the porch, where Allen stood in shadows, then said, "Mr. Frost?"

Allen assumed they were asking about his grandfather. The mailbox down at the road still bore his name—his grandmother never changed it after he died, nor had Allen bothered with it after his grandmother had vanished.

"If you're looking for Nathan Frost, he died years ago."

"No," the woman said, in a vaguely familiar voice. "Allen Frost."

"Why do you want him? Who are you?"

"My name is Rachael Young," she answered.

The voice and face clicked. The intelligent-design girl from his last class. "Oh," he said. "Yes. You've found me."

The driver's door opened and closed. A long-haired man with a white beard down to his waist came around the front of the truck. "Well now," the old man said, in a thick Kentucky accent. "You're the famous science fella."

"Famous?" asked Allen.

"My granddaughter's been talking you up for nigh on a year," said Old Man Young. "Says you're gonna have answers."

"We looked all over for you," said Rachael. "The college said you'd gone to live with your grandmother in Texas."

"Texas? I don't have any relatives in Texas."

"No shit," the gunner on the flatbed said. "Been all over this damn country, chasin' one wild goose after another. You better not be a waste of our time." The dog beside him began to snarl as it studied Allen.

"Luke," said Old Man Young. "Mind your language. Haul down the ice chest."

"Sorry we got here so late, Mr. Frost," Rachael said, walking toward him. She was looking at the sword and book. "Have we, uh, interrupted something?"

"Maybe," Allen said. "Look, I'm a little confused. Why, exactly, have you been looking for me?"

"You're the only scientist I trust," she said. "When we used to have our conversations in class, you always impressed me. I really respected you. You knew your stuff. Since your specialty is biology, we want you to look at what we've got in the cooler and tell us what it is."

Allen wasn't sure what struck him as harder to swallow—that she'd spent a year tracking him down, or that she remembered the tedious cross-examinations she'd subjected him to as conversations.

Luke, the gunner, hopped off the truck carrying a large green Coleman cooler. It made sloshing noises as he lugged it to the porch. Luke was middle-aged, heavyset, crew cut. Rachael's father?

Luke placed the container at Rachael's feet. Rachael leaned over and unsnapped the clasp. "Get ready for a smell," she said, lifting the lid.

Strong alcohol fumes washed over the porch. Allen's eyes watered. The fumes carried strange undertones—corn soaked in battery acid, plus a touch of rotten teeth, mixed with a not-unpleasant trace of cedar.

"We popped this thing into Uncle Luke's moonshine to preserve it," Rachael said.

Despite the moonlight, it was too dark for Allen to make out what he was looking at. Rachael stepped back, removing her shadow from the contents. Allen was horrified to find these crazy people had brought him the corpse of a baby with a gunshot wound to its face. The top of its head was missing. The baby was naked, bleached pale by the brew in which it floated. There was something under it, paler still, like a blanket. Only, as his eyes adjusted, Allen realized the baby wasn't sharing the cooler with a blanket but with some kind of bird—he could make out the feathers.

When he finally understood what he was looking at, his hands shook so hard he dropped his sword, and just missed losing a toe.

Allen lit the oil lamps while Luke lugged the cooler into the kitchen. Allen only had a couple of hours' worth of gasoline left for the generator; he wanted to save every last drop until he was ready to examine the dead cherub. While Luke set the corpse in the sink to let the alcohol drain off, Allen gathered up all the tools he thought he might need—knives, kitchen shears, rubber gloves, Tupperware. Rachael was outside, taking care of the dog, and Old Man Young was off, in his words, "to secure the perimeter."

"That means he's gone to pee," Rachael had explained once her grandfather was out of earshot.

To take notes during the autopsy, Allen found a black Sharpie and a loose-leaf notebook half filled with notes he'd made learning ancient Greek. As he flipped to a blank page, he said, "I can't believe you shot one of these. I thought they were invulnerable. I saw video where a cop emptied his pistol into one. The bullets bounced off."

"Invulnerable?" Luke asked. "Like Superman?"

"Sure. Bulletproof."

"You think a brick wall is invulnerable?" Luke asked.

"Is this a rhetorical question?"

"Suppose you took a tack hammer to a brick wall," Luke said. "Would it be invulnerable?"

"Close to it," said Allen.

"How about a sledgehammer?" asked Luke.

"Then, no, of course not."

"A cop's pistol is a tack hammer," said Luke, as he freed the rifle slung over his shoulder. "This is a sledgehammer. Single shot, 50-caliber. This thing will punch a hole through a cast iron skillet." He nodded toward the cherub draining in the sink. "This pickled punk never stood a chance."

"Not a particularly reverent man, are you, Luke?" said Allen. "That's pretty harsh language to be calling an angel."

The back door to the kitchen opened and Rachael came in, followed by Old Man Young.

"Whatever the hell this is," said Luke, "it ain't no damn angel."

"It looks like an angel," said Allen. "I got up close to one during the Rapture."

"Shut your fool mouth!" snapped Old Man Young. To punctuate his sentence, he spat on the floor. "*Rapture*. Rachael, I thought this fella was smart."

"He *is* smart," said Rachael.

"He's a mush-brained idiot if he thinks the Rapture has happened," Old Man Young said.

Allen was confused. "You think it hasn't?"

"I'm still here, ain't I?" Old Man Young said. "I've been washed in the blood of the lamb, boy. I'm born again! When the Rapture comes, I'm gonna be borne away!"

Allen cast a glance at the sink. "Maybe Luke shot your ride."

"Naw," said Luke. "I was at the Happy Mart when this little monster started dragging off some Hindu guy. I ran to the truck and got Lucille." Luke patted the rifle. "Saved that fella from a fate worse than death."

"But—" said Allen.

"But nothing!" Old Man Young said. "Second Samuel 14:20 says that it is the wisdom of angels to know all things that are in the earth!"

"A real angel would have known to duck," said Luke.

"And it wasn't the Rapture," said Rachael. "The creatures took people at random. Yeah, they grabbed some self-proclaimed Christians. But they also took Hindus, Buddhists, Muslims, Jews, and Scientologists. They took Tom Cruise right in the middle of shooting a film."

"Yeah," said Allen. "I saw that."

"Heaven ain't open to his kind," said Old Man Young.

"So how do you explain what happened?" asked Allen.

"Demons," said Old Man Young.

"Aliens, maybe," said Rachael.

"Government black ops," said Luke.

Allen had heard these theories before, and a dozen others. The Youngs weren't the first people to disbelieve the Rapture. None of the alternative explanations made sense. Genetic manipulation gone awry, mass psychosis, a quantum bleed into an alternate reality—all required paranoid pretzel logic to work. He was still scientist enough to employ Occam's Razor, cutting away all the distracting theories to arrive at the simplest conclusion: God did it.

"I admit, what happened doesn't match popular ideas of the Rapture," Allen said. "I've studied Revelations in the original Greek and can't make everything line up. I'm no longer convinced any ancient text has a complete answer. But I get little glimpses of insight from different sources. Maybe God used to try to communicate with mankind directly. Maybe he spoke as clearly as possible, in God language, but people weren't up to the task of understanding him. They all came away with these little shards of truth; no one got the big picture."

"Son, I'm up to the task of understanding," said Old Man Young. "The good ol' King James Version spells out everything. If you don't understand, you don't want to understand."

"If you think it was the Rapture," asked Rachael, "why would God have been so random? He took rich and poor, young and old, the kind and the wicked. It makes no sense."

"To us," said Allen. "But when I was a senior at State, I helped out on this big study involving mice. We did some blood work, identified mice with the required genes, then separated them from the general population and took them to a different lab. I wonder if the mice left behind sat around wondering why they weren't chosen. They would never understand our reasons."

"That's your theory?" asked Rachael. "We're lab mice?"

"No. But maybe the gap between our intellect and God's mind is larger than the gap between man and mice. Our inability to understand his selection criteria doesn't mean he acted at random."

"Son, you're proving what I always say," said Old Man Young. "Thinking too much makes you stupid."

Allen nodded. "Thinking too much hasn't made me any wiser or happier."

"Don't pay attention to Grandpa," said Rachael. "We need a thinker. We need someone who can study this body and tell us what it is."

"Why didn't you take it to the cops?" asked Allen.

"If the government knew we had this, we'd already be dead," Luke said.

Rachael frowned. "I think we might be endangering the

world by not showing this to the government. Not that there's much government left."

"Which is more proof it weren't the Rapture," said Old Man Young. "No Antichrist."

Which was true. America had been through eight presidents in the last year. Anyone displaying even modest leadership skills quickly became a target of the legions of Antichrist stalkers roaming the capitals of the world. What was left of day-to-day civilization was staggering on due more to momentum than to competent leadership.

"This is what the Illuminati want," said Luke. "Chaos. When they seize power, people will kiss their asses with gratitude."

"Since Uncle Luke shot it, he gets to decide who sees it," said Rachael. "Also, it's his cooler."

"I'm not the trusting sort," Luke said, "but Rachael says you're a good guy, and smart."

Allen rubbed his temples. "You think I'll know the difference between an alien, a demon, and a black-ops sci-fi construct?"

All three Youngs looked at him hopefully.

"Okay," he said. "I'll go power up the generator."

"I'll come with you," said Rachael. "Jeremiah's stalking around out there and you don't want to run into him alone."

"Jeremiah?"

"Our dog," said Luke. "He's killed more men than I have."

For a second, Allen considered whether the oil lanterns might not provide enough light after all. Then he clenched his jaw and headed for the back door. If you're going to cut open an angel, you may as well do the job right.

The corpse looked slightly yellow under electric light. Allen weighed the angel on his bathroom scale and found it barely topped ten pounds. Aerodynamics wasn't his specialty, but the cherub's wings seemed slightly more plausible. Swan-sized wings could support a swan, after all, and they weighed more than ten pounds.

Allen started his exam in the obvious place—the hollow bowl of the skull. He'd never dissected a human, but what was left of the cranium looked normal. It was bone. He recognized bone. Somehow, he'd expected angels to be crafted of material more grand.

His first real clue he was well outside the realm of known biology was when he took a close look at the torn skin peeling away from the skull. He found a visible subcutaneous layer of something that shouldn't have been there, on a human body at least. It was a thin, fibrous material, like cloth. He tugged on a frayed thread carefully with his tweezers. He couldn't pull a strand of the tightly knit material free. He could see, though, that it was porous—blood vessels and nerve fibers ran through it. Whatever this was, it had grown under the skin, rather than being implanted.

"I've never seen anything like this."

"I've eyeballed it up close," said Luke. "It looks like Kevlar. Sort of."

"Score one for black ops," said Allen, pausing to jot a few notes.

"Aliens could use Kevlar, too," said Rachael. "Stuff better than Kevlar."

Allen moved on to the wings. After twelve months soaking in moonshine, they had a dull, grayish tone. It wasn't difficult to pull a feather free. Without the body on the butcher's block, he would have supposed he was looking at a seagull feather. Intuitively, this made sense. If God had designed feathers as the perfect tool of flight, why not use the same blueprint for both angel and bird?

But flight wasn't simply a matter of having feathers, as any chicken could attest. A cherub's chest didn't have the depth to support the muscles to power these wings, did it?

He flipped the cherub over and felt its breasts. The muscles under the soggy skin were rock hard. He noted the cherub had nipples and a belly button. Was God simply fond of this look? Or was there a cycle of life in Heaven? Angel fetuses developing in angel wombs, angel babes suckling at the breasts of angel mothers?

He tried to cut open the cherub's chest. It proved impervious to the butcher knife.

"Try this," Luke said, handing him a folded knife. Allen flipped the knife open to reveal a ceramic blade, black as onyx and razor sharp.

"Fancy," said Allen. He tried it against the skin. The knife's edge scraped away the surface easily, but the subcutaneous material thwarted further advance. Whatever it was, it couldn't be pierced.

Not willing to give up, Allen tried a different approach. He peeled back the torn flesh of the skull and slipped the knife along the edge of the fibrous layer. To his delight, the torn edge yielded to the knife as he applied steady, firm pressure. Slowly, he worked the knife forward, peeling the flesh from the cherub's face, working his way down the throat. He discovered cherubs had tracheas and jugular veins. He confirmed they had collarbones. After a long, tedious operation, slicing the flesh a millimeter at a time, he peeled the angel's skin back from its torso and found . . . muscle. Bones. Fatty deposits.

Ordinary matter.

He stepped back from the table and stretched his neck. He'd been bent over the cherub a long time; his muscles were stiff.

"Want some water?" Rachael asked, breaking the silence.

"No, thank you," Allen said, staring at the flayed thing before him. It was a relief, in a way, to know what his nightmares would be for the rest of his life. An angel opened, peeled like the fetal pigs he'd taken apart in freshman biology. He had taken something divine, an occupant of Heaven, and treated it with all the respect he might show a frog in formaldehyde.

If he wasn't damned before, he certainly was now.

And yet . . . and yet he couldn't turn back. Blasphemous as it was, he was going to keep cutting. His need for knowledge overrode his fear of offending the divine. Who knew what his next cut might reveal?

The muscle of the chest looked like meat but was dense and unyielding, even to the ceramic knife. He managed to scrape off several strands of the tough muscle fibers—he would have traded every book in the house for a microscope at that moment.

He tried the stomach. The muscle here was also impervious, but a thin gap of ligament beneath the ribs showed good results when he sawed at it with the knife. In less than five minutes, he'd cut a hole into the chest cavity.

He leaned over to peer inside, seeing nothing but gray, bleached tissue—the angel's lungs? Of course, if it had a trachea, it would have lungs. As near as he could tell, with the exception of the bulletproof skin, the cherub was constructed like other animals. It had breathed air. It had fed its muscles with a complex network of arteries and veins. It commanded its body with a nervous system. What did this mean?

In frustration, completely ignoring any rational, measured approach, he dug his fingers into the cherub's chest and began to feel around. His fingers sent indecipherable signals as they pushed against objects both slimy and leathery, both hard and yielding. Was this the liver? His hand was buried to the wrist. These had to be intestines. This hard thing . . . a kidney? Feces in the gut? Clear fluid suddenly gushed from the penis. He'd found the bladder.

He turned his hand up, in search of the heart. Where the heart should have been, he found an egg.

At least, it felt like an egg, smooth, oval, hard, of a size that might earn it a Grade A Large. He wriggled his fingers around it, trying to get a better understanding. The angel gurgled as his efforts freed some last teaspoon of air from the lungs.

And then, with a *pop,* the egg came free. He closed his fingers and pulled it out with a sloppy, wet, farting sound.

His hand was covered with gray goop.

He opened his fingers to reveal something beautiful.

An ovoid object, gleaming yellow in the lamplight.

A golden egg.

Allen placed it in the Tupperware as everyone came over for a closer look.

"Told you," said Luke. "It's a cyborg. This is the power source."

"It's alien technology," Rachael said.

"The devil's handiwork," said Old Man Young.

Allen didn't know. Allen felt completely empty of opinion, thought, or emotion. Confronted with something so far beyond his understanding, he felt unreal. The egg, he'd held it, he could see it, it was reality. He must be the thing out of place.

Then, to compound his sense of unreality, the egg moved

under its own power, rocking lengthwise, coming to rest upright on its small end, seeming, almost, to hover.

The lights flickered. Allen's skin tingled as the air began to smell of rain.

"What's happening?" Rachael asked.

The lights went out.

There was a terrible hush. No one breathed. Slowly, Allen's eyes adjusted to the dim starlight seeping through the window. The faces of his guests were pale and ghost-like.

At last, Rachael whispered, "I don't hear the generator."

Allen breathed. Right. The generator. "It must have run out of gas," he said. "I thought I had enough for a couple of hours."

"It's been a couple of hours," said Luke. "You needed more gas, you shoulda said something. I got a five-gallon can in back of the truck."

"I'll help you get it," said Old Man Young.

"I'll come, too. I need some fresh air," Rachael said.

Allen didn't know if the Youngs were trying to ditch him, but he wasn't going to play along if they were. He didn't want to be alone in the kitchen with . . . with whatever the golden egg was.

They went out to the front yard. He waited with Rachael on the porch while Luke and the grandfather walked down to the truck.

He could tell she wanted him to say something. She wanted him to say there was nothing to be afraid of.

He couldn't bring himself to speak the words.

The moon was low on the horizon; fingers of shadow grasped the yard. The still air carried the footsteps of the men walking across the gravel. The winter night was silent otherwise. Except . . . except, from a distance, a soft beat, like a muffled drum being struck. Then another, somewhat louder, then louder still when it repeated an instant later. A shadow grew across the yard, and Allen understood he was listening to angel wings.

Luke heard them, too. He looked up, freeing the big rifle from his shoulder. He was looking at something Allen couldn't see, something hidden by the roof of the porch. The first angel floated into view, descending as gracefully as an owl coming to rest on a branch. This was nothing like the cherubs. This was an adult-sized angel on wings the size of a small plane. The angel's body was covered in silver armor, but enough of the face showed through the helmet that Allen judged the angel to be female. The sword by her side showed she had come for war.

Luke fired. The bullet smacked into the angel's breastplate. She didn't flinch, continuing her descent to Earth, landing mere feet in front of Luke, who was hastily reloading. With a casual gesture, the angel extended her arm, catching Luke in the chest and throwing him backward, far past the end of the truck. Luke landed limp and didn't move.

With a sudden flap of wings, a second angel swooped down, kicking Old Man Young as he scrambled onto the truck bed, perhaps going for the mounted gun.

Allen grabbed Rachael by the arm and pushed her toward the door to the living room.

"The circle!" he said. "Get into it!"

He stooped to retrieve his sword and Solomon's Manual from where he'd left them on the porch. He heard the angel wings behind him, beating once, twice. The light faded as the shadows cast by the angel's wings approached. Not daring to look back, Allen dashed through the door, leaping for the circle. He was relieved to find Rachael had placed herself inside the protective drawing without smudging the edges. Then he realized she was still moving; she had wound up in the circle purely by accident.

"Stop!" he yelled, and to his relief, she froze. "We're safe here. They can't touch us!"

"Are you sure?" she said, spinning around, looking panicked.

"No," said Allen. "But if we're not safe here, where can we run?"

He turned to face the doorway, and found it filled with the bright form of the angel. The angel walked calmly toward the circle, her eyes fixed on Allen. She approached to arm's length before stopping. Rachael clung tightly to Allen's arm, digging her nails into his biceps. Allen gripped the sword tightly, then thrust it forward and said, "I . . . I command you in the name of—"

The angel smirked and swatted the tip of the sword with her gauntlet-clad hand. The force of the blow twisted the weapon from Allen's grasp, sending it clattering across the floor.

"You have no idea what you are doing," the angel said, walking around the circle, studying the symbols. Her voice was deep and operatic, heavenly. "You've copied this without understanding it."

"Yes," said Allen, seeing no advantage in lying.

The angel completed her orbit of the circle, nodding appreciatively. She asked, "If a shaman from deep in the jungle were to be transported to a modern city, would he think of writing as magic? He would have no idea what the letters spelling KEEP OUT or EMERGENCY EXIT might mean, only that people respected them, and stayed away. He might even learn to copy the strange symbols. Tell me: Would that be magic?"

"If it isn't magic," Allen said, "I think you would already have killed us."

As he spoke, there was a distant sound of barking.

"Jeremiah!" said Rachael. "They'll kill him!"

Glancing back to the door, Allen saw the second angel stepping onto the porch. She had Old Man Young draped across her shoulder and was dragging Luke by the collar. The barking grew closer by the second.

The second angel stepped through the door, tossing her limp passengers roughly into the corner. Allen saw Jeremiah round the truck and turn at a sharp angle, skidding in the gravel before bolting toward the house.

The angel closed the door with seconds to spare. Jeremiah collided with a *thump*. A brief instant of silence followed before the dog resumed his frantic barking, clawing at the door.

The first angel said to the second, "Get the body."

The second angel nodded and vanished into the kitchen.

The remaining angel drew her sword. The weapon burst into flame. Allen cringed from the heat, holding on to Rachael to keep her from leaving the circle.

"Let us pretend I can't enter your little drawing," the angel said. "Does that make you feel safe?"

"No," said Allen. "I haven't felt safe for a long time. I've been frightened. I've been lost. I want . . . I need answers."

"Answers?" said the angel. "You're drowning in answers. Every molecule of your body vibrates with answers. You don't lack answers. You lack the wisdom to recognize them. Tonight, you've cut open an angel. You've held its soul in your hands. What did you learn?"

"I don't know," said Allen.

"You have a few more minutes to think it over," said the

angel, moving toward the interior wall. "Before the smoke kills you." With a solid thrust, the angel pushed her flaming sword through the wall. On the other side there was a bookcase. Allen heard books and papers crash to the floor. Instantly, the air smelled of smoke. Allen clenched his fists, wanting to run and pull the sword free, but fear nailed his feet to the floor.

The room took on an eerie hush. Old Man Young groaned in his unconsciousness. Rachael began to sob.

Allen noticed Jeremiah had stopped barking.

The living room window exploded inward, shards of glass flying, as a gray snarling streak of fur and teeth smashed through. The angel turned, quickly, fluidly, and a second too slow. Jeremiah buried his teeth into the angel's left wing at its junction with the back, an area free of armor.

The angel gasped, stumbling in pain, trying to knock Jeremiah free. Allen held his ground in the circle, reaching back to grab Rachael's hand.

But Rachael wasn't there.

The door to the living room slammed against the wall as she dashed down the porch steps.

Allen watched the fight between dog and angel. The angel reached back, grabbing Jeremiah by a hind leg, tugging. The angel's face twisted in terrible pain. Jeremiah hung on as long as he could, snarling, struggling, but the angel was too strong. Allen winced at the sound of bones cracking. Jeremiah yelped as the angel yanked him free. The angel spun, swinging the dog in an arc. Allen ducked to avoid being knocked over. Then, by accident or design, the angel released Jeremiah in midswing and the dog sailed cleanly out the broken window.

By then Rachael was once again beside Allen, aiming the .50-caliber rifle.

"Nobody hurts my dog," she said, and fired. It was like lightning striking the room. The shot knocked Rachael off her feet and left Allen with ringing ears and spots before his eyes.

A bright red circle appeared on the wall behind the angel's neck. The bare, armorless area just below her chin was dark and wet. The angel's eyes closed as she fell to her knees and sat there, slumped against the wall, her head drooped at an unnatural angle, her arms limp and lifeless by her side.

The room was filling with smoke. The second angel came back from the kitchen. Rachael fumbled with the bolt of the rifle, her hands trembling.

The second angel grabbed the body of the first, pulled the flaming sword from the wall, and moved back into the kitchen. Allen heard the back door open. By now, the smoke was blinding.

Rachael slipped the new round into the chamber and closed it with a satisfying clack. "Ready," she said.

"I think . . . I think you chased them off," Allen said.

"I'm willing to take that chance," she said.

"Get outside. Watch the skies. I'll get your grandfather and your uncle."

By now, Old Man Young was coughing, and his eyes fluttered open. He whispered, "I heard . . . I heard Jeremiah. Is he okay?"

"Come on," Allen said, helping him rise. "The house is on fire!"

"Weren't we outside?" he asked, sounding only half awake.

"Follow me," Allen said, dragging Luke toward the open door. To his relief, Old Man Young obeyed. Soon, Allen had dragged Luke down the front steps, down to the truck, where Rachael now manned the machine gun. Luke's breathing was ragged, but Allen didn't know how to help him. The main thing he knew about first aid was not to move a person who might have internal injuries, and he'd just dragged Luke fifty feet.

Allen scanned the skies. Bright white sparks flew into the night as flames nibbled through the roof. It wouldn't be long before the house was gone, taking his collected books, his months of notes and sweat and theories, to say nothing of his family history.

He took a deep breath and ran back inside.

The living room was oven hot. There wasn't much in here to burn, though—just the floorboards and the wall studs. It was lucky he'd stripped the room down to drywall. He pushed forward, trying to reach the library, but it was no use. The heat from the open door was unbearable. The hair on his arms began to singe.

Allen stepped back, then staggered toward the kitchen. The back door stood open. Burning wallpaper lit the room a flickering red. Dark smoke rolled along the ceiling. He could see the butcher's block, now empty. The golden egg was gone.

Allen crouched, searching for fresher air. He noticed the wet red spot on the wall next to him. Angel blood.

Walls appear solid and impervious through most of daily life. In reality, most drywall is only an adult male fist and a surge of adrenaline away from having a good-sized hole knocked through it. Allen punched that hole, then a second, then a third. His knuckles were bleeding. He grabbed the edges of the punctured drywall, grunting as he tried to break free the section splattered with angel blood. The drywall wasn't on fire, but it was crazy hot. Allen wouldn't let go. He tugged with all his strength, but the nails held tight. The wall was winning. In frustration, he screamed—a primal, animal howl of rage and pain, a sound that frightened him.

With a crack, the drywall twisted free. Allen stumbled outside clutching a three-foot chunk of the stuff to his chest.

Allen sat on the frozen ground as the house behind him roared into the night sky. He was dimly aware that Luke was awake now, sitting next to the trunk, drinking something from a thermos. He was also distantly conscious of something walking toward him, limping, panting, smelling like dog.

It *was* a dog. Jeremiah sat beside Allen. Allen looked into the dog's eyes. They were full of emotions, far more recognizable than what he'd seen in the eyes of the angel. Jeremiah was in obvious pain. Yet Jeremiah looked concerned, as if worried about Allen's health. What's more, the dog had a cocky tilt to his head, and angel pinfeathers stuck between his teeth, which combined into a reassuring vow of "I've got your back."

Allen had angel blood all over his hands and chest. Or maybe it was his own blood after punching through the wall. He couldn't tell where his blood ended and the angel's began.

Blood. He'd expected angels to be full of divine secrets, to be filled with miraculous matter. Tonight he'd seen a hint of this, of things beyond his understanding. But he'd seen far more things he'd understood intimately as a biologist—muscle and bone and blood.

Every molecule of his body vibrated with answers. Did he have the wisdom to understand them?

Jeremiah left his side to greet Rachael, who was approaching. "You okay?" she asked.

"I think so," said Allen.

"I guess it's still an open question," she said. "Whether those were aliens, I mean."

"I don't think so," said Allen.

"Black ops?"

"No," said Allen. "I think they were angels. I think they were created by God."

"Oh," said Rachael.

"I thought they would be full of divine material," said Allen, raising his bloody hands. "Of strange and wondrous stuff. And what if they were?"

"What do you mean?"

"What if they *were* made of divine material? What if we all are? You, me, Jeremiah. The ground under us, the sky above . . . what if what we think of as ordinary matter is actually the building blocks of the divine? The laws of biology, of physics, of chemistry—these are the rules God follows. These are the ways he works his will. Science turns out to be the study of his divine mechanics."

As he said the words, he believed them. He didn't know if it was deduction, intuition, or simply faith, but he felt a powerful calm settle over him. He would probably never know the "why" of God. Why the Rapture? Why take Mary? Why create angels and men and dogs? Why the world? But the "how"—the how was knowable. Before the detour of this past year, he'd learned with some detail the how. He'd thought that angels falsified science. But, studying the angel blood on the drywall on the grass, he understood that, in their ordinary matter, angels confirmed science as the path to understanding the mind of God.

"Uncle Luke thinks he's broken a couple of ribs," said Rachael, apparently not knowing how to respond to his little epiphany.

"There's a hospital in Roanoke," said Allen. "We can be there in an hour."

He stood up and carried the chunk of drywall carefully, hoping not to contaminate it more than it already was. The next step in understanding the angels was beyond Allen's expertise. But part of the fun of being a scientist was talking to people who knew a lot more than you did about their specialties. In retrospect, he'd botched the autopsy of the angel, big time. If he'd gone to experts, asked for help, who knows what they could have learned? At least he had a shot at redeeming himself. You can collect a lot of DNA from a blood-spattered chunk of drywall.

He walked toward the truck, Jeremiah limping beside him. Allen knew of a vet down the road. Hopefully Luke could survive a detour to drop off Jeremiah. In the battle between man and angel, the dog had made his loyalties clear, and deserved whatever care could be provided.

Old Man Young already had the truck revved up. They had decided that Luke and Jeremiah would ride in the cab due to their injuries. Allen and Rachael would have to ride on the back. Rachael abandoned the rocking chair and pressed up next to Allen against the cab as the truck began to pitch and sway down the driveway. From the jumbled mounds of gear, she produced a heavy quilt and pulled it over them.

It was disturbingly intimate, to be sharing a blanket with a woman with whom he'd shared such an adventure. He'd not thought about women at all since Mary was taken. He had a lot on his mind, as he watched his house burn, filling the heavens with a plume of sparks and smoke. He was, in the front of his mind, still trying to figure out what the night's events meant. But something in the back of his mind was more concerned with whether or not he should put his arm around Rachael, who was leaning her head on his shoulder.

Rachael, her voice soft and caring, said, "I'm so sorry about your house."

Allen shrugged. It was what it was. He knew, deep in his gut, that the chapter of his life the house represented was over. The house for him represented magical thinking—the notion that there were things that could happen outside the laws of science. He was almost glad to be rid of it.

"Things will be all right," he said. To his own ears, his voice was tired and thin, battered by stress and smoke. His lungs felt sandpapered, and his hands were starting to blister. To show that he meant the reassuring words, he put his arm around Rachael and drew her closer. It felt right. More importantly, the world felt right. The night had brought him a newfound faith in the essential sensibleness of the universe.

"Can I ask you a question?" Rachael said, her face inches from his.

"Sure."

"Why did you have that circle drawn on your floor?"

Allen rolled his eyes. "It'll sound stupid."

"What?"

"I was trying to summon an angel."

"Guess it worked," said Rachael.

Allen's mouth went dry. Rachael's arrival with the cherub had just been a coincidence, hadn't it? Old Man Young turned the truck onto the road and gunned the engine. Allen pulled the quilt tighter around them, to fend off the chill night air.

Afterword by James Maxey

When I wrote this story, my girlfriend Laura Herrmann was dying. Her cancer had spread to her lungs and liver; the radiation reports described the tumors as "innumerable." Still, I couldn't quite grasp why the tumors were killing her. Her

oncologist would tell us gravely that a specific tumor had dou-
bled from one millimeter to two. On a ruler, two millimeters is
tiny. What did it matter if she had things smaller than houseflies
growing in her lungs? Lungs are big things, right? So why
couldn't Laura breathe?

Four months after Laura passed away, I went to see "Bodies: The Exhibition." This is a traveling museum of human ca-
davers that have been treated with plastic to preserve them.
They are then flayed to various stages and posed to reveal the
inner workings of the body. I finally saw an actual human lung.
It was attached to a woman whose facial muscles were haunt-
ingly similar to Laura's. It was easy to imagine flesh over them
once more. Beneath the face and neck, I was able to study adult
female lungs. I had imagined them filling up most of the space
under the rib cage. In fact, they are actually squashed up rather
high in the chest. And they are small. I could easily have held a
lobe in my palm. Suddenly, the threat of tiny tumors made
more sense. There isn't a lot of space to start with. This was
further driven home when I studied a diseased lung riddled
with cancer. While Laura struggled with her disease, I would
have given anything to have X-ray vision; I wanted to know
what was happening inside her. At last, I could see. I had been
imagining the tumors as distinct objects, not really a part of
her. Instead, the preserved tumors were the body's own tissues
twisting and knotting themselves. There isn't a clear division
between the disease and the healthy tissue.

When I left the exhibit, many of my questions about Laura's
death had been answered. I felt a sense of closure. It wasn't the
end of my grief, but it was a foot on the path to that end. It occurred to me that I'd written about a similar moment months
ago, in "To Know All Things That Are in the Earth." Allen, the

protagonist, must learn to find order in a world where all he knew has been shattered. I identify with Allen when, in his frustration to understand, he plunges his hands inside the cherub's corpse and begins to root around for answers. I wanted so badly to know what was going on inside Laura. Allen finds his path to understanding by asking "how" after too long banging his head against "why." I found a measure of peace through a similar mental shift. "Why" may forever remain just outside the knowable. "How" lies within human understanding.

Beats of Seven

BY PETER ORULLIAN

Jimmy Nesbitt sat in the dark of a new moon on the Lincoln City beach and listened.

No wind.

No obnoxious birds.

No obnoxious lovers strolling.

Just Jimmy and his sound gear, capturing the roll of waves, the susurration of water over sand, the ticking of air bubbles popping as the water retreated back toward the ocean. It was the same sound he'd heard a hundred times before . . . until he detected something more, buried deep in the white noise of waves.

He looked around, irritated, expecting to see someone stomping through the sand with a portable stereo in one hand on the way to a midnight swim.

Nothing.

Even the occasional sweep of headlights had ceased, leaving the darkness unbroken and tranquil.

He was alone.

Jimmy reached quickly for his frequency filter, dialing the luminous knobs to try to isolate the pitch he thought he heard. His heart actually pounded in his chest—something music hadn't done for him in quite some time.

And it totally surprised him.

The romance—if it had ever really been there—had long gone out of this job. Recording the ocean had been the only gig he could get once he quit session work in Los Angeles and Nashville, where musicianship had been replaced by packaging and sex appeal. If the market for *Pacific Oceanscapes*—the project that would take him up the entire West Coast—weren't so lucrative, he could never have endured the mindless sound-tracking of splashing water.

He narrowed in on the frequency, methodically muting levels where he could not hear the strange sound through his headphones. The rumble of whitecaps turning over on themselves fell away; the sizzle of water creeping up wet-packed sand disappeared as well. He kept at it, eager to identify this new tone, something he hadn't heard on any other beach south to San Diego.

After several more adjustments, his parametric equalizer began to spike only in the +10 megahertz zone.

Jimmy pressed the ear cups of his Sony Pro Studio reference phones tighter against his head, sealing out further noise.

He gave a smile.

No mistake.

A trumpet.

Another sound engineer might not have known what he was hearing. But Jimmy had spent several years mixing studio jazz albums in New Orleans in the years before New Age labels started throwing money at French Quarter musicians and recording the always hilarious "light jazz."

He knew from a trumpet.

That wasn't all, though.

If a little fuzzy through the processing he had to impose to create the discreet horn sound, the tone perfectly matched a Gillespie model horn—something only the men playing on Bourbon Street or in swank Manhattan dinner clubs in the early thirties would have used. Still, a badly soldered connection, an errant grain of sand, any number of things could have caused the tone.

But not when it moved in and out of melody.

Jimmy sat, compressing his phones against his ears, tweaking his EQ, recording snippets of what he was coming to think of as a song, then playing them back against the real-time music.

They were different.

The song seemed to live in the very rattle and hum of the ocean itself.

What the hell had he found? And could he sell it?

Watery light dawned behind Jimmy in the east. He'd spent all night listening, recording, filling three hard drives with the unique tonal aberration. Life stirred around him, folks walking pets, a few morning runners. Still no one carrying a CD player or child's musical toy. And certainly no one with an instrument, let alone a Gillespie model.

If nothing more, he wanted to know where the music originated. Through the night he'd listened, trying to make sense of the melodies and rhythms. Despite the enchantment of it—or maybe because of it—any form or structure eluded him.

But the thrill that he might have captured something previously unheard raced through his blood. Sound men lived for such discoveries, and extracting it from a remote beach in a sleepy seaside town only made the mystery and improbability greater.

Then sun struck the water, rays of light spearing the thick Pacific mist . . . and the music ended.

The abrupt departure seemed as much a mystery as the sound to begin with. It didn't matter; he had it on file.

Jimmy packed up his equipment, and in the space of moments had left behind the endless turn of waves and dunes of sand for the tarmac of Highway 101.

A mile north he braked hard to a stop beside a yellow marquee announcing the sale of harmonicas, two for ten dollars. Max's Music Maven was a converted home with two music rooms and an adjoining apartment. Jimmy had met Vincent, the proprietor, just yesterday. His store hours written on a paper plate taped inside the window told him Vince opened at 10:00 A.M. This couldn't wait three hours, so he rounded the side and found a door decorated with an endorsement sticker that read, "If it ain't Gibson, it ain't nothing."

This was the place.

Jimmy began knocking, and didn't stop.

Moments later, the door swung inward. Vincent stood in boxers, his pale skin stretched impossibly tight over ribs and shoulders. Thin, scraggly hair hung down in eyes that squinted in the strengthening light.

"We ain't open, man. Come back later."

"It can't wait," Jimmy said. "I need to ask you a few questions."

"Ah, crap, you're that New Age ocean guy. Man, I'm not

having this conversation at seven A.M. I told you yesterday, I'm not going to carry mood music in my place. Try the Dirty Lap Dog or something. I got a rep."

Jimmy would have smiled to hear it if he didn't have important questions to ask. "Never mind that. Listen, I've got something I want you to hear. It's not the same as yesterday."

"You're some piece of work. I don't let my lady in this early, and you think I'm letting you in?"

Unable to hold it back any longer, Jimmy blurted, "I just recorded your little beach at the end of the D River." He waited until the aging hippie looked at him straight. "And I captured the sound of a trumpet playing a tune."

If the hippie had shown Jimmy any other response, he might have gotten back in his VW Beetle and driven away. What he saw instead was a suspicious eye peering from between kinky strands of hair.

That was all he needed to see. "You know about it? What the hell is it?"

The hippie left the door standing wide and retreated into the shadows of his one-room apartment. Taking it as an invite, Jimmy gladly followed.

Vincent poured some coffee from a pot still bearing the 7-Eleven insignia, which made perfect sense since the stainless steel coffeemaker it sat in bore the same logo. To the left in the corner, a mattress lay flat on the ground, sheets and blankets balled up on one side. A Stratocaster lay beside the bed, a litter of picks strewn around it. The scent of mildew and cat litter mingled in the air with yesterday's cigarettes. Vince lifted his coffee mug in the direction of a door at the back of the room and led Jimmy in to the music shop.

The main showroom—nothing more than a fifteen-by-fifteen deal with a small selection of guitars and amplifiers—stood in shadow. It was here yesterday that Jimmy had met Vince, this holdover from the sixties telling him that he didn't carry digital media for Jimmy's hard-disk recorder. Vince had added that electronic gadgets weren't real music anyway. The flower child hadn't bothered to show Jimmy the second music room.

Just three steps up to a second door, they passed into an elevated space smelling of dusty wood.

Filled with pianos.

At one time, it might have been a living room, maybe even a dining room. Now it had been stripped of everything but the floor planks. Even the walls were little more than studs and framing. This space wasn't about anything but the piano-forte, the clavier, and one irreparable harpsichord.

Dust lay in blankets a quarter inch deep over the tops of everything. As Jimmy and Vince stirred the air in their passage, it hardly moved the dust; the weight of time made a fabric of the accumulated motes.

The room smelled of antique wood, of metal casings and broken strings. It was like a graveyard of pianos packed so tight that only two aisles could be walked from one end of the space to the other.

"You only sell guitars and pianos?" Jimmy asked.

"And harmonicas," Vince replied.

Jimmy reached one end of the room. "I came here to ask . . ."

The words died in his throat. To the left, sitting on a piano bench facing a windowless wall, was a trumpet case propped open. Inside, a silver horn bearing the dents and scrapes of use lay cloaked in the same fall of dust that coated everything.

A Gillespie model.

Vince came up beside him. "Been here since I bought the place in '69. Old Doc Thurber told me just to leave it be. Didn't much matter to me, I don't care for brass."

Jimmy looked up at the man. "This isn't the instrument I heard. Can't be. I just finished recording it less than ten minutes ago. This thing hasn't been played in years." He ran a finger along the tubing, clearing a path across the dull finish.

"You'll need to keep an open mind about that," Vince said. "Things are different on the Pacific. Stuff has a way of being less and more than you make of it. That's no lie."

"I'd like to buy it," Jimmy blurted. "How much?"

"Ain't for sell," the hippie said. "Not to you. I can see the money in your eyes. Saw it yesterday when you came through talking about selling us the ocean on a CD." He laughed. "You realize I just need to step outside to get that for free."

"I'm not going to argue with you. What about five hundred for the horn?"

Vincent's eyebrows lifted, but Jimmy soon realized it had nothing to do with interest in the five hundred. "I won't take your money," the guy began, scratching his nipple. "But since you seem sincere, I'll steer you one port more. There's a small theater up Nelscott way, the West End Theater. Judd Jensen is always around. Oldest guy in town. He was here when this was still getting some lip." He pointed at the Gillespie horn. "Tell Judd I showed you the trumpet. He'll know what to say."

Jimmy spent several moments looking at the instrument in its stiffened velvet case, then strode the boards back toward his car. The very thought of the sounds in the waves caused him to quicken his pace.

Something about those songs.

The West End Theater was closed until 6:00 P.M.

Jimmy spent the day trying to duplicate his findings at the beach, annoyed at the bystanders asking him a lot of stupid questions. He actually threw a bit of sand at a few pesky kids to shoo them away.

But the trumpet didn't seem to accompany the waves in the daylight.

When dusk fell, Jimmy went to the theater, bought a ticket to a delightful rendition of *You Can't Take It with You,* then lingered in his seat while the other three patrons wandered out.

When the rumblings of stage props ceased, a man with thick white hair stepped out onto the stage beneath the single bulb that burned above it.

"You waiting for me?" the man asked.

"If you're Mr. Jensen."

"I am."

"My name is Jimmy Nesbitt. Vincent said I could talk to you about the trumpet," Jimmy replied.

The old man stared out on the small theater, deep-set eyes hiding whatever thoughts they might have betrayed. "That so?" He titled his head back, staring into the weak glare of the light. "You know what that is?"

"No, sir."

"Ghost light," the man said. "Every theater leaves the one bulb burning on the boards to keep the wrong kinds of spirits away."

"You think I'm a spirit?"

"Are you?" The head lowered again, leveling an uncomfortable stare at Jimmy.

"Not the last time I checked," Jimmy joked. The humor fell flat on the empty theater.

The old fellow didn't laugh, but came to the edge of the stage and out of the immediate glare. Now he was nothing more than a silhouette. "Then tell me what business you have with the trumpet, and I'll tell you if I can help."

"Just want to buy it."

"Why?"

Jimmy suddenly felt wary of sharing his story. Perhaps he was afraid people would laugh, perhaps he was afraid they wouldn't. "It's an unusual item," he said. "Is it yours?"

The man smiled then. At least Jimmy thought it looked like a smile; in the dark it was hard to tell. "What's it sound like to you?" Jensen asked.

"What do you mean?"

"Never mind, then." The old man pivoted and had almost exited stage left when he stopped and turned to look back at Jimmy. "You a musician?" he asked.

"Used to be. Now I work on the other side of the board." Jimmy began to get irritated. "Since when does anybody need to know how to play an instrument in order to buy one? No one would ever learn how that way."

The guy nodded, but not, Jimmy thought, in agreement to what he'd said. "It's been a long time," the man answered cryptically. "Maybe this time we'll get it right."

"Get what right? What are you talking about?" Jimmy got out of his seat and began moving toward the aisle.

"It was 1938!" the man yelled. The boom of his voice shattered the theater quiet, freezing Jimmy midstride. "Vaudeville lost its luster, and talented acts were starving in the streets of New York. Some died, believing movies were a passing fancy, wasting away in tenements waiting for venues to reopen at a nickel a seat. Others went upstate, taking their acts to resorts, working for room and board and lying in the beds of the rich for a little extra on the side."

The old man's hair began to shift with the trembling of his own impassioned words. "A few got out. A few went south, touring nightclubs and bars along the eastern seaboard. Some came west." He stopped.

Jimmy stood at the edge of the aisle, ready to either rush the man, feeling that he knew more than he admitted, or run from the theater, sure the coot was crazy as a loon. He did neither.

The old man continued. "George Henry found this place when his trumpet lost its appeal to both vaudeville and the New York uptown jazz community. But no one cared to listen to a horn out here, not for money. So George set to music of a different kind, learning the sounds of the earth, the sounds of nature, writing it down, learning the patterns." Something entered the old man's voice then. Fear, maybe. He whispered, the sound of it carrying in the empty hall. "There's power in that, my friend. The power to undo. George learned it sure enough."

The man held his arm toward Jimmy, pointing a finger. From the shadow at the edge of the stage, it appeared ominous, like the specter of Christmas Future pointing toward Scrooge's grave. "Anything you've heard is a gift to you, young man. Leave it be. Music isn't to be trifled with. You're either a musician or you're not. You either do it for a life, or you mock it by making it a hobby."

"I didn't say—"

"Didn't have to," Jensen cut in. "Listen if you will. No harm there. But let the music rest. For heaven's sake, just let it rest."

Then the man stepped behind the curtain, and Jimmy was alone with the ghost light.

As night closed in, a glorious sunset erupted over the western horizon. Crimson skies lit across the water, turning the ocean a thousand shades of red. Some few tourists and locals trod the beach, heading for their cars or home, and Jimmy, headphones firmly in place, sat watching it all, listening to his recordings from the night before.

Something strange in them.

The melodies were beautiful, haunting, but oddly never repeated. It was as though the trumpeter had no song in mind but simply played on and on, forever defining a new phrase, a new melody.

Some of them fast.

Others languorous, creeping slowly and marking out a passage of aching beauty.

Jimmy tried to chart it at first, replaying sections over and over. His theory was rusty, but he managed to define a few note progressions before combinations of complexity went beyond him.

The sun disappeared, and almost immediately the wind came in, cold, whispering across the sands.

The longer he listened, the less Jimmy thought he understood the music. At times, he wasn't sure it was music at all. Among other things, he couldn't find any definite rhythm. The time signature eluded him, so that he could never identify individual phrases.

Finally he stopped, putting his headphones aside and

dropping to his elbows to watch the light go completely out of the sky. For a moment, he lost himself in the reassuring sound of waves upon the sand—something he hadn't done once in all the time he'd been tracking the movements of the great ocean.

. . . learning the sounds of the earth, the sounds of nature, writing it down, learning the patterns . . . There's power in that, my friend. The power to undo.

Jimmy's gift had always been a very good ear. Any sound man worth his salt had one. Consumers rarely heard the difference, which explained the popularity of digital song downloads, in which compression technology had removed so much of the acoustic information.

Jimmy hated those. Not because they were free. Because they sounded thin.

Not like this.

The almost laughing sound of water rolling toward the beach came full-bellied, rich and strident every time. If the earth had a voice, this was surely it, and no place more certainly than this strip of sand on the Oregon coast.

But still something in it evaded him. If he could just understand.

Stories of vaudevillians, old instruments, and warnings about his own musical incompetence only made him more eager to understand what it was he heard in his recordings. They might not want to see him profiting from the music of their beach here, but they wouldn't run him off with creepy stories. The thought of it made him laugh.

Hell, he'd lived in Los Angeles for eight years; nothing was creepier than that.

Then it happened.

Just reclining there on the beach, he began to count.

Simple eighth notes.

Seven of them.

Then again.

Jimmy sat up straight, staring at the water as if he expected it to talk. With alarming regularity, the water tumbled and fell to a beat of seven. The time signature carried its own power, but could scarcely be handled by most musicians. Standard time, swing time, the three-count of a waltz, each of them could be danced to, internalized without training. Even phrases of two and five and nine fell more frequently in the music pantheon, adopted often by classical composers, used in songs with regularity.

But seven.

Jimmy counted, and counted.

When night had descended in full, something occurred to him. He quickly got his recording equipment from the car and set it up. This time, he dialed the frequency only halfway in, and listened.

There it was.

The languished melody of the horn came in musical phrases to the beat of the surf. Jimmy now heard them together as he hadn't before, and in a flurry, he began to scribble out bars of seven, transcribing the song as it wafted and sang across the great timekeeper.

So busy was he at his transcription that he did not hear the rumblings deep in the earth. He exulted at the possibility that he might put definition to something that had never been written down.

He owed it all to the bugling of a horn. He owed it to George Henry.

The sky suddenly darkened and crackled with lightning. The waves swelled; a flurry of wind swept down upon the dunes.

All in perfect seven time.

Jimmy madly went on, oblivious to the changes around him.

Soon the tumult of thunder and pounding surf and shrieking wind became a chorus he might never have imagined. His papers riffled in his hand, but he held them tight, penning the sound in his ears, marking a great melody in bars of seven.

He knew instinctively that he'd become a conductor, and his orchestra was nothing less than the elements themselves.

He held the key.

He was unlocking the sounds of heaven.

Just like a vaudevillian with a Gillespie horn.

In a fury, he put his pen back to the paper, marking out notes with haste, his hand flying across the page. The maelstrom whipped and churned, but all he heard was sevens, beautiful, indecipherable sevens.

Then he came to the end of his sheet, a single phrase yet to write, and paused as at the climax of a symphony, holding a great note before the finale.

And again he heard the old man, the minor thespian. *There's power in that, my friend. The power to undo.*

With a single beat of his heart, he knew that to decipher the song would make him forever a part of it.

Like a horn joined forever in the waves.

Jimmy shook with the feverish desire to unlock the mystery, to see his finding through to its conclusion.

As the wind lashed and the water churned, he listened to another measure of seven.

And dropped his pen.

In moments the sea and air calmed.

Jimmy loosened his grip on his opus, the pages scattering about him, carried on mild breezes to the water's edge. He fell back and grabbed fists full of sand, imagining the difference between heaven and earth.

In the moments that followed, he could no longer count the rhythms of the ocean, its voice become again a mystery to him. But gentle it came, and it lulled his senses, like any good jazz music should.

Afterword by Peter Orullian

A few years ago, I attended a writing workshop on the Oregon coast. One of the themes of the two-week boot camp was: Write fast and get out of your own way. The idea is that too many writers allow their critical voice to impede their creative voice, the result being diminished productivity.

To that end, many of our assignments were given late in the day with an early-next-morning deadline. What I learned is that most writers can do roughly a thousand words an hour. So, do the math. In three months, you should be able to write a novel—and that's if you write just an hour a day, and you're slow.

Anyway, on this particular short story assignment, I was asked to do two things: use a sleepy coastal town as my setting (part of the über assignment given to everyone) and work on "voice" (an exercise for me, in particular).

Each of the attending writers scurried into town to consider locations, gather details, look for inspiration. I hadn't needed to; I'd seen mine already.

A music store.

Which was perfect, since it got me to the second part of the assignment: voice. For me, the easiest way into voice was to go to music. I'm a musician, and for those of you who are, too, you've no need of an explanation here. For the rest of you, I'll paraphrase by saying it involves things like timbre, phrasing, dynamics, note selection. All of which should be internalized and forgotten before you try to perform; just like studying the craft of writing, internalizing it, then allowing it to come out (subconsciously) through your fingers as you pound the keyboard.

Back to the music store. There was this great place right on Highway 101 that captured my imagination. I'd thought to myself on first seeing it: How does a music store thrive in such a small community? In point of fact, the place didn't appear to be thriving. But amazingly, it had this whole large, dusty, neglected room of old pianos.

I was in heaven thinking of the possibilities for stories out of this corner of the world.

The other thing I should mention is that I'm taken with odd time signatures in music. It ain't easy to dance to something written in 7/8 or 11/8, but I don't dance much anyway.

All these things coalesced for me, as I imagined a sound engineer doing cheesy ocean-wave recordings (you see these in spas and New Age shops all the time) because he can't get another gig and is tired of the overcommercialization (and dilution) of jazz music.

Now I just needed to write it all down.

In about three hours I'd finished my story; it's really rather short. But it felt complete, as it had allowed me to get to the heart of a few things. I was happy with the cadence and the character voices, too. Plus, I'd managed to underscore my own feelings about the power of music.

Pretty Boy

BY ORSON SCOTT CARD

How do you systematically destroy a child with love? It's not something that any parent aspires to do, yet a surprising number come perilously close to achieving it. Many a child escapes destruction only through his own disbelief in his parents' worship. If I am a god, these children say, then there are no gods, or such gods as there be are weak and feeble things.

In short, it is their own depressive personalities that save them. They are self-atheists.

You know you have begun badly when you parents name you Bonito—"Pretty Boy."

Well, perhaps they named you after a species of tuna. But when you are pampered and coddled and adored, you soon become quite sure that the tuna was named after you, and not the other way around.

In the cathedral in Toledo, he was baptized with the name Tomás Benedito Bonito de Madrid y Valencia.

"An alliance between two cities!" his father proclaimed, though everyone knew that to have two cities in your name was a sign of low, not high, pedigree. Only if his ancestors had been lords of those cities would the names have meant anything except that somebody's ancestors were a butcher from Madrid and an orange picker from Valencia who moved somewhere else and came to be known by their city of origin.

But in truth Bonito's father, Amaro, did not care for his ancestry, or at least not his specific ancestry. It was enough for him to claim Spain as his family.

"We are a people who were once conquered by Islam, and yet we would not stay conquered," he would say—often. "Look at other lands that were once more civilized than we. Egypt! Asia Minor! Syria! Phoenicia! The Arabs came with their big black rock god that they pretended was not idolatry, and what happened? The Egyptians became so Muslim that they called themselves Arab and forgot their own language. So did the Syrians! So did the Lebanese! So did ancient Carthage and Lydia and Phrygia, Pontus and Macedonia! They gave up. They *converted*." He always said that word as if it were a mouthful of mud.

"But Spain—we retreated up into the Pyrenees. Navarre, Aragon, León, Galicia. They could not get us out of the hills. And slowly, year by year, city by city, village by village, orchard by orchard, we won it back. 1492. We drove the last of the Moors out of Spain, we purified the Spanish civilization, and then we went out and conquered a world!"

To goad him, friends would remind him that Columbus was Italian. "Yes, but he had to come to *Spain* before he accomplished a damn thing! It was Spanish money and Spanish bottoms that floated him west, and we all know it was really Spanish sailors who did the navigation and discovered the new world. It was Spaniards who in their dozens conquered armies that numbered in the millions!"

"So," the daring ones would say, "so what happened? Why did Spain topple from its place?"

"*Spain* never toppled. *Spain* had the tragic misfortune to get captured by foreign kings. A pawn of the miserable Hapsburgs. Austrians! *Germans*. They spent the blood and treasure of Spain on what? Dynastic wars! Squabbles in the Netherlands. What a waste! We should have been conquering China. China would have been better off speaking Spanish like Peru and Mexico. They'd have an alphabet! They'd eat with forks! They'd pray to the god on the cross!"

"But *you* don't pray to the god on the cross."

"Si, pero yo lo respecto! Yo lo adoro! Es muerto, pero es verdaderamente mi redentor ainda lo mismo!" I respect him, I worship him. He's dead, but he's truly my redeemer all the same.

Don't ever get Amaro de Madrid started on religion. "The people must have their god, or they'll make gods of whatever you give them. Look at the environmentalists, serving the god Gaia, sacrificing the prosperity of the world on her altar of compost! Cristo is a good god, he makes people peaceful with each other but fierce with their enemies."

No point in arguing when Amaro had a case to make. For he was a lawyer. No, he was a poet who was licensed and paid as a lawyer. His perorations in court were legendary. People would come to boring court actions just to hear him—not a lot of people, but most of them other lawyers or idealistic citizens or women held spellbound by his fire and the flood of words that sounded like wisdom and sometimes were. Enough that he was something of a celebrity in Toledo. Enough that his house was always full of people wanting to engage him in conversation.

This was the father at whose knee the pampered Bonito would sit, listening wide-eyed as pilgrims came to this living shrine to the lost religion of Spanish patriotism. Only gradually did Bonito come to realize that his father was not just its prophet, but its sole communicant as well.

Except, of course, Bonito. He was a remarkably bright child, verbal before he was a year old, and Amaro swore that his son understood every word he said before he was eighteen months old.

Not every word, but close enough. Word spread, as it always did, about this infant who listened to his brilliant father and was not merely dazzled, but seemed to understand.

So before Bonito was two years old, they came from the International Fleet to begin their tests. "You would steal my son from me? More importantly, you would steal him from *Spain*?"

The young officer patiently explained to him that Spain was, in fact, part of the human race, and the whole human race was searching among its children to find the most brilliant military minds to lead the struggle for survival against the Formics, that hideous race that had come two generations before and scoured humans out of the way like mildew until great heroes destroyed them. "It was a near thing," said the officer. "What if your son is the next Mazer Rackham, only you withhold him? Do you think the Formics will stop at the border of Spain?"

"We will do as we did before," said Amaro. "We will hide

in our mountain fortresses and then come back to reclaim Earth, city by city, village by village, until—"

But this young officer had studied history and only smiled. "The Moors captured the villages of Spain and ruled over them. The Formics would obliterate them; what then will you recapture? Christians remained in Spain for your ancestors to liberate. Will you convert Formics to rebel against their hive queen and join your struggle? You might as well try to persuade a man's hands to rebel against his brain."

To which Amaro only laughed and said, "I know many a man whose hands rebelled against him—and other parts as well!"

Amaro was a lawyer. More to the point, he was not stupid. So he knew the futility of trying to resist the IF. Nor was he insensitive to the great honor of having a son that the IF wanted to take away from him. In fact, when he railed to everyone about the tyranny of these "child-stealing internationalists," it was really his way of boasting that he had spawned a possible savior of the world. The tiny blinking monitor implanted in his son's spine just below the skull was a badge for his father.

Then Amaro set about destroying his son with love.

Nothing was to be denied this boy that the world wanted to take away from Amaro. He went with his father everywhere—as soon as he could walk and use a toilet, so there was no burden or mess to deal with. And when Amaro was at home, young Bonito was indulged in all his whims. "The boy wants to play in the trees, so let him."

"But he's so little, and he climbs so high, the fall would be so far."

"Boys climb, they fall. Do you think my Bonito is not tough enough to deal with it? How else will he learn?"

When Bonito refused to go to bed, or to turn his light out when he finally did, because he wanted to read, then Amaro said, "Will you stifle genius? If nighttime is when his mind is active, then you no more curtail him than you would demand that an owl can only hunt in the day!"

And when Bonito demanded sweets, well, Amaro made sure that there was an endless supply of them in the house. "He'll get tired of them," said Amaro.

But these things did not always lead where one might have thought, for Bonito, without knowing it, was determined to rescue himself from his father's love. Listening to his father and understanding more than even Amaro guessed, Bonito realized that getting tired of sweets was what his father expected—so he no longer asked for them. The boxes of candy languished and were finally contributed to a local orphanage.

Likewise, Bonito deliberately fell from trees—low branches at first, then higher and higher ones, learning to overcome his fear of falling and to avoid injury. And he began to understand later that he was not nocturnal, that what he read in the daze of sleepiness was ill-remembered by morning, but what he read by daylight after a good night of sleep stayed with him.

For Bonito was, in fact, born to be a disciple, and if his mentor imposed no discipline on him, Bonito would find it in his teachings all the same. Bonito heard everything, even that which was not actually said.

When Bonito was five, he finally became aware of his mother.

Oh, he had known her all along. He had run to her with his scrapes and his hungers. Her hands had been on him, caressing him, her soft voice also a caress, all the days of his life. She was like the air he breathed. Father was the dazzling sun in the bright blue sky; Mother was the earth beneath his feet. Everything came from her, but he did not see her, he was so dazzled.

Until one day, Bonito's attention wandered from one of his father's familiar sermons to one of the visitors who had come to hear him. Mother had brought in a tray of simple food—cut-up fruits and raw vegetables. But she had included a plate of the sweet orange flatbread she sometimes made, and it happened that Bonito noticed the moment when the visitor picked up one of the crackers and broke off a piece and put it in his mouth.

The visitor had been nodding at the things that Father was saying. But he stopped. Stopped chewing, as well. For a moment, Bonito thought the man intended to take the bite of flatbread out of his mouth. But no, he was savoring it. His eyebrows rose. He looked at the flatbread that remained in his hand, and there was reverence in his attitude when he put another piece in his mouth.

Bonito watched the man's face. Ecstasy? No, perhaps mere delight.

And when the man left, he stepped apart from the circle of admirers around his father and went to the kitchen.

Bonito followed him, leaving his father's conversation behind in order to hear this one:

"Señora, may I take more of this flatbread with me?"

Mother blushed and smiled shyly. "Did you like it?"

"I will not insult you by asking for the recipe," the man said. "I know that no description can capture what you put into this bread. But I beg you to let me carry some away so I can eat it in my own garden and share it with my wife."

With a sweet eagerness, Mother wrapped up most of what remained and gave it to the man, who bowed over the paper bag as she handed it to him. "You," the man said, "are the secret treasure of this house."

At those words, Mother's shyness became cold. Bonito realized at once that the man had crossed some invisible line; the man realized it as well. "Señora, I am not flirting with you. I spoke from the heart. What your husband says, I could read, or hear from others. What you have made here, I can have only from your hand." Then he bowed again, and left.

Bonito knew the orange flatbread was delicious. What he had not realized till now was that it was unusually so. That strangers would value it.

Mother began to sing a little song in the kitchen after the man left the room.

Bonito went back out into the salon to see how the man merely waved a brief good-bye to Father and then rushed away clutching his prize, the bag of flatbread.

A tiny part of Bonito was jealous. That flatbread would have been his to eat all through the next day.

But another part of Bonito was proud. Proud *of his mother.* It had never happened before. It was Father one was supposed to be proud of. He understood that instinctively, and it had been reinforced by so many visitors who had turned to him, while waiting for their chance to say good-bye to Father, and said something like this: "You're so lucky to live in the house of this great man." Or, more obliquely, "You live here in the heartbeat of Spain." But always, it was about Father.

Not this time.

From that moment, Bonito began to be aware of his mother. He actually noticed the work she did to make Father's life happen. The way she dealt with all the tradesmen, the gardener, and the maid who also helped her in the kitchen. How she shopped in the market, how she talked with the neighbors, graciously making their house a part of the neighborhood. The world came to their house to see Father; Mother went out and blessed the neighborhood with kindness and concern. Father talked. Mother listened. Father was admired. Mother was loved and trusted and needed.

It took a while for Father to notice that Bonito was not always with him anymore, that he sometimes did not *want* to go. "Of course," he said, laughing. "Court must be boring for you!" But he was a little disappointed; Bonito saw it; he was sorry for it. But he got as much pleasure from going about with his mother, for now he saw what an artist she was in her own right.

Father spoke to rooms of people—let them take him how they would, he amused, delighted, roused, even enraged them. Mother spoke with one person at a time, and when she left, they were, however temporarily, content.

"What did you do today?" Father asked him.

Bonito made the mistake of answering candidly. "I went to market with Mama," he said. "We visited with Mrs. Ferreira, the Portuguese lady? Her daughter has been making her very unhappy but Mother told her all the ways that the girl was showing good sense after all. Then we came home and Mother and Nita made the noodles for our soup, and I helped with the dusting of flour because I'm very good and I don't get tired of sifting it. Then I sang songs to her while she did the bills. I have a very sweet voice, Papa."

"I know you do," he said. But he looked puzzled. "Today I argued a very important case. I won a poor family back the land that had been unjustly taken by a bank because the bankers would not have the patience with the poor that they show to the wealthy.

I made six rich men testify about the favors they had received from the bank, the overdrafts, the late payments that had been tolerated, and it did not even go to judgment. The bankers backed down and restored the land and forgave the back interest."

"Congratulations, Papa."

"But Bonito, you did not go to see this. You stayed home and went shopping and gossiping and sifting flour and singing songs with your mother."

Bonito did not grasp his point. Until he realized that Father did not grasp his own point, either. He was envious. It was that simple. Father was jealous that Bonito had chosen to spend his day with his mother.

"I'll go with you tomorrow, Father."

"Tomorrow is Saturday, and the great case was today. It was today, and you missed it."

Bonito felt that he had let his father down. It devastated him. Yet he had been so happy all day with Mama. He cried. "I'm sorry, Papa. I'll never do it again."

"No, no, you spend your days as you want." Father picked him up and held him. "I never meant to make you cry, my Bonito, my pretty boy. Will you forgive your papa?"

Of course he did. But Bonito did not stay home with Mother after that, not for a long while. He was devotedly with his father, and Amaro seemed happier and prouder than ever before. Mother never said anything about it, not directly. Only one day did she say, "I paid bills today, and I thought I heard you singing to me, and it made me so happy, my pretty boy." She smiled and caressed him, but she was not hurt, only wistful and loving, and Bonito knew that Father needed to have him close at hand more than Mother did.

Now Bonito understood his own power in the house. His

attention was the prize. Where he bestowed it mattered far too much to Father, and only a little less to Mother.

But it worked the other way as well; it hurt Bonito's feelings a little that Mother could do without him better than Father could.

A family filled with love, Bonito knew, and yet they still managed to hurt each other in little ways, unthinking ways.

Only I *do* think about it, Bonito realized. I see what neither of my parents sees.

It frightened him. It exhilarated him. I am the true ruler of this house. I am the only one who understands it.

He could not say this to anyone else. But he wrote it down. Then he tore up the paper and hid it at the bottom of the kitchen garbage, under the orange rinds and meat scraps that would go out into the compost pile.

He forgot, for that moment, that he was not actually alone. For he wore on the back of his neck the monitor of the International Fleet. A tiny transmitter that marked a child as one of the chosen ones, being observed and evaluated. The monitor connected to his neural centers. The people from Battle School saw through his eyes, heard through his ears. They read what he wrote.

Soon after Bonito wrote his observation and tore it up, the young officer returned. "I need to speak to young Bonito. Alone."

Father made a bit of a fuss but then went off to work without his son. Mother busied herself in the kitchen; she was perhaps a bit noisier than usual with the pots and pans and knives and other implements, but the sound was a comfort to Bonito as he faced this man that he did not well remember having seen before.

"Bonito," said the officer softly. "You wrote something down yesterday."

Bonito was at once ashamed. "I forgot that you could see."

"We thought it was important that you know two things. First, you're right. You are the true ruler of the house. But second, you are an only child, so you had no way of knowing that in any healthy family, the children are the true rulers."

"Fathers rule," said Bonito, "and mothers are in charge when they're not home."

"That describes the outward functioning of your home," said the young officer. "But you understand that all they do is meant for you—even your father's vast ambition is about achieving greatness in his son's eyes. He doesn't know this about himself. But you know it about him."

Bonito nodded.

"Children rule in every home, but not in the ways they might wish. Good parents try to help their children, but not always to please them, because sometimes what a child needs is not what gives him pleasure. Cruel parents are jealous of their children's power and rebel against it, using them selfishly, hurting them. Your parents are not cruel."

"I know that." Was the man stupid?

"Then I've told you everything I came to say."

"Not yet," said Bonito.

"Oh?"

"*Why* is it that way?"

The young officer looked pleased. Bonito thought: Do I also rule *him*?

"The human race preserved itself," said the young officer, "by evolving this hunger in parents for the devotion of their children. Without it, they starve. Nothing pleases them more than their child's smile or laughter. Nothing makes them more anxious than a child's frantic cry. Childless people often do not know what they're starving for. Parents whose children have grown, though, they *know* what they're missing."

Bonito nodded. "When you take me away to Battle School, my parents will be very hungry."

"*If* we take you," the young officer said gently.

Bonito smiled. "You must leave me here," he said. "My family needs me."

"You may rule in this house, Bonito, but you do not rule the International Fleet. Your smile won't tell me what to do. But when the time comes, the choice will be yours."

"Then I choose not to go."

"When the time comes," the officer repeated. Then he left.

Bonito understood that they would be judging him, and what he did with the information the young officer had told him would be an important part of that judgment. In Battle School, they trained children to become military leaders. That meant that it would be important to see what Bonito did with the influence he had discovered that he had with his parents.

Can I help them both to be happy?

What does it mean to be happy?

Mother helps both me and Father, doing things for us all the time. Is that what makes her happy? Or does she do it in hopes of our doing things in return that would make her happy? Father loves to talk about his dreams for Spain. Does that mean he needs to actually achieve them in order to be happy? Or does his happiness come from having a cause to argue for? Does it matter that it's a lost cause, or does that make Father even happier as its advocate? Would I please him most by adopting that cause as my own, or would he feel like I was competing with him?

It was so confusing, to have responsibility for other people's happiness.

So now Bonito embarked on his first serious course of study: his parents, and what they wanted and needed in order to be happy.

Study meant research. He couldn't figure things out without learning more about them. He began interviewing them, informally. He'd ask them questions about their growing up, about how they met, whatever came into his mind. They both enjoyed answering his questions, though they often dodged and didn't give him full explanations or stories. Still, the very fact that on certain subjects they became evasive was still data, it was still part of understanding them.

But the more he learned, the less clearly he understood anything. People were too complicated. Adults did too many things that made no sense, and remembered too many stories in ways that did make sense but weren't believable, and Bonito couldn't figure out whether they were lying or had merely remembered them wrong. Certainly Mother and Father never told the same story in the same way—Father's version always made him the hero, and Mother's version always made her the suffering victim. Which should have made the stories identical, except that Mother never saw Father as her savior, and Father never made Mother all that important in the stories.

It made Bonito wonder if they really loved each other, and if not, why they ever got married.

It was disturbing, and it made him upset a lot of the time. Mother noticed that he was worried about something and tried to get him to tell it, but he knew better than to explain what he was working on. He didn't really have the words to explain it anyway.

It was too much responsibility for a child, he knew that. How could he possibly make his parents happy? He couldn't *do* anything about what they needed. The only thing he controlled was how he treated them. So gradually, not in despair but in resignation, he stopped trying to make their behavior and their relationship make sense, and he stopped expecting himself to be able to change anything. If his failure to help them meant the IF didn't take him into space, well, that was fine with him, he didn't want to go.

But he still kept noticing things. He still kept asking questions and trying to find things out about them.

Which is why he noticed a certain pattern in his father's life. On various days of the week, but usually at least once a week, Father would go on errands or have meetings where he *didn't* try to bring Bonito—where, indeed, he refused to take him. Until this research project began, Bonito had never thought anything of it; he didn't even want to be in on *everything* his father did, mostly because some of his meetings could be really boring.

But now he understood enough of his father's business to know that Father never hid his regular work from Bonito. Oh, of course he met with clients alone—it would disturb them to have a child listening to everything—but those meetings weren't hidden. There were appointments that the secretary wrote down, and Bonito sat out in the secretary's office and wrote or drew or read until Father was done.

These secret meetings always took place outside the office, and outside of office hours. Sometimes they consisted of a long lunch, and the secretary took Bonito home so Mother could feed him. Sometimes Father would have an evening meeting after he brought Bonito home.

Usually, Father loved to tell about whatever he had done, and especially what he had said that made someone else angry or put him in his place or made people laugh. But about these secret meetings, he was never talkative. He'd dismiss them as boring, pointless, tedious, he hated to go.

Yet Father never seemed as though he hated to go *before* the meeting. He was almost eager to go—not in some obvious way, but in the way he watched the clock surreptitiously and then made some excuse and left briskly.

For long months this was merely a nagging uncertainty in Bonito's mind. After all, he had given up on trying to take responsibility for his parents' happiness, so there was no urgency to figure it out. But the problem wouldn't leave him alone, and finally he realized why.

Father was in a conspiracy. He was meeting with people to do something dangerous or illegal. Was he planning to take over the Spanish government? Start a revolution? But whom could he meet with in *Toledo* that would make a difference in the world? Toledo was not a city where powerful people lived—they were all in Madrid and Barcelona, the cities his parents were named for but rarely visited. These meetings rarely lasted more than an hour and a half and never more than three hours, so they had to take place fairly close by.

How could a six-year-old—for Bonito was six now—find out what his father was doing? Because now that he knew there was a mystery, he had to have the answer to it. Maybe Father was doing secret government work—maybe even for the IF. Or maybe he was working on a dangerous case that might get him killed if anyone knew about it, so he only had meetings about it in secret.

One day an opportunity came. Father checked the time of

day several times in the same morning without saying anything about it, and then left for lunch a few minutes early, asking the secretary to walk Bonito home for lunch. The secretary agreed to and seemed cheerful enough about it; but she was also very busy and clearly did not want to leave the job unfinished.

"I can go home alone," said Bonito. "I'm six, you know."

"Of course you can find the way, you smart little boy," she answered. "But bad things sometimes happen to children who go off alone."

"Not to me," said Bonito.

"Are you sure of that?" she answered, amused.

Bonito turned around and pointed to the monitor on his neck. "*They're* watching."

"Oh," said the secretary, as if she had completely forgotten that Bonito was being observed all the time. "Well, then I guess you're quite safe. Still, I think it's better if you . . ."

Before she could say "wait until I'm done here," which was the inevitable conclusion of her sentence, Bonito was out the door. "Don't worry I'll be fine!" he shouted as he went.

He could see Father walking along the street, briskly but not actually *fast*. It was good that he was walking instead of taking a cab or getting the car—then Bonito could not have followed him. This way, Bonito could saunter along looking in store windows, like a kid, and still keep his father in view.

Father came to a door between shops, one of the sort that held stairs that led to walk-up shops and offices and apartments. Bonito got to the door and it was already closed; it was the kind that locked until somebody upstairs pushed a button to let it open. Father was not in sight.

The buttons on the wall had name tags, most of them, and a couple of them were offices rather than apartments. But

Father would not be having a manicure and he would not be getting his future read by a psychic palm-reading astrologer.

And, come to think of it, Father had not even waited at the bottom long enough for somebody to buzz him up. Instead he had taken a long time getting the door handle open . . .

Father had keys. That's what happened at the door: He fumbled with keys and opened the door directly without ringing anybody.

Why would Father have a second office? Or a second apartment? It made no sense to Bonito.

So when he got home, he asked Mother about it.

She looked like he had stabbed her in the heart. And yet she refused to explain anything.

After lunch he became aware that she had gone to her room and was crying.

I've made her unhappy, he thought. I shouldn't have been following Father, he thought.

And then she came out of her room holding a note, her eyes red from crying. She put the note on the kitchen table, folded, with Father's name on it, and then took Bonito to the car, which she almost never drove, and drove to the railroad station, where she parked it and got on the train and they went to Grandma's house. Grandma was Mother's mother, who lived two hours away in a small town in the middle of nowhere, but with orange groves—not very productive ones, but as Grandma always said, her needs were few and her son-in-law was generous.

Mother sent Bonito into the backyard and then cried to her mother. Bonito tried to listen, but when they saw him edging closer to the window they closed it and then got up and went to another room where he couldn't hear them without making it obvious he was trying to spy.

Yet he knew, bit by bit, what had happened, and what he had done. From the scraps of words and phrases he could overhear, he knew there was a "she" that Father was "keeping," that it was a terrible thing that Father had the key, and that Mother didn't know how she could bear it or whether she could stay. And Grandma kept saying, Hush, hush, it's the way of the world, women suffer while the men play, you have your son and you can't expect a strong man not to wander, one woman could not contain him . . .

Then they saw him a second time, sitting directly under the window where Mother had walked to get some air. Mother was furious. "What did you hear?"

"Nothing," said Bonito.

"The day you don't hear words that are said right in front of you, I'll take you to a hearing doctor to stick needles in your ears. What did you hear?"

"I'm sorry I told you about Papa! I don't want to move here! Grandma's a bad cook!"

At which Mother laughed in the midst of tears, Grandma was genuinely offended, and then Mother promised him that they would *not* move to Grandma's, but they'd visit here for a few days. They hadn't packed anything, but there were clothes left there from previous visits—too small for him now, but not so small he couldn't fit into them.

Father came that night and Grandma sent him away. He was furious at first but then she said something in a low voice and Father fell silent and drove away.

The next day he was back with flowers. Bonito watched

Mother and Father talk in the doorway, and she refused to take his flowers, so he dropped them on the ground and left again. Mother crushed one of the flowers with her shoe, but then she picked up the others and cried over them for a long time while Grandmother said, over and over, "I told you it meant nothing. I told you he didn't want to lose you."

It took a week before they moved back home, and Father and Mother were not right with each other. They talked little, except about the business of the house. And Father stopped asking Bonito to come with him.

At first Bonito was angry at Mother, but when he confronted her, Mother denied that she had forbidden him to go. "He's ashamed in front of you," she said.

"For what?" asked Bonito.

"He still loves you as much as ever," said Mother.

Which left his question unanswered. That meant the answer was very important. Father was ashamed of something, ashamed in front of Bonito. Or was that Mother's kindly-intended lie, and Father was actually very angry at Bonito for spying on him?

For days, for weeks Bonito didn't understand. And then one day he did. By then he was in school, and on the playground a boy was telling jokes, and it involved a man doing something bad with a woman that wasn't his wife, and in the middle of the joke it dawned on Bonito that this was what Father had been doing with some other woman that wasn't Mother. The reaction of the boys to the joke was obvious. Men were supposed to laugh at this. Men were supposed to think it was funny to find a clever way to lie to your wife and do strange things with strange women. By the end of the joke *both* women were deceived. The boys laughed as if it were a triumph. As if there were a war between men and women, both lying to each other.

That's not how Mother is, thought Bonito. She doesn't lie to Father. When a man comes to her and flirts with her, she sends him away. That's what happened with that man who liked her flatbread.

The final piece fell into place when they were visiting Grandma again—briefly, this time—and Grandma looked at him and sighed and said, "You'll just grow up to be another *man*." As if *hombre* were a dirty word. "There's no honor among men."

I won't grow up like Father. I won't break Mother's heart.

But how could he know that? It wouldn't be Mother's heart, anyway, it would be the woman he eventually married; and how could he know that he wasn't *just* like his father?

Without honor.

It changed everything. It poisoned everything.

When they came to him only a few days before his seventh birthday, and took out the monitor, and asked him if he'd like to go to Battle School, he said yes.

AFterword by Orson Scott Card

The character of Bonzo Madrid functions, in *Ender's Game,* as very nearly an "empty villain"—that is, a character who exists just for the sake of malice. There really are people like that in the world, who delight in the suffering of others, but I'd like to think they're rare. It's certain that they aren't very interesting. The only hint of depth in Bonzo is that he has a sense of honor, and when Ender invoked the memory of Bonzo's father, it provoked Bonzo into ordering his thugs to hold back and let him deal with Ender alone, *mano a mano.*

There was no way, within the structure of the novel *Ender's Game,* to explore Bonzo Madrid and make him anything other than a font of malice. But now, writing *Ender's Game* stories for *IGMS,* I had a chance to find out for myself just what Bonzo's childhood had been like, and why his father was such a key to his character.

I found myself tempted into weirdness, a sort of de Maupassant extravagance of eccentricity; I had to force myself to keep Bonzo's family from getting too strange. Still, in the real world *everybody's* family is strange, in one way or another. On average, families are pretty much alike, but in detail, every family does things that make people from outside the family shake their heads and wonder how any of the children emerged with their sanity.

Well . . . do any of us? Or don't we all carry around in us bits of madness acquired from our families? This does not mean families are bad—on the contrary, those who have no families merely carry around the madnesses of strangers. The fact is that everyone has an odd upbringing, with plenty of triggers leading to eccentricity (at least) or serious neuroses—or worse.

In an ordinary situation, Bonzo might have outgrown his need to bully others. But in Battle School, where competitiveness ruled and status was so clearly marked and intensely struggled for, Bonzo was driven—or drawn—to push harder than he probably would have in the kind of school he would have attended on Earth. This is partly because Battle School truly was a meritocracy, whereas on Earth, Bonzo would probably have

been in a school where his family's status would provide him
with the constant reassurance of superiority that he needed.

The tragedy, then, was that because of where they were,
Bonzo's and Ender's conflict led inevitably to a fatal climax;
had they been anywhere else, they would not have met, and
even if they had, they could have avoided each other easily.

Respite

BY RACHEL ANN DRYDEN

The wagon rumbled and crunched over the scupp shells in the sand. Each time Ann and Edward felt one of them crack under the wheels, they shuddered. The hatching could begin at any time.

The two of them sat silent and tense on the hard wagon bench, their simple black and white clothing a sharp contrast to the dun of the beach dunes and the purple shells thrusting up through the sand all around them. Ann clutched her swollen belly protectively, though she knew she would not be able to save the babe within if the scupps hatched before the wagon reached the shelter of the cliff caves.

"We left too late," Edward said. It had become a litany of sorts.

"We'll make it," Ann replied, because they had to try.

Edward whipped the scaled backs of the placid undru

pulling the wagon. Ann could have told him it would do no good; the beasts were doing the best they could already. He glared at Ann's belly before quickly looking away. His look cut Ann to the core. He's wishing I wasn't here with him, slowing him down. He wishes we had never tried to have this child.

"And if the babe comes early?" He was taking out his helplessness on her.

"I'm still glad we're having a child, Edward."

"I don't think you will be after we've been eaten alive by thousands of flying crab-things, shooting out of all of these scupp shells. Especially if we might not have been eaten if you hadn't slowed us down with a premature labor."

"I'm not going to go into labor. Edward, why are you being so hateful?" If I'd known you were like this when I met you, you wouldn't be the father of my baby.

"That should be obvious to the whole world, Ann. We're doomed out here, and we're alone, and if you weren't pregnant none of this would be happening." His arms gestured to include the horizon. Ann thought that he was pushing things a bit. The hatching would happen whether she was pregnant or not.

"May I remind you that I didn't get pregnant all by myself?" She was getting angry at his selfishness. "And that the main reason we came to Respite was so that we could have freedoms denied to us on Earth—such as having children? That used to matter to you, Edward."

"Freedom is no use if you're dead."

"I'd rather die free than live in the kind of bondage we were under on Earth. I'm still glad I came."

"The scupps are glad, too. You'll be a nice meal for them, I'm sure." His lips tightened into a thin line. He didn't look at her. She stared at him, in shock that he could be so uncaring. This place was changing him. And not for the better.

"That was completely uncalled for. You don't have to take your fear out on me."

"So now I'm a coward? I'd like to see the man who *wouldn't* be afraid in my shoes."

"That wasn't my point, Edward. I'm frightened as well. But tearing each other up is not going to solve anything, or help us survive this. I haven't given up yet. But I need you to not give up, either."

Edward said nothing more, but his lips were still tight and he began to whip the undru again. Normally Ann would defend the animals, but in this case it was either her or them, and she was tired of Edward taking it out on her. Let the undru have their turn. They had thick scales after all. And whatever Edward might do to their bodies, their hearts could not be touched by him. If only humans could protect themselves so well.

For a long time the two sat silently on the bench, not looking at each other. Ann wanted to just close her eyes. Every direction she could see only dismayed her more. Under them, ahead and behind, there was nothing to look at but the endless purple shells sticking out of the sand. To their right, eastward, the sand eventually changed to brown hills covered with drooping, dying grass. To the west lay only the sea, salty and warm, harboring its own menaces. Overhead the sun shone harshly down from a wheat-colored sky, refusing to hide any of the ugliness around them.

Ann missed their little farm. It hadn't been much, but to her it was the whole world. A few acres tilled and planted, a small, struggling crop of grain, some chickens. They hadn't even had a real house; they lived out of the back of the wagon, and put a canvas cover on it during storms. It had been adequate, or so they thought. Houses and other niceties would have to wait until there was enough food to fill their mouths and that of the offspring soon to come. If any survived.

When the colonists had left Earth, all they knew about their future home was that it was compatible with Earth's atmosphere and climatic conditions. It had only been a number on a map of stars. They had been granted one small, aging starship with which to limp through the light-years until they reached their home. The colonists had felt grateful to get it, and did not complain. The resources aboard the craft had been barely enough to support the lives of the hundred people on it, even in stasis, but they had managed to reach their destination. As a symbol of their new home, each of the colonists had chosen new names for themselves: plain, old-fashioned names. Like the Quakers or the Puritans on Earth. It was a way to return to simpler times. The landing was less than a year ago, but there were perhaps twenty women already pregnant. Ann was the farthest along.

What a privilege to conceive and bear children when she wanted, with whom she wanted. To live a simple life, free of mindless machines and the hive mind of an omnipotent government. Though the scupps were quite a trade-off to make.

As if reading her thoughts, the babe within her somersaulted. Ann gasped and clutched her stomach, then laughed. The sensation was so odd. No matter how often she felt it, she never got tired of the reminder that there was life within her womb.

Edward glared at her and said, "How can you laugh at a time like this? We could die, Ann. I thought you realized that."

Ann sobered a bit, but couldn't help saying, "Edward, if

there is ever a day in my life in which I cannot laugh, that is the day I will die."

He gave her a look that clearly expressed *you're crazy, this place is getting to you,* but he didn't reprimand her again.

The wagon jerked, much harder than usual, and Ann grabbed Edward's arm for balance. Then the wagon was still. The undru strained, trying to pull the cart along, but it wouldn't budge. Edward cursed under his breath and hopped off the bench, looking at the wheel. It had cracked on a sharp stone sticking out of the sand. The axle was broken. There was no way to fix it.

"We aren't going to make it," Edward said. He was staring at the broken axle. Finally, he sat down and began to weep. Huge, racking sobs, tearing through his body. Ann had never seen Edward express so much emotion, and was a bit shocked. Carefully she climbed down from the high wagon bench and joined him. She put her arms around him and said nothing for a time; just held him. Ann's eyes were still dry, which surprised her. If anyone had told her even a year ago that she would one day be cradling her husband, her strong man, in her arms while he sobbed his heart out to her and she remained unaffected, she would have laughed in that person's face. Yet the truth was undeniable. She was stronger than Edward.

She realized that she had always been stronger than he was, but had never before admitted it, even to herself. Instead she had borne his weaknesses alongside her own strength, defending him, excusing him. *What must the other colonists have thought of me? Knowing that I was married to a weakling, yet unable to see it?* Perhaps that was why Edward had been so eager to establish their farm so far away from everyone else. Alone with her, he could be with the one person who did not despise him. *But I do despise him. Now, when it is too late.*

Our fate is already sealed, and by my hand as much as his. Yet I must go on. I must be strong, for both of us.

After she felt he had had enough time to get himself together, she said, "Come on, Edward. We need to go."

"Go where? How? There's nowhere to go. We'll never make it."

"Edward, stop it. You're giving up. We still have the undru. And I can walk if I have to. The cliffs can't be too far off. Maybe a day's walk or so. We'll make it."

Edward just put his head in his hands in reply. Ann sighed, then got to her feet and went over to unhitch the placid, patient undru. They were native to Respite, and had taken the place of Earth oxen, which had not thrived on this planet. Large, reptilian beasts, they had short stubby tails and a broad bony plate across their head. They looked more like dinosaurs than anything else, but they were quite gentle and easily tamed. Stiff overlapping scales, like chain mail, covered most of their body, a natural protection from the claws and jaws of the myriad tiny scupp hatchlings. When the hatching took place, the undru would squat down and curl into themselves, exposing their scaly backs and nothing else to the onslaught. At least, Ann assumed that would happen; she had seen the undru, when frightened, do that in the past. The colonists had not yet been on Respite long enough to really know what to expect of many of the animals on it.

Only one man had seen a hatching and survived; he had managed to find shelter in a hole in the ground, blocking it from the inside with rocks as the scupps swarmed all around it. The scupps were purple buzzing flying discs the size of Earth locusts that had lots of tiny black claws and a mouth like a crab, except that crabs didn't fly and eat people. The man, Daniel, had returned to the cliff caves that were the landing base of the colonists and told his frightening tale. He had been exploring the coast in an area where none of the colonists had yet been, when one morning he noticed a few purple spots in the sand. He examined a few and found that they were all large shells, larger than a man's head, buried in the sand, and burrowing to the surface. Over the next few days, the shells stuck farther and farther out of the sand until they were completely exposed on the surface. There were now thousands of them. Then they hatched open, revealing the swarming death within that shot toward the sky in a cloud.

He was lucky to survive, in his hole in the ground. The others who had gone with him had not been so lucky. Only their bones remained to show they had ever existed.

Word was sent to all the outlying farms, to watch for the scupp shells and stay away from the coasts, and to return to the cliffs as soon as possible, since no one knew how widespread the hatching would be, or how many more times it would happen that season. For some reason, the scupps seemed to stay out of caves during the one hatching that Daniel witnessed. The theory was that because the caves were bare rock there was nowhere for the scupps to burrow to hibernate and transform, before again rising to the surface. The shells could be cracked with a hard blow, but there were too many for that to be effective. The colonists in the cliffs were experimenting with ways to kill the scupps before the next hatching, but so far had been unable to find anything that worked.

Ann and Edward had received the warning, but Edward insisted that they were far enough inland that they were not in immediate danger. Besides, the grain would be ready to harvest in a couple of weeks. It was probably safe to wait until their crop was ready to go back to the cliff caves. Ann had reminded Edward that they had to cut back to the coast to reach the caves; the nearest inland route was many miles longer and impassible for the wagon; a road had not yet been cleared through the thick vegetation. Edward had been confident that they could make it, though, so they had stayed. And I stayed with him. I could have left; could have made him leave. But I didn't. I thought he was the strong one then.

Yesterday morning Ann had found a purple spot on the ground near their well. Edward had examined it, and their worst fears were realized; it was a scupp shell, barely peeking through the earth. Immediately they threw their few belongings together and loaded the wagon, catching the chickens as fast as they could. They had been traveling steadily ever since, even through the night. They had only stopped for brief intervals to rest and water the undru. As they traveled, the shells became more and more plentiful. Now, as Ann looked about her, most of the shells were at least three-quarters of the way through the sand. How much longer did they have? Would it be long enough?

She tied their water skins and some of their blankets on the back of one of the undru, to serve as a sort of saddle. Undru weren't ordinarily ridden by humans; their backs were a bit too broad, and their scales were intensely uncomfortable to sit on. Ann felt that in this instance she had no choice. She couldn't walk far or fast enough to beat the hatching, and needed to ride.

"Edward, I need you to help me mount." During Ann's exertions, Edward hadn't gotten up. He simply sat, staring at a scupp shell near his feet. Now he rose wordlessly and helped Ann clamber up the back of the undru. When she was sitting unsteadily on the beast, he stopped moving again. "Let's go,

Edward." He seemed drained; the anger was gone, but so was his will to live, apparently. Why wouldn't he fight?

"Edward, I don't want to leave you behind. You are my husband."

"Some husband I've been to you."

"We don't have time for this right now. We've got to get going. If you aren't going to help yourself, help your child. The baby needs you to not give up."

"It won't matter whether I give up or not. The end result is the same."

"It *will* be the same if you don't get moving. Help me, Edward."

He said nothing, but his lips were once more in that tight line she had come to hate. He turned away. Ann finally let herself get angry. "All right. Stay here, then. I'm taking the undru. No reason for innocent creatures to die along with you. Good-bye." And if the child is a boy, I'm not going to name him Edward.

She tugged on the reins of the undru she was riding, and it started plodding northward again, its companion rumbling forward with them. They were still yoked together. She had thought about leaving one behind for Edward, but the yoke was too heavy for her, and he hadn't seemed to care enough to take it off himself.

"Wait. I'm coming." Edward ran up beside the undru.

Ann was relieved. She really hadn't wanted to leave him behind.

Now that they were moving again, Edward seemed to be more like his old self. He had always preferred action to sitting still. That was probably why he had become a colonist in the first place, to avoid stagnation.

She looked down into his face, wondering how he was feeling. He avoided meeting her gaze. *He knows that I'm the stronger one, and he can't deal with that. Has he always known that?*

The afternoon passed very slowly. There wasn't anything to do but look at their doom drawing near. No time to stop and cook a meal, so there wasn't anything to eat. The undru was very uncomfortable to ride, and at intervals Ann had to dismount and walk beside Edward. Then she would get out of breath and start to feel dizzy, and Edward would help her remount. Ann had been ill much of the pregnancy, and traveling so near to her time wasn't helping matters at all. She wanted so desperately to just give up and lie in the sand, regardless of the consequences.

But I can't do that. Not when I have a child who is relying on me.

In the evening, the pain started.

Ann didn't notice at first because she hurt all over anyway, but by full dark she could no longer put it out of her mind: Her back was aching, deeply, and she was starting to feel contractions. Edward had been right. The babe would come early. She was afraid to tell Edward about it, though, for fear of his reaction. He had been so strange lately.

I don't know if I can trust him to stay sane long enough to reach the cliffs anyway, much less if I tell him that his prediction came true. So with each contraction I'll hold my breath and try not to show him my pain.

The hours continued to pass with agonizing slowness, Ann's rhythmic pain the only thing marking the passage of time. At one point, she didn't know when, she felt her waters stream down her leg and soak the blankets on the undru's back. Ann had stopped thinking clearly a while before that. She hadn't slept in two days now, and with labor on top of her exhaustion, there wasn't much room in her mind for thoughts. She clutched the bony plate on the undru's neck to keep her balance, and half dozed even through the pain.

Edward seemed oblivious to what she was suffering. He kept his head down, looking at the shells in the dim starlight, walking beside the undru.

At long last, the sun rose over the ocean. It brought a welcome sight: The cliffs were ahead. Ann could even make out the cave openings, very small. Safety was within reach. We're going to make it.

Then she looked down at the ground. The shells were completely out of the sand now, and lay like fat upright fans on the ground, with a seam showing at the top of each one. The seams hadn't been visible yesterday. That meant the hatching was soon, very soon.

"Edward?" The sound was faint coming from Ann's throat. Her pain was suddenly very strong. She felt herself sliding off the back of the undru. Edward caught her and eased her to the ground. Ann clutched her belly and writhed, screaming. The contractions were unbearable, a continuous unrelenting agony. My mind is going to fracture. I can't do this. Edward, I can't do this. Help me.

She wasn't speaking out loud, wasn't even aware that she wasn't. She dimly heard Edward, from a long way away, say, "Ann. Ann, listen to me. The baby is coming. I'll help you with the baby, Ann. Can you hear me?" Yes. Edward. I hear you. But the words stuck in her throat as another contraction, the strongest of all, came. She could feel her child being born.

In a short time, or maybe a long time, Ann didn't know, she was holding her bloody child in her arms, with Edward leaning over her. "It's a boy, Ann," he said. That part she heard.

The baby cried, weakly. Then she heard something else. The undru were moaning.

The hatching was beginning.

Only a few feet away, Ann saw a scupp shell begin to rock back and forth. Everywhere the shells were moving. Edward jumped to his feet in terror.

"Oh God, Ann. We're too late. It's starting."

The undru began to lower themselves onto their knees, their heads pulling in toward their chests.

"Edward. Edward, listen." His eyes were wild, and she didn't know if she had the strength to make him hear her. "The undru."

"What about the undru? They'll survive without my help. We're the ones who will die, Ann. We didn't make it after all. I was right!" He started laughing. It was not a sane sound.

"Edward. Take the baby. Hide inside the undru." She pulled weakly at the knife on her belt.

Edward had one, too. At last he understood what she meant.

There was a moment that seemed to last an eternity in which Edward was obviously torn between making a run for the caves—so near!—leaving her and the baby to their fate, or staying to help his family, his flesh and blood. Ann held her breath and simply stared into his eyes, willing him to be a man, to do the right thing. Then he blinked and looked away from her, his decision made.

He whipped out his own knife and turned to the nearer of the two beasts. The undru were hooting and moaning, and trying to crunch into protective balls. The yoke was preventing them from completing their crouches. Edward was still able to get to the softer underbelly of the near one. Thank God his knife was sharpened recently. A large red gash appeared where Edward slashed at the animal. He dug his hands into the side of the undru, ignoring its

bellows and struggles to get away from him. He pulled out hand-
fuls of steaming innards, gagging and coughing at the stench and
the sight of the animal's viscera, then turned to Ann. As he picked
her and the baby up, the shells opened, disgorging their contents in
a violent spew toward the sun. He ran with her to the bleeding
carcass, and began to pull open the tough side of the creature, to
make a space for her. She tried to get him to take the baby and save
himself, but he either didn't understand her or chose to ignore her,
continuing to open the belly of the undru.

All at once, the sky darkened with teeming untold numbers of flying discs. They began to land on Ann, on Edward, on
everything. As soon as one landed, the disc sprouted claws and
a mouth. Then it began to feed on any creature in its path. The
bites were excruciating, and Ann found herself writhing around
in an attempt to beat the scupps off her body and that of her
son. They came off easily, but there were so many of them that
she would be unable to hold them off for long.

Edward shoved Ann and the baby into the body of the animal. He barely got them in, Ann shielding her son with her
body and trying to make sure the baby had air, before turning
to the other undru, to slash its belly open and make room for
himself. But he was too late. The undru had managed to complete its crouch, and now its scales were a defense against Edward's knife, as much as against the scupps.

He was forced to turn back to the first undru and try to
squeeze himself into the opening that was already a tight fit for
Ann. He couldn't get completely inside. The scupps began to
feed on Edward's unprotected back. She desperately tried to
make room for him, but he couldn't come any farther.

Edward bit his lips, but couldn't keep from screaming
with the pain. He forced his body to remain still, to block the

opening, protecting Ann and the baby. He could have run, but he didn't. Ann looked into his eyes. He hadn't been a coward after all, at the end, when it mattered. She should be the one dying, the one protecting him. She was the strong one. But she couldn't help feeling glad that she would live, despite her guilt at watching Edward die in her place.

"I love you, Edward." She had said it before. She realized now that she meant it.

"Love. You. Ann." The words were bitten out through the pain. Then one of the scupps burrowed into Edward's spine, and he suddenly went limp. His body blocked the scupps from coming farther into the undru's carcass and feeding on Ann as well, but that wouldn't hold them for long. She had to think, to be strong still. Edward's death was not enough.

Ann sobbed inside the undru, holding her son, looking at her husband, his now dead eyes staring unblinkingly back at her. She forced herself to burrow deeper into the beast, retching with the stench and hot closeness and blood. She was up behind the ribcage now, and she pressed against the lungs and heart of the beast. She found the windpipe and tore it free, letting a bit more air into the cramped space. The scupps were eating behind her; she could hear them everywhere.

Ann was nearly blinded by the darkness and the gore, but her sense of hearing was heightened. As she listened, the sound changed. The scupps were doing something different now. They were scraping against each other, shell on shell, rhythmically, hypnotically. The sounds of chewing stopped, changed to an odd vibrating hiss. The sound was frightening, but not as menacing as the chewing. She slid back down to Edward's body, or what was left of it, and peered out.

The scupps were changing. The little discs were now

completely unfurled and were more oblong than round, one side rough and shell-like, the other raw and unprotected. I must remember this and tell the others. When they are like this we can find a way to defeat them. As she watched, the scupps rubbed over and under each other, hissing, until two of them rubbed raw sides over each other and stopped, fastened together, with only the rough outsides exposed. Then others paired off, and more, until the ground was covered with very small versions of the large scupp shells, with only seams to show that what had once been two creatures was now one.

The scupp shells burrowed back into the earth, hiding themselves once more from view, as the cycle began anew.

Ann crawled carefully from the body of the undru. Its hide had protected her, but Edward had saved her. He was little more than a skeleton now, though his face had largely escaped the predations. He looked at peace to Ann. In fact, he looked strong.

She looked up at the cliff caves and saw people pouring out of them, running to meet her, now that the scupps were no longer a threat. She sat, grateful that her journey was at an end, nursing her son, waiting for them to come. The thought that life had come from so much death was soothing to her, and she rocked her son in her arms and crooned to him as she nursed.

Nathaniel was the first of the people to reach her.

"My God. What happened to Edward? How did you make it? We couldn't quite see what was happening here. I wish we could have come to help you. We had no way to get past the scupps."

He knelt beside her, concern on his face. The others examined the body of her husband, and that of the undru that had to die for her to live. The other undru was still alive, and trying to get up out of the crouch but was hampered by the yoke and the dead weight of its companion. Two of the men removed the yoke and helped the undru to its feet, then loaded Edward's body carefully onto it, to take back to the cliffs for burial.

"Edward was very brave. In the end, when it mattered. He might have made it, if only he'd left me behind and run for it. But he stayed. He was strong for me. I was too weak. I wouldn't have survived on my own."

The others exchanged glances at this, probably wondering how to compare this new description of Edward with the way they had previously viewed him. Let them never know how he was during the journey. I will never shame his memory. His sacrifice is enough, his penance completed.

"We used the undru hide as protection. In future, we should all have hides with us to use as a shield, so we're never caught like that again. I saw how the scupps mate. They're vulnerable and soft on one side, just before they join together into new scupp shells. We can use that to our advantage. This planet can still be a good home for us, for our children.

"This is my son." She held him up for everyone to see. The first child born on Respite. The hope of the future. The source of her strength. "His name is Edward."

Afterword by Rachel Ann Dryden

"Respite" kept me from attending Uncle Orson's Literary Boot-camp. At the time, I'd only finished one or two short stories and really had no clue what I was doing. Bootcamp would be a great way to light a fire under me, and OSC had been my favorite author since I first discovered him as a teenager. But I needed to come up with a one-page writing sample for my application. I recalled a disturbing dream I'd had a few months before in which

I was on a wagon trying to outrun a menace that was about to hatch and devour everything in sight. The dream made such an impression that when I woke from it, I even sketched these creatures and their life cycle—and I can't draw. I wrote only the first page and sent it off, so anxious about the application that I didn't even finish writing the story. Then Mr. Card's assistant, Kathleen Bellamy, called me one morning and said he wanted to read the whole thing. Could I send over the rest so he could read it that night?

"Sure!" I said, trying not to hyperventilate, and a frantic five hours followed. Amazingly, these two characters that began as mist in my mind came to life as soon as my fingers tapped the keyboard. I fell in love with them as I wrote, and I cried at the end. Without time for revisions, I e-mailed what I had.

The next morning Mr. Card called me in person and told me he wasn't going to let me go to Bootcamp, since in his opinion I didn't need the class, and he wanted to buy the story from me instead, for this new magazine he was starting. Mine was the first story purchased. Then he advised me to work on a novel next instead of more short stories. While I'll always disagree with him about not needing the class, I've taken his advice to heart and at the time of this writing have almost completed *Outleaf.*

One of my favorite aspects of writing speculative fiction is that established authors in the field are so willing to mentor the newcomers. Thank you to Mr. Card for giving me my start.

FAT FARM

by Aaron Johnston,
based on the story by Orson Scott Card

...IS OF HER.

HE'LL DO.

THEN WE HAVE ONLY A FEW PAPERS TO SIGN AND WE'RE THROUGH.

I'LL HAVE ONE OF THE TECHNICIANS SHOW MR. BARTH WHERE HIS CLOTHES ARE AND HE'LL BE ON HIS WAY, RESPONSIBLE NOW FOR YOUR WEALTH AND ESTATE, OF COURSE.

I KNOW WHERE MY CLOTHES ARE. I'LL SHOW MYSELF OUT.

YOU KNOW, I JUST REALIZED, MY MEMORIES RUN OUT HERE. THE AGREEMENT WAS— WHAT WAS THE AGREEMENT AGAIN?

THE AGREEMENT WAS TENDER CARE OF YOU UNTIL YOU PASSED AWAY. HOWEVER, THAT AGREEMENT . . .

IS NO LONGER WORTH A DAMN.

WHAT DO YOU MEAN?

TWO YEARS LATER.

THEY'RE COMING FOR YOU, H.

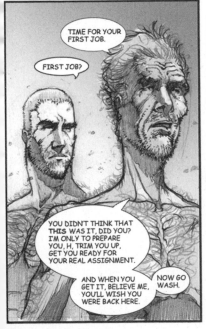

TIME FOR YOUR FIRST JOB.

FIRST JOB?

YOU DIDN'T THINK THAT **THIS** WAS IT, DID YOU? I'M ONLY TO PREPARE YOU, H, TRIM YOU UP, GET YOU READY FOR YOUR REAL ASSIGNMENT.

AND WHEN YOU GET IT, BELIEVE ME, YOU'LL WISH YOU WERE BACK HERE.

NOW GO WASH.

MOVE IT!

CRACK!

LET'S GO, H, BEFORE THE OTHER HELI-COPTER ARRIVES.

PILOT, TAKE US UP A FEW HUNDRED FEET AND STAY THERE. I WANT H TO SEE THIS.

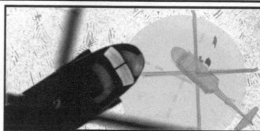

CRACK! CRACK!

SEE THAT FAT TUB OF WORTHLESS HUMAN FLESH DOWN THERE, H?

THAT'S YOU. OR RATHER, THAT'S "I." TOOK YOU ONLY TWO YEARS TO PUT THE WEIGHT ON THIS TIME. A COMPANY RECORD.

WHAT ARE YOU THINKING?

I WAS THINKING THAT THE OLD MAN CAN'T HATE HIM AS MUCH AS I DO. THAT IF I HAD THAT WHIP, I'D HIT HIM TWICE AS HARD.

HIT HIM UNTIL I KILLED HIM.

The Box of Beautiful Things

BY BRIAN DOLTON

Yi Qin came to visit Weng Hao's Grand Carnival of Curiosities on a spring day, with the air sharp and clear. She was humbly dressed, not like an emissary of the Emperor at all, and she took her place in the line, and handed over her quarter-teng piece. She looked at the tigers, pacing back and forth in their cages. She watched the acrobats perform, tumbling and swooping and spinning. She listened to the storyteller, and laughed when he recounted the tale of the Little Fisherman and the Seven Foolish Demons.

She had not come, however, to see these things. They were diversions; amusing in their way, but no more than that. No; she had come, like everyone else, to see the Box of Beautiful Things.

But not for the same reason.

There was a long line. Even though the carnival was

camped in the middle of a dusty plain, people had come from a hundred li in every direction, spurred on by rumor. Weng Hao himself was marshaling the customers. As Yi Qin waited for her turn (for no more than ten people at a time were allowed into the tent where the Box of Beautiful Things was kept), she studied him. He was a big man; bigger, almost, than his skin could withstand. His cheeks seemed distended, and his eyes were thin black slits that he could barely open. He had a long black mustache and wore gaudy silks.

His voice boomed out, from time to time. The wait is worth it, he would cry. Why, a wait of a Great Year would be worth it, to see the Box of Beautiful Things. Such things as you have never before seen. Such things as you could not even imagine! Gaze upon beauty, and let your heart lift, to know that there is still such wonder in the world!

Yi Qin had seen many wonders, and by no means all of them were beautiful. She shuffled forward as the line moved, and folded her hands together under her sleeves. Her thumb sought the point of one of the darts she kept hidden. Not yet, she told herself. Not until you can see the Box of Beautiful Things.

The sun was low in the west by the time she reached the head of the line. She bowed politely to Weng Hao, who was still beaming, and whose eyes could still not be seen. The Seven Ways taught that the eyes were mirrors of the soul. Yi Qin wondered what she would have read, if she could have seen into his eyes.

She wondered, too, what he might be able to read in hers; and looked away.

Inside the tent, there were only two lanterns. Curtains

hung, thick velvet, fringed with tassels. The Box of Beautiful Things was resting on some kind of platform. It was black, smooth and shiny, lacquered and inset with mother-of-pearl. It stood as tall as a man, as broad as a man's reach. Its doors were open wide. And inside it . . .

Yi Qin pricked her thumb with the dart, and withdrew her hand. She smeared the blood onto her forehead, drawing the sign that was the Fourth Unspoken Word: The Word That Allows the Truth to Be Discerned.

There was nothing beautiful in the box.

There was nothing inside it at all.

In front of her, nine other people were marveling, and whispering to one another as they pointed out one beautiful thing after another. Yi Qin stood slightly apart from them, and looked into the empty box. When another woman asked her what she thought of the red cheongsam, with the silver dragon picked out in meticulous detail, she smiled politely and agreed that it was exquisite. When a man loudly declared he had never seen such fine goldwork—and he was a goldsmith himself, who could only dream of creating such beauty—she nodded with the others. And, after the others were drunk on beauty, and could endure no more of it, she filed out carefully behind them. She lifted a red cloth to her face, dabbing away the blood from her brow, under the pretense of mopping up tears that had been brought forth by unworldly beauty.

Then she sat down on a rock nearby, and waited for the fall of night.

A man came to her, as the sun was just dipping behind the western mountains.

"Your pardon, lady, but the carnival is closing. You must be away from here."

"I was hoping," she told him, "that I might speak with the estimable Weng Hao."

"Master Weng Hao is a busy man," he said. "I can bear him a message, perhaps. But it is not possible to speak with him."

"I must insist," she said, rising to her feet. "Perhaps, if you tell him what I have shown you, he will wish to talk?"

"You have not shown me anything, lady," the man said.

In response, Yi Qin reached inside the bag she carried, and withdrew a tablet. The last rays of the setting sun caught the embossed symbols carved on it. The man bowed, very low.

"Your pardon, noble lady. Please, forgive me. I did not know you were an emissary of the Emperor."

"There is nothing to forgive," she told him, tucking the tablet back into her bag. "But you will tell Weng Hao that I wish to speak with him, concerning the Box of Beautiful Things?"

"I will tell him, noble lady," the man said, and bowed again.

Yi Qin sat down again on her rock, and waited. The sun slid below the horizon; First Moon followed it down, while Third Moon shone big and pale in the eastern sky.

"I am honored," a voice said from nearby. "An emissary of the Emperor himself, come to my humble carnival! Truly, this is a blessing. How may I be of service, noble lady?"

Yi Qin rose, and bowed toward Weng Hao, who was approaching, bearing a lantern.

"I would talk, Weng Hao,"

"By all means! I love to talk!" He laughed, expansively. "But this is no place for it. Come to my pavilion! I will offer you food, and rice wine, and listen eagerly to what you have to say."

"I would prefer, Weng Hao, to talk here, under the eye of Third Moon."

He bowed. "If that is what the Emperor's Emissary wishes, then that is what shall be! As a loyal subject . . ."

"Are you a loyal subject of the Emperor?" Yi Qin asked, mildly.

Insofar as it was possible to tell, behind the smooth face and inflated cheeks, Weng Hao looked surprised. "Do you doubt it?"

"If I may speak frankly, Weng Hao; then yes, I doubt it. I have seen certain things, today, which give me cause to doubt that you are a loyal subject of the Emperor. Which make me doubt, even, whether your name is truly Weng Hao."

"And why do you doubt these things, lady?"

"Because you are a charlatan, Weng Hao."

"A charlatan? If so noble a person as the Emperor's Emissary tells me, then it must be so; and yet, I do not understand. I would be grateful beyond measure if you could explain this to me."

"A thousand people come to your carnival every day, Weng Hao. They come because you have a tent in which there is a Box of Beautiful Things. But the box is empty, Weng Hao. There is nothing beautiful in illusion; in conjuring."

"In conjuring? And how, pray enlighten me, did you discern that the Box of Beautiful Things was empty?"

"By revealing the truth."

"And this truth was revealed by what means? By conjuring, perhaps?"

"Just so," she said, with a small tilt of the head. "But it is truth, nonetheless."

"If only the truth were so simple. A thousand people came

to my carnival today. All but one have left with gladness in their hearts. They will remember for many years all the beautiful and wonderful things that they have seen at my carnival."

"That they believe they have seen."

"And what is stronger than belief? Go to them, Emissary. Ask them what they saw. Tell them, if you wish, that it was but conjuring; a trick. They will not believe you. They believe what they have seen."

"They believe a lie."

"And the truth is so valuable? What is the virtue of truth, Emissary? Can you say that you have never told a lie, in all your life?"

"I have told many lies," she admitted. "Where it has been necessary. You lie, sir, purely for your own convenience. You lie to draw people to your carnival. You have fine tigers, and nimble acrobats, and talented storytellers; but there are a dozen carnivals which can boast such things. It is trickery and illusion that draws people to come here, and to place a quarter-teng piece into a bowl. You are a wealthy man, Weng Hao, but your wealth has come from lies."

"I am accounted a wealthy man by some," he admitted. "But wealth is a relative thing. I force no one to come to my carnival. It is the word that brings people here, the word of mouth. People speak of the beauty they have seen. 'You must go to Weng Hao's Grand Carnival of Curiosities,' they say. 'You must see the Box of Beautiful Things. Such beauty, such wonderful things, as you cannot imagine!' This is why they come, Emissary. They pay but a quarter teng to see things that they will remember for years to come; things they will tell even to their grandchildren. They buy beauty, and the memory of beauty."

"They buy lies," Yi Qin maintained.

Weng Hao shrugged. "If you say so. But I wonder, perhaps, if they see a truth that you cannot. You did not wish to see beauty, when you came here, did you? You wished only to uncover your truth; but your truth is a sad, mean-spirited thing. You would deprive the world of beauty, Emissary. You would steal its dreams."

Yi Qin said nothing. The night folded itself around the carnival tents. Geckos barked to one another in the dusty plain.

"Show me the Box of Beautiful Things," she said, eventually.

Weng Hao smiled. "But of course! Come, let me enumerate its wondrous contents." He rose, and carried on speaking as they walked to the tent where the Box of Beautiful Things was kept. "There is the most magnificent gold filigree, jewelry that surpasses the work of even Grand Master Lin Fu! There is porcelain, so fine that it is translucent, so delicate that even the Emperor has none to equal it. And the silks . . . colors, my lady, that you have never seen; colors that only your dreams have ever held."

"Please," she said. "Do not recount these things. Let me see for myself."

He ushered her through the opening of the tent, and followed her inside. The lamps had been extinguished; but he lifted the lantern he held, and its orange light spilled into the open box.

Yi Qin, her arms folded together under her sleeves, looked into the Box of Beautiful Things.

A necklace of gold filigree, delicate as a spiderweb, bright as the morning sun on Mount Yang. A jade dragon, smooth as water, cool as a blessing. Silks, as vivid as dreams. Porcelain, pale as milk. Pearls and rubies and feathers. Shapes and colors and textures that made her heart ache.

She knew none of it was real. Her thumb pressed, lightly, against the dart under her sleeve; but so lightly that it did not pierce the skin, and draw forth blood.

She looked into the Box of Beautiful Things for a long time.

Then she sighed, and pressed her thumb hard onto the point of the dart. With swift, precise movements, she withdrew her bloody hand, and reached forward, and inscribed the First Unspoken Word onto the beautiful black, lacquered wood.

The First Unspoken Word: The Word That Releases Hungry Flames.

Weng Hao shrieked, and flapped his sleeves in alarm, but there was nothing he could do. In a moment, the lacquered box was ablaze; spitting and crackling and consuming itself. Flames leapt to the heavy drapery, and in a moment the whole tent was alive with fire. Yi Qin walked, very calmly, out into the night air, and stood aside, watching the tent burn, watching Weng Hao's men bustle uselessly around it, for there was not enough water, here in this dry place, to have the slightest hope of quenching the fire.

Weng Hao stood in front of Yi Qin and cried.

"Why have you done this? You have destroyed it! You have destroyed the box! You have destroyed my livelihood!"

"You have a carnival, Weng Hao," she answered him, quiet and adamant against the torrent of his emotions. "You have a carnival like any other, with tigers, and acrobats, and storytellers. Settle for that, and make your living without the Box of Beautiful Things."

She was sure that, if she had not been an Emissary of the

Emperor, he would have killed her where she stood; or would, rather, have attempted it. Instead, he merely dropped to his knees. Tears spilled out onto his enormous cheeks.

"You have destroyed beauty," he wailed. "You are wicked, Emissary. Wicked beyond measure! These are not just my tears! These are the tears of thousands, who will come to my carnival, because they have heard tales of the Box of Beautiful Things, and wish only to see it for themselves; and I must tell them that it is no more. That it was burnt. That the beauty is gone, forever."

"Until you find another conjuror," Yi Qin said, quietly, calmly, "who can work such magic for you. It is not, I think, as if you lack the money to pay for such a thing? But next time, Weng Hao; next time, I advise you this. Create a little less beauty. Create colors that are wondrous, but which people have seen before. Create jewelry that is no more than the equal of the work of Master Lin Fu. You have reached too high, Weng Hao. The Emperor does not care to think that, in all his realm, there is such beauty owned by another."

Weng Hao stared at her.

"The Emperor is jealous? You have burnt my Box of Beautiful Things because the Emperor is jealous?"

Yi Qin said nothing. There was nothing she could say. She simply turned, and walked away into the night, and remembered beauty.

Afterword by Brian Dolton

1—The Title

Titles come from all kinds of places. There's a Scottish singer-songwriter called Jackie Leven who has some really great song titles (and some really great songs, though the two don't always match up). One song is called "Burning the Box of Beautiful Things" (which itself, I believe, is borrowed from a book by Alex Seago—see, we just get our ideas from other people!), which I just thought was a great image. I knew I wanted to write a story about the box. I just didn't have a clue what the story was . . .

2—The Story

Online, I hang at a writing group called Liberty Hall, run by the wonderful Mike Munsil. The site features writing challenges; you get a trigger, which may be a word, a quotation, a picture . . . anything. And you get ninety minutes to write a story. Yep; a complete story in an hour and a half. It sounds absurdly daunting, but it's a great way to get sat down, stop thinking about stuff, and actually *write*. Of course, it helps that I can dump between two and three thousand words onto a page in that time . . .

The trigger that resulted in this story was a picture of a doll, with a porcelain mask and a gold and purple robe. I looked at the trigger and, as I usually do, I didn't sit back and think, I just started writing, thinking as I went. Under ninety minutes later, I had the story. Critiques by the other members of the group helped me to hone it into the right shape, and voilà!

Just in case this all sounds ridiculously easy, I've written stories for more than thirty of these challenges (as well as a dozen others, for fortnight rather than ninety-minute deadlines). Some of them will certainly never, ever see the light of day. Others have taken weeks of thought and careful polishing, or even complete rewriting, before they've gone wandering out to market. But there's no doubt that I've been a far more productive—and, I hope, far better—writer as a result of these challenges.

3—The Character

Heh. That's another story. Indeed, that's a lot of other stories. I'm really hopeful that everyone's going to be seeing a lot more of Yi Qin. But *IGMS* was her first ever appearance (and my first ever sale), and I'll always hold it dear.

Taint of Treason

BY ERIC JAMES STONE

"**Just be** sure of your stroke, son."

Only I could hear my father's words over the jeers of the crowd. He knelt down before me and nodded to indicate he was ready. Calmly he raised his head, extending his neck to give me a wider target.

My right arm felt suddenly weak, and my grip on the sword my father had given me for my fifteenth birthday was becoming slippery with sweat. I knew he was no traitor. No one had served King Tenal so faithfully, so long, as had my father. Even as others whispered that the king had fallen to madness, Father's lips formed no ill word. He had lived to serve the king, but now stood condemned to die, convicted of treason by the mouth of the king himself—no trial necessary, no appeal possible.

I did not feel I could do this. But what choice did I have?

The son of a traitor has the taint of treason in his blood,

which can only be cleansed if the son executes his father. If the son cannot do it, he proves his own treason and joins his father in death. But my father had foreclosed that option: "You must remove the taint of treason from our family so that you can care for your mother and sisters. It is your duty to them, and the final duty you owe to me."

Perhaps the king was mad, but my father was his oldest friend and closest advisor. King Tenal had been like an uncle to me; as a child I'd sat on his lap countless times as he told me stories of the battles he and my father had fought together. He wouldn't really make me kill my father. I refused to believe that.

Turning away from my father, I knelt before the king. "Your Majesty, by your word is my father condemned to die at my hand. He has accepted your sentence, and has not spoken against it. Does this not prove he is loyal to Your Majesty? Will you not show him mercy?"

The jeers trickled to silence. The king's eyelids closed, and he muttered while bobbing his head. Snapping his eyes open, he said, "Are you . . . questioning the justice of our sentence?"

My heart fell. There was no mercy in that stare. Knowing I was a knife's edge from joining my father, I said, "Your Majesty's word is law. At your command I will slay my father."

Suddenly, King Tenal's eyes rolled up, his eyelids fluttering. A shudder ran from crown to boot and his back arched in a spasm. Two of his guards reached out and grabbed his arms to prevent him from falling out of his throne, while the royal omnimancer swiftly clapped a hand to the king's forehead and began muttering.

Then, as abruptly as it had started, it was over. He returned his gaze to me as if nothing had happened. "You spoke of mercy," he said. "Yes, perhaps it is time we showed mercy."

I stood motionless, hardly daring to breathe. Was it possible that the omnimancer's treatment had brought the king back to some measure of sanity?

Standing unsteadily, he seized a goblet from a courtier. "We will let the gods decide whether this traitor deserves mercy. We will pour this goblet of wine over his head. If he does not get wet, we shall spare his life." The king giggled and snorted as he came toward my father and me. Courtiers laughed hesitantly, but the crowd roared as the king upended the goblet, the wine spattering like blood over my father's upraised face.

"Well, it appears the gods have spoken. Execute him." Dropping the goblet, the king returned to his throne.

I stood before my father. Though wine ran in rivulets down his face, there were no tears to dilute it. "Tell your mother I love her and was thinking of her. Now carry out your duty." His voice was low but steady.

Blinking the tears from my eyes so I could see clearly to strike, I positioned my sword by his neck and drew it back. If I struck swiftly and cleanly, he would feel no pain.

I held my sword high, waiting hopelessly for a final word from the king to stay me.

"Do it." The king's words were taken up as a chant by the crowd.

I swung my sword. My father was not a traitor. The blade sliced smoothly through his neck. My father had not been a traitor. His head fell back as his body toppled forward, his blood spraying my legs—his blood untainted by treason. For generation after generation, my family's blood had never been tainted by thought of treason.

Never.

Until now.

Afterword by Eric James Stone

This story began as an exercise in a creative writing class taught by Caleb Warnock: *Show, don't tell, a person with dignity.*

I thought about various situations in which a character might show dignity, and I decided on a man facing execution. I started writing the scene without knowing much about any of the characters, except for the fact that the man being executed was going to show dignity.

As I wrote, I decided that the executioner would be a young man, new to the business of execution. The prisoner would be an old man, and would actually give friendly advice to his executioner. So I wrote the line "Just be sure of your stroke, son." (I later moved that line to the beginning.)

And then it hit me—this was not just an old man calling a young man "son." This was a father talking to his actual son.

But why was the son executing the father? I came up with the idea that it was to cleanse the taint of treason from his family, and the rest of the story flowed from that.

Originally, I envisioned a much longer story, one that followed the young man over several years as he planned and eventually carried out his treason. But Caleb pointed out that nothing in that plot could match the power of the moment when the son is forced to kill his father. So I ended it there.

The inevitable overthrow of the king is left as an exercise for the reader's imagination.

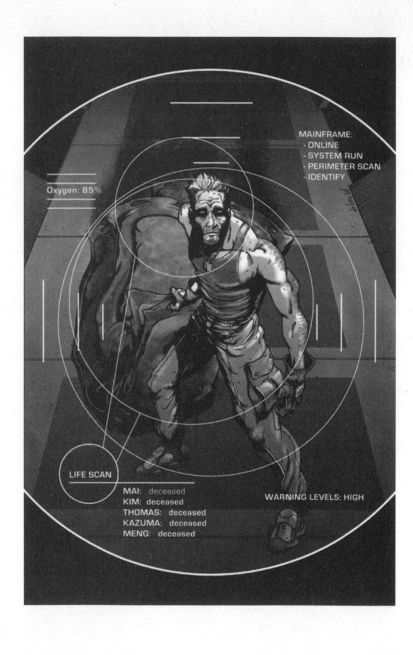

Call Me Mr. Positive

BY TOM BARLOW

Day 1,688

It was my watch. Every time I wake from deep sleep, I have a moment of panic, convinced I've slept through some event that has changed the course of human history. My father never forgave himself for falling asleep in his recliner and missing the president's announcement of our first contact with an alien race. Fortunately, though, most human change is as agonizingly gradual as interstellar flight.

This was my ninth awake period of the voyage, and we'd built up so much velocity that little news from Earth could catch up to us. Although I'd been in deep sleep for six months, there was only a couple of weeks' worth of news in the queue. No personal messages: That's why I was in the service to begin with. No strings.

I've lived long enough to differentiate "news" from the

reiterations of the same old human comedy. People continue to create arbitrary groups so they can fight with people in other arbitrary groups. Those who have a lot continue to try to convince those that have nothing that universal laws are to blame. Meanwhile, people keep butting their heads against those universal laws, and damned if they aren't beginning to bend. Once I deleted items like those from the message queue, there was nothing left.

I selected some music and soon had the cabin rocking. Control preferred it quiet, but I figured by the time I actually *heard* something mechanical going wrong in the Unit, I'd probably be dead anyway. That's what it's like in space; you're either bored to tears or being sucked into a vacuum. There's not much in-between.

These kinds of things were going through my mind, which is my piss-poor excuse for not checking on the others right away. I waited for my head to clear and my heart rate to stabilize. I showered. I had a cup of tea and a biscuit. I turned the volume up some more. Control could kiss my ass.

Then I looked at the service log.

We had a cute little routine with the service log. None of us had been awake at the same time since we left five years ago. There were six of us, and we each had to be awake for a week every six months, since that's the longest you can safely stay in deep sleep without working your muscles, eating real food, and getting some REM sleep and sexual release. (Yeah, I made that last one up. Not proven, but try to find a spacer that disagrees.) Because Control wants the Unit checked as frequently as possible, we stagger our awake periods. Because Control is stingy with the food and O_2, they restrict us to the minimum time awake.

So we spend a good portion of our waking periods composing witty log entries for one another. Unfortunately, Mai Mu, who precedes me in the rotation, thinks she's an artist and often fills page after page with her sketches. They resemble a child's picture of an elephant, every part of the body in a different scale. Or maybe Picasso.

Nonetheless, I look forward to them. Solitude lowers your expectations.

This time, no drawings. No Kuro Kazuma's haikus. None of Meng's ruminations on Goethe. No performances by Sir Thomas, who'd carefully hidden his cello the day we embarked because he knew I'd jettison it as an act of compassion for composers everywhere.

No laundry list of duties, staff evaluations, plans, or way-over-my-head technical notes from Captain Kim.

That's when I thought to check on their well-being.

Until that moment, I never realized that somewhere deep inside, I harbored the belief that losing five friends at once wouldn't be five times as bad as losing one. I suppose it was doughnut thinking; the first one is great, the fifth is blah.

It's not true. As soon as I saw the first body, I knew the rest would be dead. The readouts were there in plain sight, right in front of me when I woke up, but I hadn't bothered to look. I had just assumed everything was all right. Things couldn't be any less right.

I checked them over one at a time anyway. Every one hurt just as much as the first, or maybe more.

They weren't smashed-faceplate dead. They were peaceful-sleep dead. They looked like they'd died at about the same time, and not too long ago; there wasn't a great deal of decomposition.

I'm not a medicine man, but we've all had some basic training, including reading the diagnostics. So after I cried a while, ate a big bowl of spaghetti and half a dozen brownies (supplies being suddenly abundant), and received permission from myself to postpone the burial detail, I checked the medical histories.

They didn't tell me a lot. It was as if their bodily functions, already dialed back by deep sleep to the minimum necessary to sustain recoverable normal life, had just drifted away. The heart rates dropped smoothly from twelve to zero over the course of several hours. The troughs of the brain waves got wider and wider. Body temperature only fell about twenty degrees, to room temperature. I got excited for a minute when I saw the line on the chart start to go back up slightly; then I realized it was the heat of putrefaction.

The life support system seemed to have malfunctioned. The emergency protocols didn't kick in until they were almost dead. The stimulants, then the shocks, over and over again, only sent them into exaggerated cycles, until a cycle overlapped death. After that, we were just injecting and shocking meat.

I made a mental note to suggest to Control that the pods be equipped to automatically crash-refrigerate the dead until they could be returned to Earth.

For now, though, I had to improvise. It would have been very difficult to thread them into their suits, because they were beginning to melt a little, some skin turning slightly gooey. Instead, I removed their dog tags, zipped each into their own duffle bags, lashed them together, and tied them to the outside of the ship. With any luck, they'd still be there, flash frozen, when we got home. Slow acceleration has its good points, I suppose.

It was queer, but I didn't feel as alone then as I had when the bodies were lying next to me. I sent a report back home, although I didn't really need to; the daily readings were automatically fed back to base. There wasn't a damn thing they could do about it anyway.

It is only now, after I've slept real sleep for about two days, that I've begun to consider what comes next.

A lot of redundancy had been built into our mission. Six of us had been sent on what was essentially a two-man mission, so that we had a backup crew and a back-backup crew, just in case. We carried enough provisions for twice our anticipated time in space. At the time, I thought it was overkill. I've since changed my mind.

I'm in a quandary about resuming deep sleep. If I keep my normal rotation, the Unit would be unmonitored for six months at a time, rather than a few weeks. We could drift irretrievably off course in six months. If I don't hibernate, I'll burn up at least fifteen bioyears twiddling my thumbs alone in a thirty-cubic-meter room with nothing but my doppelgänger to keep me company.

OK, truth is, that isn't foremost in my thoughts. Fear is. I'm scared to death of returning to my pod. I'm obsessing over the fact that there are five dead people outside, who died in deep sleep for no discernible reason. If I were a gambler, I know where I'd place my bet on the viability of the sixth crew member, once he goes back under.

Day 1,692

Control equipped Mainframe with a huge entertainment library. It's come as a surprise to me just how useless that collection is. I've tried all kinds: 3-D, 2-D, role playing, fantasy. I can only take a few minutes of any of them, though. The more images of people I see, the lonelier I become. Like pornography.

Day 1,694

Tomorrow I'm scheduled to go back into deep sleep. I spent today reviewing what I know of celestial mechanics. All I accomplished was confirming that, left to my own devices, I couldn't find my own ass with two hands and a road map. I also spent some time reading up on alcohol stills and inventorying the drug supplies.

I know it doesn't matter anyway. I can't turn around now: not enough fuel. We need the mass of that sun to swing the Unit around without losing all of our momentum.

What is most frustrating is that the trip will be for naught. The original plan had some of us taking the excursion vehicle down to the planet as we passed it on our way into the system, then rendezvousing with the Unit on its way back out. Now it's going to be like walking past a pastry shop window without a penny in my pocket. A twenty-year walk.

I field-stripped a couple of the pods right down to the chassis. I found nothing. I checked the air feed and reclamation system. It was A–OK. The nutrition system worked flawlessly. I didn't see anything in the blood-monitoring system records.

Day 1,695

I actually got to the point of getting dressed, sliding into my pod, and laying my head down on the pillow. Then panic set in. I couldn't close the lid.

The faceplate looked like a giant hand about to close over my mouth. The skin jets looked like snake fangs. The rush of cool air felt like I'd stepped on somebody's grave.

Day 1,696

I began going through each of the crew's personal possessions, looking for clues or direction or, really, companionship. I started with the captain, since *I* was the captain now, and I needed some tips about maintaining crew discipline.

Captain Kim's locker confirmed my impression that he was the world's most boring man. There was almost nothing in his kit that wasn't military issue: no family pics, no diary, no awards, no jujus, no candy, no jewelry, no bronzed baby shoes. At first, all I saw was regulation clothes, an elaborate shoe-shining kit, and some old manuals from the Academy.

At the bottom of the drawer, though, I found a neck chain. There were fifteen dog tags on it. They weren't dated, but from the patina and, more importantly, by the sequence of political entities they fought for, I could see that they stretched back at least three hundred years. Kim after Kim after Kim, marching, drinking, whoring, fighting, dying in the service of the country du jour.

I took his tag off the chain around my neck and added it to his.

Day 1,697

Today I went through Sir Thomas's effects. If Kim was parsimonious, Tom was profligate. He had a marvelous hand-carved wood chess set, a Go board with moonstone and hematite pieces, an antique cardboard backgammon board, tiny playing cards featuring the faces of famous composers, and a painted sheet-metal Chinese checkers board with exquisite stone marbles. I found that disheartening; the games all took at least two people to play.

I carefully leafed through his prized sheet music collection, browned and flaking at the edges, carefully preserved in plastic sleeves. None of it was more recent than the twentieth century.

For some reason he had also packed his performance outfit, a tailored black suit, ruffled white shirt, and black boots with shiny brass buckles. Perhaps he thought he might run across an alien civilization that didn't know his reputation yet.

He also had brought a scrapbook of his performance programs, which dated back to when he was about ten. He'd never played large or prestigious venues, but rarely were there six months between performances, except when he was in the Academy or in space. I hadn't properly credited the sacrifice it must have been for him to spend years with an audience of five.

He told me before we left that, like it or not, he'd be playing for all of us, a week each six months. Since we would be asleep, there was nothing we could do about it.

"If you could just applaud," he'd said, "you'd be the perfect audience."

I knew he couldn't hear me, since he was floating outside, but I clapped for a while anyway.

Day 1,699

Opened Mai Mu's locker yesterday, but I didn't feel like writing about it for a while.

I expected to find it jammed with bad art. I'd seen the sketches, of course, but whenever we talked, which was a lot during our prep since we were often teamed up (we weighed about the same), she talked about all the other art she did: sculpture, ceramics, glass, wood carving. She made it all sound massive.

There was, in fact, a lot of art, but very little of it hers. Half of the locker was filled with exquisite miniatures of famous sculptures, each about fifteen centimeters tall. It wasn't that I recognized them all, but the name of the piece and artist was engraved on each base. There was the *Burghers of Calais* by Rodin, Modigliani's *Head,* Donatello's *St. George and the Dragon,* Noguchi's *Mother and Child, Brushstrokes in Flight* by Lichtenstein, and others. Each was in its own wood case. Each of the bases was a little worn, like someone had held it in her hands for a long, long time.

She was also a diarist, but wrote in Chinese. I couldn't read it, but Mainframe could.

I never knew she felt that way about me. She seemed so assured, so professional, so decisive, so damned competent. I could have gone the rest of my life not knowing how she was attracted to me, or feeling the regret that came with that knowledge.

Day 1,700

Today I went through Kuro Kazuma's things.

What a slob. I hate cockroaches, and thanks to his habit of hoarding crumbly cookies, we had them. You know what's worse than stepping on a roach when you walk into the kitchen without turning on the light? Waking up with one floating an inch from your mouth, and not knowing if it was arriving or leaving.

Luckily, we had enough spin to keep the crumbs from floating away, so I shook out his stuff and swept up what fell.

He had a lot of civvies for a military guy. I had a hunch he didn't bother to wear his uniform when he was awake alone. I can't say much, since I usually don't wear anything at all when I'm the only one awake.

He had some strange-looking outfits, historical stuff. There were several silk robes, which were entirely too small for me; he was a slight man. There were a couple of hats. The bright green silk fez fit me just fine.

At the bottom of his locker was a sword in a heavy leather scabbard. The long curved handle was ivory, elaborately carved with dragon heads, tails, talons, and little people in various stages of being devoured. I carefully drew the blade. It sounded sharp against the sheath, utterly smooth and foreboding.

The blade was greased to keep it from corroding. I wiped it off with one of his socks. I almost took my thumb off when I let my hand stray too close to the edge, so I had to take a half-hour break to administer first aid. Five minutes for the bandaging, twenty-five to work up the courage to look at the blood. We all have our demons.

The sword was amazingly heavy, the steel beaten so dense it felt like an anvil. I cautiously took a few swings the way I'd seen in old martial arts entertainments, and managed to neatly slice the cable to the backup environment monitor, which caused the primary monitor to immediately start whooping like a drunken cowboy. I put the sword away before I put a hole in the hull.

There were some photos in an envelope taped to the lid. I pulled them out and spread them on the floor. There was nothing written on the back of any of them, and they were mostly close-ups, so I couldn't really tell who they were by context. Many may have been of him, but could just as easily have been his ancestors. I wished I knew something about him, but we'd never really talked about ourselves. We were too busy with the jokes, trying to outdo one other, each trying to capture the audience. I tried to remember one of his jokes, but for the life of me, I couldn't. What's worse, I couldn't even remember any of my own.

Day 1,701

Last locker. Meng Ruixun. Probably the person I knew the best, since I almost married his sister, until it dawned on me that she was a raving lunatic. Meng had tried to warn me, but she had such a cute overbite I couldn't hear him.

He was the world's worst poker player, so I'd spent a lot of time in college playing cards with him. He had the money to spare, since his mother built the biggest specialty metals business on the planet.

In return, I helped him learn Western literature. I did such a good job that he soon made me feel like a dilettante. He was one of those people that could quote Goethe or Yeats or Kim-Juan off the top of his head. I can do it with commercials, but that doesn't impress people so much.

He was that way about anything he tackled: consumed. He gathered information about a topic like a whale sucks in krill.

When I found out he'd been assigned to the team, I was flabbergasted. I couldn't believe the Service would squander such talent on what would most likely be a wild goose chase.

He was convinced that he deserved a slot in the Unit, though. When we received that famous transmission, which confusingly seemed to arrive from five widely dispersed solar systems simultaneously, he didn't sleep for almost a week. It was his wild-ass theory about what it meant that prevailed after all the other wild-ass theories had been discredited. It was his research that found a way to assign probabilities to each of the systems as the true source of the signal. We were lucky that the closest system turned out to also be the most probable, because it was the only one we'd be able to reach.

In his locker, I found a letter from his mother. She'd made sure, before he left, to let him know what a burden he had placed on her heart by asking her to pull the strings necessary to get him assigned to the mission. She put it all down on paper so that he could refer back to it whenever his guilt started to slip.

I wasn't surprised to find poetry. I knew he'd been writing since he was a teenager, but he'd never shown it to anyone. After I read it, I understood why.

It wasn't bad. It wasn't good. It was poetry written by someone who thought too clearly, who always knew the route from point A to point B and never got lost.

It was, however, intensely revealing. With all the scholarship and accomplishments, he'd still found time to stop and doubt the hell out of himself.

The hardest thing was the smell. Meng had a penchant for musky, sandalwoody cologne, and it permeated his locker. It reminded me, as nothing else could, of cookouts on his patio, holding his head while he puked Coors in the dorm head, bounce-racing on Mars.

Speak of the devil—he had a bottle of Coors in the bottom of his locker. He also had a dozen empties, which disappointed me. I'd have shared with him, if I'd thought to bring some. Probably.

I waited until later in the day, after dinner, before I cracked open the beer. I sipped it all evening, toasting Meng, savoring the flavor and the memories.

Day 1,708

20 (Earth) days down. 480 (Earth) hours. 28,800 (Earth) minutes. 5.4% of a (Earth) year.

About 5,475 days left. 131,400 hours. 7,884,000 minutes. 0.36% of the remaining journey in the bag already; only 99.64% to go.

No, wait, we have an update: 7,883,999 minutes. The multiplication took me a minute.

I'm going out of my mind, which is a short walk to begin with.

Day 1,715

Since I have all day, every day, to devote to it, you'd think I could keep a decent journal. But there's something less than satisfying about recording your thoughts and actions when all you think about is how bored you are and all you do is eat, evacuate, and count the hours until bedtime.

I tried to figure out how long it would be before I could expect a reply from Earth to my incident report, but the math is still beyond me. The computer knows, but I don't know how to phrase the question. I know it'll be years, not days. Years.

Day 1,718

Maybe you thought things couldn't get much worse. I sure did. But now, I can't sleep. I've been awake for over forty-eight hours. When I'm sitting up, I feel like I'm about to pass out, but as soon as I lie down my eyes pop open like sunny-side-up eggs.

I've gotten to the point that I can watch entertainments again without intense longing, but I've lost the ability to be amused. I've discovered that the joy of the audience depends on being able to imagine, if only in the most tangential way, sharing the experiences of the characters. I've lost the capacity to pretend.

Day 1,720

Some things you might not know about space travel:

—Despite traveling through mostly vacuum, the window gets dirty.

—It's apparently cheaper to spray the food with an agent that numbs your taste buds than to make it delicious.

—Just because they spend billions and billions to build a ship, that doesn't guarantee the speakers will be worth a shit.

—If I do find an alien civilization, I'm going to ask them for an air freshener.

—Like they say about all the sled dogs except the one in front, the view is always the same.

Day 1,723

Blah, blah, blah, blah.

Day 1,724

It took me hours to screw up my courage, but I went back outside today. I needed to look into the faces of my friends again, to see if they'd died peacefully. As I did, I realized I had nothing to compare it to except my imagination.

Day 1,725

I've run out of things to put in the log. If you have a problem with that, complain to the morale officer.

In fact, if you're reading this, then you probably have corpses to deal with, so why are you screwing around? The Exec Comm is going to tell you to burn the log anyway. Nobody wants to admit they allow juveniles like me into the space service.

Just bury us as a crew and pretend we died together.

If you aren't reading this, then maybe I survived.

Day 1,728

A strange thought popped into my head this morning: Even Jesus only had to spend forty days in the wilderness.

Where that came from, I have no idea; I haven't seen the inside of a church in twenty years, and even out here between the stars, I don't sense any divine presence, just emptiness. If I were a believer, though, I might come to the conclusion that I'd been spared for a good reason: to mourn my friends' deaths. Everybody deserves to be mourned.

I hadn't admitted it to myself yet, but I was finally ready to get in the pod. Afraid my courage would evaporate if I looked at it too carefully, I let my mind go blank as I dressed and prepped the pod. I slid in, and was about to close the lid, but I couldn't shake the notion that I'd left something unfinished.

I got up and wrote these words so that the log has some sort of an ending, in case things don't turn out well. I've always hated books that end "To be continued."

I thought long and hard about these, perhaps my last words. I was looking for something profound, something you could carve on my gravestone if you want to, but couldn't think of anything. Only that I'd rather be floating dead through space with five of my friends than be alive and alone.

See you in six months. Call me Mr. Positive.

The end.

You know what's funny? The cabin? It has a night light.

Afterword by Tom Barlow

I imagine, if a person came into consciousness in the womb, he would conclude that the universe is a water-filled bag only slightly larger than his body, with a shape he could adjust with a few well-placed kicks. Or perhaps he wouldn't arrive at the concept of "me" at all, since he would have no awareness of "other."

Unfortunately, as soon as the door opens and he's rudely shoved out of his universe, he becomes aware of the other, usually via a slap on the rear end. And there's no going back.

Sartre wrote, in *No Exit,* "Hell is other people," but I think that misses the point a bit. Hell is our need for other people. Being social animals, once we identify the others, we live forever after in denial of, or acquiescence to, our yearning for them; thus the appeal of the cinematic loner, free of such shackles (and therefore something different than human; better or worse, I can't say). This is, I think, what causes us to bond together so closely in perilous circumstances, forging fellowship with people that in our normal lives we would regard with little more attention than we give to an ear of fresh corn. Note the lack of fisticuffs among residents of the space station, compared to the antics of *Big Brother* participants.

Of course, the lonely on Earth have reason to hope that over the next hill, beyond the next wave, when the sun comes up, they will stumble upon another person. With six billion souls infesting the planet, solitude is a state that must be sought.

Outer space is a different story—this story, in fact. Once man leaves the cocoon of Earth, he/she knows for sure, positively, that there is no possibility of chance encounter. Deep space travel is as close to absolute loneliness as it is to absolute zero. That, I thought, would make it the perfect setting in which to explore the depth of our attachment to one another, and what a man would sacrifice to avoid absolute solitude. As Plato said, "Death is not the worst thing than can happen to men."

One of those worse things is returning to the womb, as our hero does, only to realize he may never again be unaware of the universe outside.

T. S. Eliot said it much more eloquently, in *Four Quartets*:

We shall not cease from exploration
And the end of all our exploring
Will be to arrive where we started
And know the place for the first time.

A Young Man with Prospects
BY ORSON SCOTT CARD

"**Do you** know what I did today, Alessandra?"

"No, Mother." Thirteen-year-old Alessandra set her book bag on the floor by the front door and walked past her mother to the sink, where she poured herself a glass of water.

"Guess!"

"Got the electricity turned back on?"

"The elves would not speak to me," said Mother. It had once been funny, this game that electricity came from elves. But it wasn't funny now, in the sweltering Adriatic summer, with no refrigeration for the food, no air-conditioning, and no vids to distract her from the heat.

"Then I don't know what you did, Mother."

"I changed our lives," said Mother. "I created a future for us."

Alessandra froze in place and uttered a silent prayer. She

had long since given up hope that any of her prayers would be answered, but she figured each unanswered prayer would add to the list of grievances she would take up with God, should the occasion arise.

"What future is that, Mother?"

Mother could hardly contain herself. "We are going to be colonists."

Alessandra sighed with relief. She had heard all about the Dispersal Project in school. Now that the Formics had been destroyed, the idea was for humans to colonize all their former worlds, so that humanity's fate would not be tied to that of a single planet. But the requirements for colonists were strict. There was no chance that an unstable, irresponsible—no, pardon me, I meant "feckless and fey"—person like Mother would be accepted.

"Well, Mother, that's wonderful."

"You don't *sound* excited."

"It takes a long time for an application to be approved. Why would they take us? What do we know how to do?"

"You're such a pessimist, Alessandra. You'll have no future if you must frown at every new thing." Mother danced around her, holding a fluttering piece of paper in front of her. "I put in our application *months* ago, darling Alessandra. Today I got word that we have been accepted!"

"You kept a secret for all this time?"

"I can keep secrets," said Mother. "I have all kinds of secrets. But this is no secret, this piece of paper says that we will journey to a new world, and on that new world you will not be part of a persecuted surplus, you will be needed, all your talents and charms will be noticed and admired."

All her talents and charms. At the coleggio, no one seemed

to notice them. She was merely another gawky girl, all arms
and legs, who sat in the back and did her work and made no
waves. Only Mother thought of Alessandra as some extraordinary, magical creature.

"Mother, may I read that paper?" asked Alessandra.

"Why, do you doubt me?" Mother danced away with the
letter.

Alessandra was too hot and tired to play. She did not chase
after her. "Of course I doubt you."

"You are no fun today, Alessandra."

"Even if it's true, it's a horrible idea. You should have asked
me. Do you know what colonists' lives will be like? Sweating
in the fields as farmers."

"Don't be silly," said Mother. "They have machines for
that."

"And they're not sure we can eat any of the native vegetation. When the Formics first attacked Earth, they simply destroyed all the vegetation in the part of China where they
landed. They had no intention of eating anything that grew
here naturally. We don't know if our plants can grow on their
planets. All the colonists might die."

"The survivors of the fleet that defeated the Formics will
already have those problems resolved by the time we get
there."

"Mother," said Alessandra patiently. "I don't want to go."

"That's because you have been convinced by the dead
souls at the school that you are an ordinary child. But you are
not. You are magical. You must get away from this world of
dust and misery and go to a land that is green and filled with
ancient powers. We will live in the caves of the dead ogres and
go out to harvest the fields that once were theirs! And in the

cool evening, with sweet green breezes fluttering your skirts, you will dance with young men who gasp at your beauty and grace!"

"And where will we find young men like *that*?"

"You'll see," said Mother. Then she sang it: "You shall see! You shall see! A fine young man with prospects will give his heart to you."

Finally the paper fluttered close enough for Alessandra to snatch it out of Mother's hands. She read it, with Mother bending down to hover just behind the paper, smiling her fairy smile. It was real. Dorabella Toscano (29) and daughter Alessandra Toscano (14), accepted into Colony I.

"Obviously there's no sort of psychological screening after all," said Alessandra.

"You try to hurt me but I will not be hurt. Mother knows what is best for you. You shall not make the mistakes that I have made."

"No, but I'll pay for them," said Alessandra.

"Think, my darling, beautiful, brilliant, graceful, kind, generous, and poutful girl, think of this: What do you have to look forward to here in Monopoli, Italia, living in a flat in the unfashionable end of Via Luigi Indelli?"

"There is no *fashionable* end of Luigi Indelli."

"You make my point for me."

"Mother, I don't dream of marrying a prince and riding off into the sunset."

"That's a good thing, my darling, because there are no princes—only men and animals who pretend to be men. I married one of the latter but he at least provided you with the genes for those amazing cheekbones, that dazzling smile. Your father had very good teeth."

"If only he had been a more attentive bicyclist."

"It was not his fault, dear."

"The streetcars run on tracks, Mother. You don't get hit if you stay out from between the tracks."

"Your father was not a genius but fortunately I am, and therefore you have the blood of the fairies in you."

"Who knew that fairies sweat so much?" Alessandra pulled one of Mother's dripping locks of hair away from her face. "Oh, Mother, we won't do well in a colony. Please don't do this."

"The voyage takes forty years—I went next door and looked it up on the net."

"Did you *ask* them this time?"

"Of course I did, they lock their windows now. They were thrilled to hear we were going to be colonists."

"I have no doubt they were."

"But because of magic, to us it will be only two years."

"Because of the relativistic effects of near-lightspeed travel."

"Such a genius, my daughter is. And even those two years we can sleep through, so we won't even age."

"Much."

"It will be as if our bodies slept a week, and we wake up forty years away."

"And everyone we know on Earth will be forty years older than we are."

"And mostly dead," sang Mother. "Including *my* hideous hag of a mother, who disowned me when I married the man I loved, and who therefore will never get her hands on my darling daughter." The melody to this refrain was always cheery-sounding. Alessandra had never met her grandmother. Now, though, it occurred to her that maybe a grandmother could get her out of joining a colony.

"I'm not going, Mother."

"You are a minor child and you will go where I go, tra-la."

"You are a madwoman and I will sue for emancipation rather than go, tra-lee."

"You will think about it first because I am going whether you go or not and if you think your life with me is hard you should see what it's like without me."

"Yes, I should," said Alessandra. "Let me meet my grandmother." Mother's glare was immediate, but Alessandra plowed ahead. "Let me live with her. You go with the colony."

"But there's no reason for me to go with the colony, my darling. I'm doing this for you. So without you, I will not go."

"Then we're not going. Tell them."

"We *are* going, and we are thrilled about it."

Might as well get off the merry-go-round; Mother didn't mind endlessly repeating circular arguments, but Alessandra got bored with it. "What lies did you have to tell, to get accepted?"

"I told no lies," said Mother, pretending to be shocked at the accusation. "I only proved my identity. They do all the research, so if they have false information it's their own fault. Do you know why they want us?"

"Do *you*?" asked Alessandra. "Did they actually tell you?"

"It doesn't take a genius to figure it out, or even a fairy," said Mother. "They want us because we are both of child-bearing age."

Alessandra groaned in disgust, but Mother was preening in front of an imaginary full-length mirror.

"I am still young," said Mother, "and you are just flowering into womanhood. They have men from the fleet there, young men who have never married. They will be waiting eagerly for us to arrive. So I will mate with a very eager old man of sixty and bear him babies and then he will die. I'm used to that. But you—you will be a prize for a young man to marry. You will be a treasure."

"My *uterus* will, you mean," said Alessandra. "You're right, that's exactly what they're thinking. I bet they took practically any healthy female who applied."

"We fairies are always healthy."

It was true enough—Alessandra had no memory of ever being sick, except for food poisoning that time when Mother insisted they would eat supper from a street vendor's cart at the end of a very hot day.

"So they're sending a herd of women, like cows."

"You're only a cow if you choose to be," said Mother. "The only question I have to decide now is whether we want to sleep through the voyage and wake up just before landing, or stay awake for the two years, receiving training and acquiring skills so we're ready to be productive in the first wave of colonists."

Alessandra was impressed. "You actually read the documentation?"

"This is the most important decision of our lives, my darling Alessa. I am being extraordinarily careful."

"If only you had read the bills from the power company."

"They were not interesting. They only spoke of our poverty. Now I see that God was preparing us for a world without air-conditioning and vids and nets. A world of nature. We were born for nature, we elvish folk. You will come to the dance, and with your fairy grace you will charm the son of the king, and the king's son will dance with you until he is so in love his heart will break for you. Then it will be for *you* to decide if he's the one for you."

"I doubt there'll be a king."

"But there'll be a governor. And other high officials. And young men with prospects. I will help you choose."

"You will certainly *not* help me choose."

"It's as easy to fall in love with a rich man as a poor one."

"As if you'd know."

"I know better than you, having done it badly once. The rush of hot blood into the heart is the darkest magic, and it must be tamed. You must not let it happen until you have chosen a man worthy of your love. I will help you choose."

No point in arguing. Alessandra had long since learned that fighting with Mother accomplished nothing, whereas ignoring her worked very well.

Except for this. A colony. It was definitely time to look up Grandmother. She lived in Polignano a Mare, the next city of any size up the Adriatic coast, that's all that she knew of her. And Mother's mother would not be named Toscano. Alessandra would have to do some serious research.

A week later, Mother was still going back and forth about whether they should sleep through the voyage or not, while Alessandra was discovering that there's a lot of information that they won't let children get at. Snooping in the house, she found her own birth certificate, but that wasn't helpful; it only listed her own parents. She needed Mother's certificate, and that was not findable in the apartment.

The government people barely acknowledged she existed, and when they heard her errand they sent her away. It was only when she finally thought of the Catholic church that she made any headway. They hadn't actually attended Mass since Alessandra was little, but at the parish, the priest on duty helped her search back to find her own baptism. They had a record of baby Alessandra Toscano's godparents as well as her parents, and Alessandro figured that either the godparents *were* her grandparents, or they would know who her grandparents were.

At school she searched the net and found that Leopoldo and Isabella Santangelo lived in Polignano a Mare, which was a good sign, since that was the town where Grandmother lived.

Instead of going home, she used her student pass and hopped the train to Polignano and then spent forty-five minutes walking around the town searching for the address. To her disgust, it ended up being on a stub of a street just off Via Antonio Ardito, a trashy-looking apartment building backing on the train tracks. There was no buzzer. Alessandra trudged up to the fourth floor and knocked.

"You want to knock something, knock your own head!" shouted a woman from inside.

"Are you Isabella Santangelo?"

"I'm the Holy Virgin and I'm busy answering prayers. Go away!"

Alessandra's first thought was: So Mother lied about being a child of the fairies. She's really Jesus' younger sister.

But she decided that flippancy wasn't a good approach today. She was already going to be in trouble for leaving Monopoli without permission, and she needed to find out from the Holy Virgin here whether or not she was her grandmother.

"I'm so sorry to trouble you, but I'm the daughter of Dorabella Toscano and I—"

The woman must have been standing right at the door,

waiting, because it flew open before Alessandra could finish her sentence.

"Dorabella *Toscano* is a dead woman! How can a dead woman have daughters!"

"My mother isn't dead," said Alessandra, stunned. "You were signed as my godmother on the parish register."

"That was the worst mistake of my life. She marries this pig boy, this bike messenger, when she's barely fifteen, and why? Because her belly's getting fat with you, that's why! She thinks a wedding makes it all clean and pure! And then her idiot husband gets himself killed. I told her, this proves there is a God! Now go to hell!"

The door slammed in Alessandra's face.

She had come so far. Her grandmother couldn't really mean to send her away like this. They hadn't even had time to do more than *glance* at each other.

"But I'm your granddaughter," said Alessandra.

"How can I have a granddaughter when I have no daughter? You tell your mother that before she sends her little quasi-bastard begging at my door, she'd better come to me herself with some serious apologizing."

"She's going away to a colony," said Alessandra.

The door was yanked open again. "She's even more insane than ever," said Grandmother. "Come in. Sit down. Tell me what stupid thing she's done."

The apartment was absolutely neat. Everything in it was unbelievably cheap, the lowest possible quality, but there was a lot of it—ceramics, tiny framed art pieces—and everything had been dusted and polished. The sofa and chairs were so piled with quilts and throws and twee little embroidered pillows that there was nowhere to sit. Grandmother Isabella moved nothing, and finally Alessandra sat on top of one of the pillow piles.

Feeling suddenly quite disloyal and childish herself, telling on Mother like a schoolyard tattletale, Alessandra now tried to softpedal the outrage. "She has her reasons, I know it, and I think she truly believes she's doing it for me—"

"What what what is she doing for you that you don't want her to do! I don't have all day!"

The woman who embroidered all of these pillows has all day *every* day. But Alessandra kept her sassy remark to herself. "She has signed us up for a colony ship, and they accepted us."

"A colony ship? There aren't any colonies. All those places have countries of their own now. Not that Italy ever *did* have any real colonies, not since the Roman Empire. Lost their balls after that, the men did. Italian men have been worthless ever since. Your grandfather, God keep him buried, was worthless enough, never stood up for himself, let everybody push him around, but at least he worked hard and provided for me until my ungrateful daughter spat in my face and married that bike boy. Not like that worthless father of yours, never made a dime."

"Well, not since he died, anyway," said Alessandra, feeling more than a little outraged.

"I'm talking about when he was alive! He only worked the fewest hours he could get by with. I think he was on drugs. You were probably a cocaine baby."

"I don't think so."

"How would *you* know anything?" said Grandmother. "You couldn't even talk then!"

Alessandra sat and waited.

"Well? Tell me."

"I did, but you wouldn't believe me."

"What was it you said?"

"A colony ship. A *starship* to one of the Formic planets, to farm and explore."

"Won't the Formics complain?"

"There aren't any more Formics, Grandmother. They were all killed."

"A nasty piece of business but it needed doing. If that Ender Wiggin boy is available, I've got a list of other people that need some good serious destruction. What do you want, anyway?"

"I don't want to go into space. With Mother. But I'm still a minor. If you would sign as my guardian, I could get emancipated and stay home. It's in the law."

"As your guardian?"

"Yes. To supervise me and provide for me. I'd live here."

"Get out."

"What?"

"Stand up and get out. You think this is a hotel? Where exactly do you think you'd sleep? On the floor, where I'd trip on you in the night and break my hip? There's no room for you here. I should have known you'd be making demands. Out!"

There was no room for argument. In moments Alessandra found herself charging down the stairs, furious and humiliated. This woman was even crazier than Mother.

I have nowhere to go, thought Alessandra. Surely the law doesn't allow my mother to *force* me to go into space, does it? I'm not a baby, I'm not a *child,* I'm fourteen, I can read and write and make rational choices.

When the train got back to Monopoli, Alessandra did not go directly home. She had to think up a good lie about where she'd been, so she might as well come up with one that covered a longer time. Maybe the Dispersal Project office was still open.

But it wasn't. She couldn't even get a brochure. And what was the point? Anything interesting would be on the net. She could have stayed after school and found out all she wanted to know. Instead she went to visit her grandmother.

That's proving what good decisions I make.

Mother was sitting at the table, a cup of chocolate in front of her. She looked up and watched Alessandra shut the door and set down her book bag, but she said nothing.

"Mother, I'm sorry, I—"

"Before you lie," said Mother softly, "the witch called me and screamed at me for sending you. I hung up on her, which is what I usually end up doing, and then I unplugged the phone from the wall."

"I'm sorry," said Alessandra.

"You didn't think I had a *reason* for keeping her out of your life?"

For some reason, that pulled the trigger on something inside Alessandra, and instead of trying to retreat, she erupted. "It doesn't matter whether you had a reason," she said. "You could have ten million reasons, but you didn't tell any of them to me! You expected me to obey you blindly. But you don't obey *your* mother blindly."

"*Your* mother isn't a monster," said Mother.

"There are many kinds of monsters," said Alessandra. "You're the kind that flits around like a butterfly but never lands near me long enough to even know who I am."

"Everything I do is for you!"

"Nothing is for me. Everything is for the child you imagine you had, the one that doesn't exist, the perfect, happy child that was bound to result from your being the exact opposite of your mother in every way. Well, I'm not that child. And in your mother's house, the electricity is on!"

"Then go live there!"

"She won't let me!"

"You would hate it. Never able to touch anything. Always having to do things *her* way."

"Like going off on a colony ship?"

"I signed up for the colony ship *for you.*"

"Which is like buying me a supersized bra. Why don't you look at who I am before you decide what I need?"

"I'll tell you what you are. You're a girl who's too young and inexperienced to know what a woman needs. I'm ten kilometers ahead of you on that road, I know what's coming, I'm trying to get you what you'll need to make that road easy and smooth, and you know what? In spite of you, I've done it. You've fought me every step of the way, but I've done a great job with you. You don't even *know* how good a job I've done because you don't know what you could have been."

"What could I have been, Mother? You?"

"You were never going to be me," said Mother.

"What are you saying? That I would have been *her*?"

"We'll never know what you would have been, will we? Because you already are what I made you."

"Wrong. I *look* like whatever I have to *look* like in order to stay alive in your home. Down inside, what I really am is a complete stranger to you. A stranger that you intend to drag off into space without even asking me if I wanted to go. They used to have a word for people you treated like that. They called them *slaves.*"

Alessandra wanted more than ever before in her life to run

to her bedroom and slam the door. But she didn't have a bed-room. She slept on the sofa in the same room with the kitchen and the kitchen table.

"I understand," said Mother. "I'll go into my bedroom and you can slam the door on me."

The fact that Mother really did know what she was think-ing was the most infuriating thing of all. But Alessandra did not scream and did not scratch at her mother and did not fall on the floor and throw a tantrum and did not even dive onto the sofa and bury her face in the pillow. Instead she sat down at the table directly across from her mother and said, "What's for dinner?"

"So. Just like that, the discussion is over?"

"Discuss while we cook. I'm hungry."

"There's nothing *to* eat, because I haven't turned in our fi-nal acceptance because I haven't decided yet whether we should sleep or stay awake through the voyage, and so we haven't got the signing bonus, and so there's no money to buy food."

"So what are we going to do about dinner?"

Mother just looked away from her.

"I know," said Alessandra excitedly. "Let's go over to Grandma's!"

Mother turned back and glared at her.

"Mother," said Alessandra, "how can we run out of money when we're living on the dole? Other people on the dole man-age to buy enough food and pay their electric bills."

"What do *you* think?" said Mother. "Look around you. What have I spent all the government's money on? Where's all the extravagance? Look in my closet, count the outfits I own."

Alessandra thought for a moment. "I never thought about that. Do you owe money to the mafia? Did Father, before he died?"

"No," said Mother contemptuously. "You now have all the information you need to understand completely, and yet you still haven't figured it out, smart and grown up as you are."

Alessandra couldn't imagine what Mother was talking about. Alessandra didn't have *any* new information. She also didn't have anything to eat.

She got up and started opening cupboards. She found a box of dry radiatori and a jar of black pepper. She took a pan to the sink and put in some water and set it on the stove and turned on the gas.

"There's no sauce for the pasta," said Mother.

"There's pepper. There's oil."

"You can't eat radiatori with just pepper and oil. It's like putting fistfuls of wet flour in your mouth."

"That's not my problem," said Alessandra. "At this point, it's pasta or shoe leather, so you'd better start guarding your closet."

Mother tried to turn things light again. "Of course, just like a daughter, you'd eat *my* shoes."

"Just be glad if I stop before I get to your leg."

Mother pretended she was still joking when she airily said, "Children eat their parents alive, that's what they do."

"Then why is that hideous creature still living in that flat in Polignano a Mare?"

"I broke my teeth on her skin!" It was Mother's last attempt at humor.

"You tell me what terrible things daughters do, but you're a daughter, too. Did you do them?"

"I married the first man who showed me any hint of what kindness and pleasure could be. I married stupidly."

"I have half the genes of the man you married," said Ales-

sandra. "Is that why I'm too stupid to decide what planet I want
to live on?"

"It's obvious that you want to live on any planet where I
am not."

"You're the one who came up with the colony idea, not me!
But now I think you've named your *own* reason. Yes! You want
to colonize another planet because *your* mother isn't there!"

Mother slumped in her seat. "Yes, that is part of it. I won't
pretend that I wasn't thinking of that as one of the best things
about going."

"So you admit you *weren't* doing it all for me."

"I do not admit such a lie. It's all for you."

"Getting away from your mother, that is for you," said
Alessandra.

"It is for you."

"How can it be for me? Until today I didn't even know
what my grandmother looked like. I had never seen her face. I
didn't even know her name."

"And do you know how much that cost me?" asked
Mother.

"What do you mean?"

Mother looked away. "The water is boiling."

"No, that's my temper you're hearing. Tell me what you
meant. What did it cost *you* to keep *me* from knowing my own
grandmother?"

Mother got up and went into her bedroom and closed the
door.

"You forgot to slam it, Mother! Who's the parent here,
anyway? Who's the one who shows a sense of responsibility?
Who's fixing *dinner*?"

The water took three more minutes before it got to a boil.

Alessandra threw in two fistfuls of radiatori and then got her books and started studying at the table. She ended up over-cooking the pasta and it had been so cheaply made that it clumped up and the oil didn't bind with it. It just pooled on the plate, and the pepper barely helped make it possible to swallow the mess. She kept her eyes on her book and her paper as she ate, and swallowed mechanically until finally the bite in her mouth made her gag and she got up and spat it into the sink and then drank down a glass of water and almost threw the whole mess back up again. As it was, she retched twice at the sink be-fore she was able to get her gorge under control. "Mmmmm, delicious," she murmured. Then she turned back to the table.

Mother was sitting there, picking out a single piece of pasta with her fingers. She put it in her mouth. "What a good mother I am," she said softly.

"I'm doing homework now, Mother. We've already used up our quarreling time."

"Be honest, darling. We almost never quarrel."

"That's true. You flit around ignoring whatever I say, being full of happiness. But believe me, *my* end of the argument is running through my head all the time."

"I'm going to tell you something because you're right, you're old enough to understand things."

Alessandra sat down. "All right, tell me." She looked her mother in the eye.

Mother looked away.

"So you're *not* going to tell me. I'll do my homework."

"I'm going to tell you," said Mother. "I'm just not going to look at you while I do."

"And I won't look at you either." She went back to her homework.

"About ten days into the month, my mother calls me. I answer the phone because if I don't she gets on the train and comes over, and then I have a hard time getting her out of the house before you get home from school. So I answer the phone and she tells me I don't love her, I'm an ungrateful daughter, because here she is all alone in her house, and she's out of money, she can't have anything lovely in her life. Move in with me, she says, bring your beautiful daughter, we can live in my apartment and share our money and then there'll be enough. No, Mama, I say to her. I will not move in with you. And she weeps and screams and says I am a hateful daughter who is tearing all joy and beauty out of her life because I leave her alone and I leave her penniless and so I promise her, I'll send you a little something. She says, Don't send it, that wastes postage, I'll come get it and I say, No, I won't be here, it costs more to ride the train than to mail it, so I'm mailing it. And somehow I get her off the phone before you get home. Then I sit for a while not cutting my wrists, and then I put some amount of money into an envelope and I take it to the post office and I mail it, and then she takes the money and buys some hideous piece of garbage and puts it on her wall or on a little shelf until her house is so full of things I've paid for out of money that should go to my daughter's upbringing, and I pay for all of that, I run out of money every month even though I get the same money on the dole that *she* gets, because it's worth it. Being hungry is worth it. Having you be angry with me is worth it, because you do not have to know that woman, you do not have to have her in your *life*. So yes, Alessandra, I do it *all* for you. And if I can get us off this planet, I won't have to send her any more money, and she won't phone me anymore, because by the time we reach that other world she will be dead. I only wish you had trusted me enough that we could have arrived there without your ever having to see her evil face or hear her evil voice."

Mother got up from the table and returned to her room.

Alessandra finished her homework and put it into her backpack and then went and sat on the sofa and stared at the non-functioning television. She remembered coming home every day from school, for all these years, and there was Mother, every time, flitting through the house, full of silly talk about fairies and magic and all the beautiful things she did during the day, and all the while, the thing she did during the day was fight the monster to keep it from getting into the house, getting its clutches on little Alessandra.

It explained the hunger. It explained the electricity. It explained everything.

It didn't mean Mother wasn't crazy. But now the craziness made a kind of sense. And the colony meant that finally Mother would be free. It wasn't Alessandra who was ready for emancipation.

She got up and went to the door and tapped on it. "I say we sleep during the voyage."

A long wait. Then, from the other side of the door, "That's what I think, too." After a moment, Mother added, "There'll be a young man for you in that colony. A fine young man with prospects."

"I believe there will," said Alessandra. "And I know he'll adore my happy, crazy mother. And my wonderful mother will love him, too."

And then silence.

It was unbearably hot inside the flat. Even with the windows open, the air wasn't stirring, so there was no relief for it. Alessandra lay on the sofa in her underwear, wishing the upholstery weren't so soft and clinging. She lay on the floor, thinking that maybe the air was a tiny bit cooler there because hot air rises. Only the hot air in the flat below must be rising and heating the floor, so it didn't help, and the floor was too hard.

Or maybe it wasn't, because the next morning she woke up on the floor and there was a breath of a breeze coming in off the Adriatic and Mother was frying something in the kitchen.

"Where did you get eggs?" asked Alessandra after she came back from the toilet.

"I begged," said Mother.

"One of the neighbors?"

"A couple of the neighbors' chickens," said Mother.

"No one saw you?"

"No one stopped me, whether they saw me or not."

Alessandra laughed and hugged her. She went to school and this time was not too proud to eat the charity lunch, because she thought: My mother paid for this food for me.

That night there was food on the table, and not just food, but fish and sauce and fresh vegetables. So Mother must have turned in the final papers and received the signing bonus. They were going.

Mother was scrupulous. She took Alessandra with her when she went to both of the neighbors' houses where chickens were kept, and thanked them for not calling the police on her, and paid them for the eggs she had taken. They tried to refuse, but she insisted that she could not leave town with such a debt unpaid, that their kindness was still counted for them in heaven, and there was kissing and crying and Mother walked, not in her pretend fairy way, but light of step, a woman who has had a burden taken from her shoulders.

Two weeks later, Alessandra was on the net at school and she learned something that made her gasp out loud, right there in the library, so that several people rushed toward her and she had to flick to another view and then they were all sure she had been looking at pornography but she didn't care, she couldn't wait to get home and tell Mother the news.

"Do you know who the governor of our colony is going to be?"

Mother did not know. "Does it matter? He'll be an old fat man. Or a bold adventurer."

"What if it's not a man at all? What if it's a boy, a mere boy of thirteen or fourteen, a boy so brilliantly smart and good that he saved the human race?"

"What are you saying?"

"They've announced the crew of our colony ship. The pilot of the ship will be Mazer Rackham, and the governor of the colony will be Ender Wiggin."

Now it was Mother's turn to gasp. "A boy? They make a *boy* the governor?"

"He commanded the fleet in the war, he can certainly govern a colony," said Alessandra.

"A boy. A little boy."

"Not so little. My age."

Mother turned to her. "What, you're so big?"

"I'm big enough, you know. As you said—of child-bearing age!"

Mother's face turned reflective. "And the same age as Ender Wiggin."

Alessandra felt her face turning red. "Mother! Don't think what I know you're thinking!"

"And why not think it? He'll have to marry somebody on

that distant lonely world. Why not you?" Then Mother's face
also turned red and she fluttered her hands against her cheeks.
"Oh, oh, Alessandra, I was so afraid to tell you, and now I'm
glad, and you'll be glad!"

"Tell me what?"

"You know how we decided to sleep through the voyage?
Well, I got to the office to turn in the paper, but I saw that I had
accidentally checked the other box, to stay awake and study and
be in the first wave of colonists. And I thought, what if they
don't let me change the paper? And I decided, I'll make them
change it! But when I sat there with the woman I became afraid
and I didn't even mention it, I just turned it in like a coward.
But now I see I wasn't a coward, it was God guiding my hand,
it truly was. Because now you'll be awake through the whole
voyage. How many fourteen-year-olds will there be on the
ship, awake? You and Ender, that's what I think. The two of
you."

"He's not going to fall in love with a stupid girl like me."

"You get very good grades, and besides, a smart boy isn't
looking for a girl who is even smarter, he's looking for a girl
who will love him. He's a soldier who will never come home
from the war. You will become his friend. A good friend. It
will be years before it's time for him and you to marry. But
when that time comes he'll *know* you."

"Maybe you'll marry Mazer Rackham."

"If he's lucky," said Mother. "But I'll be content with
whatever old man asks me, as long as I can see you happy."

"I will not marry Ender Wiggin, Mother. Don't hope for
what isn't possible."

"Don't you *dare* tell me what to hope for. But I will be content for you merely to become his friend."

"I'll be content merely to see him and not wet my pants. He's the most famous human being in the world, the greatest hero in all of history."

"Not wetting your pants, that's a good first step. Wet pants don't make a good impression."

The school year ended. They received instructions and tickets. They would take the train to Napoli and then fly to Kenya, where the colonists from Europe and Africa were gathering to take the shuttle into space. Their last few days were spent in doing all the things they loved to do in Monopoli— going to the wharf, to the little parks where she had played as a child, to the library, saying good-bye to everything that had been pleasant about their lives in the city. To Father's grave, to lay their last flowers there. "I wish you could have come with us," whispered Mother, but Alessandra wondered—if he had not died, would they have needed to go into space to find happiness?

They got home late on their last night in Monopoli, and when they reached the flat, there was Grandmother on the front stoop of the building. She rose to her feet the moment she saw them and began screaming, even before they were near enough to hear what she was saying.

"Let's not go back," said Alessandra. "There's nothing there that we need."

"We need clothing for the journey to Kenya," said Mother. "And besides, I'm not afraid of her."

So they trudged on up the street, as neighbors looked out to see what was going on. Grandmother's voice became clearer and clearer. "Ungrateful daughter! You plan to steal away my beloved granddaughter and take her into space! I'll never see her again, and you didn't even tell me so I could say good-bye!

What kind of monster does that! You never cared for me! You leave me alone in my old age—what kind of duty is that? You in this neighborhood, what do you think of a daughter like that? What a monster has been living among you, a monster of ingratitude!" And on and on.

But Alessandra felt no shame. Tomorrow these would not be her neighbors. She did not have to care. Besides, any of them with sense would realize: No wonder Dorabella Toscano is taking her daughter away from this vile witch. Space is barely far enough to get away from *this* hag.

Grandmother got directly in front of Mother and screamed into her face. Mother did not speak, merely sidestepped around her and went to the door of the building. But she did not open the door. She turned around and held out her hand to stop Grandmother from speaking.

Grandmother did not stop.

But Mother simply continued to hold up her hand. Finally Grandmother wound up her rant by saying, "So now she wants to speak to me! She didn't want to speak to me for all these weeks that she's been planning to go into space, only when I come here with my broken heart and my bruised face will she bother to speak to me, only now! So speak already! What are you waiting for! Speak! I'm listening! Who's stopping you?"

Finally Alessandra stepped between them and screamed into Grandmother's face, "Nobody can speak till you shut up!"

Grandmother slapped Alessandra's face. It was a hard slap, and it knocked Alessandra a step to the side.

Then Mother held out an envelope to Grandmother. "Here is all the money that's left from our signing bonus. Everything I have in all the world except the clothes we take to Kenya. I give it to you. And now I'm done with you. You've taken the last thing you will ever get from me. Except this."

She slapped Grandmother hard across the face.

Grandmother staggered, and was about to start screaming when Mother, lighthearted fairy-born Dorabella Toscano, put her face into Grandmother's and screamed, "Nobody ever, ever, ever hits my little girl!" Then she jammed the envelope with the check in it into Grandmother's blouse, took her by the shoulders, turned her around, and gave her a shove down the street.

Alessandra threw her arms around her mother and sobbed. "Mama, I never understood till now, I never knew."

Mother held her tight and looked over her shoulder at the neighbors who were watching, awestruck. "Yes," she said, "I am a terrible daughter. But I am a very, very good *mother!*"

Several of the neighbors applauded and laughed, though others clucked their tongues and turned away. Alessandra did not care.

"Let me look at you," said Mother.

Alessandra stepped back. Mother inspected her face. "A bruise, I think, but not too bad. It will heal quickly. I think there won't be a trace of it left by the time you meet that fine young man with prospects."

Afterword by Orson Scott Card

This story was *supposed* to be about Ender's voyage to the colony he governs—a story set between the climax and the final ending of *Ender's Game*. I was going to deal with Ender's relationship with the captain of the colony ship, who assumed that Ender was intended to be a figurehead, with the captain actually calling the shots. I knew exactly how Ender was going to maneuver him out of position.

But along the way, I also figured on having Ender encounter an intensely ambitious mother and daughter among the colonists. The mother is determined that her daughter will be young Ender's best friend and then bride. Meanwhile, sensing how the wind is blowing, the mother herself makes a play for the captain of the ship.

In other words, I was superimposing a Jane Austen marry-for-status storyline on a political power-struggle story. I should have known that Jane Austen would win.

When I tried writing an opening that left the mother as an empty villain—driven by ambition alone—I found that I wasn't terribly interested in her. I'm not a fan of "comedy of humors," and so I began rewriting the opening with scenes.

I had a double problem. The mother was ambitious for her daughter, yes, but she also had to be desperate enough to join a colony and leave planet Earth forever! What would drive her to do such a thing—especially when she had to be smart and sane enough to pass at least minimal tests for potential colonists? (Surely they would not take, say, criminals or people with mental illness or other defects.)

I had no idea how to answer that question until I got to the scene where the daughter meets her grandmother for the first time. Then, seeing her knickknack-lined room and hearing how she talked to her granddaughter, I understood it all.

Sometimes you just have to write your way into a story to find out who your characters are.

But then you can easily discover that you aren't writing the story you *meant* to write at all!

Credits for the Illustrations

"In the Eyes of the Empress's Cat" illustration by Nicole Cardiff

"Mazer in Prison" illustration by Howard Lyon

"Tabloid Reporter to the Stars" illustration by Tomislav Tikulin

"Audience" illustration by Thorsten Grambow

"The Mooncalfe" illustration by Jerimiah Syme

"Cheater" illustration by Jin Han

"Dream Engine" illustration by Howard Lyon

"Hats Off" illustration by Lance Card

"Eviction Notice" illustration by Jin Han

"To Know All Things That Are in the Earth" illustration by James Owens

"Beats of Seven" illustration by Walter Simon

"Pretty Boy" illustration by Jin Han

"Respite" illustration by Nate Pinnock

Fat Farm illustration by Jin Han
"The Box of Beautiful Things" illustration by Laura Givens
"Taint of Treason" illustration by Glen Bellamy
"Call Me Mr. Positive" illustration by Jin Han
"A Young Man with Prospects" illustration by Julie Dillon